By the same author

SLIP ON A FAT LADY
PLUMRIDGE
WILD THING

The Skaters' Wal

With best wishes
to you both,
on a very pleasant

The Skaters' Waltz

visit to Gloucester

by

Philip Norman

Philip

November 1982

J'ai plus de souvenirs que si j'avais mille ans.
Baudelaire

HAMISH HAMILTON
LONDON

To my mother

First published in Great Britain 1979
by Hamish Hamilton Limited
Garden House, 57/59 Long Acre, London WC2E 9JZ

Copyright © 1979 by Philip Norman

British Library Cataloguing in Publication Data
Norman, Philip
   The skaters' waltz.
   I. Title
   823'.9'1F   PR6064.075S/
   ISBN 0 241 10255 3

Printed in Great Britain by Bristol Typesetting Co. Ltd,
Barton Manor, St. Philips, Bristol

prologue: the yellow anemone

At the end of Trinity Street, the path grew old and crooked, like cobblestones, with grass and frilled weeds and clover and dandelions springing out between the cracks. It was not a private road, but I used to think so each time I turned the corner, past the Tredegar Guest House, and saw it, waiting for me under the shower of trees that hung above Trinity Churchyard wall. In the afternoon, when I trod that bumpy pavement, trying hard to miss the cracks, Trinity Street was like a tunnel of greenery and silence which led, in all senses, to a dead end. The churchyard wall ran along the left-hand side. On the right stood a row of three blackened stone cottages, their gardens untidy with pansies and pebbles and trellises for the thin, salty roses that grow near the sea. I can still feel how my heart would sink as I reached the third cottage because beyond it was the carriage gate of Holmwood, the house where we lived. On one of the tall black gateposts, Charles, our Siamese cat, would sit and wash himself and watch for any-one who might be coming home.

Like many of Ryde's large houses, Holmwood had been built as some rich Victorian family's summer home. That was in the

1

days when Queen Victoria herself came to the Isle of Wight, and would drive from Osborne into Ryde along Queen's Road, named in her honour, and down Union Street, named for the Union of South Africa. Ryde was never as grand as Cowes nor as pretty as Ventnor; its mansions, therefore, held themselves aloof on wooded slopes to the west of the pier, invisible but for their private beaches, and 'observation towers' with views away to the roadstead where Kings and Kaisers might be yachting.

Holmwood was not quite a mansion. According to Nanny Belmayne, it had been built for a foreign diplomat; and indeed, there was something a little foreign in the combination of sour yellow brickwork and the dark orange rectangles that patterned the windows and stitched up the corners, giving the house an oddly cloth-like appearance, as of some suit a foreigner might wear. Originally there had been iron railings along the front: their removal—in the War presumably—had given the façade an uncomfortable, top heavy appearance, balanced on paths and basement windows that were like a stem barely able to support its weight. On its raised ground floor, it had bay windows; on its remote first floor, windows that were tall but straight. It had a steep roof and numerous chimney stacks. The front door was inside a porch, reached by stairs between a thick, black, flaking balustrade. It had been divided to make our flat on the ground floor, Mrs Harper's on the first floor, and two or three more—I never knew exactly how many—around the perimeter in what had formerly been the cellars and servants' quarters. Immediately behind the carriage entrance there was now a modern brick garage with a flat asphalt roof. You went through the carriage gate, around the garage to reach the side door into our flat.

Across the road, behind the stained white graveyard wall, lay the grounds of Holy Trinity, a church so big that it was practically invisible save for one huge locked door around the corner in Dover Street. Only its spire betrayed it—one of three spires visible in Ryde from the sea—and a bell that used

2

to toll, endlessly and illogically, hugely near at hand on Sunday mornings and evenings.

Over the wall in the churchyard, the tombstones had all been removed, but a few ancient ones embedded in the ground and hidden under dead leaves and pine cones. It was dark in there, in the lee of the great church, silent and sunless like a mossy room. Few people entered it other than the boy who lived at Holmwood and took a short cut through the church-yard each afternoon on his way home from school. Shallow within, the wall dropped five feet or so down into Trinity Street. He crouched there, a Confederate officer, watchful for any Union cavalry or hostile Indians who might be passing beneath. He was a boy of fixed habits and easily awakened guilt. He was not very good at jumping. He got over the wall backwards, lowering himself gingerly until he hung from the ridged parapet by his fingers; then he let go with a scrape on his bare knee, a sting in both ankles at once as he landed with his satchel on the pavement.

Trinity Street was not, as it seemed, a cul-de-sac. You could turn left at the end, beside Holmwood's garden wall, down a steep hill to Monkton Street and the low part of Ryde. A car would come along occasionally, almost stop outside the house, then skirt it with a crunch and flicker of loose gravel. The only other sound was of the trees in the churchyard, stirring gently where the breeze touched them, high up near the sun. Sometimes, late at night or in the morning, the trees would make a sound together that seemed to come from no perceptible breeze but from some impulse deep inside themselves, rising to a crescendo; breaking and then gently withdrawing, like the sound the sea made, not so very far away.

In summer, the trees awakened Louis early in the morning. His bedroom was on the ground floor of Holmwood, facing Trinity Street. His bed pointed towards the window: from his pillow he could see nothing but foliage, where the cascade stopped above the churchyard wall. He opened his eyes at the impetus of a cool and restless motion. The wind gathered all at

3

once in the trees, then the sea sound gushed through the packed gold and green ferns, tossing them together, brightening, then dimming them as the sun worked and worried its way down towards the road.

The next thing Louis saw were the pictures pinned to the wallpaper above his bed. Some were drawings he had done himself, of heroic gunfighters and hussars, but most were photographs of film stars, cut out of magazines like *Picturegoer, Picture Show* and *Photoplay*. About a hundred film stars, male and female, looked down on Louis as he lay in bed, with slanted shoulders, sepia complexions and brilliant white smiles. The picture he looked at for longest showed a male film star standing up to make a speech while a lady film star secretly wrote 'A Happy 1954' with her lipstick on his exposed shirt-front. Louis liked this picture best because the lady film star was so pretty and because, although he knew it was only a photograph, he suspected she had fallen in love with him.

He glanced round his bedroom curiously, as if searching for clues to his own life. He saw, above the rise of his green quilt, the plain wooden bed-end, and the window ledge beyond with its blistered cream sill where, sometimes, groups of his soldiers would venture daringly from the floor below. He saw, to the right, the Geyser and little wash-basin boxed in by cream panels on which Mickey Mouse had been stuck in a transfer for some other boy whose room this used to be. To the left, he saw the chair with his school clothes thrown over it, vest and grey shirt and pullover in a single concentric garment. He remembered that a book inspection had been promised this week by Charley, and that three or four of his books were still uncovered. Where in the world—in all the world—could he find some brown paper?

He knew now there was something to remember other than school. Beyond the familiar qualm of term time lay an additional fact which, last night had caused him to hope he might not wake this morning. He looked again, over his crooked quilt, through the window at a bough among the churchyard trees that he always noticed. Long and slack, bare of all but

4

a few rough-riding leaves, it drooped down almost as far as the wall, bucking and wagging sideways in a sudden breeze that seemed to blow through Louis also, causing a chill page in his memory to flutter open.

He remembered that Dad had come back to Holmwood again.

He turned his head to look at his bedside clock. The square, friendly face showed not even half-past six. Louis disciplined himself to awake at this time each morning by banging his head on the pillow six and a half times. It was part of the routine he had evolved for himself, like the long pre-school games on the floor with his soldiers; the breakfasts of cherry-ade; the long, leisurely investigations into formerly private cupboards and drawers. With numb dismay, he realised a whole epoch of his life had ended last night. That was what always happened whenever Dad came home.

'He *is* here,' Louis said, against the quilt-hem. 'I know he is. He's definitely here.'

If you did that it sometimes caught God out. God was so intent on proving you wrong about everything.

'He is—I know he is. I assure you. He's definitely come back.'

Louis got out of bed, down to the cold black floorboards. As he did, he noticed his door had been shut during the night. The door was big, and ill-fitted its frame; its handle hung out loose on a pole. He grasped it but then waited, his toes clinging to the floorboards, because an instinct advised him that if he held his breath—if he could hold it long enough to count to thirty—he might still pacify God and find that, after all, he had been mistaken. Life might still be able to go on as it did yesterday, and the day before.

'One, two . . . he *is* there, I assure you. Please God . . . five, six, seven, please, please God . . . nine, ten, I know he is, he definitely is, eleven, twelve, and forgive us our trespasses, as we forgive them . . . 'ineteen, 'enty, please, please, *please* God, twenty-five, six, sev', e', ni' . . .'

He came to thirty and let out his breath. He had done all

A*

5

that he could against the Universe. Slowly, to make no noise with the loose knob, he opened his bedroom door.

His room was situated next to Holmwood's high front porch. He peeped out across a vestibule dark with its brown walls, its black stained floorboards on which were laid irregular lengths of coconut matting. The stairs, belonging to the flat upstairs, were walled in. Light shone dimly through the glass panels, slanting up through the ceiling, with Mrs Harper's brass ornaments silhouetted against them. Mrs Harper had to come through the hall of this flat to reach the staircase to her own.

Around the shared vestibule were the doors to the spare bedroom, the sitting-room, and *their* bedroom, as Louis still characterised it, though months had passed since his mother and Dad had slept, and awakened, behind that door together. In the weeks after Dad's departure, she had slept in there alone, behind a door slammed shut in the nightly paroxysm of her grief. When she too had gone away, in carrying out her suitcase she had left the door wide open. Light shone through the doorway across a fawn carpet, from the windows to the little balcony, beyond. It was the sight which, more than any other, proclaimed the flat to be empty now, but for Louis. And Mrs Kennie, of course, who came and went, offering no threat to his independence.

Today that door was closed, sealing up the dark beside the front porch. The door of the spare bedroom was open, the sitting-room door ajar. Doors wrongly shut and open in the twilight corroborated what a change had occurred since Louis went to bed.

Down the narrow passage to the kitchen, old Nigger, the gundog, lay in his usual place. His eye glittered up through the shadow at Louis and his big tail thumped once against the skirting-board. Nigger, at least, would be happy that Dad had come home again. He must be hoping Dad would take him out, as in the old days, to shoot pheasants and partridges and rabbits and ducks and hares.

*   *   *

6

He dressed himself in a few seconds, struggling on his vest, shirt and pullover in one thick-armed garment still harbouring in its grey folds the warmth of yesterday's sun. He put on the underpants whose yellowness, while changing for PT, he tried to hide, and the faded grey short trousers, and long grey socks with the school colours around the tops which no longer pulled up high enough, folding them over black elastic garters, each in the wrong place on his leg. He put on the tie, diagonally striped in blue, red and gold, which he had had since he was in the Junior School, and which was now too small, and torn at the broad end so that a length of canvas stuff hung out.

He opened his door slowly and tiptoed down the passage, wary of the many loose floorboards, stepping with care over the place where old Nigger blackly lay. This part of Holmwood had once been used by servants only. A side door, left open day and night, led down steps, through a stone arch, to the outside path. The kitchen was to the right of this door. To the left was the toilet and a small lobby where, in their early days at Holmwood, seemingly enthused by its potentialities, Dad had built shelves to house his guns, his fishing-rods and some straw-wrapped bottles of yellow wine. On the wall outside the toilet, two mounds of coats hung, as they had for months, unworn and undisturbed. As Louis passed, he always looked at a certain coat of his mother's that was camel-hair, with a belt and a brown silk lining. Sometimes he would stop and finger the silk lining and remember her, walking with her dog, Melody, down country lanes long ago, before they had moved to the Island. Her camel hair coat was the last link with a refinement which had otherwise disappeared from her life. Louis wondered why she had not taken it with her, but, instead, left it hanging, as if in loyalty, next to the pale brown leather sleeveless over-jacket which Dad always used to wear when he went out shooting.

The bathroom, beyond the kitchen, overlooked the big garden that had been divided among the flats. As Louis went in, a sudden warmth struck his face from the sunshine the bathroom had already trapped. He thought, as he did every morning,

7

how terrible it would be were anyone in his form at school to see the cracked lino, the bath, on its stumpy legs, stained near the plug hole, with the Ascot above it; the stale loofah, the dry pumice stone and chips of petrified soap. His toy boat, the Frog 'Drifter', lay, scuttled, on the bath rim. Not for three or four weeks had there been any obligation to have a bath.

He touched his face briefly with the almost dry flannel. No toothpowder was left other than a faint pink halo round the tin, unyielding to a more energetic brush than Louis's. Thinking about Charley's book inspection, he forgot his greater unease until, turning back to the basin, he met the eye of the man on the razor-blade packet that stood wedged behind the cold tap. The man wore a steep collar and short black moustache, and had signed the blue packet with his name, Gillette. It was the brand of razor-blade which Dad always used and which—like brushes and razors, like the very act of scraping lathered cheeks—seemed to Louis to be the prerogative of Dad alone. The packet had lain there, wet and rusty, through all the weeks since last Dad had had occasion to shave at home. Despite its dreadful significance to Louis this morning, he looked at it also with a little surge of familiar excitement. He remembered when Dad would send him out to Timothy White's, impressing on him that vital formula 'six Blue Gillette blades', and how he would hurry, balancing the words on his tongue.

By seven o'clock, he was ready to start for school. He sat in the kitchen with his satchel beside him on the red and white checkered plastic tablecloth. He sat stiff-backed, as if already in class, and felt summer creep in under his pullover arms, his tight sock-garters and the earpieces of the spectacles he wore. Occasionally he moved his leg, for the seat had grown sticky underneath him. His eyes remained fixed on the small electric clock which his mother used to say, unavailingly, was too high on the wall for her to see. Each time the second hand swept round and the minute hand jerked forward a notch, he felt his heart give a tiny reciprocal jog of apprehension. It was ten, now twenty, now twenty-five past seven. At half past, in the distance, he heard the Town Hall clock chime once. On a usual morning, he would have passed the Town Hall by now.

Not until almost ten to eight did the moment come that he was dreading. At the far end of the flat, a door opened, then quietly closed. Footsteps started to come along the passage to the kitchen.

They were the footsteps which had returned last night, as Louis always knew they would, along Trinity Street from whatever business had so long detained them. Out of the tree-filled silence had come, at last and when least expected, that soft, rapid, rustling noise which did not grow gradually, like other footsteps, but seemed to spring up all at once nearby, like a pounce. Louis, lying in bed, had time only to shut his eyes tight and make himself rigid before the footsteps reached the landing outside his door. He had lain, not even breathing, as Dad came in and looked down at him, touched—so Louis powerfully sensed—by some pathos in this counterfeit sleep. A kiss, rasping yet tender, was placed on his forehead. The footsteps had withdrawn then, pulling his bedroom door closed.

The footsteps were getting nearer, passing his bedroom door. He heard a loose floorboard creak, and felt his whole body wilt with fear as if after all this time he were about to be discovered in some furtive, forbidden act. As the footsteps came on, he strove to arrange his backbone, hands and feet in the posture of innocence, to expel even from his mind all that might be incriminating or unseemly, rendering every thought down to the same guiltless blank. He stared at his satchel, at the house-badge in his coat-lapel, as the footsteps reached the end of the passage, pausing to step over the place where Nigger lay. Nigger's tail thumped against the skirting board, and a grotesque shape passed before Louis's eyes as Dad came round the corner, down two steps beside the food cupboard and into the kitchen.

For a moment, such was his evident fatigue, he did not even seem to notice Louis. The eyes that were pale hazel brown stared at nothing while Dad yawned steeply, jutting out his lower lip and pushing both hands up the peak of black hair

9

which his wartime flying helmet had made. How many times had Louis seen that same gesture—Dad's fingers smoothing his white temples as though to wake were harassing beyond endurance. Yellow smoking stains still coated his cigarette fingers on the inside. On his other hand, Louis saw again the plain gold ring which, having the Belmayne family crest and motto on it, excepted it from Dad's dislike of personal flamboyance.

He wore only his trousers and undervest, and the red leather slippers which had stood empty so long under the wardrobe he preferred to call his 'compactum'. He had never owned pyjamas, considering them in some way unmanly, preferring to sleep—as evidently he still did—in his vest alone. This half-dressed state was the familiar interim between sleep and his later protracted labour with Blue Gillette blades. Bluish stubble, thicker than Louis had seen on any other man's face, coated his chin and his dimpled cheeks like a mask hooked on behind each ear. Black hair grew on his chest in a thick tangle spilling out through his vest's white arc. And terror reached back into Louis to see Dad's dark chin and hairy chest, and smell again the smell Dad brought with him from sleep—the odours of a pipe gone cold, and yellow fingers, and his alien, pyjamaless night.

'Hello old son,' Dad said, as if they had last met yesterday. His voice was the one Louis remembered, light but low with the burden of his thoughts. The lips, in the thick stubble, were pale and sensitive, though not all speech came easily to them.

'Hello, Dad.'

'How are you, son'

'All right thanks, Dad.'

"Getting on well at school?'

'Yes, Dad.'

'Good-o.' Dad yawned again, smoothed back his widow's peak and said: "Want some breakfast?'

This was why Dad had goaded himself into his trousers from the deep, exhausting sleep following his journey home.

10

'Okay, Dad.'

'What does Mrs Kennie gen'rally give you in the morning?'

Cherryade, thought Louis desperately. Orangeade. Lime-ade. Dandelion and Burdock.

'A boiled egg, Dad.'

'Roger,' Dad said: the Air Force word meaning 'Good'.

He went out to the food cupboard and returned with the solitary egg that was there. He filled the kettle under the tap; then he filled a little saucepan. He could remember where everything was kept. Mrs Kennie had left tea-leaves in the pot, and Dad emptied it out and shook it, making the vest wobble loosely under his arm, and then rinsed it under the cold tap, swirling clean water through it time and again as if even this small job involved the full expertise of his hand and eye. When Dad rinsed a teapot, you knew no one had ever done it before in so scientific and thorough a way. As he did so, his tongue emerged to rest on his top lip like a small pink moustache. Thus did he signify all moments of concentration.

" Not too hard, not too soft. That's how you like your eggs, isn't it?'

'Yes, Dad.'

'Roger.'

He made the tea and spread margarine on some sliced bread he found, at the same time diligently watching Louis's egg as it boiled. His slippers, with the pale spats of his feet inside them, rustled to and fro in the little kitchen as he fetched sugar from the cupboard, hunted for a teaspoon and used a skewer to unblock the salt. Not only the kitchen but the whole flat seemed filled with unwonted noises. Floorboards creaked, untrodden upon, and doors stirred in their frames. Outside in the corridor, old Nigger's tail thumped with pleasure against the skirting-board. Even Charles, the Siamese cat, sensing the novelty of this morning, came upstairs from his new home with Mr and Mrs Scovell to walk springily round his empty food bowl, parrying Dad's legs with his tail and crying like a baby.

'Now, come on tiddles,' Dad said. 'I don't want to go treading on your feet.' He stooped down to move Charles aside with

11

his hand. The fantastic thought occurred to Louis that Dad, in some incomprehensible way, relished the enigma of his sudden homecoming, his nonchalant preparation of breakfast as if this were just an ordinary morning without the months—or was it years?—that intervened. Once, only once, Louis ventured to ask a question. He asked whether Mrs. Kennie would be coming today, and Dad said, 'No, Louis' in a clipped voice that precluded all further inquiries. The epoch of Mrs Kennie had ended. No more than that need concern him.

In front of him now was the egg which Dad had cooked him and which, just in time, he remembered to broach in the manner prescribed by Dad, tapping it lightly round the neck of the shell. He dug with his spoon through marbled white, to an eye of warm, sticky gold. It was—for Dad could do no less—a perfect egg. Louis did not want it. That was the only trouble.

He put down his spoon, swallowed hard and said:

'Can I go now, Dad?'

'Finished?' The black-matted chest overhung Louis as Dad leaned across to inspect his eggshell. 'No you haven't. Look—you haven't eaten up any of those nice white horses.'

'I've had enough, Dad.'

' "Had enough!" ' Dad echoed jovially. 'Come on now. Finish the nice white horses. That's the best part.'

Louis picked up his spoon again. He lifted out another curve of egg. It felt heavy in his mouth, and oddly metallic, and his chews mingled, somehow, with his faster and faster heartbeats. The time, he saw, was nearly ten past eight. His glasses misted over with the force of a horrified sigh.

The months had not lessened Dad's ability to read his every thought.

'In any case, old son, it's much too early yet to set off for school. You might just as well finish your egg up and drink up your tea.'

'I can't eat any more, Dad, honestly. I've got to go.'

'To go *where*, Louis?' The hazel brown eyes looked suspiciously at him.

12

'To school.'

'At eight o'clock in the morning!'

'It's *gone* eight o'clock—'

'It's only ten past eight, Louis. You don't have to be there until nine. What's the point of setting off so early?'

'I always do—'

'Then it's *stupid* of you, old son', Dad replied with the vehemence which always brought out the small impediment in his speech. 'That's *schoopid* of you, Louis. You don't have to be at school until nine o'clock. You could set off from here at—at ten to nine, old son, and still get to school in *ample* time."

'But—'

'But me no buts, Louis.'

'I—'

'There's just no *point* in it, Louis. There's no *point* in setting off for school at ten past eight. What's the *point* of it —just tell me, what's the *point* of it, old son?'

He was staring at Louis now. His eyes were hazel, but if you argued with him, a yellow shape suddenly came alight in them, like an anemone, flowering larger and brighter the more persistently you tried to argue. There was no *point* in it, Dad said again, with lips that on each letter p made a little, thudding explosion; and Louis saw, gleaming in Dad's pupils, the yellow light which, for as long he could remember, had signified both a challenge and a warning.

the beginning: castles in the sea

Someone has picked me up to show me the big ships in Portsmouth Harbour. From the rail of the Island ferry, I can see them all around us, lying in bays and corridors, the thin roof-shapes of battleships and destroyers, the spires of aircraft carriers, put away tidily until war breaks out again. Our boat is not moving yet—the harbour still flows past us on its flat and flickering tides. High astern I can see the draped masts of Nelson's *Victory* in her dry dock behind the railway station. I can see tugboats and barges, and the tiny Gosport ferry as it darts across the harbour packed with people, all standing. Out beyond the dredgers, I can see a long boat rowed by boys from the sea-training school. A faint cry from the longboat reaches me on the wind, and I look at the faraway cluster of sailor hats, feeling glad I am here, safe on the ferry, not out there learning to be a sailor.

We clear the harbour slowly, leaving the big ships behind. Portsmouth seems derelict—a city of tumbledown wharves and tall, narrow pubs overhanging the water's edge, and slipways down to beaches of black slime. We pass minesweepers, numbered in pairs, and the ship called HMS *Vernon*, so long at

14

anchor that she has changed into a concrete wall. The shore folds back slowly, now into grey battlements and a corner turret above a steep, shingled beach; now suddenly it recedes to a distant promenade where a fairground stands, marked by its big wheel. Where the harbour is only horizon, passing a light that flashes from an invisible point, we escape, at last, into open sea.

The Island, six miles away across the Solent, lies wrapped in a long, grey, coast-shaped cloud which barely seems to advance as we traverse sea lanes crowded, like a busy street, with Navy craft and ocean liners and cargo ships and thin, rusty-sided tankers, all making their way through the channel between Spithead and Southampton. We can see launches and speedboats and pinnaces and sailing dinghies that buck valiantly up and down, and yachts in slim, white clusters, and lolling buoys as well as the other sort of buoy, like a bird in a drowning cage. Sometimes we see a ferry like ours, black and white and yellow-funnelled, passing near us on its return voyage to Portsmouth.

We are sitting under cover on a polished wooden seat, its boards so deeply curved that only my heels touch the edge. On the wall above us, in a stout, seagoing frame under thick glass, is a picture showing us how to put on a lifejacket if the boat sinks. One man has been photographed in several poses, here holding the lifejacket above his head, here tying it behind his back, here standing triumphantly aproned and tied. I can tell that he belongs to the forties, with his sharp face and skinny wrists, even though his picture will still be seen on all the boats many years from now. Melody the cocker spaniel sits close to us, unhappy on the grinding deck boards. On the seat beside us is a basket which, from time to time, emits a low, scandalised cry. Charles the Siamese cat is inside. He has cried like this all the way down from St Neots, and his blue eyes squint out furiously through the gap under the lid. Nigger the gundog has travelled ahead of us with Dad. Eilian says they'll be waiting for us when we get to the other side.

The boat seems to move unaided by human hands. There are no sailors on the deck, no smoke defiles the funnel or the

15

uncaptained bridge. We are driven by the scream of gulls, hovering over our long, rough wake, and by a humming, grinding, incessant power deep below: the high bows jump the waves like hurdles and the broken sea speeds under the rivetted sides as if a fast river flows with us over the dishevelled plain. The boat excites me because it is like a toy; I want to play with it in my hands. I feel excited to see the radar, spinning slowly among clouds that pitch and swing. I love the white curved chimney things that stand open-mouthed around the deck. Eilian does not know what they are for. I'm certain I could draw them if I tried. The thought of drawing stays in my mind like a sudden little fire amid the wind.

We have gone below now, carrying the cat basket, forcing Melody down the double staircase. I am standing at the open top half of a square door in the ship's side, looking at the sea, a few inches beneath, plunging and lifting under sheet after thrown sheet of snow-speckled foam. I am looking out at the forts, built in a string across the Solent to protect its shipping. The forts are square and dark, like burned loaves. Three of them stand in the sea between here and Spithead—or is it four? One more, or less, is there each time I look. One has receded, another has come suddenly close, although never close enough to study it clearly. Looking at its black shape, I feel afraid, as I do if I think about ghosts. I wonder if the forts have soldiers on them. Or whether, as some people will tell me, they are garrisoned by dead men.

I love how neat and clean the boat is below decks. To get into the toilet you step over a high step to a black and white tiled floor. The refreshment saloon has green leather couches and armchairs, and tables with ledges to stop your teacup sliding away. In the corridor is an open door through which you can look into the engine-room, down among spotless silver turbines, to the ship's uninhabited, floorless, roaring and hammering heart. A wind rises from the engines and fans against my face, like a smell of hot ice-cream.

Now we must be coming close to Ryde. The grey cloud has

become a green cloud embedded in a long, wet coast. At either end stands a shadowy headland, each with a second headland just visible beyond it. A town materialises, through the rain-smeared porthole, under three church spires. We can see how hilly it is, the houses piled on top of each other, the main streets dropping like waterfalls to the sea front. We can see woods banked up to east and west, and the high towers of houses hidden by woodland, and the wall that runs above the dull, thin glint of the beach.

But first of all we can see the pier which comes slantwise out to meet us. We can see its length from the density of green railings on it, and the tramway and railway lines along it, with a signal box half-way down. We can see the pierhead, floating on its hedge of grey pontoons, and the dome of its railway terminus and, to the right, the larger dome that was visible before any other pierhead detail. We can see the cranes, the luggage trucks, the parked cars, advertisement hoardings, and the people waiting in a group for the boat to arrive. I can see Dad at the railings with Nigger, off the lead, beside him. We wait in front of an open gate as the berth comes alongside and a rope is thrown down to a man standing with his hands on his hips. He picks up the rope and pulls it, slowly drawing the boat towards him over the gap of sea like crowds that kick and writhe under blue-black snow, churning, thumping, now only hissing as the propellers stop.

That was in 1947. Louis knew it was still the forties because the sky was so grey. He was then four. He had been told by his mother that they were on their way to live on an island. He felt excitement, but a little afraid, in case the island were wild or cold. He imagined himself sent out for a walk with Eilian, his Irish nursemaid, along a wide, dreary beach, with a castle in the distance. But, of course, Ryde did not look at all like that as Dad drove them along the pier and up through the town. For the first time in his life, Louis realised the tendency of life to turn out to be other than he imagined it.

The boat journey, so memorable, so definitely the start of

17

an epoch, failed to assert itself as a starting-point in his life. For Louis, in 1947, moving to the Isle of Wight was part of a pattern of sudden uprootings and vivid changes, an uncertainty of destination that had already become his main method of characterising his own existence. Though for the present they might be living in Ryde, he had little doubt that they would shortly move on, as before, to some equally far distant and original new home. His expectancy did not diminish as years passed, summers passed, and still the move was unaccountably delayed.

Not that the Island failed to imprint its special character upon him. Each school he attended taught him incessantly where in the world it was located—the little distorted diamond, turned sideways in the sea, close under the bottom coast of England. He knew the position of Ryde, on the edge of the diamond, a little to the right of the long split in its northern point; he knew also that Ryde, apart from its pier, was the least celebrated of the Island resorts. In the season, a big wooden map hung outside the coach offices, showing in highly-coloured caricature form, Carisbrooke Castle, the Needles, Keats Green, Shanklin Old Village, the whale skeleton at Blackgang Chine, and all the beauty spots and historical curiosities which brought visitors from the mainland on holiday throughout the summer. In this respect Louis was unlike a visitor: he had seen few of the places illustrated on the map. In six years, he had scarcely ventured outside Ryde. There was never time, because of 'the Season'.

Yet the longer he lived here, the deeper grew his impression of a temporary home, a life misrouted and in abeyance. He felt no affinity with Isle of Wight people—the upper class, hidden in yacht clubs, the far more plentiful lower class with the dreadful accent he had been forbidden to copy. To the sea and beaches he was indifferent; the countryside did not exist for him. He was surprised to hear his mother, even at the time of her greatest unhappiness, say what a pretty place the Isle of Wight was, when you got away from Ryde.

Most temporary did life become in the season itself, as the

18

overcrowded ferries slouched to the pierhead, white and yellow through a hot sea haze. The frenetic summer months ought by right to have abolished thought in any dimension beyond the besieged and panic-stricken *now*. And yet this was when Louis heard the fondest stories of mainland life—how lovely it *used* to be in the years preceding their move to the Island, before, and briefly after, his own arrival in the world.

'Used to' had a specially fond and pleasant sound when Dad said it.

So he, too, formed the habit of looking back, regretting that he had missed the nice times, the happy years. His sight— not good—grew blanker with the dullness, the interminable sunshine of present and future. But inward eyes hungrily devoured what tatters of those early epochs his mind could remember, before this endless summer. He lived most vividly at the cold, grey threshold of his own life, sometimes assisted by dreams.

The Island was the present, moored immobile back behind the pier's long dark iron arm. The past was out there, beyond the pierhead, beyond the water and the walls and chimneys of Portsmouth, under a wide glow at night, which seemed to come from all the rest of the world.

He knew he had been born in London, 'during the War'. He remembered nothing of this much-discussed epoch, although he had been told he used to sleep in the Tube stations during air raids. His earliest memory came from The Porcupine, the pub where they had lived after Dad crashed his aeroplane, hurting himself so badly that he had had to leave the Air Force.

The Porcupine was in Charing Cross Road. He remembered standing outside it on the corner, looking at its sooty upper windows while the noise of long ago hurtled and spun around him. His mother's voice repeated, until he understood: 'Look! There's Eilian! Cutting sandwiches! Look, see? *There* she is! Cutting *sandwiches*!'

He remembered going out with Eilian in bright sun. You

19

knew that it was London sun. 'I've come for the Rations,' Eilian said.

He went to school already. He remembered a stone walled passage inside the school, and a teacher, Irish like Eilian. His mother told him the school was in Covent Garden. He remembered the face of a little black boy there who frightened him so much that he cried at night. He went to the teacher and asked not to have to go out and play. 'You see, there's a little black boy . . .' The teacher's face came down next to his as she listened.

He remembered Dad only in one brilliant, inexplicable incident. He was standing with Dad in the ticket concourse of a Tube station. He had often dreamed of this ticket concourse, and even wondered if he had been there only in a dream. He remembered the squared pattern of the tiles on the ground and the lighted machines rattling as they coughed out the tickets for trains. He was standing with Dad at the central ticket-office, conscious that Dad knew, and was talking to, the men inside. He himself looked up, trying to see behind the counter. And then, through a lighted aperture, came a bundle of every comic that was sold on the bookstall, all for him from someone he did not know, dozens of comics all twisted in a roll together.

'We were right opposite the Hippodrome,' his mother told him.' I used to take you into Ivor Novello's dressing-room. You always used to say to him, "Uncle Ivor: have you got any grapes?"'

'What did he say?'

'He used to say, "No Louis, I haven't got any grapes. But I *have* got some coconut ice."'

Louis enjoyed hearing about the Hippodrome and Ivor Novello. He imagined his mother going to see shows that were called *The Dancing Years* and *Perchance to Dream*. There was a song called 'We'll Gather Lilacs', which Ivor Novello had written, and which reminded Louis of her, and made him hope that her heart, too, would learn to sing again.

'I sometimes used to leave you with the Ballet girls, 'They'd look after you if Daddy and I went out. And you went in the

20

lorry with Daddy when he took all the drinks down for Ivor Novello's garden party. Don't you remember the lovely house he had at Sunningdale called Redroofs?'

Louis almost remembered. He saw sunshine at the very threshold of his life. He tasted tinned fruit and ice cream—tinned plums with stones, staining the ice cream. He saw blue, clear water, and pink bodies floating stickily on the top, and breathed a faint recollection of his own fear, in case they made him go into the swimming pool.

Then, soon afterwards, they were leaving The Porcupine. His mother told him they were going to live in the country, at an hotel called The Cross Keys. He remembered her describing, quite excitedly, the big keys that hung on the wall outside. He tried to remember what it had been like during this, the briefest but happiest time of all.

It was the forties then, and always winter, cold and grey, but with log fires cracking and snapping and spitting in several places through the long hotel lounge. There were tapestried settles and warming-pans, belts of horsebrasses and brass jugs in alcoves, and chiming clocks, and logs, crumbling in old brick hearths, all waiting for them when they got back after Dad had finished shooting.

But he had not finished yet. He was walking, with Nigger, away from the car in which Louis and his mother sat. Dad walked away from them with his gun down a long, muddy lane with bramble bushes on either side. His shoulders were rounded—deliberately, it seemed to Louis—so that the hem of his coat and his brown leather overjacket hung unevenly in folds. His head, with his straight pipe, thrust forward into the wind, conveyed both the earnestness of his purpose and the absolute necessity of his pursuing it alone. As he walked, his head moved from side to side, making each step a minor statement of defiance.

Later, he came back along the lane, followed by Nigger. His gun was broken, so that the jointed barrels hung down over his forearm.

21

'I got a rabbit,' he said.

But he did not smile or seem pleased, or show them the rabbit he had shot. He put it in the boot of the car, then he walked back to the front again. He bent down and grasped the starting-handle, and his white face flew upward as the handle turned. He grasped it again, and again his face jerked, unsmiling, remote from them even then on that cold afternoon in the country, where, supposedly, he had been happiest.

On Thursdays, when the Market Square filled with stalls, The Cross Keys stayed open all day. Early in the morning, when the grey frames stood joined in lines, waiting to be clothed with their canvas, Fred Cambers took cups of tea round to the bedrooms, wearing leather leggings and carrying his cap under his arm. Fred's brother Stanley—who had wanted to be a jockey—drove the little bus that went to the station to collect new guests. And there were German prisoners in grey shirts and caps, digging up the old stable-yard.

'Look! Daddy's bought ever such a lot of little chicks!'

Louis raised his eyes to the squeaking yellow clouds. The mealy smell of the chicks, even the word 'chicks', would now always remind him of Dad. And *Chicks' Own*, the comic they bought for him every week.

'Daddy's bought a pony and trap. The pony's for you to ride.'

The pony was called Snowy. He was white and old and rather irritable. He was kept in a field belonging to a friend of Dad's called Uncle Teddy Hopperton. Louis put out a hand with half a green apple for Snowy, keeping his thumb pressed under his index finger, as his mother had told him. As the grey, damp lips grazed his palm, he hoped with all his heart that he would never be made to sit on Snowy's back.

'Daddy's building a cottage!'

'All by himself?'

'Yes. He's building a cottage at Great Staughton.'

They went in the car to see the cottage Dad was building. A white wall and plump thatched roof showed among the trees in a curving drive. Dad walked up to look closer at the cottage

22

while Louis and his mother sat and waited in the car.

There always seemed to be some fresh piece of news arising from Dad's energy and enterprise, his restless aptitude for every part of living in the country.

'What do you think! Daddy's bought an island on the river.'

They went in a punt to see the island that Dad had bought. When Nigger jumped off the landing-stage into the punt, he stood helplessly in the middle, making it slap from side to side in the water. As the punt went up the river, Louis put his hand over the side: he remembered how the water, yellow-brown, like Dad's eyes, slipped gently between his fingers. He remembered standing on the grassy island, watching while Dad fished. Dad caught several fish, but then he always threw them back into the water again. He knelt, as Louis stood watching, and separated their mouths from his line, tenderly, as if he had never meant to hurt them. He looked up, saw Louis watching him, and smiled.

'How are you?' he said. 'My old cockalorum.'

Dad was the manager of The Cross Keys. Louis's mother helped him, working shut away in the 'private office'. There was a cook called Mrs Prince, who used to march around the kitchen with Louis in time to military music on the wireless. Then Mrs Prince stole the knives and forks, and had to leave. After that, Louis's mother did the cooking, too.

He went up the courtyard towards the kitchen to find her. She and Ena, the maid, were pulling the inside out of chickens. Every so often, in the wet red entrails, they would discover an unlaid egg.

'Where's Daddy?' Louis asked.

'Gone out shooting.'

Now she was typing out the day's menu on the old typewriter in the 'private office'.

'Where's Daddy?' he asked.

'Gone out fishing.'

She was helping to make the beds upstairs in the long passage over the archway.

'Where's Daddy?'

'Away on business.

Louis remembered standing one evening under the hotel archway, waiting for Dad to come home. The Market Square was empty of stalls. He looked towards the river bridge that rose steeply out of the square, into the worlds beyond, and was moved and excited by the thought that Dad was there, somewhere, 'on business'. Smells and evening sounds in the hotel behind him made him glad he lived here, even though he would soon be sent to bed. There was a Women's Institute dinner for eighty people tonight. His mother had to do the cooking, because another cook had been caught fiddling and had to go away.

He is led through uproars of movement and light, holding Eilian's or his mother's hand. He sees his own four fingers in a row, holding on. He wishes they went in the grown-up way, with the knuckles outward-facing.

Voices speak over his head. Sometimes a face comes swooping down close to speak to him. Sometimes they speak about him as if he is not there.

On his own level, there is no one else—only the face. He has glimpsed it, as he is pulled by the hand through the rushing and light, returning his gaze from mirrors or shop windows. It is pale, unsmiling, cocked a little on one side. Gradually, Louis learns to look for this face, and gradually, to recognise it as his own.

The face is the perpetrator of acts whose consequences continually astonish him.

He has evidently bitten a piece out of his glass of lemonade. He is standing under the hotel archway, with the seam of darker cobbles running down the middle. There are stiff, harsh bubbles in his nose. His mother is bending over him, shaking him to and fro by the wrist. She is wearing her grey costume, with the little brooch in the lapel. She is wearing her blouse with the little pink stripes.

'You *bit* it! You *bit* it! In *temper*!'

24

'—did you go round asking the German prisoners to give you money?'

The German prisoners, working up in the stable yard, in their funny loose grey shirts and caps, smile at everything Louis says to them. There is a puddle with a purple rainbow on it. There is a green apple with oil smeared on the skin. He asked if he should eat the oily apple, and the German prisoners said 'Yes'.

He has heard his mother say that she doesn't like the milkman, who brings the milk in two big churns on the back of a tricycle. She has told Dad she wants to change to another milkman. But just after the war, you are not supposed to change milkmen. Next time the tricycle is there, Louis goes out and tells the milkman he is going to be changed.

The crime is too grave for a smack. His mother speaks gently to him to convey the enormity of it.

'Mummy and Daddy nearly got put in prison because of you.'

They go in the car, one winter afternoon, to Bedford. In a tiny, dark room, cold hands pass on either side of Louis's face. The hands withdraw, leaving a pinchy, thin pressure on his nose, and curling behind each ear. The optician calls him a good boy. The pressure continues as they walk back to the car, with Dad walking in the road, outside the parked cars. Louis glimpses the face again that day in a shop window. It, too, is wearing round spectacles with little pink pieces clutching its nose.

Now he is standing in the double bedroom, just above the big gold keys. They are dressing him up as a Red Indian, to ride on Snowy's back in the St Neots Carnival procession. In his new spectacles, he is dressed in a brown costume fringed with blue beads, and a feathered headdress; and all the time, he is suggesting how, even at this late stage, the Indian costume might be converted into a cowboy costume.

'If I could go and get my holster, we could use a little bit of string . . .'

Now they are putting brown stuff over him. The face in the

25

wardrobe mirror is also brown. It looks out at him in its spectacles and warpaint, horrified at being a Red Indian and having
to ride on Snowy's back.

'There! Doesn't he look nice!'

'*Doesn't* he look nice!'

'Can't I go and get my holster, and tie it with a little bit of
string . . . ?'

He goes to Cedar House School in Cambridge Street. It is a
girls' school, but with boys in the babies' form. They have
to keep quiet while the 'big girls' are doing exams.

The sand-pit is full of roadways, made by their hands. You
can take your cars to school, to play with in the sand.

A boy is showing his car to somebody as Louis comes
up. Seeing Louis, he turns away, shutting the car in his
hand.

'I'm not going to show *you*,' he says over his shoulder. 'I'm
not even going to *look* at you.'

Louis walks out of the sand pit, towards the trees. Cold
waves of mortification wash over him, shutting out the noise
of Playtime. *I'm not going to look at you.* He is *you*: a detest-
able thing. Vision is lost from his throbbing face as his feet
carry him away in steps that lead to nowhere.

It is his first intimation of the power of life to discomfit
him, to frighten or horrify him in a momentary stopping of the
heart. He will dream many times of the sandpit and the toy
motor car. But in his dream, the other boy turns to him with
tears in his eyes. 'I'm only making a little roadway,' he says.
And Louis feels his own eye fill with tears at the sadness in the
other boy's voice.

Then there is the moment when the world above ceases going
about its business and turns inward on him, putting on bright
lights overhead. He hears water in the basin, running fast, and
sees big, hard hotel towels unfolded. He knows these auguries,
yet still pretends not to see them. He walks away with a throbbing face, and the footsteps that lead to nowhere.

He hates it when his mother washes his hair. He struggles
and cries, no matter how quickly she does it, no matter how

many times she assures him the soap will not go into his eyes. Nothing can take away the horror when his head goes under water; of feeling his head pulsing with soap, and soap trickling near his eyes, then the teacup of warm water tipped against the side of his head; but, worst of all, his own voice beyond the rushing water and his tightly-shut eyes, screaming at her to stop. Dad says he must still be a baby for crying when they wash his hair.

And he is afraid of a word—'Ardingly', the school where they are sending him when he is older. They have been to see it already, and to 'put his name down'. There were big boys sitting along the top of a wall, reading newspapers. One day, he knows, he will be abandoned on those strange lawns : the big boys will put down their newspapers and come after him all together.

And every night, there is night.

It comes, after tea, with pitiless regularity. He knows it is coming when Ena the maid puts the lights on around the big lounge, and lights twinkle around in the little snug bar and his mother goes up the yard to the kitchens to taste the soup. In the brightening, savoury-smelling hotel evening, only he is an anachronism. Big clocks strike everywhere, inviting his sentence to be pronounced, as always, in the form of a joke :

'Time *somebody* was in bed.'

'In bed by six for *somebody*.'

He discovers that words have power to bargain against his fear, if only he can gasp out the right formula in time.

'Please. Five more minutes.'

'All right—five minutes more.'

' . . . Another five minutes.'

Now the five minutes are all expended. He is lying in his bedroom at the end of the corridor, awaiting familiar horrors. There will be burglars and murderers—they wait only for the moment when Eilian goes downstairs. Covering his head brings no escape. Swooping and swinging through the darkness inside his eyelids will come the face of the little burnt boy he remem-

27

bered from the hospital where he went to give his comics away:
the face covered in bandages, all but its eyes and its bright red
open mouth.

'What are you doing, Eilian?'

'Folding up a pair of my drawers.'

'When you go, will you leave the door open?'

'All right.'

'Bumping the spare bed?' That is as far as the door will
open, to let in most light from the passage. In time, the words
have a power to comfort him as he lies, crouched and not
breathing, awaiting the zigzag hordes:

'Will you leave the door open bumping the bed?'

One person broke every rule. If Dad bathed him, he was
allowed to have water so deep, it touched his chin. When he
couldn't pull his vest over his head, Dad said: 'Get into the
water with it on.'

Sometimes he got into Dad's deep bath. Dad taught him the
words of 'Phil the Fluter's Ball' and 'Three Old Ladies Locked
in the Lavatory.' He sat half-floating on Dad's legs, and his chin
slapped the water as he sang. He wasn't afraid then to show
his winkle to Dad.

Dad was not away on business today. In the hotel office he
had spread out all his guns and fishing-rods to clean them.
The guns were kept in cases like canvas jodhpur legs. The
rods were rolled in soft green canvas, tied by green string.
With loving, delicate care, Dad slid forth the gold-ringed
polished pieces that connected to make a rod that was higher
than the ceiling. Dad's fishing-rods filled Louis with greater awe
than his guns: they were so bright, so slender he knew he only
had to touch one for it to break. He must never touch anything of Dad's.

When Dad was there, they had their breakfast together in
the little lounge that looked across the Market Square. Louis,
this morning, had already got down from the table. He knelt
on the brocade window-seat, using the ledge as a road for a
little milk cart, bought for him in the Market. The milkman

stood with his whip on a square green metal base. At the table, Dad was saying:

'*Other* men's sons do it. Oliver Squire's sons do it. As head of the household, Laura, I consider that I'm entitled to *some* degree of respect.'

She came across to Louis at the window-seat. She was wearing her grey costume—the one she always wore.

'In future', she said, 'Daddy would like you to try to remember to call him "Sir" '.

He had slipped in the stable yard and hurt his knee. He showed the place to Dad in the little snug bar. Dad pushed his leg away, saying: 'Aah—that's nothing, is it? It's nothing.'

The graze burned through him. He saw his own blood shining in a pink and white web.

'It's *nothing* is it. Don't be soppy—it's *nothing*.'

Dad knew none of the special codes. He did not know that the door had to be left open until it bumped the spare bed. He occurred in Louis's life like a strong wind, obscurely glorying in its power to destroy ordinary conventions. His coming filled Louis with excitement that was also anxiety—for some reason, when Dad was there, he became conscious of his own small silhouette, his weakness and paleness, the bareness of his legs against Dad's rough tweed, but above all, conscious of his inability to bend Dad, as other people, to his will. For words had no power when the hazel brown eyes looked at him: he felt his thoughts founder and his voice fail and fade beneath a curt and crushing logic.

'Dad, I can't eat any more of this.'

' "Can't eat any more!" Of course you can—eat up. That's the *best part*.'

Dad confused everyday life no less by means of wonderful presents and surprises. The night he came home across the River Bridge, he brought with him a sword in a red tin scabbard, tied with yellow cords. His presents took no account of Christmas or birthdays—at any moment, he might put his arm around Louis's shoulders and draw him aside to whisper, 'I've got something for you', or take him out, along the wide pavement to

Clayton's toyshop to buy a rubber gun, a bus conductor's set or a horse with a bandy-legged soldier that cost 'one and fourpence halfpenny each.' Other presents, too munificent for Louis even to comprehend, were 'put away' for him until he was older. It seemed that Dad, on his many journeys away from St Neots, worked ceaselessly for his benefit, now and in the future. The long, twitching rods would be his one day—a fact which did not diminish his fear of them. Even the island on the river would one day belong to him, and the £21 that had been put for him into the bank.

He knew himself enough to feel unworthy of such goodness. For he cried at grazes that were nothing and, at meal-times, choked on the best part; he had not, like other men's sons, acquired the habit of calling Dad 'Sir'. Worst of all was the crime that seemed second nature to him—the crime of 'being deceitful'. For Dad, wherever he was, had a method of finding out any secret.

'You listened to *Dick Barton, Special Agent* on the wireless when I told you not to, Louis, didn't you?'

'Yes'.

'That was deceitful. Go up to your bedroom and stay there for being deceitful.'

He lay on his bed, looking out through the window at the wall of Plum's Bakery, not moving for hours, thinking of the affronted rage in Dad's eyes, the shape of Dad's mouth when he said 'deceitful'. His deceit lingered on that day, and the next, when he asked Dad to buy him the rubber dagger at Clayton's.

'You were deceitful yesterday. You get nothing for being deceitful.'

Dad was not always solemn. In the afternoon, when Louis came home from school, Dad would ask what they had for lunch today at Cedar House.

If Louis replied 'Tapioca pudding', Dad would open his big dimples and laugh and say, 'Your name's Tapioca.'

'It's not.'

'Yes it is—look at Old Tapioca.' On the days when they had had semolina, Dad would call Louis 'Old Semolina'.

30

'Look at old Tapioca. Look at old Semolina!'

Or he would say: 'You're a twerp.'

'I'm *not*!' protested Louis, horrified.

'Yes you are—you're a twerp. You're a looby.'

He sang in a high wheedling voice: 'Louis Belmayne is a loo-by. Louis Belmayne is a loo-by.'

Or beckoned to him in a funny foreign voice, saying: ' Come a leetle bit nearer. Come a *leetle* bit nearer.'

Once within the radius of Dad's arms, terrible things could happen. Dad might hug him suddenly close and, with irresistible strength, rub his dark, rough cheeks up and down Louis's fair pale one. Worse than that was the agony of the Big Tickle, when Dad lunged and gripped him round his bare knee so hard that ticklishness changed to a screaming paralysis, for, bare-legged against Dad's fragrant and overwhelming manliness, to struggle was even worse than to stay still.

But often Dad wanted to kiss and hug him. You never knew if it would be a Big Tickle or a kiss. All at once, Dad seemed to be overcome with gentle love: he drew him tenderly past his knees, into the rough softness of his coat and his pipe. He laid his terrible cheek against Louis's kissing him again and again, in the clean-smelling pipe fragrance, and murmuring:

'Bless your old cotton socks. Bless your old cotton socks. *Bless* your old cotton socks!'

Late in the afternoon, Louis would see him sitting by the fire alone in the hotel lounge. The setting was one in which Louis preferred to picture him throughout the epochs that followed—surrounded by beams and warm hearth bricks and horsebrasses and brass jugs, with Nigger, the gundog lying peacefully at his feet, that must have been the moment when Dad was happiest of all. Why then, as Louis approached him, did he seem so deeply sad? His face pale and pointed in the firelight, he sat in the big chair with one leg crossed high on the other, and stared into space and tapped his fingers on the arm—little men, kicking pink legs in a feverish dance unrelated to the stillness of his face. Why was he so sad, Louis wondered. Was

31

he pining for the brilliant places that lay somewhere beyond the River Bridge? Was his sadness in some way connected with Louis himself, for so little resembling other men's sons? Was he staring at Louis and, deep inside that pale, tragic brow, thinking and thinking all about him? Or was he not even aware that Louis stood in the lounge beside him?

Louis's mother came up then and steered him off, saying: 'Daddy wants to listen to *Variety Bandbox* on the wireless.' Both of them withdrew on tiptoe.

They stayed at The Cross Keys only eighteen months. Yet it seemed at the time as if Dad would be happy to remain there for ever, particularly when extensive renovations were put in hand. The kitchen was moved from its old place under the archway, separate from the hotel, to the top of the courtyard. The lounge became the dining-room, connecting with this new kitchen by a passageway. The old kitchen became a bar with a redbrick hearth, and glass cases for the medieval keys which the German prisoners had dug up. The alterations were carried out by the brewery which owned the Cross Keys, but Louis did not know this—or, indeed, that the hotel was not Dad's own property—until many years later. At the time, the excitement of workmen and ladders and aprons and paint, all seemed to originate from Dad alone; it appeared to Louis that Dad in person carried out most of the work.

Eilian, the Irish girl, met Wilf, who worked at Dudeney and Johnson's the grocers. Wilf brushed his hair straight back and smiled, even when nothing was funny. He now accompanied Louis and Eilian on their walks across the scrappy common inside the town. Louis, to his annoyance, had to wait about while Eilian and Wilf sat down near the hedge for long and tedious intervals.

Charles the Siamese cat arrived, and instantly ran up the chimney in the Montagu Room, where the Masonic dinners were held.

Then Uncle Cal, Dad's brother, came down to St Neots to stay, and soon after that, Louis was told by his mother that they would be leaving the Cross Keys to go and live on the Isle of Wight.

'Why are we going there?' he asked.

'Daddy's going down to help Uncle Cal in a business.'

He remembered how this explanation subdued any regrets he felt at leaving the Cross Keys. It seemed yet further proof of the nobility in Dad's nature to be going to the Isle of Wight to 'help' Uncle Cal rather than for any mercenary or self-seeking purpose.

The alterations continued during their final weeks in St Neots. Now the workmen were redecorating the big bedroom, directly above the gold keys, where Louis's mother and Dad usually slept. This meant that they had to move to a temporary room at the other end of the passage, opposite the one in which Louis slept. It must have been at this time that Louis heard the strange, unforgettable thing happen outside his door.

It happened partly in a dream. He remembered lying in bed, and the sensation both of sleeping and waking. The door stood open as Eilian had left it, bumping the spare bed next to his own. He lay and looked at the comforting pillar of light, and listened to the gentle uproar of evening in the hotel below. Lately he had heard someone say that the passage was haunted by a 'grey monk' from the olden days, but, for some reason, the thought comforted Louis instead of frightening him. He found it almost pleasant to think of the grey monk gliding past his bed and through the wall.

He lifted his eyes once again to look at the light. He realised that his mother and Dad had both come upstairs, although not yet to bed; they were standing and talking outside his half-open door.

Dad's voice said:

'I hear that you've broken my . . .'

Louis did not hear what it was that had been broken. Probably some slender, shiny fishing rod.

'*You* broke my . . .'

His voice did not seem angry. He spoke to her in a thoughtful way, as if only pretending to mind about the thing she had

33

broken. His voice said: 'You're going to suffer for that.'

Her voice replied: 'I suffer when I've done nothing, Emile.'

He said again, in the same voice, thoughtful, almost teasing:
'You're going to suffer and *suffer* . . .'

Then another door closed behind them, outside his door, in
a light that glowed far away, down the years.

amber and bobby and edward the eighth

Now someone else is holding his hand. Deep in the winters of the past, he is going for a walk with someone who is not Eilian or his mother. He sees his fingers held beside a coat with big squares over it, of dark and of paler brown.

The street is dim with cold, and a grey wind blows against his watering eyes. A man walks along the gutter towards them, pushing a cart full of dust. The figure with Louis bends down to speak to him, pulling his hand against the big, squared, soft-feeling coat.

'Would *you* like an ice-cream?'

That was when he first remembered Nanny Belmayne. She was looking after him because his mother had to go into hospital up in London for a few days. When the button came off his coat, Nanny Belmayne did not sew it on again. She fastened his handkerchief to him with a big safety pin. They went on a bus to see his mother in hospital, and the nurse let him get into bed for a few minutes next to her.

When they came outside, Nanny Belmayne asked if he would like an ice-cream. He stood beside her at a tricycle with a white box at the front, watching as his ice-cream was unwrapped

35

from a sticky paper roll. A moment later, he saw it topple off the cornet and lie, like a melting moon, in the heap of tawny dust the roadsweeper had made.

Then came the part he did not understand. He did not get into trouble for having dropped the ice-cream. Instead, he found himself being hugged, there in the street in front of the ice-cream tricyclist and the man with the dustcart. He felt big, dry smacking kisses around his brow and forehead, and heard a voice telling him how much it loved him, not once but over and over again:

'Bless you, my loved one, my little lamb, Nan loves you so much. He's his Nan's little bit of all right, isn't he? He's his Nan's little bit of all right and her little bit of fluff and little bit of fat bless his dear sweet face.'

He could not understand why anyone should love him so much. He had done nothing, so far as he knew, to deserve the adoration that descended on him from this astonishing figure in its light and dark squared coat, into whose care he was periodically committed, who continually picked him up to kiss him, who bought him ice-creams whenever he wanted one, and often when he did not know he wanted one, stooping down to ask him if he would like an ice-cream in a voice as low and reverent as if she were saying her prayers. She always bought one for herself as well. They walked along streets in winter, eating their ice-creams together. She laughed when a man shouted, 'God bless your stomachs!'

Slowly, still in amazement, he began to love Nanny Belmayne back.

He loved, first of all, the face that kissed him. It was a round, red-cheeked face with a turned-up nose and eyes that slanted upward, and long dimples, just like Dad's, in either cheek, and a wide dimple like his in her chin. In appearance she was less like Dad than like his brother, Uncle Cal, her eldest son, but Louis was still far from such distinctions. To him, Nanny Belmayne's face was pre-eminently like that of a Bisto Kid. When he first saw the Bisto gravy packet, his heart nearly stopped to see the larger Bisto Kid sniffing the aroma of Bisto gravy just as Nanny Belmayne would, with rosy cheeks, snub nose tilted in the air, eyes closed to signify aroma, and appetite for all the same things that Louis liked, such as vinegary cabbage or oranges with lumps of sugar in them, but also for the exotic, outlandish things Nanny Belmayne liked, such as stout and applecores and bananas sprinkled with red cayenne pepper.

When he sat on her lap, and she hugged and kissed him and told him how much she loved him, his overwhelmed senses could scarcely distinguish her face. He could see nothing but the grey lump high up on her left cheek that had two long white hairs waving out of it. Her lips were dry and cold-feeling. The rosiness in her cheeks came from tiny flecks of red that stayed there, in or out of doors, winter and summer. Her face had a smell like no other in the world, cool and dry and old and leathery, an aroma deriving in equal part from her skin, her hair, her coat, her hat, her handbag, her house and her history, and subtly suggesting in addition her mats, her cats, her Red Indian dolls, her staircurtain, her dog's dinner, her cacti, her meat-safe, her cornplasters, her box of rattlesnake teeth, her walking sticks, her junket-moulds, her satin bloomers, and all else about her that was unlike anybody else.

The grey lump on Nanny Belmayne's cheek and the smell of her face remained in Louis's mind through all the months when he and she were forced to be apart. For already he loved Nanny Belmayne, as she loved him, more than anyone in the world, and longed, as she did, for the next time he would go up to London and stay with her up in Clapham Old Town.

After they had moved to the Isle of Wight, going to stay with Nanny Belmayne entailed a journey of some complexity. Louis had first to be escorted by his mother or by Dad from Ryde Pier across to Portsmouth on the boat. At Portsmouth Harbour, below the masts of HMS *Victory*, where gulls screamed and swooped about the long station canopy, he would be put on the train for Waterloo in the care of the Guard.

The guard, for this duty, had something slipped into his

hand by Dad. It was always a different guard but Louis's agitation was such that various guards merged into a single personality, with gold around his hat, silver coat and waistcoat buttons in many vertical seams, like a hussar, a pocket watch, which he pulled out of his waistcoat pocket repeatedly, and a strong aroma of trains and of stations. He showed no animosity to Louis for having been placed in his charge: he allowed Louis to travel, if he wished, in the guard's van, among the crates and parcels and parcelled-up bicycles. He often lent Louis a pencil with which to draw. A guard's pencil had a very blunt point and a pink rubber sunk deep into its chewed gold metal cap. He conversed with Louis in a voice imperfectly heard above the train noise: they said 'Pardon?' to each other for mile after mile. Sometimes the guard even invited Louis into his private sanctum, within the metal cages, offered him a tiny, strong peppermint from a tin and allowed him to look through an instrument like a tilted mirror in which the fields and trees and towns flew past in the wrong direction.

Louis received these kindnesses with indifference. All that concerned him about the train was its power to remove the distance between himself and Nanny Belmayne. Such was his nervous longing, it seemed to him that the train was almost malignly unwilling to carry out its task. After leaving Portsmouth Harbour, it proceeded at no more than a walking pace beside the streets of sailors' houses, the parks and football ground. A few moments later, it drew into Portsmouth Town, the secondary station that hung on corrugated bridges above the city centre. The journey had not yet even begun.

Between Portsmouth Town and Haslemere lie an infinite number of miles. Louis has left the guard's van now, and is sitting in his own compartment. Nobody else is there. The thick red upholstery feels rough and warm against the backs of his legs. He has read all the comics Dad bought for him, and drawn on every possible piece of paper. He looks out, beyond the red *No Smoking* triangle, at the flat lands, and dwindling reminders of the sea. He looks at his own face, pale and un-
38

smiling, reflected in the glass beside him like a piece of finger-nail or a rushing fragment of the moon.

From Guildford to Woking, the train rattles and raps with compensating haste. The guard comes along the corridor, clips his ticket and asks if he is all right. But, from Woking onward, a terrible fitfulness steals over the train once more. They are now at the very edge of London. Louis can see blackened houses next to the line, and the first red bus, passing under a bridge. Already, to his eyes, the whole landscape suggests Nanny Belmayne. Every window is like her kitchen window; every back garden, every clothes-line is like hers. But the train, with maddening sloth, glides through widening estuaries of track, passing other trains, then being overtaken by them : stopping, or nearly stopping, then imperceptibly gathering speed. His whole body, his arms, his legs within their elastic sock garters, urge the train to move. He begs God to do it. He whispers to himself, 'We're not moving. I know we're not moving. We're standing still. I know we're standing still.'

They are moving, past the walls etched with the words *Brand's Essence*. They have stopped again, opposite the long black figure in a cloak which advertises Sandeman's Port. There is a glimpse of Parliament, and Big Ben gleaming in the sun. At last the rounded signal box proclaims 'Waterloo $\frac{1}{2}$ mile'. His face pressed against the compartment window, he sees the far end of the train uncurling into the station mouth, under low-lying glass mountain-peaks.

He sees her, just before she sees him, waiting outside the ticket-barrier. He sees her broad shoulders, her coat with the big squares, her squashy green hat with a hatpin in it, her face searching for him among the crowd released from the train, all down the avenue of open compartment doors. 'Nanny, here I am!' Now she has seen him, and he runs towards her. The ticket collector takes half his ticket. He is in her arms, feeling the big, dry kisses smack against his face, his ears, his glasses and school cap, breathing the heavenly smell of Nanny Belmayne's coat and handbag, and hair and skin and feet.

Together they cross the vast indoor pavement where pigeons

39

fly and settle under the high-girdered glass. Waterloo is *her* station, built for the single purpose of welcoming Louis into her world. The brown bookstalls, the luggage office, the shifting and slapping indicator-boards, all seem to have a kinship with Nanny Belmayne; a complicity in the plans she has made for Louis during his stay. Above the platform entrances, he sees the poster that is half a statue—the man in a tall hat and topboots, 'Born 1821—still going strong', striding along quickly, as if to keep up with them, smiling and holding his monocle in his eye.

'There's old Johnnie Walker,' she says, as if alluding to some personal friend.

They go into the Underground together, to the Northern Line. Deep and snug and windy, the Northern Line belongs to Nanny Belmayne: other people travel on it only by permission. The escalators break like a waterfall under the wide painting of the girl on the Ovaltine farm. Louis and Nanny Belmayne go down, standing on the right. Tall-necked lamps ascend to the left of them and, to the right, the angled showcases with advertisements for Coruba Rum, 'Make Mine Myers', Phillips Soles and Heels, 'Anzora cream and Viola Masters the Hair'. At the bottom, Louis tenses himself to jump over the dangerous place where sharp teeth devour the subsiding steps.

They stand on their platform in the strong, warm London wind. There are angular chocolate machines along the platform, which have not functioned since 'before the War'. On the curved tunnel wall, beyond the deadly rail, is a picture of two little children in hoods and leggings, walking hand in hand along a tree-lined road that has no end. Next to it is the picture of a lemon with a face, crying. Even the lemon's weeping face seems to Louis to resemble Nanny Belmayne's. 'What Made the Lemon Squash?' the poster asks, as she might well have done. Their train is coming with a change in the wind, a rumour of sound, a white light darting along the dingy and curved white tiles, a gust preceding it that makes the long lamps jerk and sway in the tunnel roof.

Trains on the Northern Line have interiors of deep green
40

and seats upholstered in scarlet and black. Louis and Nanny Belmayne sit side by side on the sideways seat, their elbows on scarlet leather arm-rests. Louis can see himself reflected in the window opposite, his face, his cap, his school scarf against the rushing, cabled darkness. Nanny Belmayne is visible beside him in her coat and beret, her face, doubled by the refraction of the glass, inclined towards his as if she is listening carefully.

So they sit together, past Kennington and Oval, past Stockwell and Clapham North, to Clapham Common, where the lines northbound and southbound do not have separate platforms but come out of tunnels on either side of the same platform.

The milk is the sea. The pieces of puffed wheat are ships of the Spanish Armada, storm-tossed by the tilted dish. Louis always has puffed wheat out of this dish even though the word 'Porridge' is written inside its buff-coloured rim. He catches the brown-seamed galleons one by one, condemning each to run onto a reef when the milk around it flows into his spoon. As the milk grows less, the pattern on the floor of the dish is cloudily revealed. It is a group of flags, and yellow and red heraldic beasts, rampant beside the portrait of a brown-tinted young man. Louis once asked the identity of this young man, and Nanny Belmayne replied that it was Edward the Eighth. 'He's the poor Duke o'Windsor now,' she added gravely. This suggestion of tragedy always returns to Louis's mind when he sees the young man's face surfacing through the sugary milk, and appearing the more sad and unlucky for having been slightly scraped away by porridge and cereal spoons.

It is the first morning of his stay with Nanny Belmayne. He is sitting with his puffed wheat at the kitchen table while Nanny Belmayne, at the curtained stove, cooks the fried potato which traditionally forms the second course of his breakfast at Orlando Road. Behind him is the kitchen window and beyond that, fixed to the roof-tiles, is the meat-safe where Nanny Belmayne

41

keeps her bacon and dripping. Turning in his chair, he has a view of her long back garden with the crazy paving that Dad laid for her and the little fruit trees planted for her by Dad. Then comes her rockery, and the back wall of a turquoise-coloured tin shed, beyond which lie all the kingdoms of London.

The kitchen is full of potato steam and the noise of spitting and cracking. Nanny Belmayne's face, as she turns round from the stove, seems even rosier than usual, slightly enlarged by heat and concentration. Catching his attention, she opens her eyes wide, so that the whites show, and breaks into a little war dance, looking at Louis over her shoulder, moving her bottom so that the pleat in her skirt sways to and fro, and waving the kitchen-slice above her head.

Louis is entranced but a little scandalised, just as he is when Nanny Belmayne runs out into the road to pick up horse manure on the coal-shovel, or crosses the road forgetting her Kerb Drill, or eats an apple, core and all.

'Let's all go down the Strand,' sings Nanny Belmayne as she waves the kitchen-slice. 'Let's all go down the Strand—*and have a banana*!'

'Nanny! What would your West Country ancestors say if they could see you doing that?'

'Shall I ask you a riddle?'

'All right, Nanny.'

'What did the rheumatism say to the arthritis?'

She always has a riddle to ask Louis when he comes up to stay. Her rich West Country voice, undiluted by years in London, particularly enjoys pronouncing 'th'arthritis'. And, of course, it is the very essence of Nanny Belmayne humour that rheumatism and arthritis shall be thought capable of holding a conversation.

Louis cannot guess what it was that the rheumatism said to the arthritis.

'It said "How can we get out of this joint?" '

She brings his plate across. It is the Edward the Eighth plate again, with a bit of puffed wheat still sticking to the rim.

42

'There you are,' she says, with a wink. 'Get outside o' that, and you won't do badly.'

'Nanny?'

'Yes my little lamb? What my little love?'

'When will we be going up to the West End for a walk round?'

'Soon, loved one. Please God an' all's well.'

That is the pleasure that lies in the future. For the present, he has fried potato, browned on top, a fried egg with pepper over it, bacon crisped into little ram horn shapes. He has Nanny Belmayne all day today, tomorrow, the next day, the next day and the next day. The joys of present and future break out in him like the egg under his fork, they whirl with the potato steam in his head. The sad, spoon-scraped face of Edward the Eighth stares up through a gap in the potato at the infinity of his happiness.

Nanny Belmayne lives at 71 Orlando Road, Clapham Old Town. As you come along Orlando Road from the shops in Rectory Grove, her house is the last but one on the right. That, at least, is its position since the War, when the Germans dropped a bomb on Orlando Road, leaving a crater which now extends from the house next to Nanny Belmayne's up to the corner of Klea Avenue. Nanny Belmayne was away when the bomb fell. She was down at Hornchurch, helping Uncle Cal to run a sweet shop. Fortunately, Dad had boarded up her windows for her, and they were not even broken in the explosion.

When Dad and Uncle Cal were little boys, they used to occupy the whole of 71 Orlando Road. But when Dad and Uncle Cal went to fight in the War, it proved too much for Nanny Belmayne to manage by herself. So she gravitated upwards, letting the ground floor to tenants. Consequently, for all that 71 Orlando Road means to Louis, it does not signify to him any special sort of exterior. There are two bay windows, one above another, painted cream; a front door with a misty glass pane, surrounded by lozenges of coloured glass which

43

reflect the front hall in dark red, blue and green. A laurel bush stands in the front garden, together with two dustbins. The coal-hole is near the front-step. The wall, recently rebuilt for Nanny Belmayne by Dad, is of large grey bricks, painstakingly but unevenly cemented.

The ground floor is let to a Mr and Mrs O'Rourke. Mr O'Rourke is Irish. He is a huge, slow, snuffling good-natured man who works as a glazier and whose only other pastime seems to be sitting in the small back kitchen, that used to be Nanny Belmayne's, waiting for his dinner to be ready. His wife—who is not Irish—calls him 'Paddy'. She is short thin, white, cheerful and always busy. She wears a turban on her head and, in the mornings, a pinafore of violet flowers with only her underwear beneath. To Louis, she typifies all the women to be seen in Orlando Road and along Klea Avenue, scrubbing front door steps, polishing brass door knockers, going shopping in the Brixton arcades, or standing and gossiping, in their turbans and their tight-waisted, soldierly-looking coats with velvet collars, straight after the era referred to, not without affection, as 'The War'.

Mr and Mrs O'Rourke's kitchen is shared with a large quantity of cats. There are cats sitting on the chairs or underneath them; there is often a cat reclining on the grey enamel cooking-range, where Mr O'Rourke's dinner is being cooked. Of these many cats, only one—Toby—actually belongs to Mrs O'Rourke. The remainder belong to Nanny Belmayne, but are looked after and fed by Mrs O'Rourke. There is Korky, the oldest, there is Amber, and Judy and Judy's daughter, another Judy. Mrs O'Rourke feeds them all on liver, boiling it in a number of saucepans on the stove next to Mr O'Rourke's dinner. The lower part of 71 Orlando Road is pervaded by this thick, meaty but strangely unappetising odour.

Nanny Belmayne's domain begins at the top of the first flight of stairs, its boundary a curtain, hanging across between the stair wall and the place where the banister turns. The curtain, the pattern of which cannot be seen in the darkness, is thick and rough, and so long that it trails on the ground above

44

the top stair. One of Louis's delights is to entangle himself in the curtain and the darkness round it, treading its slackness underfoot, rolling and twisting himself, walking against it, along the passage towards the kitchen, so that the curtain brushes his forehead, flows through his hair and drops down again behind him. It has a rich, sour, catty smell, and the hem, as it brushes his face, feels a little wet, where the cats have been.

Grandpa Belmayne is dead. To Louis he has always been so. He was in the Navy, and 'went down' with his ship in the Irish Sea in 1918, while Uncle Cal and Dad were still only babies. Nanny Belmayne, when the sad news reached her, was suffering from one of her 'mugraines', an affliction which, to Louis, had somewhat savoury overtones, like puffed wheat, or perhaps shredded wheat. But evidently a 'mugraine' is painful, since Nanny Belmayne shuts her eyes merely to remember it.

'Lou!' She tells him in a hushed voice. 'I was in such pain! I wouldn't have cared if the *whole* of the Germany army, with fixed bayonets, had come marching through my bedroom.'

A picture of Grandpa Belmayne hangs at the top of the house, on the landing outside Nanny Belmayne's bedroom. It is an oval-shaped yellow-tinted photograph, in a black, carved wooden frame. Grandpa Belmayne has a short, pale yellow moustache; he wears a Naval cap not much bigger than Louis's school cap; his eyes seem gentle and preoccupied. Nanny Belmayne speaks of him always with the greatest pride. 'He was a Master Mariner, y'know.' At these moments, she, too, has a touch of ships and the sea about her. She points out to Louis the sequence of Grandpa Belmayne's navigational and Masonic certificates which still hang, one below the other, down the rosebudded wall next to the stairs up from her sitting-room. By her account, Grandpa Belmayne was a noble and kind and infinitely gentle man, the source of those virtues in both Dad and Uncle Cal, whose very death showed tact and consideration. For, though undoubtedly sad, it left Nanny with

45

a pension and some buildings she was able to rent to United Dairies. Nor could any of her extraordinary later life have happened but for Grandpa Belmayne's obligingness in being torpedoed.

Nanny Belmayne's house is full of things acquired by Grandpa Belmayne during many sea voyages. There are buffalo and antelope horns, fixed to the wall on wooden shields. There are carved wooden mugs from South Sea Islands, now full of old crayons or lumps of orange sealing wax or counterfoils detached from postal-orders. There are elephants' tusks, with string threaded through them; and a little pillbox she has shown to Louis, full of rattlesnake's teeth. Outside her sitting-room door is a tall, thin receptacle, full of dusty canes and silver-banded walking sticks and, standing among them, a length of stained yellow bone-like substance with serrations along either side—the saw from a saw-fish, brought home by Grandpa Belmayne from the sea.

After Grandpa Belmayne went down with his ship, Nanny Belmayne never remarried. She is not married to Uncle Tony, although he has lived at her house, since 'before the War'. To Louis, Uncle Tony is exactly like the kindly-looking old shoemaker you see on the Tube advertisements, recommending Phillip's stick-on soles and heels. He has a little, grizzled, squared-off moustache and he looks at you, as the shoemaker does, over the top of half-moon spectacles. He is gentle, different, kind, modest and short-tempered. When he kisses Louis, he imparts a faint, fresh whiff of what Louis privately terms 'Brickwood's and Whitbread's', acquired on his nightly journey home from the City. He and Nanny Belmayne hug and kiss one another, and argue with one another about the washing-up as though each is embarrassed by the other's goodness and kindness.

'*I'll* do that, Gerry dear.'

'Gerry is short for Geraldine, Nanny Belmayne's first name.

'No, *I'll* do it, Tony dear.'

'Oh—*Gerry*, dear!'

'Oh—*Tony* dear!'

In the daytime, Uncle Tony puts on a grey Homburg hat and goes to work outside the Old Town. He is already up when Louis is awoken by Nanny Belmayne, in her big bed with its swinging side arms of brass and its two tall turrets like sultans in brass turbans. She brings him up a cup of tea with a Rich Tea biscuit balanced in the saucer. She sits on the edge of the big bed, holding the saucer steady while Louis lifts off the cup to drink through the biscuit-edge, soft and brown-wet in his mouth. The front door at the bottom of the house shuts behind Uncle Tony. Now Nanny Belmayne belongs to nobody else.

She has waited weeks for him, getting things ready. She has bought him the new Mary Mouse book, and the new Sunny Stories. She has bought the sweets they both like—Murraymints and Barker and Dobson fruit drops and Butter Brazils, all sticking and clotting together, unwrapped, in the sweet-tin with the cavalier's head. She has bought tall bottles of Hooper Struve ginger beer and Tizer, and Peter's Original Milk Chocolate, and Blenheim apples and William pears. She has made junket for him in a rabbit-shaped mould, and put it to set in the bath. She has brought him a drawing-pad and pencils and a pencil-sharpener. The new point of the first pencil hovers above the first starched white page, symbolising what spaces of joy now lie ahead.

She reads to him from the Mary Mouse book: the adventures of Mary Mouse, Mummy Doll, Daddy Doll and their children, Melia, Pip and Roundy.

'Pip is going to have a birthday. He will soon be four. How very big!'

'Nanny.'

'What, my lamb?'

'I did miss you when I went back last time.'

'And I missed you, my love. Nan missed you ever so.'

'I was sad on the train, Nanny.'

'Oh, so was I. Nanny nearly cried.'

'Did you, Nanny?'

47

'I did. Nanny came home afterwards, and she nearly cried because she missed you so.'

Louis is awed to think of that.

He spends the morning in her kitchen, filling up the pages of the new drawing book. Her kitchen is at the end of a passage, next door to the bathroom, on the first floor. In the midst of London, it retains the homeliness and solidity of kitchens she has described to Louis in her native West Country. The big table, with its green baize cloth, is surrounded by chairs with arms and wheelbacks and seats shaped to fit your bottom. Beside the curtained stove and sink is a marble-topped washstand—one of Nanny Belmayne's numerous wash-stands—with a bread-bin marked 'Bread' standing on it. There is a black fireplace surrounded by a copper grate, which can be reduced into sections, and a high mantelpiece crowded with china ornaments : ivory back-scratchers, old calendars, letters, penholders and other unreachable objects. On the wall around the table hangs a series of humorous illustrations, extolling the benefits of electricity through characters from history. One illustration suggests that, if King John had had an electric washing machine, he might not have lost all his jewels in the Wash. Another affirms that, if King Alfred had had an electric cooker, he might never have burned the cakes.

Bobby, Nanny Balmayne's terrier, moves about the kitchen, bumping into things. He is blind; his eyes completely absent. Wild cats in the street tore them out, leaving behind two empty sockets of parched-looking, yellowish fur. He moves with an air of great patience, bumping now into the table-leg, now into the fender or the lemonade-cupboard; now stopping and fatalistically altering his course. His black-spotted white coat is smooth, like a toy dog's. If you touch him, a growl vibrates distantly through the stubbly warmth.

Life at Nanny Belmayne's suffers from none of the disruptions of home or his other grandma's house, where people come and order him to move so that they can dust or Hoover under the table. Nanny Belmayne seldom wants to Hoover or dust. She sits beside the wireless set in the low chair where

48

Bobby the terrier sleeps at night, and reads him the story of Mr Pink Whistle, who pinned notes on people's back, saying 'I'm a thief' or 'Take care—he bites.' In a minute, she stops, and goes out of the kitchen, down the passage, and Louis hears her calling over the banisters in a deep voice: 'Mrs O'Rourke!' For Mrs O'Rourke goes to Brixton to buy liver for the cats in the arcade. Bobby has liver, too, but Nanny Belmayne cooks that for him with her own hands. A big grey saucepan stands on the stove, steaming and bubbling and jumping its lid up and down, filling the kitchen with that rich and ragged, meaty smell. Louis bends closer down to the page. His nose almost touches the paper and his eyelash, the tip of the pencil. His feet fidget in delirium of joy among the stools under the table. His bottom propels the little chintz cushion, tied to the bars of his chair, back and forth ceaselessly over the seat that is worn smooth by generations of West Country bottoms.

Now she has returned. Her arms are round him, filling his head with the Nanny Belmayne smell; a huge kiss goes off like a cannon-shot against his brow.

'Bless you! Bless you my lamb. His Nan loves him and loves him so much. He's *so* good when he comes up and stays with his old Nan. You'll sit there, amusing yourself for hours, bless your dear heart.'

Later in the morning, they go out shopping in the Old Town. Nanny Belmayne fetches a string bag which she enlarges with waving fingers. She fixes on her beret, driving a long pin through her head to secure it. They go down Orlando Road with Bobby, on his lead, bumping into lamp-posts first, then reversing and cocking his back leg like the elbow of a violinist.

From the opening at the bottom of Orlando Road, there are shops extending along the line of the original Clapham village street, widening into a square named The Polygon, where buses stop to have their numbers and destinations changed. The road bends round, among shoals and outcrops of the Common, past a paddling pool where, according to Nancy Belmayne, several little children have been drowned in only a few inches of water. Louis must promise her he will never go near the paddling pool. He hardly dares to look at it as they pass on the other side of the road.

Around the small green dome of Clapham Common tube station stands a complex road junction, known by the name of its principal pub, The Plough. For the trams to Stockwell or Balham and buses to Brixton, you have to go to the Plough. The tube station stands among bushes on an island between Clapham High Road and Clapham South Side with its raised pavements and its sense of a loftier, racier metropolitan life. Over there is a big hotel called The Alexandra, and a long-fronted shop displaying the legend PRAMS-TOYS. But it is so far away, beyond the silver rails and silver road studs and the shuffling and clanging trams. He knows he belongs on this side, with Woolworth's and Maritime House and Bravington's jeweller's shop, gabled like an Elizabethan manor house.

From 'Louis Hislop', a wavy-haired confectioner whose sweets are fastidiously arranged on paper doilies, Nanny Belmayne buys New Berry Fruits and quarters of Barker and Dobson's fruitdrops and Butter Brazils. She buys Canadian Brand notepaper in Woolworth's, and a new drawing-book for Louis, as well as a whole *box* of dark green Venus pencils. From Mr Brill's off licence, she buys stout in black bottles, lined up on the counter by Mr Brill, whose khaki gloves have no fingers. At the butcher's, she buys sausage meat and a duck's egg for Louis's breakfast tomorrow. In Rectory Gardens, he holds his breath when they cross over the road so as not to pass Tomkinson's the newsagent, where Mr Tomkinson was rude to Nanny Belmayne, and where she will never again in her life set foot. The greengrocer has a tiny, earthy cockpit just at the bottom of Orlando Road. 'Five pounds of potatoes' thunder into Nanny Belmayne's other shopping bag, then back they go up Orlando Road, towards the bomb-site at the top. Bobby the terrier has decided that he doesn't want to walk, so Nanny Belmayne drags him along with his front legs stiff, his bottom trying to sit on the pavement, his empty eye-sockets stubbornly cast down.

For lunch, she cooks sausages, boiled potatoes and cabbage. Louis will not eat cabbage anywhere else but at Orlando Road. She gives it to him on a separate dish, with vinegar and pepper, and Edward the Eighth. She turns round from the curtained stove, her face rosy in the cabbage steam, and suddenly asks:

'Why's a bird like a bank manager?'

'Nanny, I don't know.'

'Because he goes hopping from branch to branch.'

'Nanny?'

'Yes, love. What, my loved one?'

'What happens if I can't eat any more?'

'Eat what you can,' she tells him. 'And can what you can't.'

For pudding she brings him a wedge of suet, obliterating the tragic face of Edward the Eighth. She fetches the tin of Golden Syrup, its interior a silver cylinder, with a floor of shining gold. She plunges in a tablespoon and brings it out twisted up with Golden Syrup, then lifts it high into the air, trailing a slow golden column from the tin that grows slender as she folds it round the spoon, round and round until the last thread is sucked in. Then she tips the spoon the other way. The thick gold slips downward, and breaks over the suet and piles there, sliding to encircle it, as Nanny Belmayne flourishes the tablespoon up high again, and twists and twists it until the last glittering thread has broken.

After lunch every day comes a ritual dear to his heart. Nanny Belmayne takes him from the kitchen, along the passage to the top of the stairs where the dark curtain hangs. They go up four steps to a higher landing, where the white enamel plates of two closed doors glimmer through the shadow. One of these doors is to Nanny Belmayne's sitting room. The other is to Uncle Tony's room. They go into Uncle Tony's room. It is bare save for the bed, the fireplace, and Uncle Tony's slim yellow wooden shoe-trees standing at the edge of the carpet. Nanny Belmayne reaches to a high shelf and takes down a Toby jug in a dark green coat with a foaming china mug balanced on one knee of its scarlet breeches. She winds

51

it up with a key underneath and holds it out while the music inside plays a little plinking and plonking tune that to Louis is poignant and mysterious.

'Where did it come from, Nanny?'

'Your Daddy brought it home, my love.'

'When was that?'

'Oh—one night before the War.'

'Will you wind it up once more?'

'I will, love.'

'What do you think it's saying, Nanny?'

'I think it's saying "drink it up, drink it up, drink it up".'

When she puts the Toby jug back on its high shelf, the music cuts off with a click. 'That'll be yours one day,' she tells him.

Sometimes after lunch, Nanny Belmayne has a visitor. It might be Auntie Jeff, an old lady she knows from Wimbledon, or Aunt Kate from Hungerford or some other member of her wide acquaintanceship of old ladies. Louis sits under the kitchen table, listening to Nanny Belmayne and her visitor discussing rheumatism and arthritis—now robbed of their power to make jokes—and corns and bunions and the mild winter and meat coupons and Dr Manley and Mr Churchill. Dr Manley is Nanny Belmayne's doctor, a saintly man whose every observation she repeats in a kind of trance of gratitude and respect. And Mr Churchill won the War. Nanny Belmayne's voice is hushed as she speaks of this good, gentle man who has made a point of personally watching over her and all her family, including Louis himself. Sometimes it is almost as if Mr Churchill is sitting there, having a cup of tea and a Rich Tea biscuit, in the house that has been preserved by his personal intervention.

And naturally the visitor hears what a clever boy Louis is; how he travels up from Portsmouth to London in the care of the Guard; how good he always is when he stays at Orlando Road—he will sit and draw and amuse himself for hours. The funny little things he has said are repeated by Nanny Belmayne for the visitor's benefit—the funny thing he said about a

52

sunhat in Oxford, and the funny thing he said yesterday on the tram. These funny little things, dating back to his babyhood, are like a treasury in Nanny Belmayne's mind. And once, she tells the visitor, he stood up and bowed left and right, just like the cat he had seen in a cartoon film.

They are talking about bunions and the War again. The light fades in the window behind her meat-safe—he can hardly see Nanny Belmayne's face. He can only hear her voice, so kind, so gentle, so thankful for kindness and gentleness in Mr Churchill and Dr Manley.

'You know what they say, don't you—that the only good German's a dead German.'

Now the visitor has gone, and Nanny Belmayne, in the funny, low slung chair next to the kitchen table, settles down for her afternoon rest. Bobby has gone to sleep against the long copper fire-surround, his eyeless sockets closed, snoring gently. The firelight gleams on the big aerial clothes-horse which Nanny Belmayne has lowered on its string pulleys from the ceiling and festooned with teaclothes and Uncle Tony's collarless shirts and his vests and long johns, and Nanny Belmayne's own vests and her large, pink satin, elasticated bloomers.

Louis is underneath the table. Leaning on one musty, doggy-smelling footstool, he re-reads his new Mary Mouse book by the light of the fire alone. He can barely distinguish the red and black illustrations. He can smell the strange aroma, like sour toffee, of the glue between the pages.

'Nanny.'

There is silence.

'Nanny, are you awake?'

'Yes, love.'

'Nanny, where's Mrs O'Rourke this afternoon?'

'Gone to be a soldier.'

He wonders if Mrs O'Rourke, in her flowered pinafore and turban, with so many saucepans of liver to watch over, could really forsake those responsibilities for a military career.

He stares from under the tablecloth into the fire until he

53

can almost see Nanny Belmayne's face there, twisting and flickering up and flaring among the coal.

'Nanny.'

A silence. He says, louder:

'Nanny.'

'What, love?'

'Where *is* Mrs O'Rourke this afternoon?'

'Gone to see a man about a dog.'

'Are we going up to the West End tomorrow, Nanny?'

'Yes, my lamb. Please God and all's well.'

He wants to be excused. He goes out of the kitchen, down the passage to the toilet in its alcove at the top of the stairs. Above and below the stair curtain, the house is dark and still. The name printed inside the toilet bowl is Claro. He believes that, after he has pulled the chain, something will happen to him unless he can get back to the kitchen before the flushing noise stops. Holding the chain down, he opens the door, getting as far outside the toilet as he can; then he lets go; in a single bound, as the lever clanks up in the cistern, he reaches the kitchen door, saved from a faceless retribution by the glint of firelight through the glass.

Mrs O'Rourke has not gone away to be a soldier after all. Her voice, calling to cats below the banisters, signifies the end of afternoon:

'Toby! Toby, Toby, Toby! Judy! Judy, Jud-ee! Korky, Korky! Tob-*ee*! Aah, there he is, love him! Toby, Toby, Toby!'

They start for the West End directly after breakfast. They cross over by the bomb-site at the top of Orlando Road, then they go along Klea Avenue, where the houses are tall, like mountain fortresses, with airborne front doors, and porches and bay windows striped in white and vermilion.

Louis wears his brown school raincoat—for he goes to Partlands now—and his brown, blue and white scarf wound around his neck twice, tucked into his raincoat-belt in front

54

and behind. Nanny Belmayne wears her coat with the big squares, a cameo brooch and her squashy green beret, pulled down straight over her forehead, giving her the appearance of some big, genial Maori or cannibal chief. One of her hands holds Louis's: in the other she carries a string bag full of Butter Brazils, Blenheim apples and other necessary provisions.

At the Plough, they catch a number 88 bus. They sit downstairs on the sideways seat. The conductor says 'Hold tight' through his nose, helping an old lady by the elbow up the cabin step as the bus jumps forward.

'A tuppenny-ha'penny and a penny, please,' Nanny Belmayne says in a rich and jovial West Country voice. Even the conductor, detaching a pink and a green ticket from his wooden frame, seems to share in the excitement of starting out for the West End. Sometimes the conductor is a black man. As he continues down the bus, collecting fares, Nanny Belmayne nudges Louis in the ribs and whispers loudly: *'He's* looking a bit black about something.'

Despite all the years that Nanny Belmayne has lived in London, her attitude, to all outside Clapham Old Town, remains that of the explorer. They capture a front seat as soon as they can, close behind the driver and his big, flat wheel. As the bus descends from the foothills south of the river, they can see the Thames all round them, sparkling brown. They go across Chelsea Bridge, and Louis looks up, as he always does, to the tops of the bridge columns where fat little gold galleons gleam in the winter sun.

'I'm going to get you one of those ships for Christmas,' Nanny Belmayne tells him.

Her tone is jocular. Yet to Louis it is entirely possible that Nanny Belmayne can climb the cables to the summit of Chelsea Bridge and return with one of the galleons to be put into his Christmas pillow-case.

By now the bus is crowded. Several ladies are standing in the aisle with shopping baskets and bags. Louis feels sorry for them because they are not going to the West End. He is

55

surprised when Nanny Belmayne discourages him from offering his seat to one of the ladies, as he has been taught.

'You sit where you are,' she whispers to him. 'You paid for your seat the same as everybody else.'

In Whitehall, they see a Horse Guard sitting high aloft in his plumed and scowling helmet. His sabre rests on the side of his breastplate. They go past the white thing, in the middle of the road, which makes Nanny Belmayne suggest Louis remove his school cap.

'What *is* that thing, Nanny?'

'It's the Cenotaph.'

'What's it for, I mean?'

'It's for all the poor soldiers and sailors who died in the War.'

They get off the bus in Trafalgar Square. They are walking and kicking flocks of grey and violet pigeons into the air with their feet. The new, big, breezy London swirls above them at the summit of the square, and rushes below them, through the archways into the Mall. The fountains, all around them, fling up skirts of silver water to try to damp the noses of the four smug lions on their plinths. 'There's old Nelson up on his column,' Nanny Belmayne says, as though speaking humorously of an old friend.

It is the same with statues. Nanny Belmayne knows the identity of all the statues, raising mildewy hats or swords or riding petrified chargers under the noisy, splashing, bus-roaring, taxi-racing West End sky. 'That's Mr Gladstone. And *that's* Mr Asquith.' To Louis, the character of several British Prime Ministers will always be determined by the extent to which they were approved or disapproved of by Nanny Belmayne. At Apsley House, where the Duke of Wellington once lived, they climb the big marble staircase, under a vast chandelier, and Louis looks over the balustrade at the statue of Napoleon with no clothes on but a thing concealing his winkle that reminds Louis of nothing so much as a big stone cauliflower. He remembers how Nanny Belmayne nudged him the first

56

time they climbed that staircase, and how sure he felt that she had been actually acquainted with the Duke of Wellington once; and perhaps even directly concerned in putting Napoleon there with a cauliflower over his winkle.

They go to Buckingham Palace, hoping to see the King and Queen and Princess Elizabeth and Princess Margaret. Along the front of Buckingham Palace there are circular windows at intervals which, Louis thinks, must be toilet windows. How do the King and Queen make up their minds which of these many toilets to go into? They never see the King and Queen and Princesses, just as they never quite see the Changing of the Guard, but to Louis this does not matter. The thing he loves is standing beside Nanny Belmayne, holding her hand, feeling the cold wind in his face and the oval shape of a Murraymint inside his cheek as they look through the railings together.

'Are they in there, Nanny?'

'If they'd have known *you* were coming,' she tells him, 'I'm sure they'd have made a point of staying in.'

'*Would* they, Nanny?'

'Not half they would,' she says fervently.

Her personality, far from diminishing outside the Old Town, has grown miraculously to encompass the whole of London and its monuments. She has the power, wherever they go, to grant, instantly, Louis's most extravagant wish. When his wish is to see a prehistoric skeleton, Nanny Belmayne takes him straight to the Natural History Museum: it is as if the woolly mammoth in the entrance-hall has been produced by her casually from among the Butter Brazils and Blenheims in her string bag. When he wants to go to a museum in which there will be nothing but toy soldiers, she takes him to the United Services Museum in Whitehall. Outside, she shows him the head of King Charles—another acquaintance of hers, he deduced. And while he runs distractedly from one display case to the next, Nanny Belmayne sits waiting for him, in the United Services Museum, in the Victoria and Albert or the Science Museum, in her coat with the big squares and her

57

squashy green beret and hatpin, her string bag settled on the floor between her large, button-sided shoes.

She takes him next to the Zoo. There is a rhyme which she always recites on their way.

'We'll go to the Zoo and we'll see a Gnu. An elk and a whelk and a wild Em*u*.'

They stand watching the monkeys, who leap and scowl and flourish bottoms as pink as seaside rock. Louis thinks that if he had a pink bottom, he would go to any lengths to conceal it. Nanny Belmayne can pull a face just like a monkey if she wants to. Louis feels himself overwhelmed by a recurrent but hopeless desire to have a monkey for a pet.

'I used to have monkeys at home when I was a girl,' she tells him.

'You *didn't*, did you Nanny?'

'We did, you know. When we lived down at Bath. Monkeys we used to have. And greyhounds, my father kept.'

'What were the monkeys like?'

Nanny Belmayne wrinkles up her little nose.

'They'd cling on tight to you and then they'd go and wee wee all down your front.'

In the lion house, she showed him the lion which had been given to Mr Churchill. She seems so proud that Louis feels she herself must have been concerned in choosing for Mr Churchill this most original present.

But best of all, Louis likes the Aquarium. He likes the dark corridors of mock stone, the floating, dark windows full of silver stripes, flickering and swift. He is frightened but fascinated by the eels, their turned-down mouths and bright, disgusted eyes. In particular, he loves the sea-horses. He is, for some reason, charmed by the jaunty little creatures, sailing curved but upright, among the turning fish shapes and the gravel that wriggles with half-buried things.

'I've got a sea-horse at home,' Nanny Belmayne says casually.

'Nanny—you *haven't*!'

'Yes I have. I've got a sea-horse, *and* I've got a sea-cow.'

'Where did you get them from, Nanny?'

'Your Grandpa Belmayne brought them home from the sea.'

'Will you show them to me, Nanny?'

'I will, my love. Nan'll show 'em you tomorrow.'

Now they have arrived in the true West End. They are climbing out of the Tube into Piccadilly Circus, towards Swan and Edgar's department store, leaning dizzily at the summit of the twisted tunnel stairs. The sight of the Wrigley's chewing gum sign causes a stir of recognition deep inside Louis, like coming home. And Eros, naturally, is an old friend of Nanny's.

When Nanny Belmayne walks, her feet turn outward, as if to communicate her newness and innocence in the big city. She forges with untiring energy through the crowds at the end of Louis's arm; at times, heedless of traffic, plunging out into the road. 'Nanny!' he protests, losing his voice in the wind. 'Remember your Kerb Drill!'

They walk along the inner side of Regent Street, seeing themselves pass next to the plaster dummies in high shop windows. Louis, by this time, is holding in his free hand an animal constructed from balloons, both round and cylindrical, twisted up together. And in his heart the excitement leaps into fear, because they must be getting closer to Hamley's. Nanny Belmayne, of course, wants to go to Hamley's as much as he does. She knows a little rhyme about it, which she recites as they draw near. 'Hamley's toys—for girls and boys.' Yet his chief sensation is of dread, lest something shall happen, before they get there, to remove Hamley's from the surface of the earth.

Hamley's is not merely a shop: it is a whole department store of toys. Its ground-floor windows exhibit a myriad of toys, given life by hidden electric current. There are bears that nod and trains that rush, and aeroplanes that fly and dogs that bark and dolls that walk. Up above, in a long second storey window like an aquarium, are giant animals and dolls, so inconceivably expensive that Louis dares not even raise his eyes to look at them.

59

Inside Hamley's, a spiral staircase ascends to firmaments of toys. Louis ignores them all in his desire to reach the department on the right of the staircase. This department is entirely devoted to soldiers. The very walls are made of soldiers —of thin red boxes piled up like bricks behind the counter, showing sets of five or ten or twenty-five, with legs secured to a yellow background by string, mounted or on foot, marching, running, trotting, cantering, galloping, shouldering or presenting arms, firing from a standing, kneeling or lying position. There are also tall cabinets of unboxed soldiers, exquisitely lifelike, idolatrously accurate in dress and equipment, but these, he has been told, are 'collectors' models'. A single figure can cost as much as ten shillings.

Nanny Belmayne sits on a bench in the middle of the soldier department while Louis decides which soldiers to buy. There are so many boxes, so many silhouettes uncertain to his poor eyesight that at the last, a sort of panic overcomes him: he is not sure if the box he has indicated contains the soldiers he really wants. Brown paper envelops the yellow lid with its flourished signature *W. Britain*, its picture of battle honours won by the regiment he has chosen. 'Eight and eleven, please,' the salesgirl says, just as Louis glimpses at an upper level a set of Russian infantrymen in overcoats, or Zulus, or motorcycle dispatch-riders or Foreign Legionnaires, or Royal Canadian Northwest Mounted Police that he meant to buy last year but somehow, in a similar panic, did not. Now it's too late, again.

Afterwards, they go to a cinema called the Cameo in Great Windmill Street. This, in Nanny Belmayne language, is called 'seeing a Walt Disney'. She has great affection for Walt Disney, whom she has presumably encouraged to make his cartoon films about Mickey Mouse, Pluto and Donald Duck. You enter the Cameo through a door immediately below the screen, and then stand and wait for a seat to become vacant, with the cartoon happening overhead in soft, high flickers and bumps. Often it is so crowded that Louis and Nanny Belmayne have to sit in seats apart from each other. They see

60

Tom and Jerry, Bugs Bunny, and Sylvester the cat, chasing and somersaulting, nearly mute above the crowded, laughing, noisy little auditorium. They see The News, and sometimes, a Charlie Chaplin film. Louis is fascinated by Charlie Chaplin, not only for the funny way he walks and eats spaghetti, but for a sadness that can be felt in the mime and flicker of his world. At the finish of one film, as Charlie walks away with his big boots and his walking stick, a voice on the film says solemnly, 'The world will never forget Charles Spencer Chaplin.' Surely, Louis thinks, this cannot mean that Charlie Chaplin is dead. Surely, with a name so beautiful as Charlie, he could never die.

At Lyons Corner House afterwards, eating the Welsh Rarebit they always have for tea in the West End, Louis asks 'Nanny, when were Charlie Chaplin films made?'

He feels sure that, in some former existence, she must have been acquainted with Charlie Chaplin.

'Ooh, I don't know. About twenty years ago, love.'

'He isn't dead, is he, Nanny?'

'Oh no, loved one. He isn't dead.'

'I am glad he isn't, Nanny.'

It is now late afternoon. When they come out of Lyons Corner House, they have what Nanny Belmayne calls 'a walk-round'. Sometimes she calls it 'having a mooch-round'. They walk through the little streets behind Piccadilly Circus, going nowhere in particular and eating Wall's ice-creams, even if it is winter. The hard brick numbs their tongues, still cindery with the taste of Welsh Rarebit. They go along pavements with gratings that have kitchens underneath. Louis smells a gust of yellow foreign gravy, and feels thankful he has been with Nanny Belmayne to Lyons Corner House.

In Charing Cross Road is a statue they always seem to pass after dark. Nanny Belmayne stops and looks gravely at it. Louis can see only the thin straight outline of a lady wearing a funny, folded thing on her head.

'Who is it, Nanny?'

'It's poor Nurse Cavell.' She tells him how the same wicked Germans who torpedoed Grandpa Belmayne also shot Nurse Cavell for the crime of being kind. Though it happened long ago, the outrage is still fresh to Nanny Belmayne. He remembers what she said in her kitchen : that the only good German is a dead German.

They stop near a corner entrance and look in at more beautiful chandeliers. This is the Plaza cinema, and Louis has been there to see a film on an earlier expedition with Nanny Belmayne. He remembers, as they crossed the brilliant foyer, how his feet sank down into the carpet.

'There's the Plaza, Nanny,' he says with pride.

'Some people, you know, call it "The Plat-za".'

'They don't, do they, Nanny?'

'Yes, they do, you know.'

'It's a ballet film,' he says.

'Nanny?'

'What, my lamb?'

'I don't like ballet-dancing much, do you?'

'No,' she concurs. 'I think it's all a lot o' bally-hoo.'

'Do you like Bob Hope, Nanny?'

'No,' she answers fiercely.

'Why not?'

'He kissed the parson's bald head.'

Louis does not understand where or why Bob Hope kissed a parson's bald head, or how Nanny Belmayne happened to witness it. But he comprehends perfectly that, in Nanny Belmayne's eyes, it was a gratuitous, facetious and irreligious thing for Bob Hope to have done.

She nudges him again, because a black man is walking down the street towards them. Then she whispers loudly : 'He's looking a bit black about something!'

One afternoon, outside a snuff shop in the Haymarket, they discover a pile of silver tins that have been thrown away. Louis stands waiting while Nanny Belmayne wades among the cardboard boxes, collecting up tins and putting them into her string bag, as the gleaming black and purple, dark red and dull gold bus and taxi, West End night comes rushing and hooting and roaring to engulf them.

They are back again in Nanny Belmayne's kitchen at Orlando Road. The Old Town, outside the little domed Tube station, welcomes them home as if from some city far away. A single light shines over the green tablecloth, with the white cloth and supper things spread over it. Uncle Tony, back from work, is sitting in his chair at the table with his collar off, shredding out tobacco from cigarettes he has smoked during the day, and putting them carefully into a tin to be made into fresh cigarettes tomorrow. Louis is sitting in his chair, with his back to the window. His new soldiers stand around the butter-dish, along the yellow border of the cloth. He is drawing pictures of the Duke of Wellington. Life seems too short for all the pictures of the Duke of Wellington he hopes to draw.

Nanny Belmayne sits in a low chair at the other end of the table, reading the copy of *The Star* which Uncle Tony has brought home from the City for her. She wears thick, shallow tortoiseshell spectacles which, settled half-way down her nose, give her face a fierce, almost devilish expression. Her spectacle case, the metal showing through one denuded corner, lies next to her on the tablecloth. If she comes to an interesting paragraph in *The Star,* she reads it aloud to Uncle Tony and Louis. Bobby the terrier is asleep by the fire, growling softly in eyeless dreams. And outside the window, beyond the darkened meat-safe, beyond her rockery and the corrugated shed, the soft thunder, the warm yellow glow of London seals them safely in together.

Even when Louis goes to bed, the day has not yet ended. For he sleeps with Nanny Belmayne, always, in her big bed in the bedroom at the top of the house. He lies in her feather mattress, not knowing which way to turn because every way is so comfortable. Nanny Belmayne puts a night light on the edge of her wash-stand. He can see its glow reflected in the big bed's two tall turbaned brass foot-posts, and in all the brass rods and joints and curlicues and columns between.

'When are you coming to bed, Nanny?'

'I shan't be many minutes now, loved one.'

'How many minutes, Nanny?'

'Oh, about five.'

'Five minutes, Nanny?'

'Five or ten minutes, my lamb.'

Outside the door, as she begins to go down the stairs, she calls back to him: 'Another lovely day tomorrow.'

'Don't be long, Nanny, will you?'

'I won't.'

Her voice grows softer as she descends: '. . . 'nother lovely day tomorrow.'

The flannelette harbours a faint whiff of the Nanny Belmayne smell. He can see her dressing-table, and the photographs of Dad and Uncle Cal standing on it. He can see her rocking-chair, her dressing-gown hanging up and the wardrobe in which she stores her bottled plums. He knows that here he is at the very heart of her domain. But he is also by himself at the very top of the house, with two dark landings and an infinite quantity of banisters between Nanny Belmayne and himself. The night-light shines, too, on the iron framed pictures of Jesus hanging on the Cross, and of Nanny Belmayne's West Country ancestors, hanging in alcoves around the green-tiled fireplace. Some may have died in the very bed in which Louis lies, now not daring to move or to look beyond the edges of the eiderdown. The hot-water bottle with its knitted cover slips away under his feet, and he wishes he did not remember the prayer which Nanny Belmayne has taught him, with its disquieting clause:

'If I die before I wake, I pray the Lord my soul to take.'

With joy and thankfulness, a little later, he hears Nanny Belmayne coming up the stairs again, to bed. There is a creak as she mounts each stair, then a smaller secondary creak as she pauses on each one for a rest.

She is not cross to find Louis still not asleep. They go on talking about tomorrow as Nanny Belmayne undresses, moving back and forth between the turrets at the foot of the big bed.

Standing in front of her dressing-table, she unhooks her corsets at the front, then stands for a moment in her pink slack vest and her baggy pink satin bloomers, scratching her back and the top of her bottom-crack with the point of her long-handled comb.

Next, she goes across to her wash-stand. She doesn't believe in having too many baths, preferring what she calls 'a good wash-down'. She pours water from the jug into the basin; a moment later, she pours the water into the bucket underneath the wash-stand. 'There!' she sighs, as though at the conclusion of some difficult and tiring ordeal.

She returns to the dressing-table and removes the grips from her hair, so that, gradually, it abandons the compact shape on top of her head and creeps down her back in a long, dark coil like the draught-excluder downstairs. With one movement of her comb she flicks it all forward, completely obliterating her face. A second flick, and it is once more hanging all the way down her back.

She makes little noises—'*Eugh!*' 'Ugh!'—as she puts on her nightdress, and often murmurs, '*Isn't* it cold!'

She says 'isn't it cold' even in summer. They pretend it is always cold late at night, to make bed more safe and cosy.

She blows out the night-light on the wash-stand. Louis hears her coming through the darkness to the left-hand side of the big bed. There is a pause; then he hears the fierce pattering noise as Nanny Belmayne wee-wees into what she calls her 'chamber', or the 'Po' or 'the Edgar Allan'.

'Eugh!'

The edge of the feather bed near him heaves downward beneath her weight.

'There!' she sighs.

Or she says with a sigh: 'Peace came to Peckham!'

Louis stares gladly into the darkness with eyes wide open, thinking about ghosts and Death and bandaged faces and all the things that can never harm him now.

'Eugh!' sighs Nanny Belmayne next to him. 'Eugh! Ugh! *Isn't* it cold!'

*   *   *

When Nanny Belmayne was a little girl in the West Country, they had giant acid drops for a halfpenny each.

'I used to suck one all morning,' she says, 'until my cheek was ribbons inside.'

Every time her father had a drink, whether it was beer, whisky or champagne, she and her sister used to be given their own special portion in a little glass.

'Where did you live in the olden days, Nanny?'

'We lived at Harewood House, Bath. A lovely big house it was with a farm and a dairy. I used to go out into the dairy early in the morning when the butter was all there, unsalted, and cut myself off a big piece an' eat it, as big as this.' She shows Louis the size of the butter pat as big as the space between her crooked first finger and thumb.

'We might be living there still if my father had taken a bit more care of his money, bless him.'

Louis is astonished that even Nanny Belmayne should confide that to him.

'Was your father very strict, Nanny?'

'No-o, he was lovely. Whenever I came home, he used to say to me "Geral'! When you go away, I lose my right arm!" '

It gives Louis a somewhat confusing picture of Nanny Belmayne's father, drinking beer and champagne, driving his horses to Market and continually losing and regaining his right arm.

Sometimes in the afternoons Louis goes with Nanny Belmayne into her best sitting-room, on the landing next to Uncle Tony's bedroom. It is here that she brings out the sea-horse to show him from a shelf of her china cabinet. He holds it up by its light, ribbed tail, disappointed that it is so unlike the creatures that charmed him at the Zoo. It has been dead for even longer than Grandpa Belmayne.

Nanny Belmayne reaches up to put it back in its place. Louis, standing beside her, looks in through the open door at the cherished objects ranged on three or four shelves—at the orange china greyhounds, standing or reclining; at the china black baby eating water-melon, the little green china house,

66

the pug dog's head with a china fly crawling on its brow. He can also see the egg-cosy and the back-stitched place mat which he made for her by himself in the handwork class at Partlands School.

'Nanny, can I have a look at that cannon up there?'

'Not just now, loved one.' She quickly closes the door, shutting away the mugs and greyhounds and china houses, and turning the little key.

Or they sit together on Nanny Belmayne's cold, blue-flowered best sofa, looking at the photograph albums she has lifted out from under the single bookcase. Beside them is the cabinet wireless that does not work. On top of the wireless stands a wooden toucan which sways, if you push it, on a magnetised perch. An old gentleman called Mr Dunwoody made the toucan. Nanny Belmayne unflaps the thick gilt album clasps. Beyond the lace curtain, Louis can hear the eerie cry of the rag and bone man passing along Klea Avenue, at the top of Orlando Road.

What a big family she had. The thick pages reveal them, framed in ovals or squares or little arbours or archways, some decorated with a spray of hand-painted flowers. Some are palely defined in death-yellow, some in dark vermilion, richly detailed. The ladies wear bustles and puffed-out shoulders and strange little droplet earrings. The men wear open coats and high shirt collars and trousers that trail behind their shoes. Some stand against painted backgrounds. Some lean against columns. Some sit. Some stand behind chairs in which others are sitting. All stare forth at posterity with the vague-eyed regretfulness of the dead. 'This is your great-great-grandpa Belmayne,' Nanny Belmayne tells Louis. 'This is your great-great-great-*great* grandma Phillippeaux. By her account, the half-bearded faces, the flat noses and almost ape-like jaws, commemorate lovable and loving hearts who, although inclined in moments of stress to go mad and put revolvers in their mouths and then pull the triggers, would all have loved Louis and hugged and kissed him, just as Nanny Belmayne did, if they had survived to make his acquaintance.

67

Her enthusiasm does something to reassure Louis about being alone with the photographs in her bedroom after he has gone to bed at night. But he still thinks of dead people, including his own ancestors, as harbouring a grudge towards the living.

She tells him how lovely it used to be in the West Country when she was young—what lovely new crusty bread they used to have, and all the butter, for there were no ration-books or 'points' then; and the cheese and Victoria plums and roast beef and cucumber with pepper sprinkled all over it. Her eyes bright with appetite and affection, she sketches the outline of those days with an extended arm, and her accent grows more pronounced—she says ' 'tis' for 'it is' and ' 'twas' for 'it was'.

Louis loves to hear her talk about the West Country. He wonders if it is still as it used to be, full of delicious things to eat and people with lovely accents and kind hearts, as kind as Nanny Belmayne herself. She has promised to take Louis there for a holiday one day soon.

'We'll take a coach from Victoria. And we'll go all over—Shepton Mallet and Glastonbury. You shall see the place where Nanny used to live. We'll go to the Abbot's Kitchen. And we'll do Bath.'

'When will we, Nanny?'

'Soon we will, loved one. One day soon, please God and all's well.'

Grandpa Belmayne was much older than Nanny Belmayne when they got married. She was only eighteen but he had two children from his first marriage. He had ceased by then to be a Master Mariner. Before the First World War, he took Nanny Belmayne to help him run the Talbot Hotel at Bampton in Oxfordshire. It was there that her two sons, Uncle Cal, first, then Dad, were born. An early aeroplane, Nanny Belmayne says, once came down in the field at the back of the Talbot Hotel.

Details of Grandpa Belmayne as a living person remain somewhat scanty. He was a wonderful man, Nanny Belmayne

68

says, and a wonderful, kind and loving father to Uncle Cal and Dad. She says he wore a gold signet ring, which 'went down' with him in the Irish Sea. And when he became annoyed, as he sometimes did, Grandpa Belmayne used to grind his teeth loudly together.

'Your Daddy does just the same if he gets upset about anything: you can hear his teeth grinding away together, bless him, just like his Dad before him.'

Both of Nanny Belmayne's sons were christened with very long names, some of them French, in recognition of Grandpa Belmayne, whose mother was French; others commemorating Nanny Belmayne's West Country lineage, the male members of which possessed names of almost comical solemnity and ungainliness.

'Your Uncle Cal's full names are Calver Claude Phillippeaux Belmayne. And your Daddy's are Emile Theodore Hummerstone Belmayne.'

The habit of many Christian names has been continued in Louis himself. He is called Louis after Grandpa Belmayne and Emile after Dad, Calver after Uncle Cal, and Theodore because there used to be Theodores in the family. Louis hates his first name—it sounds so weak and liquid, like dribble— *Louis*. His initials, L. E. C. T. Belmayne, remind him of letters on goods wagons; in full, they seem like a crowd of people standing and disputing his real identity. He knows he ought to be proud of the names he bears. His own favourite name— that of a two-gunned cowboy in a film he has seen called *Coroner Creek*—is Ernie.

After Grandpa Belmayne went down with his ship, in circumstances of unspecified heroism, wearing his gold signet ring and, doubtless, grinding his teeth with irritation, Nanny Belmayne was left alone with two baby boys and two slightly older stepchildren. Her response showed characteristic flair: she took them all to America to live. They travelled to America on a boat which gave you as many prunes as you could eat for 15 cents.

They lived in Seattle, in a wooden house. They saw Red

c*   69

Indians dancing, and received brown, blue-beaded dolls, which are still in the top back bedroom. Sometimes, when they went on picnics, bears would come out of the forest and eat up the food while they hid in a car which they used to call a Tin Lizzy. Dad, who mispronounced words as a little boy, used to call it a 'Tin Liddy'.

They came home from America after two years. But Nanny Belmayne's two stepchildren, Harmer and Eunice, both decided to remain in Seattle. Eunice died, becoming 'poor Eunice' in her oval album frame. But Harmer survived, became a bank messenger and grew into a god. He now lives out in California, and sends Nanny Belmayne parcels full of peaches and corned beef in unfamiliar tins, and, sometimes, embroidered cowboy shirts for Louis and his cousins. The one he sent Louis the last time had 'Hopalong Cassidy' on the pocket.

Louis is fascinated, above all, by her stories about 'the twenties'. He will never lose his passion for the age when cars looked funny, and buses had open roofs and large, smooth wheels, and policemen's coats were buttoned all the way up and ladies laughed strange, fond laughs from the sides of obscuring hats. It was a world which he imagined to have existed all at the flickering pace of a Charlie Chaplin film— he blinks his own eyes very fast to try to imagine twenties life. Its chief virtue was that it was not separated from 1950 necessarily by Death. If Louis looks at an old photograph, he says hopefully, 'When was that, Nanny? About 1925?' The people may still not have been claimed by the cloud-eyed kingdom of the dead.

She tells him what fun everyone had during the General Strike, when students came up from Oxford and Cambridge to drive the buses. 'They'd take you exactly where you wanted to go, and every fare was sixpence. And in Woolworth's *everything* used to cost sixpence.'

She and her two little boys lived in Chelsea first, as Louis remembers each time they go on the bus over Chelsea Bridge. After she shows him a Chelsea Pensioner in the street, he has a confused but vivid picture of Nanny Belmayne existing in perfect amity with old, red-coated men.

She lived in Gunter Grove, and danced with artists at the Chelsea Arts Ball. She knew an artist called Le Shay, who came from New Zealand and whose grandmother—so she assured Louis with wide eyes—used to be a cannibal. Nanny Belmayne cooked meals for Le Shay and gave him things for his cough. He, in return, did paintings and drawings for her. He did drawings of both Uncle Cal and Dad as little boys, with feelers and wings, like insects. He drew a picture of Nanny Belmayne herself in a wide-brimmed hat, having her future read in a crystal ball. The fortune-teller is promising her, 'a dark man, a blond man, a red-headed man, a piebald man . . .'

In Nanny Belmayne's best sitting-room, above the fireplace she never uses, there hangs a larger and more enigmatic work by Le Shay. It shows a figure seated, with downcast face, in a confusion of sunlight and blue shadow, cradling one knee within its clasped hands. 'He always said that was the way I used to sit in front of the fire,' Nanny Belmayne says, from which Louis gathers that the blue picture is a portrait of her. Yet it is evident, for all the figure's daubing and dappling, that it is not wearing any clothes. Louis finds himself drawn to this painting, not knowing why. It does not make him happy to look at it. He feels uneasy and furtive, yet he cannot stop wanting to look.

Nanny Belmayne bought 71 Orlando Road in 1927. She sold sewing-machines for a living then. Uncle Cal and Dad went to Manor House School on Clapham Common as boarders, but coming home every weekend.

She has kept all their toys. Louis sits and reads strange old waxy annuals, dated 1924 and 1926, about characters unfamiliar to him, such as Teddy Tail and Tiger Tim and Pip, Squeak and Wilfred. There are teddy bears which belonged to them. Louis tries, from their facial characteristics, to determine which bear belonged to Dad and which to Uncle Cal. Up in her bedroom there is another more ancient bear, close-

71

cropped, mounted on iron wheels. You pull a leather tab in its back, and it utters a single, remonstrating grunt.

She tells him how clever they were at school. All their reports, for every subject, said 'Excellent'. And 'Conduct—excellent'. At Prize Day, between them they won every prize, and had to hand some back to give the other boys a chance.

'Your Uncle Cal swallowed a gooseberry. We had to send for Doctor Manley. And, do you know—that Doctor Manley counted every *pip* in your Uncle Cal's motion until it had all gone!

'Your Uncle Cal had his pockets sewn up at school, for putting his hands in his pockets. And your Daddy cut them open. He told the headmaster that *his* Daddy had always put his hands in his pockets, and so why shouldn't his brother Cal do it? Bless him. He gave all his white mice away to a little friend. And then cried himself to sleep that night.'

She has often shown Louis photographs of the little boy who did such sweet and impulsive things. This other little boy, of thirty years ago, is Louis's only rival for her worship. His hair is cut in a fringe; he wears a jersey with a square-shaped neck. Louis can recognise the channel that is in his upper lip and the wide dimple, like Nanny's own, which cleaves his chin.

Whom did she love most, when they were little—Dad or Uncle Cal? She loved both of them as much, in the same inordinate degree—yet there is a special adoration in her stories about Dad because of the speech impediment from which he suffered as a little boy. According to Nanny Belmayne, he could not speak at all until he was almost three years old. After that, he pronounced many words wrongly. She did not correct him, but rather cherished his struggles to talk in a treasury of sweet little misguided sayings.

'If you asked him at meal-times if he'd wanted something, he used to shout out "Yeppease, yeppease!"'

'When we lived over in Gunter Grove, if he heard some-one at the back door, he used to shout out, "letten in, letten in!"'

72

' "My Mummy's honey tarts", he used to say to people—he said it to Mrs Maxwell at Manor House School. "They're *ludley*," he used to say, "they're *ludley*!" '

And with the impediment went a kind of comical gravity, even as a little boy. He was conscientious, even then, in doing things for Nanny Belmayne and looking after her—just as today Louis had seen him kneel in front of her to take off her walking shoes and put on her slippers.

'He always used to be such a help to me if I wasn't well. I used to lie up in bed with one of my mugraines. I used to be in such pain—I wouldn't have cared if the *whole* of the German Army had come marching through my bedroom with fixed bayonets. Your Daddy used to bring me up a hot-water bottle for my feet, the lamb. He was only a little boy, but he'd still look after me. If there was a lot of washing-up and your Uncle Cal usen't to want to do it, your Daddy's little voice used to say, "No wonder the poor ting's got a headache with all that washing-up." '

Upstairs, on her dressing-table, there are photographs of the grown up men into whom these two, dear, brilliant little boys have metamorphosed, standing among the tortoiseshell boxes and long-handled combs. On one side is Uncle Cal in Army battledress, with his strange, bright, staring eyes. On the other side is Dad in Air Force uniform. He always looked so beautiful in his uniform, Nanny says. On his forehead, the dark ridge of hair is a little shallower. His expression, as he looks into the room, is gentle and wistful, like the little boy who said 'ludley' for 'lovely', and who, so generously and thoughtlessly, gave all his white mice away to a friend.

Louis is overwhelmed with a love for Dad that he has never felt properly before. He resolves he will try to show it to Dad in the future without becoming embarrassed or tongue-tied. He wonders whether it would make Nanny Belmayne love him more if he, too, were to mispronounce some of his words.

*   *   *

73

Now, of all the pleasures in life with Nanny Belmayne, he has only one left of each. One more bus journey to Brixton with Mrs O'Rourke to buy liver, and a toffee apple at Tubby Dave's Corner. One more conversation with Mr O'Rourke, snuffling and mild, smelling of plaster and putty, who calls Walt Disney 'Walter Disney'. One more journey with the empty bottles to Mr Brill's off-licence. One more Sunday-morning stroll with Uncle Tony to buy a quarter of loose Smarties from the shop in Rectory Grove. One more listen to the Toby jug in Uncle Tony's room, and one last go with the big, easy jigsaw puzzle, left by his cousins, called Hiding from the Giant. One last settling down with Nanny Belmayne in her big bed, when he lies, unwilling even to blink for fear of sacrificing one instant of warmth, comfort, safeness, the smell of the sheets, the feeling of her close to him in the great feather bed, and the friendly whirls and flashes in the darkness round them.

They sit together, too unhappy to speak, in the deep green Tube train, watching the stations that go the wrong way now— Clapham North; Stockwell; Oval; Kennington; he remembers how happy he felt when he last saw that same advertisement on the tunnel wall for Idris lemon squash. The escalators go the wrong way, clambering, clumbering in their ignorance up under the girders of Waterloo. Johnnie Walker, born 1821, is still going strong on his plinth, with top hat and coat-tails flying, but now Louis cannot bear to look at him.

He is sitting by himself in the train, with heat coming from under the bench, against the backs of his legs. He can feel it through his socks, and smell the rough, warm, red-upholstered smell you find only on the Portsmouth trains. Nanny Belmayne stands outside the window across the aisle, waving to him, even though the train has not yet started. Whistles keep blowing but still the train will not move. Two people have offered to look after him during the journey. They are being seen off by a black man. Through the window, Nanny Belmayne pulls a face, with eyes wide, in reference to the black man. Now the train is moving, she is sliding away from him, still waving.

Now he sees other people, smiling, waving. The man in the compartment stands up, so close that Louis can see the holes in his raincoat buttons: not waving to the black man but smiling and holding his thumb up in the air. The train moves out into daylight.

He can still smell her cheek, and feel her brooch against his face when she hugged him: 'Goodbye my lamb. Goodbye my little bit o' fat. Come up and see old Nan again soon.'

At Portsmouth Harbour there were gulls, wailing and sliding beneath a smeared and joyless sky. The ferry lights shone bleakly along the mooring below the long ramp. Anguish began in earnest now, in the privacy of the sea wind as he stood and watched the widening harbour, the minesweepers and masts and HMS *Vernon,* the faraway sparkle of the Big Wheel at Southsea reiterating the distance he now was from any prospect of happiness. It was already too dark to see the Solent forts. He stood below deck, looking through the door into the engine room far below, and the strange, hot ice cream-smelling warmth in his face beat away the tears he could not yet cry.

The Island moved up slowly, out of rain. First came two headlands; then the long wall of packed iron legs out to the pierhead and its shining-wet dome. Bleak white lights shone over the berth where they docked, and where someone would be waiting to meet him—what did it matter who? With a sidle, a bump, a bell, a flight of wet ropes, a slither of gang-planks, drawn over the black and hissing gulf, the ferry delivered him home.

In the little flat at the top of Ryde, his mother was waiting for him, with the electric fire on and Charles, the Siamese cat, indifferent to all arrivals and departures, with fishy breath, basking in front of it. She wore a new housecoat, tied at the waist. She gave him chocolate biscuits for supper, and then allowed him to lie in bed with the door wide open, listening to *Calling Paul Temple* on the wireless from the sitting-room.

75

'Steve!' Paul Temple said. 'The girl in grey has been murdered!' And Louis, listening to Paul Temple's theme music, felt the tears burst out and saw them blurring the light outside his door with the fringe along the edge of his bed-rug. He cried most of all at the thought of how Nanny Belmayne tonight must be grieving for him. 'Nanny nearly cried.' He thought of her words in a voice hushed with sadness, and of the grey smudge with its two white hairs high up on the cheeks of her sad, kind face.

Late that night, his mother came and bent over him as he lay crying and begging to be sent back to Nanny Belmayne.

She straightened up again with a sigh. Louis saw the outline of her floating in his tears.

'All right, don't cry,' she said in a dull voice. 'Stop crying now. We'll try to get you up to London again as soon as possible.'

master of ceremonies

The Forties, with their wan and wintry light, had finally rolled away. 1950 was printed on the front of Louis's Christmas annuals. He wondered if time would ever again pass so rounded and perfect a numeral. He felt excited because it was 1950, because he would be seven soon, but most of all because it was Saturday morning, and he was out in the car with Dad.

In those days, like many men who had been in the Air Force, Dad drove a very old car. It was a Wolseley, black and long and lofty, like a hearse—for which, indeed, it sometimes used to be mistaken. Dad had bought it very cheaply soon after coming to the Island, and had devoted many hours to 'doing it up', so that now only five or six swings of the starting handle were necessary for the engine, under its ancient, tapering bonnet, to set up a low, rather bronchial but at least continuous note. Dad drove the Wolseley, not from necessity as he made clear, but in appreciation of its historic worth, its superiority over cars that were merely new, or convenient to Ryde's hilly streets. Frequently, though it might seem to be running satisfactorily, Dad would dismember it again in the

77

yard behind the High Street, lying for hours underneath it while Wilf, the assistant he called his 'Aircrew', knelt as close as possible with the hurricane lamp. 'She sounds a bit better now,' Dad would concede, at last. If you had been in the Air Force, you always called your old car 'she', just as you said 'ruddy', not 'bloody' if you were angry.

They were driving down Union Street, the steep main street of Ryde, fifty years too late to see Queen Victoria in her carriage. They were passing Colenutt's the grocers, and Beti's Café, and the Galleon Restaurant, and on the other side, Yelf's Hotel and Tap, and the Royal Squadron Hotel, the strange, empty Royal Victoria Arcade, and the crowds that climbed uphill past ordinary 1950 cars, parked one above the other. At the bottom of Union Street, the sea stood between crowding shopblinds like a cold, blue wall, its ascent checked only by faint grey mainland chimneys. The *Queen Mary*—or perhaps the *Queen Elizabeth*—passing through the Solent to Southampton, hung softly over the town, suspended in dim firmaments of deep water.

Louis sat with Dad in the Wolseley's narrow chauffeur compartment, where both leather seats spilled out stuffing, and spars of the woodwork hung, vibrating, from historic-looking nails. Nigger lay alone in the rear cabin, which was upholstered in dust-grey plush and equipped with matching silver umbrella stands. An oval yellow window, lodged in the dusty roof fabric, gave only partial vision of the following traffic.

Dad stopped the Wolseley several times on their way down through the town. He got out, over the wide running-board, and Louis stayed behind with Nigger in the back, watching Dad stride uphill to the bank or the chemist, his green tie fluttering over his shoulder. Once, Louis got out as well, and accompanied Dad along a lane and up the steps to a loft to see Mr Boynton, the signwriter. While Dad spoke to Mr Boynton at the end of the loft, Louis stood, looking at the beautiful coloured writing balanced on its pencilled framework in half-finished cards and posters, envying Mr Boynton his lovely job and wondering where Dad and he would be going next. All

78

car journeys with Dad had an element of surprise. At any moment, he might stop the car, brusquely walk away, and return, bringing the toy that Louis desired most in the world. Louis never asked Dad for things—he told his mother, and Dad found out: the present, when it came, was invariably accompanied by a small pang of guilt. It happened just like that with the little model stage-coach he had wanted so badly —the one with four horses, and doors that you could open and close.

Towards the bottom, Union Street abandoned its regal descent and lapsed into a nearly perpendicular gradient to which the last shops clung like climbers on a rock face. Here, long ago, the Royal Pier Hotel had stood on its promontory beside the pier, jutting inward to form a narrow alley from Union Street into the Esplanade. Proud and famous as it once was, the hotel had not long survived the coming of the motor car. Some people in Ryde could still remember what crashes there used to be at the bottom of Union Street when drivers, unable to manage the sharp turn, went careering on into the Royal Pier Hotel, or across the private gardens which, in those days, ran down to the western sands.

The gardens were public now, and a wide, safe turning, lined with reddish pavement and flower borders, flowed through the site of the Royal Pier Hotel. Yet its memory lingered, in the gap it had left and the suddenness with which the unscreened pier was now revealed. As Dad brought the Wolseley gushing round from Union Street on to flat road, the pier caught Louis's eye and raced with it on iron legs half a mile out to sea. It was a clear morning, and, far away, he could just see the outline of the dome at the pierhead. The effect was of a figure, bent low and labouring among yachts and shipping, in a meadow of silver sea haze.

From the pier entrance, a wide pavement sloped gently down to the road. There a crowd of taxi-drivers stood all day, waiting for the boats to come in, and customers to emerge, shortly, afterwards from the station exit beside W. H. Smith's. The Wolseley mounted the ramp and moved gently through the taximen, up to the brick towers, like twin porters' lodges, which flanked the pier gates. Under the glass-roofed gatehouse, two men stood behind the IN turnstile, collecting boat tickets and pier tolls. One of them, recognising Dad, left his post and came to push open the two parts of the gate which admitted cars to the pier. Dad, of course, paid no toll. Carefully, probing with his tongue, he fitted the Wolseley between the IN and OUT turnstiles, at the same time leaning forward to smile and salute the ticket collector as if he were an old and valued friend. The Wolseley crept out of the gatehouse, past the green mesh barrier of the tramway station. It drove across the remaining concrete and, with a sharp 'Belp!' noise, crossed the loose metal stud that lay where the planks began.

The tide was out that morning as they drove along the pier. To east and west, beyond the slipway ends, lay miles of sand, the foreshore that was like some dark, wet ocean, with the real sea cowering far in the distance, underneath Portsmouth. Louis remembered the first time he had driven along the pier, the disappointment he had felt to see those long, weak horizons, so little like the seaside illustrated in storybooks. Today, in winter, the outlines were firmer but the desolation seemed all the more. The pier carried him outward through a dead land where dinghies lay on their sides, and ragworm had been dug from freshly-opened graves, and forgotten breakwaters showed themselves again, in bleak resurrection through the sand.

There was a 5 m.p.h. speed limit for cars along the pier, which Dad observed with punctilious care. Beyond the silver statuette on the Wolseley's nose, the planks made a highway of vertical seams that shifted gently to and fro because of the light that came up through them from the beach. On either side were iron railings painted green, a lyre shape endlessly-reproduced below the rail and, above it, an interminably-repeated green knob. At first, Louis thought it would be possible to count the knobs—then one escaped, then five, then fifty then all became one green knob, removed and deftly replaced by a conjurer's hand.

Throughout the winter, the pier carried on the task for

which it had been built. A boat had lately arrived from Portsmouth, a few people walked down the pier, strung out across the planks in combat with colliding sea winds, not pleased to meet the big, careful car that nosed among them. To the right, across a broad seam of iron, a crimson train, also on its way to the pierhead, stood still and let the steam from its engine melt in the sea air. As Dad passed the train, the pier tram passed him, banging over its open frame between the railway and the planks. In the second car, the driver sat backwards, accompanied by a small white dog.

'Why don't you try to beat the tram, Dad?' Louis had once asked.

'Because there's no *sense* in trying to beat the tram, Louis.'

A four-sided shelter with a pagoda roof, standing out from the pier on a balcony, marked the half-way point. By now the town and its three spires had grown small in the Wolseley's yellow rear window; the headlands, in receding, seemed to have crept forward on either side to close up the circle of distance and sky. Eastward, the black forts stood in line through deeps that barely cleared the tideline. Louis counted three forts today—or was it four? A fourth fort was definitely there, beyond the others, like a small, bruised cloud. He shivered, not without pleasure, to think how the forts changed places in the sea with their garrisons of dead men.

He could see the pierhead clearly now, spread beyond the causeway in two equal and dissimilar portions. He could see, at one end, the deckchair office, the square white yacht club tower with the ship's mast on it; and at the opposite end, booking halls and platform roofs and crane-tops, and the ferry's mast and yellow funnel embedded among the breastworks of the pier station. The tram on its return journey dashed past just then. Louis opened his mouth to say something but, seeing Dad's face, closed it again. Prickles of excitement were sweeping up his back and the backs of his legs. He was certain now that a new epoch in his life was about to begin, and that, whatever it was, he would find it at the end of the pier.

Near the end, the railway and tramway forsook each other.

The train, passing a branch of signals, looped off to the right and vanished into its terminus behind a long yellow screen. The tramway continued ahead, rather proudly, running up into an elevated station. Two separate piers, in effect, belatedly revealed themselves, along opposite sides of a triangular gulf with the Pavilion standing at its head. Not until this point, as you drove along the pier, did the Pavilion come into full view.

It was in full view now to Louis. He could see its long legs standing in the sea, and its circular body, patterned all round with high windows, and the big dome, visible so far away on sea or land, now revealed to be the colour of fish-skin and covered in crescent-shaped tiles that overlapped one another like the scales of a fish. Against it on one side stood a smaller satellite dome and the sun-roof that covered the little tramway station. On the other side, the yellow railway screen curved clear, disowning kinship. For in those days, before Dad took its decoration upon himself, the Pavilion, too, was painted in the Southern Railway colours of yellow and green. Several long streams of water, from the various toilets and kitchens it contained, fell down to tumble the draughty shallows around its feet. On the high rim that ran around the base of the dome was a long yellow placard which bore, in green letters, the words:

RYDE ROLLER-SKATING RINK

Low tide reached its limit under the Pavilion. Beyond lay oily depths and dangers, and the ferry's keel. The tide was turning, even now, through the Pavilion's legs and stumps of legs, back across the estuary over long dark weeds that swayed in unison against the shallow sand floor. Faintly in the wind, Louis could hear the noise of millions of small, fretful waves, and another noise—from the windows round the Pavilion—a muffled roaring, rumbling and rolling.

He is sitting on a chair at the Pavilion while Dad puts on his very first pair of skates.

He has his first skate on already, strange-feeling and heavy

82

under his left foot. He can smell its wooden wheels and leather straps, and the piece tied over his toe, which has a raw smell like animal skin. He holds tight to his chair in case his one skate should pull him off and rattle him away to his death.

He cannot speak because he is so excited, and because of the noise. It is the same noise he could hear across the estuary, but magnified now to a rage in his head. It is the noise of skaters—the clash and stamp and slew and slither and scramble and bark and bang of skate wheels by the hundred on the Pavilion's wooden floor.

He looks in awe and gratitude at Dad, kneeling in front of him, resting his other foot up on one knee. Dad's head is bowed low, as if in fealty to a king. The ridge of dark hair rides on tiny, arching wrinkles, so intense his concentration even on this small technical job. His cold pipe slants against his cheek and the skirts of his shooting waistcoat brush against the floor. It occurs to Louis that Dad's sole aim in opening a roller skating rink has been to give him this Saturday morning surprise.

'I am excited Dad,' he says, breathlessly because he is a little afraid of trying to roller-skate.

Dad has finished lacing the second skate over his toe. Now he fits the long, pale tying-thong round Louis's sandal-strap, jerking it through the buckle until it stings his instep like a whip.

'There,' he says. 'Beautiful.' He takes his pipe from his mouth and stands up.

'It's too tight, Dad.'

' 'Course it isn't,' Dad replies.

'It is.'

They are shouting at each other now above the noise. Dad's eyes tremble as his white lips shout: 'It is *not* too tight, Louis.'

Why does he always make Dad angry? Why, even on such a morning as this, did he have to make Dad angry?

Uncle Cal, Dad's older brother, was an awe-inspiring figure

83

to Louis. He was taller and heavier than Dad, in build resembling some of the bulkier ancestors in Nanny Belmayne's picture album. His black hair grew in a peak like Dad's, but a shallower one since Uncle Cal had never been obliged to wear a flying helmet. His eyes were his most prominent feature, dark brown and small and intense, like the button eyes in his old teddy bear. The dissimilarity Louis had noticed between Dad's and Uncle Cal's teddy bears seemed to have been carried into their whole lives. For Uncle Cal knew nothing about car engines or countryman's pursuits. His posture was upright, dignified and slow. He spoke without difficulty in measured, quiet words, accompanied by a slight nasal exhalation. This snuffling sound, indicative of large mental power, was to become more pronounced over the years as Uncle Cal's physical exertions diminished and his weight increased.

Louis could remember, long ago at Hornchurch, being told a story by Uncle Cal. The story consisted of a number of questions to which the answer was always the single word 'Bones'. A man, said Uncle Cal, had been walking along a street at night; he turned round and what did Louis think he saw following him? 'Bones.' He went on a little further, then again turned round. What did he see this time? 'Bones'. Louis had often thought of that dark street; the uneasy man, pausing under a street lamp and looking back. It was an image inseparable from that of Uncle Cal's face next to his own—the bright button eyes that frowned when they smiled, and Uncle Cal's voice, slow, dignified and snuffly, telling him: 'Bones. That's what they were—bones!'

He remembered, too, in Uncle Cal's house, a picture that used to hang on the upstairs landing which showed a number of dogs queueing up on their hind legs, like men, to wee wee against a tree. Louis knew it was a French picture because of the writing underneath, and because each dog wore a grimace of amusement. It was a part of Uncle Cal's strange humour that wee wee, if accompanied by French words, was not rude but humorous in some superior, well-travelled way. In Uncle Cal and Auntie Rita's bedroom hung another French picture,

84

this time of a little boy wee weeing into a pond from which a frog was leaping in alarm. Underneath were some words deciphered by Louis, in time, as:

Ne buvez jamais de l'eau.

Uncle Cal's wife, Auntie Rita, was less inscrutable. Dark-eyed and hook-nosed, she had at one time operated a lift at Derry and Tom's department store. She was a strict Catholic and, in her own words, *highly strung,* the more so since a car accident had damaged one of her wrists, bestowing on her £900 in compensation, and a nervous habit of winding coloured chiffon around her wrist to conceal what she imagined to be its deformity. Marriage to Uncle Cal could not but heighten the tension of those anxious strings within Auntie Rita: she lived a life of damaged devoutness in back rooms, of suffering and gin and tonic, and chiffon and nerves, despite which, occasionally, a native cheerfulness could assert itself. It was Auntie Rita, possibly to counteract all the French pictures, who hung up in the toilet a little varnished notice that advised: 'Don't worry. Stick a geranium in yer 'at and be 'appy.'

Uncle Cal's cleverness had revealed itself with least complexity at school, where he won every prize for foreign languages. Nanny Belmayne had told Louis how the headmaster, Mr Maxwell, used to take her aside and speak to her in whispers of Uncle Cal's brilliance. With reverence she would describe to Louis Uncle Cal's independence of spirit at home—how he refused to help Dad do the washing-up when Nanny Belmayne herself was suffering from one of her 'mugraines'. 'Bless him,' she would say fondly. 'He used to pass the house on the other side of the road in case I saw him and wanted him to go down to the shops for me.'

When Dad became an aeronautical apprentice, Uncle Cal travelled abroad. He had fought in the Spanish Civil War, Nanny Belmayne said proudly, and had 'caught the last Dreadnought that ever left Spain.' While not understanding the reference, Louis appreciated that this had been an entirely typical thing for Uncle Cal to have done. During the real War,

85

he had been 'in Intelligence': he had travelled to Italy and had once seen Mussolini hanging up by the heels. From the tone of her voice Louis deduced that Mussolini was an acquaintance of Nanny Belmayne's, whom she had possibly even persuaded to hang himself up by the heels for her elder son's amusement.

Uncle Cal was also famous in the family for playing practical jokes, especially with chairs outside occupied toilets. On New Year's Eve, he dressed up as a lady with a beauty spot printed on his cheek. Auntie Rita and her Catholicism were a target for many of Uncle Cal's jokes—he alluded to nuns, for example, as 'currant buns'. It was said of Uncle Cal—not without pride on Nanny Belmayne's part—that he had not wanted to allow Louis's two cousins to be brought up as Catholics, and had avenged himself on Auntie Rita and her religion by cutting his toenails into her dinner.

Since leaving the Army, Uncle Cal had engaged in varied business enterprises. First, using the compensation money from Auntie Rita's road accident, he had invested in a concern called the Wandsworth Marble Works. After the Wandsworth Marble Works became bankrupt, Uncle Cal applied his powerful, polylingual mind to a little sweet and tobacco shop in Hornchurch. This proved too much for him to manage alone, and so Nanny Belmayne came down from Orlando Road to run it for him. Extending the stock to Flit fly spray, Beecham's Powders, cornplasters and—for favoured customers—clothing coupons, she made the shop a great success. Auntie Rita would stay in the back room, having 'turns' and making ice-lollies in eggcups.

It was at about this time that Uncle Cal, for reasons that would never be known, caught a train from Waterloo and took the ferry from Portsmouth to the Isle of Wight.

He came ashore at Ryde, walking along the pier into what was virtually a foreign country. Throughout the War, the whole Island had been a restricted area, accessible from the mainland only by special permit. Big guns pointed out up the Solent from the seashore playgrounds like Puckpool Park and antisubmarine nets trawled the bays at St Helens and Seaview. Ryde pier itself was a vital installation, guarding the route of a possible German landing at Southsea. The Pavilion, formerly a theatre for summer shows, was turned into a barracks for Royal Navy signallers. Plane-spotters gazed seaward and skyward around the dome.

In Ryde, just after the War, Uncle Cal met a nice man in the bar of the Albany Hotel. The nice man's name was Mr Harrison. He told Uncle Cal that he and his partner Mr Cooper rented the pier Pavilion, lately vacated by the Royal Navy signallers and now once more a place of entertainment. Under Mr Harrison and his partner, it was a theatre no longer but a restaurant and café. Mr Harrison must have taken a great liking to Uncle Cal, for, not long afterwards, he offered him a partnership in the Pavilion, to replace Mr Cooper who wished to leave the Island. After a visit to Nanny Belmayne in London, Uncle Cal was able to accept this offer.

At first, the partnership did well. Holidaymakers were flooding back to the Island with money to spend but little on which to spend it. The Pavilion café, which gave very little for rather a lot of money, had had one busy season already; it now had a second, with Uncle Cal in charge of it, even though his talents were unsuited to catering. However rushed the café staff might be, Uncle Cal preferred to sit at one side, writing little poems about how busy it was, occasionally chuckling to himself at the adroitness of his own rhymes.

The next summer—that would have been 1947—the season proved slightly less busy. Mr Harrison came to Uncle Cal and regretfully announced his intention of leaving their partnership. In future seasons, the Pavilion and all attached to it would be for Uncle Cal to operate by himself.

The autumn of 1947 marked Uncle Cal's first visit to Dad at St Neots. All through that winter, when there was snow first, then floods, Uncle Cal returned to the Cross Keys again and again and had long discussions with Dad behind the door of the private office. Louis remembered standing in the dark lounge outside, watching the light under the door, knowing that he must on no account go in. There was snow built up along the pavement round the Market Square, but all the fields by the river, and Dad's little island, that would be Louis's one day, were buried under the silver flood tide.

As Louis heard it afterwards, his mother had not wanted to leave St Neots. She had flu at the time, and Uncle Cal sat on her bed, in the room just above the gold keys, and talked to her for a long time, telling her how pretty Ryde was; how much money he and Dad could make from the Pavilion, quickly and with what comparatively small inconvenience. She still resisted, even when Uncle Cal promised her she would not have to work at the end of the pier. She and Uncle Cal never seemed to like one another very much. She complained that he didn't wash enough, and that he laughed at his own jokes.

Dad was almost persuaded not to go. On the night of a big Masonic dinner at the hotel, leaving the preparation of eighty meals to Louis's mother, he went up to London to ask Nanny Belmayne what she thought he should do. Uncle Cal, as it happened, had left Orlando Road just a day or two earlier. Nanny Belmayne declined to interfere—she never wished to do that. She only said it was her dearest wish before she died to see her two boys in business together.

You go in through the pierhead tramway station. Beside the ticket barrier stands a wide timber porch, low-fronted and gloomy, like the way into a cave. Two glass-paned doors, that can swing either outward or inward, lead to the short, twilit entrance hall. Here the skates are given out. A metal counter runs down the right-hand side, with shelves of drab skates behind it, and Dad and his helper Wilf, taking money, throwing it into saucers, spiking tickets, then looking for skates, and handing them over with interlocked wheels, the lace-ends snapping on the metal counter-top. Above their heads, the Pavilion's grand staircase—now least-used among its thoroughfares—climbs past the boarded ceiling, into darkness.

88

Doors in a second row, speared on long bolts, open in—or rather, out—to the floor of the old theatre. How were the players heard, or even noticed in that huge auditorium, far away on their little open stage? The theatre seats have gone, carted off by the hundred, but the stage remains, together with scenery from its final pre-war show—Venetian gondolas. The stage is encircled by a promenade balcony, standing on eight long wooden posts around the floor. Above the balcony, more enormous still, and hollow, lies the dome.

The noise under the dome is stupefying. A close-packed throng of roller-skaters travels round the floor, inside the balcony posts, past the long pierhead doors, past the long windows, past the stage, past the forgotten scene of Venice, a perpetual and fruitless and unsteady chase. On the right, in front of the shoreward windows, are beginners' bars, where grotesque figures scramble hand-over-hand against a background of railways and sea. There are shreds of music playing somewhere and at intervals, a voice can be heard, deep and blurred in the tangles of noise, saying:

'Please keep to the right. Ladies and gentlemen, *please* keep to the right.'

Saturdays are the busiest of all. Throughout the morning, the packed trams sway and slither up into their terminus, adding to a queue of people that already extends past the entrance-hall, their coat-lapels fluttering in the sea-wind that sweeps the platforms from end to end. Often on a Saturday, the supply of skates is exhausted. Then Louis, struggling on the beginners' bars, is requested to give up his pair so that another little boy or girl can have a turn.

He sits on a chair against the wall with the cream soda and bag of crisps that are the reward of self-sacrifice. His feet feel funny without skates, as if he has forgotten how to walk. He watches the sailors, skating in bellbottom trousers, and the girls in ankle socks who skate with their arms wrapped desperately around one another, and the tram boy, trying to skate in his serge waistcoat and green shirt, stamping and groping with his fingers for the floor. There are faces looking down

89

over the balcony, and faces all along the bolted doors from the open pierhead. Skate noise drowns everything—the boats from Portsmouth, the trams that come to meet them; even the sea itself, so close under the rink floor. But sometimes in docking, a ferry bumps a distant berth. Then the whole pier, on its thousand legs, quivers a little in admonition.

Louis sits and watches, and pinches his lemonade straw, and listens to the voice, rising through the uproar again—the blurred voice entreating skaters to keep to their right. Suddenly he realises it is Dad's voice, transmitted by microphone from some secret place behind the Venetian gondolas.

'Please keep to the right, ladies and gentlemen. Ladies and gentlemen, *please* keep to the right.'

Louis learned to skate in the company of a woman named Phyllis. She was barmaid at The First and Last, the pub at the end of the pier—so named because it could serve you your first *and* last drink on the Isle of Wight. It was part of the Pavilion, though as yet not under Dad's control; a single narrow room, with three pairs of doors, facing towards the ferry berths. It had a marble-topped bar with fancy mirrors behind, and at one end, a coal stove with a crooked pipe that arose into the ceiling. Porters from the railway station often sat huddled here.

Phyllis wore a black costume with square shoulders, a white frilly blouse and a handkerchief pushed up her sleeve. She worked the beer-pumps with one big, then one little pull, smoking a cigarette and coughing gently. Whenever she and Louis met, she said 'Hello, Lewis.' That was how Isle of Wight people always pronounced his name.

Behind the bar, up three steps, was a room that led into the Pavilion's main hall. Through the door, Louis had seen an armchair, an electric fire and a clothes-horse with stockings hung on it to dry. Sometimes there was a smell of kippers, if Phyllis was cooking her supper. A smaller adjoining room contained the backs of three beer barrels and a wooden hatch that opened directly into the sea. It was said that Phyllis, if she
90

wanted to be excused, did not bother to come out to the Ladies'
in the Pavilion, but simply lifted the hatch and did it there.
She was the first person Louis ever knew who fell upstairs
instead of down. That was when Phyllis was tiddly.

Louis was not allowed to go into The First and Last. Even
if everyone else was there, he had to wait outside. He stood on
one leg first, then the other, wondering whose breath had
coated the door-glass into the shapes of dolphins and sea-
serpents; at times advancing conspicuous little portions of himself over the threshold until someone inside the bar noticed
him and brought him out a cream soda and crisps. Phyllis sold
Smith's crisps, the rare and lovely blue and red greaseproof
bags squashed down in a tall glass jar. He shook the crisps
to salt them by jumping off the bottom step from the tramway
entrance.

When The First and Last had no customers to serve, Phyllis
came out into the Pavilion and put on a pair of skates. She
had never skated in her life before, and seemed very keen to
learn, even though she was so old. Together, she and Louis
pulled themselves up and down between the beginners' bars
near the Pavilion's shoreward windows. This was after dark,
when the rink had first opened for the evening. There were
lamps on, in little gilt clusters, all round the walls under the
balcony. The dome above their heads was dark. For fifty years
already, it had defied all illumination.

Then Louis found courage to let go of the beginners' bars
and roll forward to the nearest balcony post. Around its
sculpted base it wore a green canvas jacket laced with string,
like the canvas Dad used to wrap up his guns. Dad had fitted
jackets to all the posts, to stop them being chipped by skate
wheels.

'Come on Phyllis!' he shouted.

But Phyllis, this evening, seemed to lack her usual resolution.
Before coming to the end of the pier, she seemed to have been
to a wedding. Attached to her coat lapel was a spray of white
flowers in a twist of silver paper. Louis had helped her to
stand up straight several times already, and had breathed the

91

heady perfume of ladies when they have been drinking gin and orange or gin and It or gin and lime.

Phyllis did not seem to be listening to him. Her forearms hung over the bar like stockings over her own clothes-horse, and her skates turned inward, helplessly locked together. She coughed gently through the cigarette in her lips.

'Look, Phyllis—watch me!'

His courage increased. He found he could let go of the post and stumble a few yards to one corner of the stage. The whole stage was black with dust, undisturbed since the last seaside show. Using the stage for support, Louis found himself moving with his skate wheels for the first time in alignment, not curving inward to trip him. The dust from the stage rose up through his fingertips into his mouth. It tasted thick and sour, like sunshine left mouldering for years in dirty crevices.

'Look, Phyllis!' he shouted.

'Look, Phyllis, you can even go backwards if you hold on to the stage. Like this, Phyllis—watch!'

Phyllis had launched herself from the beginners' bars. She rolled forward to the balcony post and embraced it with both arms, the curved ash still unbroken at the end of her cigarette. There the momentum ceased. Phyllis, still holding tight to the post, sank slowly down it until she sat on the floor, her eight wheels revolving, her tight, shiny black skirt rolled back from her dark and dusty knees. 'Be quiet,' she said mildly—now the ash did fall from her cigarette.

'Look, Phyllis—I'm not even holding on at all now. Look, Phyllis, I can skate! I can skate, Phyllis! Look, Phyllis, Look, Phyllis! Look!'

Uncle Cal had found them a place to live. At the very top of Ryde, in the narrowest part of the High Street, he had acquired an entire building—a shop that could be turned into a café, with an empty flat on each of the two floors above. The building even had an archway: it was like St Neots in this one respect. Behind the archway lay a piece of waste ground, strewn with old bottles and tins. On the facing pavement stood Johncox's, a busy fishmonger's shop.

Having exerted himself so far, Uncle Cal seemed to disappear. The relationship between Dad and him had always been variable, as one would expect between such disparately-gifted men, and it appeared—though it was never actually said, and Louis did not dare to ask—that Dad's arrival on the Island to 'help' Uncle Cal had coincided with a disagreement between them. For some two years, until a brief reconciliation in 1952, the subject of Uncle Cal was vehemently not mentioned by Dad, nor was it to be mentioned to him. Uncle Cal was certainly still living in Ryde—he had a house in Haylands and a Morris car, as slow and portly as himself, which Louis sometimes saw about the town.

And yet despite this estrangement, Dad continued to 'help' Uncle Cal with unstinted vigour. The skating rink had been Dad's idea—his most inspired one in any epoch—to make use of Uncle Cal's gigantic pierhead premises during the winter. It was Dad who procured the skates, engaged the staff—still a modest one then—and built shelves and the skate counter, and another counter for the Tea Bar. It was Dad who put in hand the conversion of the High Street shop into a café, and who, at the same time, worked to make ready the Pavilion for its next summer season.

The emergence of the Wolseley from the archway into the High Street was always something of an occasion. One of the fishmongers from Johncox's had to stop the traffic to let Dad come out. Forward, up over the pavement outside Godwin's, then back until they nearly scraped the arch, then forward the big car went again with Dad's arms whirling across each other on the wheel and his tongue pressed on his lip, and old Nigger in the back, looking excitedly this way and that, his own tongue shaking like pink ham behind his teeth. One more turn, and they had done it. The fishmonger's assistant stood back. Mr Johncox himself raised his straw hat in tribute.

Louis sat in the grey plush back compartment with Nigger

D

and the umbrella-stands as Dad drove along the pier. There was so much room, he could lie down with his head against the back seat and still be unable to touch the little fold-up seats with his foot. He remembered sitting in the back of another car when they were at St Neots and his mother was receiving driving lessons from Dad. They were going across the railway line and Dad, looking wrong in the passenger seat, said, *'Don't* stop'—she had immediately stopped with a jolt. On car journeys, she used to make little jokes, but ceased doing so when silence greeted them. Louis remembered her voice saying, *'That's* a very neat haystack.' Now she did not speak to Dad on the way down the pier, nor he to her; nor either of them to Louis.

Empty of skaters, the Pavilion was a chilled echo. The wind tugged at its boardwork walls and window-frames, and rattled its long rank of doors in their bolts. The pierhead outside was sunny, but the dome made its own pale daylight. Louis felt his shoulders shiver as they crossed the floor in a clatter of dog feet. The dome stirred and creaked with the blustering outside, and he could hear the wind upstairs as it moaned through the restaurant and kitchens and still-rooms and stores, and the sea, threshing all around him and underneath him, like snakes hissing.

Dad had established his private office in one of the old dressing-rooms beside the stage, at the top of a little wooden staircase. Here Louis's mother worked, sitting at a big roll-top desk, with the yellow screen of the pierhead railway station looming through the net-curtained window behind her.

She did the 'books' and the 'wages' and typed letters on the steep black typewriter they had brought with them from the hotel. Louis had seen notebooks full of strange, wiggly shapes she had written down, and sheets of paper he was forbidden to draw on—notepaper with a heading in green letters, *Harco Ltd.* It was the name of the company formed between Uncle Cal and Dad but deriving ultimately from the names of Uncle Cal's two vanished partners, Messrs. Harrison and Cooper. To Louis, who did not know this, the word was as evocative of

Dad as fishing-rods and guns and gold tobacco tins, and blue official sealing-wax, and rolls of purple tickets, issued to skaters, and the name printed inside each wooden skate-wheel, *Hamoco*.

Once, in the drawer, he had found some scarlet badges with gold safety-pins behind them, and the letters MC written on them in gold. He asked his mother what the letters stood for, and she replied, 'Master of Ceremonies.'

The words excited Louis. Even they reminded him somehow of Dad—solemn yet with a promise of the unexpected. He asked Dad if he could wear a badge with MC written on it.

Dad looked at him as if he had said some stupid thing.

'Why should you?'

'I like them, Dad.'

'Why should *you* have one? *You're* not a Master of Ceremonies.'

There were workmen upstairs, redecorating the restaurant that overlooked the Solent. Louis stood watching them as the wind beat and rattled the shuttered balcony doors. They were sawing and planing wood, and whistling with an echo that sang off the panelled walls. One of them was whistling 'Cherry Ripe' and another one was whistling 'The Sabre Dance'. The workman who always spoke to him said 'Hello Lewis'—again Louis noticed the low-class pronunciation of his name. He was enthralled by the workmen, by their unrepentant dustiness, their chalky faces, their blue overalls tapestried with paint-marks. He coveted the tools they used— the plane, uncurling fragrant, pencilly frills of new wood; the polished mauve grip of the saw. His interest was aesthetic —he knew he had no aptitude for carpentry. When they gave him a piece of wood to saw, his arm and eye grew tired before the blade had cut half-way. He thought with shame of the fierce accuracy with which Dad sawed wood, steadying it with one foot, and his attentive tongue, lunging down and down until the sawn block fell among its own dust on the floor.

Dad had ordered him not to worry the workmen.

He stood in the middle of the Pavilion floor. This whole

95

expanse was his—to do what? He stretched his arms wide and spun himself round, making a clicking, gargling noise in his throat. He stopped, listening to the waves in the estuary, and the clap of the typewriter from the dressing-room up the little staircase, and the sawing and planing in the distance, behind the balcony. Everybody was doing something. Everybody else was busy.

'Come on, Nig,' he called, and the old black gundog immediately got up from beside the windows and came plodding out over the rink towards him. There were grey patches like elephant hide on his shoulders and tail, and he had been run over, patiently, several times. Even when the electric fire fell on him, Nigger lay still until it had been lifted off again. Nigger always came when you called him. But Melody, the cocker spaniel, never left the private office when Louis's mother was there.

He knelt, with Nigger beside him, in the centre of the floor, his cheek against Nigger's soft ear, his eye travelling around the distant walls. He felt a strange communion with the builders of the Pavilion, as if they had been men exactly like Dad—there was something of Dad even in the high panels that masked the boardwork and the curve of windows along the estuary, with their upper freize of yellow and red glass diamonds. Louis sometimes wondered if the Pavilion had stood all these years just waiting for him, as tides unnumbered roared and changed underneath it. A gauntleted finger, pointing to Exit, directed his imagination to the days when ladies wore bustles and life blinked in black and white with the rapidity of a Charlie Chaplin film. A strange feeling came over him when he looked at the stage, and the scenery behind it, and tried to imagine what show put on here had required a scene representing Venice. He wondered if his dreams might already have brought him here, to live in a painted dimension among the pale, tilted towers and gondola prows.

He remembered what Dad had said to Wilf about the Navy signallers quartered in the Pavilion during the War. Dad had shown him the name which one of them had chalked on a backstage door—Sergeant Swindells. He had heard Dad telling Wilf about all the stolen cigarettes which the sailors were said to have hidden at the top of the dome. Could the cigarettes still be there, behind the tiny crossed bars under the glint of coloured glass at the summit? He frightened himself by pretending he had to climb up inside the dome to search for them. He pictured himself starting off from one of the columns around the balcony—easily at first, but climbing higher and darker in the mesh of yellow girders until he hung completely upside down, unable to go further or to return.

He went through the entrance hall and stood outside on the tram station, waiting to see the boat come in. Both ends of the station were open, one to the track, the other to the pierhead and the white-lipped waves beyond. There was soft sand under the tram buffers and the water in the red fire buckets, one of which reflected his face, shivered with the shadow of the wind. He watched the boat approach jauntily, circling the pierhead from the west. He stood at the barrier watching as, from the infinity of iron, consuming one iron rectangle after another, came the flat green front of the tram.

The tramboy jumped from the first car the very moment it drew level with the platform, and ran down to open the gate which let the passengers out. 'Hello Lewis,' he said, laughing.

The tramboy had black hair and slit eyes like a Chinaman, and holes in his uniform that were never darned. Sometimes, if the tram was empty, he would turn a somersault between two leather hand-straps. Once, Louis had seen him wearing holsters and shooting two silver cap guns. When Louis asked his name, the tramboy said: 'Peter.'

He pronounced it 'Pidder'.

'Peter . . .'

'Charley,' the tramboy amended, still laughing with his slit eyes. He would never tell Louis if his name was Peter or Charley. Then he said: 'How about comin' to the fair with me, Lewis?'

'Where?' Louis asked

'Over Pompey.'

That was the lower-class name for Portsmouth. Louis remembered the glimpse of a fairground as the boat left Portsmouth—the big wheel, turning on the harbour shore. He breathed in with joy at the thought of going there with the tramboy.

'Wait a minute. I'll just go in and ask somebody.'

The tramboy smiled and shook his head.

'No, don't do that.'

'I've only got to go in and ask my mummy if I can.'

'No, don't do it just yet,' the tramboy said, pulling the long gate shut after the boat passengers.

'When shall we go to the fair, though?'

But the tramboy only blew his whistle and looked back at Louis, and laughed again as he stepped neatly into the departing tram.

An epoch reached its end when Eilian, the Irish girl got married.

She had looked after Louis since they lived in London, at The Porcupine. His mother did not have time to do it as well as helping Dad in the bar and restaurant, so Eilian was brought over from Ireland in the time before Louis's memory began. She had been with them during the Victory Parade, when Dad sold seats in the windows that overlooked Charing Cross Road. She had put Louis to bed upstairs through all the hectic wartime days when Dad fought Canadians with a truncheon weighted with lead, and compounded his own green cocktail in the cellar, and strolled behind the circular bar with watches for sale strapped along his arm from wrist to elbow.

At St Neots, Louis had grown accustomed to a life apart, hurried by Eilian past the doorways of places where he could not go. He felt his own presence to be insidious in the hotel, likely to undermine its delicate structure of bars, cellars, kitchens and private office. His mother and Dad—when Dad was there—appeared to him as distant figures, deeply engrossed among strangers and drifting smoke. They slept at the other end of the hotel, going to bed and getting up in their

98

own private tunnel of time. He remembered once in the summer slipping into their room behind old Fred Cambers, who took round the morning tea. The blinds, above the gold keys, were drawn; a breakfast tray had been pushed from the low divan to the carpet. Louis felt an atmosphere of scalding bad temper when his mother's voice, in the half-light, said, 'Thoroughly enjoyed that—I don't think!' Something else in the room disturbed and repelled him—something to do with the white sheet, and the hollows it made around their entangled legs.

By day Eilian took him for walks; by night, she put him to bed. She shouted at him, but seldom smacked him. While bathing him, she told him about Killarney, where she and her sisters lived, and promised she would take him there with her one day to show him how beautiful it was. He shared the sense of longing in the songs that Eilian sang about Galway Bay and Dear Old Donegal and Erin's Green Isle, and the place, which must be so beautiful he thought, where the Mountains of Mourne came down to the sea.

Sometimes Eilian took him with her to church. He stood next to her in gloomy light, watching hundreds of candles and smelling a sweet and burning odour. He looked at the candles with eyes open through folded hands, praying for he knew not what while Eilian whispered and whispered beside him. What was she whispering so desperately, and why did he have to do a curtsey at the pew-end and, out in the porch, dip his hand in a stone bowl of water? Sometimes a man in white and gold robes shouted furiously down at them from a high opening among the candles. 'It's Our Lady's Day! And not *one* of you has brought a flower!' No one had told Louis you had to bring a flower. In consternation, he put all his money—eightpence—into the plate that was offered. Later, when they were standing up, he cried out, 'Eilian! When are they going to give me my money back?'

In the afternoon, Eilian used to have a rest on the spare bed in Louis's room. As she lay there, he would approach and roll back her skirt to look at her knees. Eilian was asleep—she must have been, for she lay quite still—and so Louis rolled

99

up her skirt further still, beyond the metal clips on her stockings, to where dark bands turned into cold, white skin, and where brown hair mysteriously grew. He would wander away, and return again to look again, and touch and even rest his face against the hair, sniffing its salty, meaty smell. Often it seemed to him that Eilian's eyes were open—but if so, why did she never pull her skirt down and tell him off for doing that? She lay still in her blouse in the darkened bedroom that looked out to the ivy-covered wall of Plum's bakery.

Eilian came with them to Ryde, and so did Wilf, from the grocers in St Neots, now her fiancé. Wilf wore grease on his hair, which was brushed straight back; his lips were always parted, never quite into a smile, and when he spoke, a tight lump jerked up in his throat like a lift rushing to the top floor. Wilf had left his job in St Neots to work for Dad on the Island. He was now one of the family. If he wanted to go to the Gents', he said, 'Excuse me. I'm just going to ventilate my testicles.'

Eilian and Wilf were married at the Catholic Church in the High Street, next to the Scala cinema. A lot of Eilian's sisters came over from Killarney for the occasion. Louis liked the sister named Kathleen best. He thought how nice it would be if Kathleen could look after him now, and have a rest on the spare bed in the afternoon.

To his relief, the priest did not shout at him this time for having omitted to bring Our Lady a flower. He sat next to the priest at the reception, and made him laugh, and Eilian's sister Kathleen laugh, with all the funny things he said. Wilf's brother, Alf, read out the telegrams in a hushed and grateful voice above a plate of little sandwiches without crusts. 'With every good wish and happiness for the future stop many congratulations stop Squadron Leader and Mrs Belmayne and Louis.'

Wilf had been given the job of running the café newly-opened by Dad (and Uncle Cal) at the top of the town. The name of the café was The Creamery. It had a strip-light hanging on chains from the ceiling, a counter topped in purple
100

lino, a slot machine, a tea-urn, and tables and chairs borrowed from surplus stock at the Pavilion. It had two steamy shop windows and a steamy glass door on which a little cardboard notice hung. One side of the notice said: 'Open. Come in for your Horlicks.' The other side said: 'Closed. Call again for your Horlicks.'

For a time after their wedding, Eilian and Wilf lived on the top floor, above the flat where Dad and Louis and his mother lived. Then they moved into furnished rooms around the corner in Green Street. Wilf gave up The Creamery and went to the end of the pier to issue skating tickets. Eilian stayed at home all day, sitting next to the big rented sideboard with the clock that Dad had given her, and her wedding photographs, and statues of Jesus and Mary, blue and white and red and halo-gold, like prizes in a hoopla stall.

After Eilian, Louis was placed under the charge of a Mrs Souter. Her reign was short but unforgettable, because of the bumps that grew on her face. She had one enormous bump on her cheek and a second equally enormous bump on her forehead, as well as all the tight little baby bumps above her eyebrows and under her chin. Louis knew he ought not to look at Mrs Souter's bumps, but the more he tried, the more they transfixed his sight. The two main bumps hung before him, taut and faintly luminous, as he sat on the edge of the bath and Mrs Souter sponged his knees—he could even smell a terrible bump-like smell from them, reminiscent of cold, empty eggshells. The week he spent in Mrs Souter's care was characterised by mutual constraint, each of them seeming anxious to spare the other the smallest inconvenience. Louis never found out where she lived, where the bumps had come from, or if Mrs Souter had a family accustomed to her bumps, or possibly afflicted by bumps of its own. Mrs Souter vanished from his life one day, without explanation, and her place was taken by the next in a series of many familiar strangers.

There was also Margaret Mitchell, whose mother worked as a waitress at the Pavilion in the season, and whose father worked there sometimes as chef. Margaret had a long nose and a dark red winter coat. She knew people who rode on the bus platform and jumped into the road before it stopped. Sometimes, she would take Louis for tea at her house in Elmfield, where her mother, a little woman with a huge head, like Wee Peem in the Beano comic, gave him chocolate marshmallows for tea. Margaret and her mother were recognisably of the lower classes, yet Louis, on his visits, was struck by the neatness of their house, which overlooked a paddock with two horses in it.

Most memorable of all was Mrs Proctor, who ushered in a striking religious epoch. Mrs Proctor looked like somebody else's grandma. She wore a blue coat, buttoned across her right shoulder, and a matching peaked cap, the ensemble uncannily resembling the uniform of an officer in the US Cavalry. Louis could not resist the thought that, instead of sitting on his bed and making him say his prayers, Mrs Proctor ought to have been defending Fort Tomahawk against the might of the Sioux nations.

'Gentle Jesus meek and mild who was once a little . . . it's quiet out there, sergeant. Yes. Too quiet. Can you handle a carbine now without getting careless. Those fire arrows will blow up the powder magazine, sergeant. Amen.'

At night, when they left the end of the pier, Mrs Proctor would take Louis to a hut near Ryde St John's railway station, to a meeting of the Christian Brotherhood. He had to stand in a crowd that smelled of raincoats and sang hymns with choruses he had never heard before, and intoned garrulous and agitated prayers. There was another boy on his own level, crop-headed and ape-featured, who grinned out at Louis from among the hymns and raincoats while shadowing the bizarre catechism with his mouth.

One night, when it was more crowded than usual inside the hut, two men stood on the platform and conducted a strange oratorical argument about a brown envelope, which one of them had taken from inside his coat.

The envelope seemed to have been posted directly from God. At the same time it promised to reveal something to the

102

discredit of one of the two men, for he had now sunk down upon a chair with his elbow on a green baize tablecloth. The other man stood over him, waving the envelope, and saying sternly, 'I *know* what's in this letter. I'm going to open it and read it to everybody here.'

The seated man groaned to hear this, and buried his face in his hands, then peeped up at the envelope through his fingers.

'There's a message in this letter!' the first man said.

The seated man groaned behind his fingers and croaked: 'Hallelujah!'

'Shall I open it?'

'Don't open it,' croaked the seated man.

'Open it then!' he groaned, suddenly changing his mind.

Everyone in the hall, including the other boy, and Mrs Proctor in her US Cavalry officer's coat, shouted out: 'Open it!'

The man who held the envelope waved it and cried: 'Hallelujah!'

Louis saw the little straight lines all round Mrs Proctor's mouth, where her false teeth were, as she shouted out 'Hallelujah!' with the others.

The envelope was not opened. Instead, they sang a very long hymn. Mrs Proctor ceased looking after Louis soon afterwards, and Margaret Mitchell, in her red winter coat, came back again. His mother said that people found him 'a handful'.

going to the pictures at night

After his seventh birthday he is allowed to go to school by himself. No one is up yet in the flat; at the last minute, before he sets off, his mother comes out in her nightdress and searches angrily through her purse to find fourpence and a sweet coupon, to buy himself something for breaktime in the little shop next door to Johncox's. The same toothless old woman is there every morning, lurking behind the high glass counter in which Banjos and Crests and Spangles lie muddled up together. Louis imagines this old woman to be growing fonder of him the more often he comes into her shop, and the longer he takes to decide what he will buy. It is always a Banjo, 'two crisp wafer biscuits covered in milk chocolate—4d and one point'. Points are coupons from the ration book you have to give in exchange for sweets. The letter o in Banjo is a black man's mouth, rounded in a song of praise.

'Goodbye,' he says, raising his cap to the toothless old woman. When he feels he knows her better, he raises his cap and says: 'Goodbye. I hope it keeps fine for you.'

It is still very early in the morning. All up the High Street ahead of him, the shops are closed, and voices reading the eight o'clock news float out of open windows, mixed up with the sound, and smell, of cooking bacon. In the greengrocer's window, a yellow cat reclines on a couch of cabbages, eyes shut in a beatitude for its sun-warmed nose. The breakfast smell makes Louis think of Nanny Belmayne, and the breakfasts at Orlando Road, and rouses in him a premature craving for the Banjo bar in his satchel—an ache all along his jaw for chocolate and the snap of slatted wafer biscuit. He touches it among his books, feeling the cool firmness of the silver paper. He has taken it out and, guiltily, as if opening a private letter, he breaks the seal across the o of the black man's singing lips and eats both fingers and the chocolate seam that joins them. They are gone in a moment, leaving despair. Now he has nothing to look forward to at break. His tongue ransacks his mouth's wet ribs, imploring the taste not to disappear.

At the Health Stores, where the shops end, Ryde ceases to be a thing of climbing and endeavour. The High Street becomes Swanmore Road, like a crowded river flowing out upon the bosom of a lake. He passes the London Hotel, resenting the inaccuracy of its name, lettered in white across a blackened wall. Across the road is the IN gatepost of the Isle of Wight County Hospital, and as he passes Louis always looks in, up the drive towards the glass-domed children's ward, and remembers the little burned boy he saw in a hospital so long ago with bandages covering all but his scarlet lips. Another boy shook his head in such a sad way when Louis asked him, 'Would you like some comics?' Each morning, he feels thankful he is not in hospital, being cut open, or waking in the dark to find nurses in big, folded headdresses standing like ghosts around the foot of his bed.

He walks on, following his long-legged shadow up the big, slanting avenue—Swanmore Road now merged with West Street—towards the elm trees above Partlands. On a meadow-wide junction, the lands truly part, drifting off in high and low roads to Ashey and Haven Street. The sky above the elms is flat and wide as an extra road, silent but for the rooks

105

circling their black nests among the veined and glinting top-most branches. Louis stands and looks up, trying to imagine where the quiet blue highway might end. This sort of sky makes him think of Dad, who has dared to fly higher than the highest clouds. And yet Louis himself knows he is afraid of heights—afraid even to look any longer at the rooks' nests in the elms.

He turns right here, skirting the gravelled forecourt of the Partlands Hotel. He walks up Partlands Avenue, along a steep path of single paving stones. On one side of him is the grass verge; on the other, a ditch almost hidden by long grass, nettles and dock leaves, the hedge beyond thronged with thistles and sad white blooms and the flowers, like elm trees formed of greenish white lace, which Louis calls honeysuckle, and dandelion clocks, their time half-told by the breeze, and green, hairy burrs like caterpillars, capable of flight. He looks down in surprise to find one sticking to his sleeve.

'Do you like butter, Mary? Let me see.'
'Do I?'
'Yes, you do.'
'Do you like butter, Gay?'
'Do I?'
'Let me see—yes.'
'Do you like butter, Louis?'

He is flying high over the ground against his chest. Far beneath him lies the city of flat daisies; the daisy faces uplifted to see him fly past, his aeroplane the sound of a mower he can hear.

He looks up to see Mary Smythe holding the ritual buttercup towards him. Mary Smythe wears a cage of rods around her leg; her sock is grass-stained at the ankle where her foot crookedly touches the ground. For some reason, her caged and crooked foot allows Mary Smythe to win the Sack Race every summer.

She laughs with a gurgling sound. She is always laughing, even though she cannot walk properly or play Rounders.

106

'Yes, you like butter Louis. Do I?'

Form One has gone outside with Miss King, through the blistery door to the playing field beyond the garden. It is not a lesson—more a conference, of the kind that Miss King frequently calls during the day. They listen to her, kneeling or sitting, in clumps of white and sky blue, along the front of the old tin sports grandstand. Ladybirds walk softly on their arms and patiently traverse their pointing fingers, or burst without warning into body-splitting flight. They are counting the spots on a ladybird to tell its age. They are tying daisies together in chains, and sucking pink clover for its fugitive sweetness; searching under one another's chins for the tell-tale shadow of a buttercup. Their knees and elbows are numb with the print of grass, their finger-ends wet from pressing into daisy stalks.

Louis is in a group with Roger Sim and Gay Goudge and Mary Smythe, her leg in its cage lying sideways on the grass. A little to one side of them is Robin Burnett, who used to be his friend when he first came to Partlands School. Louis knows that Robin Burnett has a big fort at home, built for him by his father, and that he calls orange squash 'cordial' : no more than that remains of the epoch of their friendship. To Robin, perhaps, even less, for he is kneeling up and staring away from Louis, across the field into some stern, private perspective. He is very good at playing the piano. His demeanour is as grave and plump as when he walks forth in a concert and settles his music on the piano to play. He is condemned as 'proud' yet envied for the Smith's crisps, reward of virtuosity, which he brings to school each day for break.

Roger Sim is Dr Sim's son and Gay Goudge is silly. She has red hair and freckles, and she cries when she gets the tummy-ache. Sometimes she forgets where she is, and calls Miss King 'Mummy'. Once, she told Miss King she didn't like jelly because it wobbled.

Instead of Gay Goudge, Louis would rather be sitting next to Janice Bennett. She patted the grass beside her, and he wanted to, but something at the last minute made him frown,

107

as if he had not seen her, and step over her to a place where he did not want to go. He can see her now, beyond the porcine mouth of Robin Burnett, her chin resting on her raised knees. He knows she will have arranged her dress in such a way as to cover her knees but to show the underneath of her legs.

Miss King is telling them about the Half-Term Holiday. She is standing up in front of them, as she always does, like someone saying a poem, her arms straight by her sides, her feet together so that the frilled tongues of her brogue shoes are in perfect alignment with their neat little bows. Her voice, diminished somewhat by trees and insects and murmuring air, still carries without effort to the back of the assembly. It is a firm, steady, friendly voice, touched with an alluring huskiness, a voice on tiptoe, poised to exhort, congratulate or sympathise. To its hearers, it promises excitement and gaiety; a hope of adventure in the most commonplace procedure. So it is with the Half-Term Holiday, the particulars of which are to be circulated in a typically exhilarating manner. Later on, they will copy out the announcement themselves on paper slips, and this afternoon take the slips home; a hundred hastening postmen, not one in any doubt that he or she is Miss King's personal and favoured emissary.

Louis feels for Miss King, as all do, an undisclosed and respectful infatuation. His heart lifts proudly each morning to see her slim, straight shape bringing order to the chaos in cloakrooms, and her shiny black hair, its plaited bun revealed as she turns round in the garden with a whistle between her lips. He adores her neat clothes—the navy blue jumper so flattering to her dark complexion, the tartan skirt which sometimes has a little matching scarf. He has looked for hours from his desk into her sunburned face, admiring its straight black brows, its big, astonished brown eyes, the small, squared mouth that seems always to be keeping back a secret or a smile. He yearns, as all do, for the benison of that smile, bestowed on well-eaten dinner or an unusual Dinky car; he dreads, as all do, the disfavour she hardly shows. Disappointment, wounding those dark eyes, can pierce a shouter or a spitter to the heart. Uproar

108

becomes silence, wild with remorse to see lips pressed together where her smile used to be, her wrinkled forehead seeking to recollect, on their behalf, what solemn pledge has been forgotten.

How could anyone forget? It is written in white letters round their blue and brown blazer badges, encircling the figure of a skylark. It is written also in the brown metal badges they wear pinned to their dresses or shirts. It is the motto of the P.N.E.U.—The Parents' National Education Union, to which Partlands School is affiliated. All over England, it seems, there are other schools which learn the same sort of lessons, and wear blue and brown uniforms, and take the skylark as a symbol of endeavour, and share the motto, repeated now for Miss King, a low murmur among the low and murmuring trees:

'I am, I can, I ought, I will.'

'Oh, come on!' Miss King says, with just a little rueful frown.

Louder, slower, their voices say: 'I am, I can, I ought, I will.'

Partlands School belongs to Miss King, and her sister Miss Stella. It is their own house in Partlands Avenue—their ground floor invaded by classrooms and cloakrooms and charts and tadpole jars, their scullery by milkcrates and piled-up paint palettes, their garden by a square of blue asphalt and the swings. Miss King and Miss Stella live upstairs, descending each day from a region inconceivable to those who tread the lino corridor beneath.

Miss Stella does not look like Miss King's sister. She is as stout and fair-skinned and elderly-looking and prone to annoyance as Miss King is slim, dark, youthful and calm. When Louis first saw her, he was conscious of having met Miss Stella before—the grey curly hair, the pink cheeks and spectacles, and hands in cardigan sleeves, clapping for silence awoke echoes of schools he had previously attended. At Partlands, Miss Stella is the clear embodiment of authority, invoked by Miss King where matters of discipline arise. 'Miss Stella has

109

noticed . . .' she will gravely begin, '. . . and I have, too,' she will admit, almost reluctant to corroborate what Miss Stella has noticed. Yet it is Miss King ultimately who requests that whatever misconduct Miss Stella has noticed shall cease. Hers is the final authority, unenforced by clapping hands, maintained in her trusting brown eyes, wielded in such subtleties as her pre-emptive right to be known by her surname, where Miss Stella employs a familiar, somehow junior form of address. It has even been said that, despite all appearances, Miss King is actually *older* than Miss Stella. Michael Hambly, by the overgrown turnstile, insisted, against fierce opposition, that it was true.

Each day under Miss King begins with alertness and looking forward. At nine o'clock, in the two communal form rooms, they wait behind their desks, listening in silence for the music to begin. There it comes: the muffled strump of a military band. They lead out in order—Bluebirds, the baby form, first, then Transition, then Forms Two and One. They march, swinging arms, up the shiny brown passage and wheel right, past the scullery steps, down an avenue of shrouded coat-pegs into a dark little varnished room. Miss King and Miss Stella are waiting there already, in front of the window with the school gramophone playing on the floorboards between them. Miss King greets them standing to attention, as they march in and line up in front of her and, on the floor by her feet, the white label of the gramophone record flicks round and round.

They have hymns first, accompanied at the piano by a lady called Mrs Russell. They sing about the Green Hill Far Away where the dear Lord was crucified and which, for all this sad coincidence, sounds an agreeable place to Louis; he pictures the mound of dark grass in a pleasant evening light. By contrast, Good King Wenceslas, in a season of warm excitement and pasted paper chains, evokes a scene of harrowing bleakness. His heart shivers to think of the freezing place that is 'right against the forest fence, by St Agnes fountain'. But this morning it is summer; their arms are uncovered, their socks short, and 'All Things Bright and Beautiful' seems to celebrate

110

the pansies that turn smudged faces upward along Miss King's and Miss Stella's garden path. Mrs Russell comes in to play the piano for them every morning. Then she goes away again. She wears a pale grey costume with a brooch on one lapel, and does not trouble to take off her hat indoors.

As their voices die away, Miss King joins her hands in front of her tartan skirt, bows her head and says:

'Let us pray.'

She says this every morning, making it appear a novel and original suggestion. They join their hands together like hers, bow their heads and concur:

'Let us spray.'

Miss King prays alone first on their behalf. She is speaking to God in her husky, friendly voice, and the birds are singing in the little trees outside. God made the birds and He made Louis; He made the world and everything in it, even Gay Goudge. Few pictures of God are available, but Louis has seen one in a book. It showed God sitting in Heaven on a cloud; He wore a beard in numerous scrolls, like rolled-up maps round His chin, and He waved two pieces of lightning fiercely above His head. Despite His alarming appearances, God is very kind. He only lost His temper when Adam ate the apple. He will forgive all the wrong things Louis does, like wee weeing in the bath and cutting up woodlice and thinking 'bloody' and telling fibs and even opening his eyes during the prayer to study his own folded hands and the pattern of his sandals on the floor. Those standing at the back of the room near the piano, report that Mrs Russell does not close her eyes at all during prayers. But presumably God will forgive Mrs Russell for doing that.

They say Our Father in a chorus. The words, learned at the starting-point of memory, re-assemble in images familiarly baffling. 'Hello by Thy name; thy kingdom come.' 'Give us this day our daily bread' sounds too modest a request to Louis, who would rather the bread were coated with honey or chocolate spread. 'Forgive us our trespasses' reminds him of crisps—the Smith's crisps that Robin Burnett will produce

111

at breaktime, sharing them with no one else, haughtily shaking and shuffling the golden fragments in their bag to salt them. 'As we forgive those that trespass against us' reminds him of the noise made by Robin Burnett, eating crisps. He is now exceedingly hungry, and the Lord's Prayer, containing nothing more to eat, descends into anticlimax. 'And lead us not into the station: butdeliverusfromevil' heralds only the headlong slip and slither through 'The Power and the Glory' to *Amen*.

The eyes rustle open, to see Miss King outlined darkly at the window. They wait, straight-backed with joy as she draws her brows together, placing her head on one side to find the least reproachful words for what she has to say.

'Miss Stella has noticed . . . and I have too, that some of you people are coming to school much too early in the morning. I could hear somebody shouting in the scullery at about eight o'clock today. Some of you are arriving before Miss Stella and I have even finished our breakfast.'

Miss King's voice is warm with good humour, even admiration at the effrontery of these dawn arrivers. Louis was among them—his, possibly, the cry that rang so loudly off the wide, shallow scullery sink. He is fascinated by the thought of Miss King and Miss Stella at breakfast in their secret upper rooms, eating marmalade darker than he has ever seen before, which they take from a glass dish on long, thin silver spoons.

All morning, the little house echoes quietly with lesson noises, the scrape of chalk, the powdery rub of blackboard dusters, the closing, opening of desks, snap of pencilbox lids, swirl of brushes in paint water, doors opening or shutting on the murmur of things repeated, footsteps on lino, pattering laughter, sudden silence, the clanking of a toilet chain. At breaktime, bottles jingling in the metal milk crates, feet jumping on asphalt, screams of pursuer and pursued, swings in chorus like the irregular beat of a squeaky heart, stilled by the curt whistle blast; the queue, out of breath, re-adjusting socks below the scullery door, stigmata fading on the hand
112

of the person who was 'He', the swing seats empty, the high and low swings, rocking on their chains, slower and slower to rest.

Miss King teaches History, Writing, English Grammar, Reading, Picture Study, Tables and Handwork. Standing with her feet together at their end of the bay-fronted room, next to the sunlit window-blind, she tells Form One about nouns and adjectives, subjects, predicates, the use of which are exemplified through the adventures of John and Mary; she turns, to reveal the dear little bun behind her head, and shows them on the long blackboard how to join a letter y with an a, and reads with them from a gluey-smelling book the story of Tom Tit Tot, and the man who wasted all his three wishes; she tells them about the poor wounded soldiers nursed by Florence Nightingale in the Crimean War and about Raphael and Velasquez and Leonardo da Vinci and Dürer, whose works are reproduced with notes on glossy little white sheets. When Louis looks at *The Praying Hands,* or at Mona Lisa, smirking from her bower of dark woods and uphill rivers, he can remember Miss King's exact words, even to a little pause she sometimes makes, putting her face so prettily on one side as she searches for a phrase: 'It makes us think that . . . perhaps the artist could not have won Mona Lisa's heart.'

Miss Stella teaches Nature, Arithmetic, Bible, Painting, Patterns, Music and Movement and Environmental Studies. By the same subtle order of precedence between the sisters, it falls to Miss Stella to deal with such topics as the habits of the reed warbler, the adventures of Bombo, a little African boy, the slaying of the Philistines by Samson, Joseph's Coat of Many Colours and the yachts called redwings which put into Bembridge Harbour. These subjects promote a restive atmosphere with much going to be excused, and are attended by frequent clapping of Miss Stella's cardigan cuffs, and her voice exclaiming: 'Form One—be *quart*!'

She tells Jeremy Mitcheson off for writing his name in the wrong place on the paper.

'*Look* what you've written—"Bombo's village in Jeremy

113

Mitcheson". That's just silly, isn't it! Bombo's village in Jeremy Mitcheson!'

At rare moments, they see a more rollicksome side of Miss Stella's disposition. They are sitting round her feet in the dark little piano room, listening to a wireless programme of music played on pipes and drums. Suddenly, Miss Stella lifts her hands from her lap, puffs out her cheeks and twiddles all her fingers in a straight line as if she is playing a flute. When they laugh, she lifts a cautioning finger and goes 'Ssh!' against it. But in a minute, she does the same thing again—she puffs her cheeks out, twiddling all her fingers and bouncing her lap up and down. There is a second gasp of laughter. 'Ssh!' she goes, putting her finger on her lips. 'Ssh, Form One— *quietly.*'

They line up in twos outside the scullery at ten to one, ready to march down Swanmore Road to the London Hotel for lunch. The two who stand up straightest on the asphalt are given the honour of leading the column. Before choosing the leaders, Miss King holds up a piece of paper she has retrieved from the path, and says:

'Who's eaten a sweet and dropped this?'

She uncrumples and spreads out the sweet paper to look at the writing on it.

'A Minto. Come on,' she says encouragingly. 'Who's eaten a Minto?'

Her eye reviews the straining chests, the concave backs, the faces turned in agony to the chimneypots.

'I think . . . I *think* . . . Louis, a-and . . . *a-a-and* Janice can go first today.'

He sees his face again in the Partlands photograph—the one Jeremy Mitcheson spoiled by turning round. He finds himself in the second row, underneath the row of people who stood on chairs. His hair is brushed flat with water; his school tie hangs over the head of a kneeling girl. His is the face in spectacles held steeply on one side, as if harbouring some coy secret

114

against the photographer. Mary Smythe's crooked leg has been covered by a corner of her lap. Jeremy Mitcheson, in the cross-legged front row, has no face at all, and a head as wide as a concertina.

Janice Bennett says he is the handsomest boy at school. Each day she brings him a blue Turf cigarette card with a film star on it—Old Mother Riley or Gene Autry or Frank Sinatra as the Kissing Bandit. At breaktime, she follows him around the garden, telling everyone she wants to marry him when she grows up. Louis returns her admiration by jumping over flower-beds to escape her, or pretending to faint with horror on the path. Then he looks round to make certain she is still following him. His secret dream is of Janice Bennett with her dress tucked inside her knickers for gym, kneeling on his chest or putting her arms tightly around his neck.

He gets stars all the time for the pictures he draws. He knows how cars and houses and horses and mountains 'go', and cowboys' hats from the top, and swords, epaulettes and the extra coats on cavalrymen's shoulders. He is used to working with a little crowd behind his chair, feigning indifference to the gasps and sighs and sniffs and moans of admiration.

'Look!'

'Oooh—look!'

'Isn't it good!'

'They go *just* like that!'

'Will you do me a shop, Louis?'

'Will you show me how a roof goes, Louis? Please. Oh, *please*!'

He has got stars for history and writing and tables, and for learning the whole of a poem entitled 'The Ugly Little Man'. From his part of the desk, he can see his name on the chart, and all his stars marching out across the squared arithmetic paper. He thought Miss Stella would give him a star in Bible for his illustrated account of how Samson slew the Philistines with the jawbone of an ass. Samson looked dashing in epaulettes and cavalry boots while the Philistines wore the dark blue of English Naval ratings. His book was returned

115

with 'Very Fair' written beside the composition, and underneath, in Miss Stella's terse writing: 'They were not dressed like this, Louis.'

He is good at elocution. People laugh when he says his poem in front of the class. He is in the play they are going to act on Sports Day at the end of term. He plays Jack and Claire Thomas plays Jill. Richard Gould plays Mustard Seed, an elf; his brother Peter is A Little Rosebud. Every time Peter Gould appears, even if he is puffing like a train, they all have to say: 'Aah—it's the Little Rosebud!'

When Jack and Jill examine the magic cloak, Mustard Seed has to say: 'This is the new Utility model.'

Out on the playing field, they rehearse their words while the deep-voiced lady who teaches elocution directs them from an upper row of the old tin grandstand.

'Where's Mustard Seed? Come on, Richard—it's you? What are you doing?

'Making a daisy chain.'

'Don't make a daisy chain, please. Now: all together. "Aah—" '

'Aah—it's the Little Rosebud!'

'Jack and Jill, buck up. Where are you? You're lost in the forest. Mustard Seed is sitting on a toadstool, *not* making a daisy chain. Come on Jack—"My name . . ." '

'My name is Jack and this is Jill. We live . . .'

'*Point* to it, Jack. "We live in the castle on the hill." And Jill is crying not smiling, Claire—because you're lost in the forest. Comfort her, Jack!'

How silly Claire Thomas looks. Why couldn't Janice Bennett be Jill instead of Claire Thomas with her fringe and crooked collar and stumpy teeth and screamy voice? Why should she be Miss Stella's pet, just because she lives in a house called Five Ways?

'Comfort her, Jack!'

Jack whispers to Jill through gritted teeth: 'Don't cry. It's all right.'

'*Comfort* her, Jack!'

116

'Don't cry. It's enough to make a cat laugh.'

'No, Louis, *don't* say it's enough to make a cat laugh!'

He is not good at French and English Grammar, which are done in the same writing book at Partlands School. His exercises are returned with Miss Mason's soft, pink crosses through them, or sometimes a reluctant star. He is not good at piano with Mrs Aitchison, who was Miss Mason until she got married last month. For many lessons now he has striven to master the tune called 'Porcupines'. He sits in the dark little piano room, trying to remember which is the bass and which the treble clef, with Mrs Aitchison beside him in her pink cardigan, her thick lips compressed, waiting and waiting to turn over the page. But the keys outside Middle C remain as featureless to Louis as bitten chocolate cream.

In handwork, he cannot do back stitch, however many times Miss King tries to show him. Now she has kept him in after school to show him again. She is standing over him at his desk, so close that he can smell her tartan skirt, and a chalky, sunshiny fragrance that seems to come straight from her dark skin. Her long fingers push the needle through the unfinished place mat once more, and he pretends to watch, although shame and panic have unfocused his eyes. He plunges the needle in, digging about with it in the faint hope the stitch will go backward on its own. Once, in desperation, he jerked his arm up— he accidentally struck Miss King on the cheek. Deaf with horror, he crouched in his desk as her brown eyes looked steadfastly down at him. But all she said was, 'Oh, I *shall* get cross with you in a minute.'

His failings haunt him in constant review, poisoning his stray triumphs and showing him, at some exuberant moment, the pitiful outline of his true self. He cannot hit the ball in Rounders, or catch it. When they all have to run across the field, and the fast runners move out from the line with billowing shirt backs, a deep hopelessness comes over him—he wants to trip and sprawl, exempted, over the daisy clouds. He cannot swing high on the swing, as even Gay Goudge can; just to watch the others swinging up and standing horizontal near the

117

sun, makes his heart swerve in terror and his face shrink back into his shoulder. He cannot leapfrog or make grass squeal by blowing on it or find bird feathers for Nature or undo hard knots in his shoelace. Janice Bennett would not want to marry him if she knew the silent sobs that rend him, left behind in the cloakroom with one foot up the bench, his feeble fingers plucking at the knot, after everyone else has run outside.

Janice would not call him handsome if she knew the fear that haunts his every schoolday—the fear of having to do a number two at school. He pictures himself with horror, sitting on the chilly white pedestal with the green door locked and feet walking to and fro on the stone floor under the partition. Then someone will notice the shut door, a crowd will collect, Miss Stella will arrive and say, 'Who is it in there?'

One Thursday afternoon they had played rounders with Miss Stella, running from stump to stump over clouds of daisies. Afterwards, Louis stood with Roger Sim, Michael Hambly and others at the turnstile in the cold shade of the grandstand wall. Cut grass and clover juice lingered like an addiction, paralysing the will. For a little while, they were powerless to go back through the garden, to reality amid the cloakroom pegs.

They were discussing several things—a three-leaf clover that Roger Sim had found, and why it was that picking dandelions made you wet the bed, and what you called the green, sticky burr things that hung on the hedge yet seemed to roll or climb or float into every department of life. According to Jeremy Mitcheson, who had picked one off his arm, the green things were alive. Being Jeremy Mitcheson, he boasted that he had put one into his ear for a joke. All the girls laughed at that. Then Michael Hambly, the biscuit-stealer, said he had put one into his mouth.

'I put one on my leg,' Roger Sim said.

'I put one in my eye,' said Michael Hambly.

A brilliant elaboration occurred to Louis. He said: 'I put one up my nose, and it danced with all the bogeys.'

118

A scream of laughter greeted this. He laughed himself at first, picturing the furry plume within his nostril, sedately waltzing with the terrible objects that dwelt there. He stopped laughing, but the others did not. With sudden unease, he looked at their distorted faces, their blaring mouths, their eyes empty of all but gleeful horror. The laughter would not stop. It went on and on, tinged now with accusation. People who had not heard asked for the remark to be repeated to them. In gradually mutating form, it became the talk of Partlands School.

'He said he put one up his nose . . .'

'—who did?'

'Louis did.'

'Louis did.'

'Louis Belmayne did . . .'

'—Louis Belmayne said he put one of those green things up his nose, and made all the bogeys dance.'

'—he put one up his nose and it danced all the bogeys.'

Claire Thomas heard it and smiled, showing her stumpy teeth. Then, still smiling, she said: 'I'm going to tell Miss King.'

'—he put one up his nose and danced all the bogeys.'

'—and all the bogeys danced up and down.'

His face blushed hot, then cold, as he heard Claire Thomas's words. Boys at Partlands could not 'tell', but girls could, and did, and were considered virtuous for it. He realised that Claire Thomas had been smiling at something other than the joke, and staring at him from under her fringe with narrowed, triumphant eyes. He wished, too late, that he had been nicer to her in the play.

'Please don't,' he heard his own voice say quietly.

She nodded her head.

'I am going to.'

'Please. No.'

'I am in any case.'

Shock was cushioned initially by disbelief. He walked home that afternoon with a brisk step, like someone feeling cheerful and happy. Later on, as he lay in bed, his breath began to come in little horrified gasps. He fell asleep to dream of the boy with the sad voice in the sandpit, and of lighted ticket machines, rattling in an Underground station: he had been kidnapped and was being carried by a stranger across a floor of big, shiny squares. Then, among the queue at the ticket office, he saw Miss King in her tartan skirt and scarf. Everyone in Assembly was turning round to look at him; he saw Miss King outlined against the window and heard her voice say: 'In future you won't be allowed to be in the P.N.E.U.'

Next morning he crept to school earlier than ever, under elms motionless with dread, his eyes averted from the hedge. In Assembly, he sang loud, to drown his quaking heart, then shut his eyes tight and tried to draw the Lord's Prayer around him for protection. He was not denounced—on the contrary, the day began auspiciously: he got a star for composition homework and two more for drawing, and Miss Stella gave him a mint toffee as a prize. Save for the faintest whisper of dancing and bogeys, the scandal seemed to have subsided. As the day went on, and still Miss King was not told, he felt for Claire Thomas a surge of gratitude and affection. His reliance on her made her fascinating to him—he wondered what she had for tea at night and what time she went to bed; he tried to imagine her at her house, Five Ways, sitting on the knee of a kind and handsome Daddy. When Claire Thomas herself received a star for patterns, he was glad: she leaned back from a line of skyblue dresses to look at him and smile, as if tele-pathically responding to his goodwill. Then, toothlessly, her mouth shaped the taunting words: 'I *am* going to tell Miss King. I am. I am.'

He never knew exactly when she told Miss King, or what words she used that no dancing bogeys should be associated with herself. At the end of the afternoon, Miss King led him out of Form Two, along the brown corridor to the Bluebirds' cloakroom. They sat like old friends, side by side on the wooden seat with shoebags against their backs. Miss King's big brown eyes seemed to stare for an eternity at him in the macintosh twilight as she told him he must never say such a thing, ever again.

After school he sometimes walks down Partlands Avenue with a bigger boy called Peter Woodnutt, whose life at school is blameless and whose nose is so long, it seems to cut his smile in two. They walk along Swanmore Road a little way together, but then Peter Woodnutt turns left into a long avenue of white houses standing apart from each other behind high dark brown wickerwork fences. Louis watches him walk away, under the stained fences, his socks turned neatly over to show all three school colours, his big, scuffled attaché case in his hand. A nice tea will be waiting for Peter Woodnutt at his house, and afterwards he will play out on the lawn until bedtime. How can he walk along so calmly? If Louis had a lawn, he would run to it, skipping and shouting.

His own journey lies along West Street this time, past the rear of the Isle of Wight County Hospital. On his way, he stops to look through the gate of a big cemetery situated conveniently opposite the casualty department. Gazing over a metropolis of gravestones, he always thinks the same thing— how can the world possibly contain so many dead people? The crosses and angels, the rounded stones like grey thumbs, the veined black, gold-lettered tablets, or plain grass mounds covering the newly-dead, conjure up in his mind a faceless host, age-blind and chin-bearded, from untold family albums, extinguished at the same moment, bursting at the same moment from the grave, scattering earth and gravel and pages and pressed flowers from them as they advance. Even in bright sunshine after school, with holiday-makers at the bus stop, he is visited by fear of death, of dying, and of dead people and their spite against the living. Opposite the cemetery there is a shop with gravestones in the window and stone angels standing crookedly on the pavement outside. The shop's name, *W. H. Ellery, Monumental Masons,* makes Louis think again of death and church and grass mounds and crosses, and feet dragging to his bedroom door, and faces swinging

121

through the dark, pursuing him with dead and furious eyes.

Crossing the road, he turns right down Green Street, where the huge, dim letters SWS are painted on a wall. Green Street grows gradually steeper: his ankles tell him he is returning to Ryde's mountain slopes. At the bottom he comes out into the High Street, a few doors up from The Creamery. Green Street, unchecked by the traffic signals, plunges on past Timothy White's into a valley of low class streets and Council schools. Down there, too, somewhere is the hut where the preacher would not open his letter from God.

Close to the corner there is another café, named Jacqueline's. Established in the High Street before Dad opened The Creamery, it seems nonetheless both presumptuous and fool-hardy for daring to compete with any business owned by Dad. As such, it has a powerful attraction for Louis, who on his way home invariably pauses outside Jacqueline's Café to peep for a guilty moment through the window. The walls inside are pale green and decorated with paintings of hula hula girls; there are mirrors and a jukebox, and sometimes Louis fancies he can hear the mournful sound of Hawaiian music. This afternoon in Jacqueline's window someone has put an orange and blue cardboard advertisement for Paxo stuffing. A chef smiles merrily as he proffers a turkey on a plate. The slogan beneath, 'Paxo for happy meals', has been altered in hand-writing so that now it reads: 'For happy meals . . . come to Jacqueline's.'

Across the narrow street, Mr Johncox in his straw hat is energetically wiping down his empty fish slab while his assist-ant, Mr Cass, sweeps grey soapy water down to the kerb. Mr Johncox and Mr Cass both look across at Louis as he loiters just short of the archway leading to home. They do not know that in his thoughts he is far from Ryde; that, through the archway his mind's eye sees, not waste ground and broken bottles but the black and white gables of an hotel yard. Nobody knows how much he longs to be living in St Neots again, or how

122

ashamed he feels of the place where home now happens to be.

The voices argued in another room. He could hear them through his bedroom wall and again, circuitously, by way of unclosed doors. There was his mother's voice, angry and accusing, and Dad's voice answering her in a calm, tired way, as if some well-known and wearisome topic had been raised. He knew, from listening before, how their voices always changed. Attack in hers became defence—a gradually desperate clinging to the justice of her assertions—while Dad's voice, patiently reasoning and rebutting, burst into accusing rage. Louis knew he ought not to listen, so he bowed his head and covered his ears, shutting out all but abstract sound; their voices came now to him as two substances, ever meeting and recoiling, incapable of forming any blend. Sometimes he thought it might help if he cried—then they might both come and find him and forget their quarrel in comforting him. But they never heard, and never came. He raised his wet face to see doors still ajar in the same way, still forming the uncrossable gulf between his world and theirs.

He knew they had been happy once, somewhere back in the 'used to' time before he was born. They had been happy during the War, when Dad was in the Air Force and used to take her to dances in the Officers' Mess. There was a certain photograph which seemed to Louis to personify that original happiness, when the forties were brand new, before he, and a resultant weariness, had been added to their lives. They were standing together at the Air Force station on the day Dad's squadron went away to France. She looked so pretty with the camelhair coat slung over her shoulders; she held a striped box in her arms and a cigarette between her fingers. Dad wore his peaked cap at a slant and his dimples were all smiling around the pipe between his teeth.

That was how Louis preferred to think of them still—happy and carefree, with only the War to worry them, and that sort of white-windowed building in the background that looked like a block of London flats. He wished them to go on being

123

young, and ordained for each what he considered to be the perfect age—thirty-five. As such they were, to him, the epitome of a grown-up man and lady. He felt sorry for those at Partlands whose Mummies and Daddies were not thirty-five and nice-looking like his, but plain and low-class and dowdy and, in some cases, pitiably old and decrepit. Pam House, for instance, had a bizarre white-haired and rubicund Daddy who came to Sports Day wearing baggy linen shorts: he won a bottle of barley water in the fathers' race, and vaulted out of the grandstand and bowed low to Miss King as he received it. How grateful Louis felt not to be Pam House, with her crimson face and ghastly smile when this happened. He was glad they were too busy at the pier to come to Sports Day and see him in the play. Indeed, they knew nothing of it: Louis had not delivered Miss King's circular. He felt they would not be interested in the egg-and-spoon race, the sack race and book-balancing race, and he was anxious to spare them the embarrassment of singing 'God Save the King'.

They were no longer happy together—even he knew that for certain now. Except in rows, they hardly spoke to one another, communicating, when it was absolutely necessary, in curt, flat voices, as if each grudged even this small wastage of words. Most strongly did Louis feel the conflict between them on mornings after they had been out somewhere—perhaps to a dance at the Porthole Club—and he found a shrivelled balloon or unopened packet of paper streamers left for souvenirs outside his door. Going into their bedroom, he could feel stale fury in his mother's flung-off dress, Dad's trousers enveloping a chair-back, and grubby and flattened cotton wool snowballs, raffle tickets that had won nothing, and other such unsatisfactory souvenirs. Conflict lingered even as they slept, their faces on the low divan turned apart, their legs knotted up in battle under the single sheet. A terrible smell, like the smell of Mr Johncox's fish shop, hung in the darkened room, and something in the twilight and the look of their tangled legs, made Louis walk quickly to the other end of the flat, as far as he could go.

He knew that his mother still loved Dad very much, though she might not show it—in his whole life, Louis was to see only one kiss pass between them. He knew she loved Dad from the way she talked of him when he was not there. She told Louis how Dad used to tease an old lady who lived at Nanny Belmayne's by putting a piece of soap into her mouth while she was asleep—or sometimes orange peel teeth—and how he used to write Grandma Cussons cheques that couldn't be cashed for three months, and make her drunk with Gin and It. But Grandpa Cussons, and all the Streatham aunts and uncles, 'thought the world' of Dad, she said. To her friends, on every subject, she quoted Dad's opinion. 'Emile says . . .' she would begin, or: 'Emile reckons that . . .' Louis remembered when he and she had been on the point of leaving someone else's house and, at the final moment of doing up their coats and saying goodbye, his mother had suddenly turned and said, 'Emile reckons that Al Jolson and Eddie Cantor *really* knew how to sing.'

He knew she did not like the flat above The Creamery, with its yellowish rooms and veined green lino, its bathroom and back bedroom looking out over waste ground, the tiny kitchen, situated halfway along the hall, and the oversized pantry where bluebottles came in the summer. She had always hurt herself easily, and the kitchen did its utmost to trap her: it put out heavy grey stove legs and arranged cupboard doors and knife drawers to trip or stun her: from his bedroom, Louis could hear pots and pans crashing, and her infuriated *hoh*! sound, as though the whole world—himself included—had joined forces in her persecution. Once, walking in bare feet, she had trodden on a needle, pointing upwards from the coconut mat, and then rounded, screaming, on him as he looked in horror at the bright blood. He hated it when she didn't bother to be pretty, and her mouth drooped and her eyes closed in suffering. Unlike Dad, she often smacked him, but was sorry soon afterwards: she would take him, red-legged, in her arms, and kiss him and call him her Lou-Lou. He cherished the moments when she liked him, washing his knees so gently

E

and telling him a story about Roy Rogers or the days when she was a little girl. If she had put him to bed herself, he would lie still, not wanting to disturb the bedclothes where she had tucked them in.

At first she did not have to work down at the Pavilion. Such had been Uncle Cal's promise and, for a while, it was kept. Louis had heard rows about it, her voice insisting, 'I've got to look after *him*'—meaning Louis. Dad allowed her to stay at home, but all through the first summer season, he made her cook breakfast, not only for Louis and him but also Wilf and Eilian, then still living in the top floor flat, and dinner for them when they came home at night. Dad also took away her Hoover for some unexplained duty at the Pavilion. Even after she had yielded to persuasion and gone to work there herself, the borrowing of her Hoover remained a source of bitterness to her. It did not recover from its pierhead duties, for ever afterwards creaking and roaring as if still picking up splinters from bare floorboards.

She was still at work in the afternoon when Louis came home, mounting to the flat with his eyes closed so as not to see the peeling and ragged staircase—he pretended he was Blind Pew in *Treasure Island*, or some heroic cavalry officer blinded in the War. Each day, as he came in under the arch-way, his heart shrank to imagine what Miss King would say if she knew he did not live in a proper house. And Janice Bennett, who would doubtless transfer her hand in marriage to somebody with wide lawns at home. On the few occasions he had been to tea with anyone from Partlands, Louis had stood looking at any photographs he could find of his host or hostess outside on the lawn. How could they bear to stand still for the photograph, he wondered. Why did they not run and jump and roll about on the grass?

The flat was empty when he came in through the glass-paned door. From his bedroom, he heard a soft bump, and Charles the Siamese cat came flowing over the green lino to meet him with upraised tail and inquiring blue-eyed scowl, and the low cry that was like a siren wound by a handle. The
126

dark tail waved; blue eyes watched Louis as he poured himself a glass of orange squash and looked in the pantry to see if there was a biscuit. So another epoch shaped itself—in the weak flavour of orange juice, and shortbread biscuits he did not really like, and Charles's brown face and harsh miaouws, and the sound of traffic, below in the High Street, and of a stiff broom sweeping water down the pavement outside Johncox's.

Sometimes the flat became crowded. Nigger lay like a low black mountain range across the hall and in the kitchen Melody drank from her bowl with draggled ears floating on the surface of the water. Then Melody had her second litter of puppies, and there were little squeaking black or golden bodies around her in her basket, and puppy claws slithering over the lino, and pools and pointed sausages lying in corners. There were angry noises from the kitchen, brushes striking dustpans, and the damaged Hoover spat and crackled to a background of tumbling bathwater. Above all, there was a smell—that unique smell, compounded of pipes and soap and Player's Navy Cut, clean shirts and shut windows—which announced that Dad had come home.

He always got up late—at weekends, not until almost lunch-time. He would then lie for an hour or so in the bath, making no attempt to wash himself, just lying in the deep water, supported on his elbows, and staring sadly down at thick, black, wet-curly hair all over his chest. He did not lock the bathroom door or even shut it, and Louis often came in accidentally and saw him lying there. On these occasions, Louis could not help but look at the thing that grew between Dad's legs. It was something like the thing Louis's mother called his winkle, but so much longer and thicker, resting among black hair in a spread and swaying cloud; it was fierce and ugly and threatening in one way but in another, as it floated sideways, somehow defenceless and sad-looking.

'Big winkle, Dad,' Louis had once remarked chattily.
'Don't be rude, Louis.'
'Does that mean you do a big wee wee?' he persisted. But

Dad only said, in the same solemn voice: 'Don't be rude, Louis.'

Sometimes he did not get dressed all day. He sat in the sitting-room in the chair that was his alone, wearing his camelhair dressing-gown—the one Nanny Belmayne had bought him—with his slim, white legs crossed, his pale feet like spats in his red leather slippers, smoking his pipe and reading a copy of *The Field*. His love of shooting and fishing had not abated in his new life among roller-skates, and the sitting-room had become a sort of shrine commemorating these pursuits. The Peter Scott wild duck picture now hung over a built-in electric fire. His guns lay on top of a walnut linen press that almost touched the low ceiling. On the cream bookcase, lined with countryman's encyclopedias in tattered, fawn-coloured paper, stood a grey bronze bust of Rameses, the Egyptian Pharaoh. The sitting-room had a bay window, looking out into the High Street, which—like Louis's room next door—had been fitted with cream-coloured metal bars. Along the windowseat, back copies of *The Field* were spread in an overlapping path to show a dozen black titles in exact alignment. At the end, a full cover was displayed—the one felt by Dad to be truest to country ideals. It depicted a spaniel holding a dead pheasant in its jaws, but with a sad and soulful expression, as if it had never meant to harm the pheasant.

Often, as he sat there all day in his dressing-gown, Dad would be in a mellow and teasing mood. He would parade Louis in front of him and demand that he sing a song or recite a poem learned at school. Louis did so, torn between dread of the 'big tickle' and hope of some sudden munificence—a whole half-crown, perhaps, to buy comics at Dimmer's, next door. Dad liked to read his comics, especially *Film Fun* and *Knockout*. He would even sing as he sat there, in a voice that seemed almost too high-pitched and delicate to belong to so manly a man. He would sing 'Phil the Fluter's Ball', or 'Three Old Ladies', or the song that always made him smile, with its chorus: 'The end of me old cigar—hoorah, hoorah, hoorah!'

128

At other times, he did not even read—he only sat there, staring in front of him and tapping his fingers in a pattern ever-changing on the brocaded chair-arm. Then, the bust of Rameses, with its pointed chin and high forehead and stony, sightless eyes, standing on the bookshelf next to him, seemed to Louis like a cast made of Dad's own unseeing and melancholy face. As always, he wondered why Dad's face managed to look so sad when his fingers performed so perky and inventive a dance; as always, too, he was unsure whether Dad even saw him standing near, or noticed when his mother came and moved him away.

'Why?' he whispered to her in the passage.

'Daddy's worried.'

'Why is he worried?'

'Ssh. It's something to do with Daddy.'

They had their meals at an oval table near the window. Dad sat doing his crossword puzzle as Louis watched his mother bring in plates and vegetable dishes from the kitchen. When she put the first plate in front of Louis, Dad looked up from his newspaper. The peak twitched on his forehead, and he said:

'You always serve *him* first, Laura. I'm head of this household—I think you ought to serve me before you serve a child.'

Dad sat sideways at the head of the table, with his legs crossed, leaning over his place like someone bridging with difficulty some ever-widening gulf. He ate very quickly, snatching the food from the end of his fork, chewing it briefly with a flutter of the nerve in his forehead, swallowing in big swallows that seemed almost too wide for his throat. Whatever had been cooked for him he ate with a critical frown, his eyes staring alternately into his plate and over to the crossword puzzle on the strip of folded newspaper beside it. Completing this puzzle daily, in the paper that no one else was allowed to read, imposed a solemn silence on mealtimes, and Louis watched the frowning over clues, the murmuring of them aloud, the gradual infiltration of white squares, with vague trepidation, as though Dad were undergoing some ritual examination on his and his mother's behalf. Equal seriousness

129

accompanied the weekly filling-in of what Dad called 'my Littlewoods', a paper full of tiny checks, smaller than one would use for arithmetic, in which Dad, after much careful reflection, carefully drew a tiny nought or a cross—symbols which, by their very simplicity, hinted at a system so vastly complex that even Dad could keep abreast of it only by the most ferocious concentration. His stern abjurations to Louis's mother not to forget to post 'his Littlewoods' deepened in Louis's mind the sense of threatening external forces which Dad alone kept at bay and which, at mealtimes, left him drained and haunted. His long struggles had brought about a distaste even for letters which, at the breakfast table, he would receive in what seemed to Louis to be glorious abundance. He watched in disbelief as Dad opened each letter, glanced once at its contents—invariably a single sheet with figures printed on it—then tore it into small pieces. Sometimes a letter came in a brown envelope printed with the words On His Majesty's Service, suggesting to Louis a summons to Dad to use his talents in some way for the good of the country—even possibly a communication from King George VI himself. Yet these were the very letters that Dad tore up with greatest bitterness, often not bothering even to open them.

The end of his newspaper, the edge of his cork table mat and his dessert spoon seemed to form yet another defensive perimeter. From here he maintained the protocol in serving, protected the sacred outpost of his personal Escoffier sauce and made certain his tea was never strained. All through the meal, Louis could feel sidelong glances from Dad flickering over him to ensure his obedience to a rigid code of manners. When eating a boiled egg, he knew he must vanquish the inclination to batter in its cranium, and must open it, as Dad opened his, in a series of galloping, methodical taps around the edge. An ethical conflict surrounded the fork-prongs whose concavity, correct when left uppermost in the placing of knife and fork together, became objectionably incorrect when used for what seemed to be its natural shovelling process. Sternest censure descended on Louis if ever he tried to impersonate

130

one of Dad's own mealtime customs—sitting sideways, for example, or reading. '*Not* at the table, old son,' Dad would say in a voice of weary disgust, and then return to the book open on his knee.

Louis detected signs of tension in his mother who, at breakfast, seated next to him at the bottom of the table, would at times lean towards him, holding a piece of toast with her little finger extended and looking into his plate—a gesture of concern which, Louis divined, was not entirely for his benefit. In time he recognised it as the preamble to those uncomfortable moments when she had a request of some sort to make to Dad. No doubt it was her reluctance to add to Dad's burdens which made her speak in a headlong and brusque way, like an attack made desperately for form's sake. Louis himself figured in these sorties, peremptorily unnamed, as was her habit, often in the form of a threat. 'He's got to have some more shoes,' she would tell Dad accusingly, or: 'It's time he started going to Sunday School.' A thing she had often said lately was, 'It's high time we got him christened. He's nearly eight. I suppose you *want* a little heathen for a son!' Anguished at his power to worry Dad for so trivial a reason, Louis stared down at his blushing face in a spoon, and then his face upside down on its reverse.

Or she would say, in a colourless voice, examining her nails: 'I shall need some extra money, Emile.'

This made Dad give a little jump, and swing his crossed legs still further from the table. The nerve twitched in his temple, making the whole peak shift up and down on his forehead.

'What *for*, Laura?'

'The housekeeping.'

'Well, *I* haven't got any money!' Dad said in a horrified voice.

Louis found this statement extraordinary. For Dad usually had so much money in his pocket. Louis had seen him plunge his hand in deep down, then bring it out and open his fingers to show a lovely silver quilt of half-crowns, florins and shil-

131

lings, enough to buy all the new annuals on Dimmer's trestle table, or giant Plasticine or soldiers or smoky marbles by the regiment. It was terrible to think of Dad's pockets now empty— his trousers pockets and the leather-piped pockets of his coat, not jingling any more when he walked, not able to buy any more presents or cream sodas or crisps. Louis looked at his mother, wondering whether it was 'the housekeeping' which had brought about this catastrophe. Dad seemed to think so, for he would compel her to account for all that she had spent so far in the week. She included the things she had bought at Woolworth's for Louis—the picture history book about Roman Britain, the pencil or drawing-book or yet another pencil-sharpener. 'And,' she concluded, 'I bought him a pencil-sharpener he wanted.' Guiltily Louis remembered how he had pestered her to buy him the pencil-sharpener inside a globe of the world. And the globe was now choked with pencil shavings, and he had not yet found out the way to empty it.

As darkness came, his life and theirs again diverged. His path lay inexorably, through a borrowed five minutes, to the cul-de-sac of his bedroom. He lay in bed, watching the light that shone through his door, listening as they got ready to go somewhere. Beyond the flat door, at the bottom of the ragged stairs, the world had begun the night-time life that was pro-hibited to him. He wondered if they were going to the pictures tonight—to the Scala, perhaps, or the Commodore? They often went to a place called the Porthole Club, a name full of such romance to Louis that he wondered if it could exist by day at all, or whether it appeared only after dark, half-ship, half-shore, as he pictured it, built out, with a flagstaff, over dark and whispering waves. His thoughts flew in bright-lit vistas he had never seen, charged and crackling with the night's endless vitality. He despaired to think of his own banishment, the imprisoning bar of the sheet across his chin, and how many hours he must lie, watching that same light like a lantern in the passage, sometimes hearing a scrape or a rustle from the sitting-room from whoever had been paid to stay with him until they came home.

132

That was the rule—it could be broken sometimes on a thrilling scale. Such moments, depending on Dad's whim, were never announced. On any evening, resigned to bed at seven, Louis might find himself being tied into his coat and scarf, then bundled out of the flat so quickly, he knew nothing until he was in the street, and remembered having glimpsed his shadow escaping among banister bars thrown against the tattered wall by the light in the café below. The rest was like dreaming—it had the same half-familiar foreignness, the same fretfulness and speed. Only the cold of night around his cheeks and his cold, smoking breath told him he was really here, caught up unnoticed in the crowd of dark figures that hurried along the High Street as though towards some common objective, through a world remodelled in black or blazing light, past Dimmer's the stationer's, unrecognisable now but for a few dim writing pads; past Fry's the bakers, its long shelf empty of cakes and loaves; past Nash's 'fish and chip saloon', with its hissing and crinkling, and two fish like spiny footballs hanging in the window; past the Catholic Church, where Eilian and Wilf got married, looming up like some great gravestone, its damp shadows growing round it like moss. He knew where they must be going, but he dared not ask, or even think the words. Though his feet hurried, he held his breath and kept his fingers still inside his mother's hand for fear his presence might suddenly be noticed.

They passed the Scala, and he saw people buying tickets, and the smiling old man in uniform who opened the door when you went in; a moment later, they passed the end of Star Street, and he saw the Commodore, moored in its dark tributary street like a huge gold, glowing hearth. The High Street dropped away beneath them now in an avenue of shop windows brilliant with uninhabited life. In time to his footsteps and the cold puffs of his breath, the voice inside him—the voice that always tried to hoodwink his Destiny—kept saying:

'We're not going to the Theatre Royal—I know we're not. We're not going to the Theatre Royal. I can assure you. I can assure you.'

E*   133

He told himself this—just to be sure—even when they had reached the little square at the bottom of the High Street and had climbed up the steep, purple-edged steps of the Theatre Royal beneath its iron verandah, and he and his mother stood waiting while Dad bought their tickets. The narrow foyer, familiar to him from many an afternoon visit, seemed mysteriously perfumed and softly lit, like a stage, from the corners, and the lady in the pay window wore a fur coat round the shoulders of her scarlet uniform, as if selling tickets and Butterkist and Sun-Pat nuts were only a temporary occupation, and she, too, would soon be going out somewhere for the evening. She fascinated Louis with her sulky, dark eyes and her magnificent nose, her hair piled richly in a heap over her ears; for some reason, he wanted to bury his nose into the shining fur she pinched about her while haughtily pressing the button that made two joined three-and-nine tickets and one shilling one clatter up through her metal desk. 'Thank you,' she said in a voice which, though distant and disdainful, had the same thrilling drawl as the voice of a film star.

They went through more doors, into a sleep-silent upper foyer, its green wall hung with pastel portraits of Alan Ladd, Robert Taylor, Betty Hutton and Gregory Peck, then Dad ushered them through a dark red curtain that had a door behind it. Beyond the door hung a second curtain blacker than night, either end of which led into the cool and listening dark of the auditorium. There they stood and waited for a moment, and Louis felt afraid they would never find their way to their seats. Then, close beside them, a light was switched on: the usherette took the tickets from Dad and examined them in the beam of her red-cowled torch. Her face, illuminated from below, was startlingly like the lady in the pay box. She had the same nose and haughty eyes; the same hair, piled up above her ears, the same air of exotic condescension. Louis wondered if they might be sisters, recruited from some special, drawling dynasty to rule over every department in the Theatre Royal at night. Could they even be both the same person, transmuted from her paybox and fur coat, to walk regally down

134

the dark aisle ahead of them, leading them with a torch-arc on the ground?

He liked it best when they arrived half-way through a film. He loved to feel himself drawn slowly towards comprehension, his eye expanding to accommodate the figures on the screen, his ear tuning gradually to the huge, quiet wavelengths of their speech. And when this film finished, there would still be a part of it to come. He thought gladly of the hours ahead, and the journeys his eye would make, through the rest of this film, and then another one, and then newsreel and adverts and ice-cream intervals and trailers, and finally the interrupted half of the first film that would make plain to him the hap- penings that were so inexplicable now, and introduce charac- ters already familiar, and proceed towards an ending he already knew, by way of scenes growing inexorably towards the one which had witnessed his own arrival. But the awful moment of leaving was too far even for Louis to contemplate. He was still here, at the very start; everything was yet to come. His delirium had passed: he felt only restfulness and joy as the screen drew him out of his own thoughts, into a world where the worrying was done by other people.

He felt so happy to be in the brightened darkness, feeling the greater dark that filled the universe outside. Frequently during the film he would turn from the screen and look around him for sheer joy at being there, and glance along the faces that watched behind him, and all the faces watching in all the rows, glad to be at one with so many. He would look up through the projector beam, with its drifting continents of cigarette smoke, to the dim heights above the balcony, and then down again, along the steep side aisles where faint lights, like nightlights, glowed among the pillars. He would look at the glowing walls, the green Exit sign above a muffled door, and at the square-faced green clock whose distorted numerals and muzzy hands endorsed forgetful- ness of time.

As much as any film he loved the panoply of 'the pictures'— emblems and images that remained the same whatever the

135

programme. There was first, revealed by gently-parting curtains, the trademark of Isle of Wight Theatres Ltd, its initials IWT growing by trick photography into the shape of the Island itself; and then the certificate of the British Board of Film Censors, to Louis's grateful eyes suggesting a quiet and vaguely benevolent body of men; and then the bright, brief crackle of the 'U' or the 'A' certificate. There were the symbols proclaiming the source of the film itself—a plump-necked, petulant MGM lion; the Columbia lady holding aloft a long-rayed star; the strange, sparkling pylons of RKO Radio Pictures. His heart soared with excitement, when the newsreel came, to see the furious Pathé cockerel, British Movietone's glittering pantheon, the Gaumont British town crier, ringing his bell and shouting with his hand to his mouth among a collage of plunging battleships, windswept Royalty and sport of every kind. He loved the trick writing that preceded the trailers, when days of the week leapt one by one to form a pile inside the Island silhouette, no less than the trailer itself, miniature of a film to come, defaced by slanting words and exclamation-marks. He loved the trailers, both for the excitement they promised and for the feeling of continuity they gave to his own existence. It gave him confidence in the future to see it measured out in leaping letters, which formed, at last, a pile of words so deep, the Island's silhouette could barely contain that final heart-warming assurance:

ALSO
FULL
SUPPORTING
PROGRAMME
INCLUDING
LATEST
NEWS
ITEMS

In the interval, when weak lights came on, and wan magnificence was revealed, and faint music played, and the cloudy green clock concealed unfathomable lateness, the screen above the ice-cream queue gave notice of films coming to the Theatre Royal so far in the future that no trailers were yet available. Only the title could be seen, lettered against a swirling grey, red-shadowed background like the pattern of a chocolate or a dream. Louis watched the dark, slow, wrinkled curtains draw shut upon the last of them which, for a moment longer, shimmered beyond the lighted folds, to his sleep-heavy eyes resembling a glimpse ahead down all the years of his life.

On other nights, Dad did not come home to the flat in the evenings.

Louis lay in bed, listening to the wireless in the sitting-room and to his mother as she moved around from the kitchen to the other bedroom. When she came into the passage, he called to her:

'Are you going out somewhere?'

'Only down to the Scala to get some cigarettes.'

She meant the little cinema a little way down the High Street, past the Catholic Church. They didn't mind if you went to the paybox just to buy cigarettes.

'Are you coming straight back?'

He heard her hesitate.

'Well . . . I might go down and meet Daddy then.'

He would be alone in the flat. He knew he would be afraid. Yet for the moment, it did not matter. He could smell perfume and her long-pointed nail stuff—he even thought he heard her singing to herself as she moved about the flat. Taking her at her word, he imagined her walking down the High Street, and Dad coming from the Esplanade up Union Street to meet her. He could picture the roll of Dad's shoulders as he came uphill, and his solemn face and the pipe in a corner of his mouth. They would meet in the little square, outside the Theatre Royal, with the old horsetrough in the middle. Then they would be together, in love again, as in the wartime photograph. It made him happy to think of that—even though just now she had almost told him a fib about how long she would be out.

137

'Will you open my door?'

'It is open.'

'Bumping the bed. Will you open it wider, bumping the bed?'

He watched the light in the passage, a little black lantern, and thought about different films he had seen. He thought about *Samson and Delilah,* how thirsty he had felt to see the mauve wine; and about all the songs in *Annie Get Your Gun,* and the sad song in *Showboat* that almost made him cry. He thought how he had laughed to see doors shutting by themselves after Harvey the invisible rabbit; about all the fighting and horseracing in *The Quiet Man,* the miscarriage of justice in *A Boy, A Girl and A Bike*; he thought about *Shane* and *Scrooge* and *The Card,* and his own distress during *Coroner Creek* when the cowboy lost the fight whose name was Ernie and who wore the two pearl-handled six-guns.

He drifted towards sleep listening to a man's voice on the wireless. 'We are now taking you into the Palm Court of Grand Hotel . . .' Violins played a swaying tune, and he pictured somewhere bigger and more beautiful even than the Cross Keys. He saw lights and white tablecloths and menus. and people going in and out. He heard plates clinking, and savoury sounds from the kitchen, and a murmur of voices against the violins, and fell asleep wishing that he still lived in an hotel.

He has woken up again.

It isn't morning yet. The light in his eyes comes from the moon. The sky over the chimneypots is nearly blue, and the sharp, clear moon lights this side of the High Street, leaving Johncox's and the shops on the other side buried under an awning of dark. The moon shines straight through the barred window on to his pillow.

Next to his bed is a locker with his cocoa mug standing on it. The mug is buff-coloured; it has a sleeping face and stands on the blue plastic lid that is its nightcap. His mother sent away for it with labels from Bournvita cocoa. He had to drink

138

a lot of Bournvita to get the mug, and to use it, he has to drink a lot more. He does not like Bournvita, but he loves the mug, with its flat, tasselled nightcap, more than any other of his possessions. It is the first thing he looks at on waking, its face still tranquilly asleep in the moonlight.

The whole of Ryde is asleep, yet he is conscious of intense activity outside his bedroom door—which somebody has closed. He can hear a funny scuffling noise, like the noise Melody's puppies used to make. He can hear Dad's voice and other voices, and see footsteps flickering to and fro across the light under his door.

Should he get up and show himself? He remembers doing that once at Orlando Road—coming all the way downstairs, past the Masonic certificates and the buffalo horns, and finding Nanny Belmayne and Uncle Tony still up in the back kitchen, both sitting in the light that shone on the green tablecloth. And Nanny Belmayne looked up and said delightedly:

'Hel-*lo*, my little lamb!'

He gets out of bed and crosses over the cold green lino, thinking about the puppies—how they lay so warmly around Melody in the basket, making a chewing, squelching sound, and all the puddles they left on the lino. The black one he wanted to call Midnight and the one with the tiny white spot, Twilight. Then one afternoon when he came home, all the puppies had disappeared.

He stands and waits a minute, a little afraid—because that scuffling noise has started again—then, very quietly, he opens his bedroom door.

The first person he sees is Wilf, Eilian's husband. This is no surprise, for Wilf often goes out to places with Dad at night and comes back to the flat afterwards. He is standing in the passage just outside Louis's bedroom door. His back is half-turned: Louis can see just the edge of the smile he always wears, and the greased points of his brushed-back hair lying in a row along his neck. He is wearing the blue suit he wore on his wedding day. He must feel uncomfortable in it, since

139

he flexes his arm before raising his hand in bewilderment to scratch the back of his head.

Wilf is watching—and Louis, just behind him, is watching—a fight taking place around the front door of the flat. The big glass pane in the door has been broken, and a long, cold, claw-shape of dark shows through from the staircase beyond. Under the single black lantern, Louis sees his mother and Dad struggling together and shouting, and the leather oval on Dad's elbow, like another screaming mouth. She is trying to open the shattered door and Dad, to pull her back along the corridor to their bedroom. In the dim, sour light, their struggle is like a dance, back and forth over the thick doormat—where presents were left on Louis's birthday—now all crooked under their feet, and budded with lumps of green door glass.

They are shouting—but, such is the imbalance of this forbidden hour, he hears their voices less clearly than the scuffling noise on the mat. Standing unseen in the crack of his door, he wonders if it is a dream: he blinks his eyes, and finds he is still here, the light is still there, the figures still there, struggling in front of the shattered door. So is Wilf, who has again flexed his sleeve to scratch his oily head elaborately, as though to draw attention to his own embarrassing predicament. But they do not seem to notice Wilf. Their appeal is directed to some greater witness for the outrage each has suffered, to the great wrong perpetrated by the other. A single phrase, stirred up among her screams, takes shape as the cause of their combat:

The gun on the bed.

He can hear that same phrase again and again. His mother's voice screams it in terror; Dad's scornfully shouts it back. The same phrase again and again in the voices that form two elements in Louis; the voices that can neither yield nor coalesce:

'Oh no, I didn't . . . the gun on the bed.'

'Yes, you did. You . . . the gun on the bed.'

'No, I didn't, Laura . . . the gun on the bed. It was you . . . *you*, Laura . . . the gun on the bed.'

'It was *you* . . . I didn't . . . the gun on the bed!'

140

'It was you! You!'

'You!'

Dad is much stronger than she is. He is pulling her off the doormat, along the hall. She is leaning back from him, as if she can no longer be bothered to stand upright, and crying with a face crumpled up like paper, and shouting,—'Wilf, get the Police or something! Wilf—why don't you get the Police or something?'

Louis wonders if Wilf will get the Police—and what they will say about the gun on the bed, and the broken glass. Will the Police be cross with him, too, for getting up so late at night?

But Wilf only stands there in his wedding suit, flexing his sleeve again, and again, in bewilderment, scratching the back of his head.

mohawks and figure-eights

He first saw Olwen on a Sunday afternoon, when it was windy in the Solent and the sea beyond the tram station was dark blue and covered with white waves, sparkling and flashing like the teeth of angry little dogs.

Louis stood alone on the rink. It was only just after lunch, and he could hear the sound of dishes being washed in the Tea Bar and lift ropes being pulled up to the kitchen. He was thankful because lunch was over and because he had succeeded in escaping the meat fat packed away under his fork. A whole afternoon of skating now lay ahead which he was reluctant to erode even by one single step. So he stood still on his skates, with one foot behind the other in a braking position, and listened for the two-five boat, and the rasp of the tram that would come to meet it, bringing the first club members. He felt so happy, he even stopped breathing, to make this moment last. Then he thought he could hear the sea itself, hissing under the Pavilion floor, and the wind that shook in the door bolts and blustered against the balcony windows and seemed to scratch for admittance far up in the dome, where dust and darkness drew the arching girders together.

142

Somebody was already here. An automatic door in the distance slammed shut, and he heard skate wheels rustling over the floorboards in the long corridor that led from the ladies' toilets out into the entrance hall. He expected it to be Joyce or Patsy Fry, or another girl club member ahead of the main party, but instead, a lady he had never seen before came skating out to join him on the rink. One brief step, on one foot, brought her to the middle where she stopped, angling her second skate lightly behind the first. Though the Pavilion was empty, high and low, it seemed like the beginning of a performance.

She was the best skater Louis had ever seen. As soon as she began, he knew that she was no recent learner, no stumbling graduate from beginners' bars, but someone to whom movement on skates was inborn and effortless. A few quick running tiptoe steps were the only movement she seemed to make. She wore white boots, mounted on small silver wheels, which carried her along like two tall white yachts in a narrow channel, each continually overtaking the other, while her body in a bright pink jumper, lay back in flight, her arms resting quietly on the current that flowed beneath them. She was such a good skater that Louis watched her for some time before he noticed the astonishing thing about her. Below the pink jumper, she wore a dark grey pleated skirt that finished two inches, at least, above her knees. Her legs, down to her white boots, were bare.

The sight of these legs made feelings run through Louis. Strange, sharp, worried, puzzled, inquisitive, tingling, itchy feelings. He had always known that, somewhere in the world, there were ladies who did show their legs, not accidentally as his mother might if her housecoat fell open, but calmly, even defiantly, in the midst of everyday happenings. He had seen pictures of them on book or magazine covers—one in particular haunted his thoughts who sat in only her underwear with a tommy gun on her knee, staring out of the picture at him with a furious frown. And in the magazine called *Lilliput*, which Dad sometimes bought, he had found photographs of

143

ladies with nothing on at all, smiling and stretching themselves on beaches or in shadowy attic rooms. He stared at these pictures in secret, endlessly, murmuring their incomprehensible captions to himself—*Sweater Girl; Woodman's Daughter*—not knowing why he wished he had been there in that attic or on that beach, where long grass grew up through drifting and wrinkled sand.

Now, at last, he had found her—a lady who showed her legs, and did not care if you looked. He watched her as she circled the wide rink, the big legs, bending, stretching from the grey skirt that fluttered back to show matching grey knickers, and again he felt that nice and yet nasty spasm; a desire to look and look, but also to look away in horror. He caught up with her face at last and studied it, just as she turned, with a swing of skirt-pleats, and continued, skating backwards now, keeping watch carefully over her right shoulder. He decided she was pretty—then he could not be sure. Her features were thin and rather grim, her nose long, and inclined to redness, her mouth set firm as if she herself did not approve of the legs she was showing. Something about her face made Louis think that people were being very unkind to her, but she had resolved to endure it without complaint.

Christmas 1950 had been a time of exciting rumours. Late at night, after he was in bed, there were skating galas at the Pavilion—a Fancy Dress Night, an Old Tyme Night and, on Christmas Eve, a 'Krazy Nite' when Dad, by some mystical use of wrong spelling and exclamation marks, had aroused the trundling masses to some inconceivably wild skateborne celebration. Sitting up in bed on Christmas Eve, Louis had heard Wilf come to the flat door, bringing a message from Dad. Because it was Christmas Eve, Dad wanted him to go back down to the Pavilion and watch the Krazy Nite. But his mother said he had better not; he had just had a bath, it was cold out and Father Christmas was expected. He could only try to piece together what he had missed with paper streamers
144

and shrunken balloons gathered up later from the rink floor, and crushed squeakers and punctured miniature policeman's helmets and coloured snowballs, soiled and flattened by the wheels that had rolled over them.

1951 started with stormy weather. There were strong winds and ceaseless rain that made the pier planks glisten like varnish. Portsmouth withdrew behind a veil of dark squalls that hid all but the shapes of the forts in the deep-sea channel. Day after day, the big waves rolled in, as though from the wake of some huge ship; agitating the little boats moored inshore, flinging themselves suicidally over booms and breakwaters to rise and recoil in glittering shell-bursts against the undefended front. This was the winter when a small chain pier at Seaview, a mile or so around the coast, was blown into the sea overnight, and even the strong rampart of the Eastern Gardens lay in pieces, like dripping dominoes on the grass.

In these inauspicious times, at the age of seven and three-quarters, Louis was eventually christened. What with the War, and then the Victory Parade, everyone had been too busy to arrange it when he was a baby. Lately, he had come to dread the subject, both for its power to cause rows and for fear that his head might soon have to be pushed underwater. How he envied Prince Charles, Princess Elizabeth's baby, whom he had seen on the newsreels with the beastly thing already over and done with.

Eventually, Dad bit at his pipe-stem and snapped, 'Oh well —get him christened if you want!' The ceremony took place in a large, cold, windless church watched by the sixty-odd pupils of the Sunday School which Louis recently had been compelled to attend. He stood on a step and had his head guided down until his ear touched the water in a shiny brown stone bowl. The robes of the Canon who christened him were as lacy as the curtains in Nanny Belmayne's best room. Water splashed into his ear and leaked down inside his head as the singsong, disinterested voice ratified his names in all their frightful abundance—now he was, indisputably, Louis Emile Calver Theodore Belmayne. Dad could not come and see him

145

christened because of being busy. That night his mother let him stay up after seven, and stand at the counter in The Creamery drinking a cup of coffee made with Camp essence. The kilted soldier whom the bottle-label showed sitting outside a tent, and the Indian servant who waited on him, were the other guests at the christening party.

Throughout those bleak and rainy and empty days it seemed to Louis that Dad became busier than ever. Summer remained always on his mind and, when the skating rink was closed, he devoted himself tirelessly to making the Pavilion ready for next season. Upstairs, in the Ocean Restaurant, he had a workshop, for mending and oiling the hundreds of slot machines he had inherited from Uncle Cal's partners, which would stand in the Pavilion during the summer. Sometimes he would work for hours beyond locked doors, with only Wilf for company; up there, on other days, half-mended and gaping machines would await his ministrations. For he could never remain long in the same place. Each day, however stormy, took him on a dozen journeys from the pierhead, through straining crosswinds, to the shore, driving the Wolseley or the little green van he had lately acquired, on some compulsive but unexplained errand. He had taken lately to long consultations with Mr Boynton the signwriter, and Louis clamoured to go with him, just for the chance to wait at the end of Mr Boynton's loft, close to where the wooden steps came up from Union Lane, and to study the half-finished posters and placards. One day Dad brought away a set of notices for next summer which Mr Boynton had printed in four lines of red letters on yellow. The notices were for the Ocean Restaurant, and each one said: 'Only Food Purchased Here May Be Consumed On These Premises.'

Secretly, Louis hoped that Dad might plan to revive the theatrical shows which used to be held at the Pavilion before the War. He was drawn irresistibly towards the little uncanopied stage, still jutting bravely out into the great vault now robbed of its nine hundred seats: when the rink was empty, he would stand resting his arms on the dust-black

146

rim, staring up at the backcloth of a Venetian scene, left standing since the very last pre-war pierrot show. The stage was forbidden to him, unless a ball had bounced there. Then, on his skates, he was allowed to crawl up the little side staircase and tiptoe around on his rubber toe-stops, peering among the stacked scenery, feeling and tasting the dust which was as soft as black silk. Once, lifting a dustsheet, he discovered an ornate leg and, lifting it further, the yellow keys of a forgotten grand piano.

One day, when he was brought to the Pavilion, a hammering noise came from out on the rink. As his mother helped him off with his coat in the entrance hall, he could see Dad in the distance half-way up a tall stepladder, and Wilf standing below—then he saw Mr Boynton, the signwriter, standing on the rink with Wilf. It was unquestionably Mr Boynton. Even without his glasses on, Louis could not mistake the grizzled hair that formed a peak something like Dad's, the trousers so high-waisted and wide, it looked as if Mr Boynton were entering the Sack Race, and the tiny cigarette, hidden inside his hand, which Mr Boynton smoked by repeatedly kissing his thumb in a chef-like gesture of approbation.

Now Mr Boynton threw down his cigarette and trod on it, and then he and Wilf picked up something huge and square and whitish that had been leaning against the stage. They shouldered it first, then pushed it up the wall beside the stage, as far as their arms could reach, and Dad, leaning back from the stepladder, started to hammer again in a stern, regular, rhythmic tattoo, each heavy blow of which was interspersed with a light one as its echo returned from the high depths of the dome.

Louis's mother rotated him with an angry sigh. In his preoccupation he had dragged out the whole lining from inside his coat-sleeve.

'What are they doing, though? I want to go and look.'

'No—come straight up to the staffroom.'

'What are they doing?'

147

'Only something to do with Daddy—come away.'

'But I want to help.'

'You can't. It's only for grown-up men.'

'What *is* it, though?' he insisted.

'Daddy's had a freize painted.'

The word startled Louis: he had heard of it already. At Partlands, they had done freizes with Miss Stella in the babies' form. To hear a school word at the pierhead moved him with some of the same excitement as seeing Mr Boynton transmuted thither from his loft in Union Lane. Was it possible that Dad had found out about the Partlands freizes? For a moment, Louis even wondered whether Dad, in his reverie, acquired some magic power to see directly into the little classroom with its parchmenty windowblind, its tadpole jars, its illustrated adventures of Old Lob the farmer, and even to look over Louis's shoulder at the patterns he had made in little pencil paths along the top and bottom of the page . . . But of course: Dad's was not that kind of freize. Nothing of Dad's was ever the usual kind.

Dad's freize was a line of these big, whitish canvas panels fastened high along the wall behind the stage and out along each of the two flanking walls to form a continuous background for a sequence of giant figures. Beginning on the left-hand wall there was a Scotsman, supporting himself on a crooked stick and waving a whisky bottle; next to him came a tall-hatted Welsh lady, then a French gendarme striking an attitude of reproof towards the Spanish matador who was his neighbour. Behind the stage, where Venice used to be, circus clowns turned cartwheels and rode one-wheel bicycles, a tail-coated ringmaster held out his arms towards a circus lady, with wide eyes and brown legs, who in turn proffered a paper hoop towards a smiling chimpanzee. Out around the opposite wall were painted a cowgirl, a Red Indian chief, a peg-legged pirate with a parrot on his shoulder, and finally, a Zulu in a long grass skirt, waving a spear while protecting himself with a pointed shield. The company was so diverse that one did not immediately notice the feature which all had in

148

common and which gave the freize its theme. For each figure—even the Zulu; even the clown standing on his head; even the chimpanzee—wore roller-skates.

'Oh . . . isn't it *good*!' Louis said, looking up at the freize, pulling rapturously at the hem of his short trouserleg. 'Isn't it good! It's *jolly* good!' He hoped Dad could divine from these words what awe and gratitude were together rushing through his heart.

Despair soon followed that first elation. For as his eye voyaged yet again along the freize, he saw the hopelessness of his own desire to be an artist when he grew up. How pitiful seemed his small stock of skill compared with the virtuosity that could depict, with equal ease, a Scotsman's sporran, a gendarme's cloak, a ringmaster's collar, a pirate's tricorne hat and turned-back cuffs, a Red Indian's headdress, the sharp bone through a Zulu's nose. He wished he could steal one small fraction of Mr Boynton's brilliant technique for showing shoulders sideways, fingers gripping, legs running and leaping, and the right number of whirls to put inside a person's ear. He gazed with covetous admiration at the sheer vitality in the figures—the speed and urgency suggested by their dilated eyes, their red-flushed faces and grinning mouths, their skates whirling like Catherine wheels in mid-air, among shell-bursts of blue and red.

Louis asked Dad whether Mr Boynton had given his freize a title. Dad replied that it had no special title, but one could permissibly call it 'Skaters of All the World'.

Olwen was only a customer at first. She belonged to the skating club which met in the Pavilion on Sunday afternoons, when there wasn't a public session.

Sundays at home had become a thing of the past for Louis and his mother. By eleven o'clock each Sunday morning, as the church bells rang up through Ryde, they would have left the Esplanade and be on their way in the Wolseley through thudding crosswinds, out into a grey meadow surly with white-capped waves. Pier shelters that drifted in sequence between

149

the darting rail-knobs, the signal-box out on the railway, the two-car tram dashing past on its outward journey, were all unremarked incidents on a journey as natural and inevitable as going home after a night in some stranger's house. As they neared the end, where the railway and tramway branched apart, the Pavilion rolled into view, as familiar a sight to Louis, with its terraced windows and grey dome, as any other part of his shifting, migrating home-life. Often by now, his mother and Dad would have stopped speaking to each other. Sunshine, chancing in the estuary, lit up the dome suddenly with the unspecific promise of something nice today.

The club members began arriving from about half-past two. Girls came hurrying in groups through the entrance hall and straight down the long corridor to the Ladies': you could hear them talking and laughing around the corner, and the slam that made a penny drop in the automatic door. The boys sat round the edge of the rink, lacing on their skates with their faces between their knees like people recovering from dizzy spells. The figures in the freize grinned down as one and then another skater took to the floor, their crackling wood wheels accompanied by brisk hand-rubbing and jovial cries of pain. It was bitterly cold under the dome until you had been skating for at least a quarter of an hour.

For Louis, this began as the epoch of his long trousers. His mother made them out of brown corduroy to go with the real skating boots Dad had just given him. The boots were black, with white laces that crossed over and green rubber stops, for braking, under the toes. He could hardly sit still while Wilf did up the laces for him, hooking them through the avenue of little black tin petals, higher and higher; taking them round through a loop at the back, then tying them, above each tightly-bound instep, in a strong double bow. It felt lovely, that first moment of standing up, tall on his eight silver wheels, looking down and seeing no bare knees: just pipes of brown corduroy hanging over his stubby boot-toes. In the midst of pleasure, he sometimes felt sad to think that one day he would have grown out of his new skating
150

boots; that this epoch, like his corduroy long trousers, could not last for ever.

He skated with hands in pockets, carelessly, crossing one foot over another in instinctive obedience to the rink's perpetual curve. Skating was so natural to him now, he hardly remembered the days when he had struggled with Phyllis the barmaid up and down the beginners' bars. Skating had proved to be one of the things he could do so well as to obliterate for a space those many things he could not do, like backstitch, eating meat fat and parsnips, and tying his own shoelace. Out here on the rink, such shames and panics fell from him. His skill felt like a spring, wound up in each tightly-shod ankle: one step was enough to carry him into this restful, perpetual motion for mile after circling mile. A pleasant breeze blew in his face and, after a few more minutes, he began to feel warm. He would not have known he was moving at all but for the dome, resting huge and dark against his eyelids, turning and turning ceaselessly above.

All his friends were here now—he could see Joyce and Patsy and Lofty and Iris with her arm in a sling—she had broken it on the rink two weeks ago—and Mr Crichton Wells in his neat little blue suit and waistcoat. Mr Crichton Wells was a chartered accountant from Binstead who carried accountancy into skating—he only did figure-eights, in front of a mirror, again and again as though his plump little body were in the grip of some relentless calligraphist. All afternoon, whatever else might be happening on the rink, Mr Crichton Wells stayed on his little private island of floor near the office steps, gliding back and forth with his arms balancing and one leg stretched out behind him, passing and re-passing his reflection in the mirror, his chin held up like a fist his black moustache shortened in a smile of satisfaction.

Because of his boots and long trousers, the club members treated Louis as one of them. He called them by their first names, although they were grown-up; because they were low class and he was high class and the boss's son. So they had to let him go first when they skated the Conga, past Mr Crichton

151

Wells and his mirror, in and out of the balcony posts. He liked
to stand around with them at the edge of the rink while they
talked, staring at Iris's brown ankle socks and Johnny Brading's
tightly-rolled up sleeves and the funny pointed thing in Lofty's
neck that flew up when he swallowed, then down again. He
folded his arms as they did, nodding in agreement with whatever was being said, at times glancing proudly down at his
hidden knees, his smart boot toes and a blue vein that made
his wrist look exactly like a grown-up's.

Frequently during the afternoon he would skate back over
the rink to the brightly-lit entrance hall where Dad, behind his
metal counter, mended skates and held court to a large, fascinated crowd. Club meetings, for some reason, found Dad
always in a good humour; and the club members, who had
seen him no other way, were captivated by his charm and
good looks, his countryman's clothes, and the strong yet manly
fragrance which adhered to him. Louis was as captivated as
anyone: he would stand with the others, listening and laughing, amazed that such geniality could have metamorphosed
from the pale, sad face, the tapping fingers on the chair-arm
at home. He would do his best to catch Dad's eye in the crowd
—possibly to take a message across the rink, couched in the
old-fashioned phraseology which Dad employed when in a
good mood, in front of people. 'Go to Mr Crichton Wells,
give him my best compliments and tell him . . .' Louis skated
proudly off, carrying Dad's best compliments like a cup full
to the brim.

Olwen was there all through the bleak opening months of
1951 on the rink every Sunday without fail. She always came
in by herself, her cold fingers loosening the knot of a highly-
coloured headscarf, emerging from the Ladies' a long time
afterwards in a skating outfit that was different each week—
dark green or pale grey, or sometimes black with a gold pattern spreading downward from the neck, and dark stockings
with hard black seams and black lumps all over them like the
leeches which stuck to Humphrey Bogart in the film *The*
152

African Queen. All her outfits had in common that high, straight neckline which seemed to rule off her stern face from her shockingly abbreviated skirt and the cold, thick legs that fell out beneath. She did her hair in different ways, sometimes fastening it down with a band across her forehead, which had a shallow peak; on other Sundays scraping it upward with coloured combs into a shape somewhat resembling the ears of Mickey Mouse. She never said hello to Louis—dumb with shyness himself, he felt that she, too, was rather shy. But how could she be shy of him and still show him her legs? The question racked him its rippling sweet and ugly sensations as, each Sunday, he watched Olwen circle the rink alone, her high white boots stepping softly forward, forward, now backward with a twist of skirt pleats, a flash of matching knickers that made a hook twist deep inside Louis—skating backwards now, and forwards again and backwards in a rapid, knees-bending dance-step. There was a certain tune, called 'The Skaters' Waltz', which always seemed to play over the rink loudspeakers while she practised. It was played by violins, crackling and far-off, in large sweeps that matched the cold, smooth lunges of her legs; there was also something sad in it, reminiscent of that look on Olwen's face as if somebody somewhere was being very unkind to her. Though they never spoke, she knew Louis was looking at her. She must know he was looking at her legs. Sometimes, by accident, their eyes met for an instant; and it seemed to Louis, in his own confusion, that Olwen's air of pathos intensified, her head retreated into her shoulders as if that unknown persecutor had seized her neck roughly from behind. Each of them would then hurriedly look away.

He found out her name by seeing it in the club membership book—'Olwen Rumsey'. It had been written there by Dad with a firmness and flourish Louis was to remember during the confusion which grew up later around Olwen's name.

His mother, to begin with, took quite a liking to Olwen. Previously she had evinced little pleasure in club afternoons, which as a rule she would spend doing office work for Harco Ltd in the distant right-hand stage dressing-room. She had

153

tried skating, but soon fell down—how Louis had laughed to see her sitting there with her legs stuck out in front of her, all eight wheels still aspin. Dad saw as well, but remained in the entrance hall, busy on a pair of skates he was mending. He *could* be very kind to people who fell; especially to the girl members.

Olwen was a little older than a girl: that was one reason why Louis's mother talked to her. And Olwen gave her a chance, which did not often occur, of voicing an independent opinion. As they watched the roller netball game in the Pavilion, Louis heard his mother say cautiously, 'That Olwen's very good . . .' Finding that statement to be unchallenged, she went on: 'Yes—very light on her feet. That Olwen's *very* light on her feet.'

She found it interesting, as many did, that Olwen came originally from Birmingham. She herself had never been to Birmingham, as far as Louis knew, but she knew *about* Birmingham and would talk to Olwen about it almost with relief, as though she had made some further small progress towards independence of view. Louis, for his part, could never quite remember whether Olwen came from Birmingham or Liverpool. Birmingham was a word like her face, gaunt and red-nosed with a mouth quirked down at the corners. But Liverpool was a word like her voice when eventually he heard it—the voice which was both soft and plaintive and which drew out every vowel into a kind of grimace.

Olwen had come to Ryde from Birmingham—if it wasn't Liverpool—just after the War, with her whole family. She had a lot of grown-up brothers and sisters, Louis's mother told him, as well as a little sister, aged six. That was how she had first come to the Pavilion, bringing the little sister down to skate on Saturday mornings.

She herself came skating so often that she began to assume semi-official status at the rink. Dad had originally employed two men to help him keep order but both, after sudden disagreements, had abandoned their red jerseys and gone to work elsewhere. The crowds, in any case, were not as great as they

154

had once been; and now Dad relied on casual help, where he or Wilf were not available, for such jobs as sweeping up or taking tickets at the tramway-entrance. Louis's mother, Eilian the Irish girl, Margaret Mitchell, even Grandma Cussons on a visit down from London, had, at different times, found themselves co-opted to assist Dad in this way.

At club meetings now, Olwen took charge of admissions— a job which made it necessary for her to arrive even earlier on Sunday afternoon. She was initiated by Dad, as were very few, into the mystery of the lights that could be turned on inside the Pavilion from a column of brass switches next to the doors. He held Olwen's arm and reached up with it to show her what switch operated the wall lamps; the coloured lights around the promenade balcony; the four spotlights that shone into the dome, a little way.

It was clear that Dad admired, as they all did, Olwen's superiority over any other skater on the rink. If the hall was not crowded, he would leave his counter and stand at the partition doors, watching her intently as his fingers crawled by instinct for tobacco inside his oilskin pouch—watching and watching her, his pipe still unlit, as she practised incessantly, figure-eights, pirouettes and jumps. He would put on music for her, and extra lights, even if she were alone on the rink, and for all his bitter complaints to Louis's mother previously about the electricity bill. Sometimes, as Olwen practised, he would watch her in private, from his broadcasting room on the left of the stage, through a hole he had drilled through the eye of the painted Scotsman in 'Skaters of all the World'.

Faint intimations had reached the Pavilion already of a larger, mainland roller-skating world where championships were held and examinations set for medals graded from bronze to gold. People in the club were always telling Olwen she was good enough to seek some such official recognition. During that winter, it reached Louis's ears that Olwen, with Dad's encouragement, had in fact begun to train for the bronze medal figure skating test.

This enthusiasm on Dad's part was the more remarkable

155

to Louis considering how he himself had always signally failed to impress Dad with his skating. At each new accomplishment he would shout out a premature 'Look Dad!' but then immediately regret calling Dad's steady-hazel-eyed gaze upon himself. If Dad stood and watched him, the trick became unrepeatable; his wheels would collide or stick together. 'I can do it—honestly. I *could* . . .' After a few more tries, Dad walked away with Nigger shambling faithfully at his heels. 'I used to be able to, Dad . . .' How he hated that silly dying note in his own voice.

If Dad gave him praise at all, it was in an oblique and pessimistic way. He would sometimes show Louis copies of *The Skater* magazine, to which he now subscribed, to help Olwen. Between the adverts for shoe-whitener and Hamoco wheels, there were the results of the latest championships and pictures of medal winners—some of them boys and girls not much older than Louis. One girl, called Jeanette Aldweg, jumped for joy, kicking up her skates behind her after winning a gold medal, as the picture-caption said, 'at the ripe young age of eleven'. Dad's manner implied that Louis could win a medal, too, if he really tried; if he gave up playing netball with Smudge and Lofty and, like Olwen, applied himself to ceaseless figure-eights. But Louis knew he was 'no good' at figure-eights. Growing bored on the first curve, he invariably lost the momentum needed to carry him back through the second. Anyway: what was the use? Jeanette Aldweg had won her gold medal at eleven. He was nearly eight, and had not yet even begun. And he did like playing netball with Smudge and Lofty.

One Sunday, when he had stopped on the rink, Dad came over to him and put an arm around his neck, drawing him aside in the way that could be prelude to a secret, or to the present he wanted most in the world.

'If you were to ask Olwen nicely,' Dad murmured into his ear, 'I think she might teach you how to do The Mohawk.'

'What's that, Dad?'

'The Mohawk? You know what The Mohawk is. Watch
156

Olwen turning and you'll see. The proper way to turn round in figure skating is called The Mohawk.'

'I already know how to turn round, Dad.'

'You don't do it properly, Louis,' Dad said severely, withdrawing his arm.

'I can Dad—watch.'

Dad watched Louis's version of a turn; then, with faint disgust, he said:

'Anybody can do it *that* way, old son, with your feet stuck out all over the place. Why not learn to do it the right way? Olwen will very kindly, if you ask her *nicely,* show you the proper way to do it.'

Olwen, that afternoon, was practising figures on a part of the rink, near the stage corner, which by now seemed to have become consecrated to her private use. Watched by the clowns up in the freize, she jumped from the left foot, then twisted in mid-air to land on her right, travelling backwards with her arms crossed on her chest, her left leg stretched behind her. As her skirt pleats fell forward, you could see right up to where her legs stopped in arches of chilly white.

She braked when she saw Louis standing near, trying to decide on a method of address. She seemed to know already what he was supposed to ask. Without speaking, she skated a little distance away from him, and halted, standing up on her toes. She started forward on the left foot, then brought her right foot round behind her, shifting her weight to it and bringing the unwanted left foot up with a neat little kick. That was the proper way to change from skating forward to backward. That was The Mohawk.

Olwen skated back to Louis, braking with one foot behind the other: for the first time, he realised, she was speaking to him directly:

'Go on,' the plaintive little voice said. 'You have a try at eet now.'

He couldn't do it; his mind was made up, even though Olwen demonstrated The Mohawk to him again and again. She even went through the steps with him, holding his hands above

F

his head. Now he lost his balance completely, his eyes swerved away from her knees and his skate wheels ran outward, a silly sound, 'Ooer!' escaped from him. Stumbling against her, he put out his hand and, for an instant, actually touched one of her bare legs. To touch it felt like touching snow.

Olwen caught up both his hands again, lifting his arms above his head, dancing him about on his skate wheels until he could stand properly again. He saw her face smiling grimly down at him through the tangle of their arms. 'You made a nice mess of *that*,' she said. 'Didn't you?'

At five o'clock Wilf shut the swing door to the tramway station, holding it steady with his foot as he drew the long bolt into place. The lights went out all round the rink, leaving just the brightly-lit doorway to the Tea Bar, through which came wafting a cindery toast smell, accompanied by the sound of a busily-scraping knife.

A lot of people always stayed behind to tea after the club meeting. They came drifting into the Tea Bar, flat-footed, a little dazed after two hours' constant propulsion, rubbing their hands and smiling nervously, uncertain whether they really ought to have stayed behind. Three or four small tables would have been pushed together and spread with red gingham restaurant cloths to seat all the people Dad had asked to stay to tea.

Tea was the only meal Louis liked—the only one guaranteed not to contain some ordeal of meat. There would be beans on toast or tomatoes on toast—those funny tomatoes from the big tins with hard yellow pips that got under your teeth—and yellowish tea full of bubbles from the urn. If there were sardines on toast, Louis was still allowed to have beans. He was also allowed to sit down still wearing his skates. If he forgot about them and moved, he could feel his wheels trundle away from him under the table.

At these public teas, Dad was a remote figure, like some monarch presiding—albeit sideways—at the long checkered feast table, his sovereignty expressed in dishes slightly different

158

from those served to his subjects. At tea time some special dainty from Colenutt's High Class Grocers, would be brought out for his use alone from its ostentatious hiding-place on a shelf of the service-lift. 'Where's my belly of pork?' he would say curtly to Louis's mother, or: 'What have you done with my Gorgonzola?' It was part of the reverence in which Dad was held by his guests that he alone could find appetite for those blubbery strips of white fat, or for cheese so mouldy that anyone else would have thrown it away. Louis saw him hold the reeking paper under Olwen's nose, smiling as she turned away in disgust. But Olwen was smiling as well, to think that Dad could eat such strong-smelling cheese.

Olwen stayed to tea every Sunday. At twenty-past five, preceded by keen winds of scent, she would emerge from the Ladies' dressed all in black, her hair again remodelled by grips and brightly-coloured slides. On foot she was somewhat less graceful than on skates. She walked with her face turned upward, her bottom thrust out so far that it bent her skirt-pleats, stumping along on black felt flat-heeled slippers, each of which bore a little gold ornament on the toe. She gave an appearance of shyness, holding back from the tea table, perching on the edge of a bench nearby and twisting a little golden purse in her lap. Then Dad would notice her and frown at her in a joking way and beckon her to the chair beside his at the top of the table, while Louis's mother, and any helpers she might have, passed the plates over the lino-topped counter.

In those days Olwen seemed companionable to Dad chiefly because she came from Birmingham. 'Oo—Ber-ming-gum!' he would say, exaggerating Olwen's slight intonation and at the same time suggesting some comically lugubrious quality on the whole of Birmingham and its population. Olwen never seemed to mind being teased about Birmingham. She only smiled, a wintry little smile, and carried on with the knitting in her lap. She was always knitting, cardigans and jumpers and twinsets for her little sister or herself in bright pink or bright orange wool; her needles clashed and clicked together while everybody laughed at Dad's Ber-ming-gum joke; her

159

eyes remained downcast and that slight smile drew her top lip down, as if she knew what to say in answer but was purposely holding it back.

Olwen's presence at the tea table instituted a ritual which, no less than the bright tube lights and black toast crusts and tomato pips, personified this epoch of late winter afternoons. The ritual began with Player's cigarettes, the brand which Dad smoked often in preference to a pipe. After smoking his last cigarette, he would pick up the empty packet, on which a bearded sailor, framed inside a lifebelt, stared pensively between two old-fashioned warships. He would then slide out the snug silver paper lining, shaking grains of cigarette tobacco from its corners. With one hand he would flatten out the embossed cardboard tray, turned over to its greyish underside, while his other hand unclipped the Yard-o-Led pencil from his inside coat pocket. Then, to Olwen and the others sitting near him, he would explain some new plan he had for an improvement to the Pavilion, illustrating it with a diagram on the white of the cigarette packet. Louis struggled to see, too, as the plan took shape in short, brusque strokes of the propelling pencil—the method which Dad had evolved for lifting or lowering something, for chiselling a hole in something or transporting something from point A to its perennial destination, point B. Although it was Wilf who would assist him to carry out the plan, Dad seemed most interested to know if Olwen considered it feasible. Their two foreheads looked down together at the drawing, Dad's crested by its long black peak, Olwen's with the hairline flattened harshly by a little girlish ribbon, and Louis could not help but notice how ill-matched were Dad's coat, with its leather-patched elbows, and the golden yoke-like ornament spreading from Olwen's neck, her coloured combs and hair-ribbons and the bright pink of the wool which lay in her lap. He glanced across at his mother, thinking how much nicer she still looked, although she seldom bought new clothes nowadays, or had time to get her hair done.

*   *   *

160

He wants to be excused. He gets up from the table, with a clatter of the skates he has forgotten he is wearing, and skates a little stiffly out of the Tea Bar, away from the light and voices and toast smell and the small electric fire; around the edge of the darkened rink, deserted but for the figures along the freize, and coats left twisted sideways on chairs with skates abandoned underneath. He goes out through the darker entrance hall, past Dad's counter and the dusty shelves and the carved post of the grand staircase which turns and rises, through the ceiling, to the kitchens, the balcony and incalculable gloom. He draws back the long bolt and slides himself round the end of the door to the tramway station. The nearest Gents' is out here, next to the main doors, at the end of yet another twisting corridor.

The tramway station, under its glass roof, is empty and dark. Sand, heaped under the tram buffers, looks as pale as snow, and the water in the fire buckets crawls with the sea wind that sweeps the platform from both ends. Though the wind shudders through him, he stands by the ticket barrier for a moment, looking down the rail and tram lines to the shore, where a few lights now twinkle steeply in the town, under a streak of cold silver sky held lingering by the three church spires.

He skates along the corridor into the Gents', feeling a queer sensation where his wheels pass from a wood to a concrete floor, and arrives in a high-ceilinged room buried somewhere between the Pavilion and the tram platform, where the hard floor sparkles like spilt sugar in the blinded light of a window overlooking nothing. He steps up in his skates to the end place, between big, white-glazed wings. Once again, he does not bother to undo his buttons as Dad has told him he should, but merely drags up a corner of his trouserleg and underpants. It makes him feel even colder to see the sluggish yellow wee wee in the channel, falling out through the hole and drifting slowly down, through a weed-hung cross girder, into the sea's boiling green eye. Surely this moment is too cold, too windy and draughty and stale-smelling

161

—for it smells in here of old men's winkles—ever to drift on with the rest of time.

Returning to the Tea Bar, he finds the long table empty. Everyone has gone over to the windows. Three or four windows are open, and people are grouped around different windows, looking down at something in the estuary.

He has pushed his way to the front of the crowd in the middle window. At the next window, Dad is leaning over the sill, taking aim with a rifle. Louis still cannot see out properly, so Johnny Garner, who rides the drop-handle bicycle, lifts him up to stand on a chair and holds him as he leans out of the window, and points to show him what Dad is shooting at in the sea.

'See it, down there! There! See?'

Louis can see it now. Far below, an empty mustard pickle jar is floating slowly away from the Pavilion's stilts, a dab of bright yellow among the crawling blue-grey waves. Dad, in yet another divine change of mood, has evidently thrown it out of the window and is using it for shooting practice with one of several sporting guns he keeps backstage.

With Johnny Garner's arms tightly round him, Louis leans out of the window. The wind snatches his hair up and tears the breath from his lips, but still he looks out into the roaring cold, watching the tide as it carries the yellow jar away from the Pavilion, towards the converging pier-legs and the shore. 'Please God: don't let it get away!' In one eye he can see the open window next to his, and Dad's white forehead looking out, his eyes closed to take aim: with a *crack,* barely audible in the wind, the rifle jerks up again in Dad's hand. A white spurt rises in the sea; the jar tilts forward but continues on its course. *'Please,* God . . .' How good it feels to be safe up here with arms holding him, not down there, looking up for one last time at the lighted windows before the angry shallows close over his head.

Crack: *crack.*

A hit! The bottle bursts in a yellow cloud, flaring briefly, now dwindling as the shattered glass sinks from view. Every-
162

one at the windows is clapping and cheering, and Louis claps too, and shouts 'Hurray!' like audiences of children do it on the wireless, because he is so proud of Dad for hitting the jar.

'It's all goo now.'

That was what Dad said as he brought his rifle inside and fastened his window, and the two other windows were fastened, shutting out the wind. To Louis it was the most enchantingly funny thing he had ever heard. He laughed about it until his stomach ached: even then he could not stop laughing to remember that word, *goo*. He was still laughing about it later after he had changed back into his ordinary shoes and was collecting empty cartridge cases from the windowsill while Margaret Mitchell waited to take him back to The Creamery to bed. He walked towards her still weak with laughter, his feet flapping as they always did after skating. At that moment it seemed to him that the wonderful epoch might go on for ever.

Then Olwen started to work for Dad officially. Her job was to teach skating and keep order generally at the rink. Louis grew accustomed to seeing her on weekday afternoons as well, silently patrolling, at times stooping forward to assist some helpless boy or girl. Her uniform, a dark red velvet skating dress, made her look trim and capable, almost pretty with her gaunt shoulders softened, her hair simply framing her face and less of a chapped nose than usual, for spring would soon be here. Her knickers, too, were maroon. Louis glimpsed them as she bent forward to teach the little boy or girl, and he dragged his eyes away in horror from her hard black stocking seams.

Olwen had a husband. The fact was revealed suddenly to Louis one night after he had been taken to the pictures at the Theatre Royal, when, instead of going straight home, he found himself following Dad up the semicircular front steps of the Crown Hotel. It was a special treat, his mother told him gravely: he could sit with them in the bar as long as he made no sound or gesture to betray his presence. She treated

163

him as a pariah at this uncharted hour of night, but to Dad he became a hero: it was while sitting in his secret corner, eyes smarting from smoke and tiredness, that Olwen's husband was pointed out to him. Olwen's husband worked as barman at the Crown Hotel. He was a big, blond haired man with a tea-towel over his shoulder, at that moment, near closing-time, engaged in kicking a beer crate along the floor. A little later, he came across to collect the empty glasses from their table. He had a big face with a turned-up nose, and big, stubby fingers that dived into the foam-flecked glasses, gathering up several at once in either hand. 'Hello, Lou,' he said in a friendly voice, even though they had never been introduced. Then Louis saw Olwen as well, sitting on a stool at the end of the bar. Her hair was flattened under a pink band, her legs were crossed, so that you could see a crease behind each of her knees; she clutched a coat around her shoulders with a reproachful expression, as if she was cold, or had just been rescued from drowning and been ordered to sit there and wait until somebody brought her a cup of cocoa.

From now on, Olwen and her husband—whose name was Jack—became Dad's closest friends. Although Jack worked in a bar, it did not seem to make him tired of bars, and he and Olwen became frequent visitors with Dad to the pierhead pub, The First and Last. If they were not to be found in The First and Last, they might have gone to the station buffet, on the far side of the pierhead, which was tended by a deep-voiced woman named Hilda. That part of the pierhead, with its naked lights and unknown ticket-collectors and strange, bright, squirty Gents', was an alien country to Louis. He loitered outside the buffet door, which shut firmly on a spring, impatient for Dad to notice him and bring him out something.

To be adopted as Dad's close friend meant embarking on an intensive tour of all those brightly-lit places where Dad went after dark, which were so alluring to Louis as he lay impatiently with bedclothes tying him down. He knew that Olwen and Jack went with Dad to Yelf's Hotel sometimes, or to the Crown or Spencer's Inn, or sometimes to the Bodega, the Greyhound or the Royal Esplanade Hotel. It was nice to picture them all standing round Dad, listening to him, then waiting as he politely broke off his stories of the Air Force to hand more money across the glittering bar. On certain nights, Dad took Olwen and Jack in a big party that also included Eilian and Wilf, and Mr and Mrs Stiles from the Crown Hotel, to the Porthole Club in Seaview. Louis knew that because of an accident that happened to Olwen's husband Jack one night on the way there. He had been travelling with Eilian in the Wolseley's long rear compartment, sitting sideways on the carpet with his back against the door. As Dad drove round a corner, the door flew open and Jack disappeared. Nobody in the front knew anything about it until Eilian pushed back the sliding glass panel and said in a nervous voice: 'O, Squadron Leader Belmayne—Jack has gone!' He was discovered lying in the road about half a mile back. He had to be taken to hospital for stitches to be put into his head. The episode was recounted to Louis by his mother as a stern warning never to lean against a car-door.

On other nights, they all came back to the flat and had a party there. Louis had seen the traces next morning—the big glass ashtray filled with cigarette-ends; the middle doors of the linen press open to reveal a plundered array of bottles and soda siphons. Sometimes he awoke in the middle of the night, drifting up from sleep to hear voices outside his door— that same voice, pleading over and over again, 'Oh, don't be *mean,* Emile . . . don't be *mean*'—or the sound of frying from the kitchenette, or loud thumps and bangs coming from the sitting-room through the wall above his head. The explanation came later—how Dad had cooked bacon and eggs for everyone in the middle of the night, or how Olwen, encouraged by Jack, had given a demonstration of cartwheels and handstands on the carpet. Nor was his own shut door a defence against these remote nocturnal games. Once when he awoke, he was not in bed at all, but being carried in Jack's arms up the dark staircase to the empty top floor flat, where he found

F*   165 himself next morning, lying in just blankets on a camp bed. Olwen and Jack had stayed the night, sleeping in his little bed, without night-clothes.

At the rink, Olwen could sometimes be seen bending over a particular little girl in a miniature skating skirt like her own light grey one and a pink jumper the hue of peppermint rock or Olwen's bright pink nail-polish. The little girl wore white boots laced up under her brown, bony knees, even though she had not learned to balance yet: she only hung like a puppet from Olwen's hands, clicking and stumbling and laughing in a high-pitched voice that carried across the floor.

Louis asked his mother if that was Olwen's daughter.

'No—her sister,' he was told. 'That's Gaye, Olwen's little sister.'

He thought it rather strange for Olwen to have a sister young enough to be her daughter; beyond that, to begin with, the little girl hardly impinged on his notice. It seemed one more instance of Dad's generosity to his staff that, while Olwen worked at the rink, her little sister should be allowed to come down and see her and skate. The little sister came, as a rule, on Sundays, spent a couple of hours, was then fetched by an Esplanade taxi to be returned to Olwen's parents' house, somewhere on the west shore. A certain ceremonial attended her departure, Louis noticed—a packing of small valises, a tying-up of paper parcels at the skate counter while the taximan waited, and then a lengthy sometimes tearful goodbye between Olwen and her little sister half-way down the corridor to the Ladies'. Anyone would think the girl preferred her big sister's company to that of her real Mummy and Daddy. But it was none of his affair. Olwen's little sister, being only six, was beneath his notice. He did not feel obliged to speak to her, nor to acknowledge her presence on the rink, save by skating past her with ferocious solemnity to indicate high-mindedness of purpose that would not be understood by anybody of six. At intervals he saw her being guided by her big sister, with a look of grim amusement, towards the Ladies'.
166

Olwen's little sister frequently wet her knickers: a fact which the adult world seemed to view with amusement.

An afternoon came when he was compelled to form a closer acquaintanceship with Olwen's little sister. Dad had invited her to stay to tea, and Louis found himself sitting opposite her at the bottom of the checkered banquet-table.

He inspected her with frigid distaste. She was not at all like her big sister. She had a funny dark skin that put Louis in mind of Spaniards or Red Indians, and a large, brown, downward-pointing nose. In her hair she wore several ribbons which looked as if cats had been chewing them. Pathetically small, she had been provided with a heap of cushions gathered from all over the Pavilion. As Olwen lifted her into the chair, her skinny brown legs, taking hold around the cushions, reminded Louis of the long, stretchy legs of monkeys at the Zoo. If somebody spoke to her, she did not answer, but threw herself backward on her cushions and uttered a high-pitched giggle that made her nose shrivel up at the bridge. Half-way through tea, she sat up straight and let out a shrill giggle for no discernible cause: and at the far end of the table, Olwen arose with an expression of humorous resignation. Only when she had been lifted away did Louis's nostrils detect, from the heaped cushions, the odour of wee-wee.

Later on, as a special treat, there were cakes—éclairs, cream horns and cream slices brought down the pier for Dad by a daughter of Fry's the bakers. As Louis reached across the table for the éclair, a voice said: 'Ladies first!'

Dad was looking down the table at him, and everyone else had paused to look at his hand, almost touching the chocolate éclair.

'Ladies first!' Dad said again, playfully.

A blush took his face in its searing hands, and he looked weakly at the plate of cakes—at the smeared, burnt mouth of the cream horn; the ruffles of cream escaping beneath coconut-sprinkled wings—and from the fancy cakes to Olwen's little sister. Inexpressible despair took hold of him to think that she might take the éclair—that *she* would taste the brittle shell

167

and its circle of cool yellow cream. That was what she planned
to do even now as she laughed, wrinkling up her big nose
then flinging herself back on her cushions.

'I *say*—he likes the look of her, doesn't he!' Dad said,
pretending astonishment. 'He can't take his eyes off her, can
he?'

The avenue of faces turned to stare at Louis again. To those
faces, truth had no appeal; his voice, protesting 'I *can*' was
drowned in their knowing smiles. He sat there, coffined in a
blush, waiting with his head down for the moment to pass so
that he might go around the club members and speak to each
of them in private, explaining that he *could* take his eyes off
Olwen's little sister—it was only Dad's joke to pretend otherwise.

'My son and heir,' Dad said proudly. 'He's going to be a
chip off the old block one of these days.'

Later on, waiting with Margaret Mitchell in an unlit tram,
he re-lived the horror of that moment, as he looked out over
the dark platform to the long sign that eternally advised 'Drink
and Enjoy Lipton's Tea'. At least Peter—or Charley—the
tramboy knew nothing of his humiliation: that was one good
thing anyway, he thought as the whistle blew. The tram burst
from its station; he sat with Margaret under the jogging hand-
straps and watched the Pavilion's terraced lights climb away
up the estuary, aching with unhappiness now because he had
not obtained any reassuring word with Dad—only a Roman
salute from deep inside the railway buffet. Yet his trust in
Dad remained unassailed. He felt certain that Dad did not
really like Olwen's little sister. It had been only from politeness to Olwen that she was asked to stay to tea. As they passed
the middle shelter, he persuaded himself that, if he could hold
his breath and count thirty bangs of the tram on its rail, he
would never have to see Olwen's little sister again. 'Twenty-
four—five—six—sev'—eigh'—ni—' and here to save him
came the Esplanade, the station canopy lit by freezing lamps,
the boat passengers running for buses down a thunderous
wooden slope.

Next Sunday after the club meeting, Olwen's little sister

was again invited to tea. At five o'clock, Louis did his best to escape, clattering off on his skates among the chairs as Gaye was hoisted on to her cushions. His mother said, in her curt Pavilion voice: 'Come on—both you kids down here.' And Dad, pursing his lips, agreed:

'That's right. Put the two lovebirds together.'

Strange to say, he had never hated anybody before. Childhood reserves hatred for its inferiors, and Louis, who until now had lived alone in a valley between grown-ups, was at first only bewildered to discover himself thrown repeatedly— and, by Dad, roguishly—into the company of Olwen's little sister. How could his life have suffered this encroachment? He, who hitherto had only been himself—who had even tried to kick the shadow from the end of his shoe—found himself, with nightmare suddenness, relegated to the sphere of this creature, barely able to walk or speak—barely even born —this creature across the tablecloth, fidgeting about and smiling with its cheeks and its nose, but not somehow, with its strangely blank brown eyes. At this second tea, when she asked for 'egg on bread', Louis felt hatred crystallize suddenly within him, a new emotion, sharp and clear and far-sighted, like a telescope coming into focus. He hated even the little metal link that held the buckle on each shoulder of her dungarees.

'Ooh—look at him!' Dad said, and everybody looked. 'He just can't take his eyes off her, can he?'

Her knickers, visible under her stretched lap, were grey with wetting—he looked away, gouged with disgust to think of that grey, damp, place ever bubbling in the join of her legs. In time he came to recognise two distinct kinds of wee wee smell that clung to her. One was the smell of new wee wee, a green, dark, stalky smell like cabbage boiled for too long in the pot. The other was the more pervasive smell of old, dried-up wee wee, the sour and yellowing smell of her skin, her clothes, her hair-ribbons, her dolls, and all in her immediate habitat. He remembered a story they had read at Partlands about a 'wee, wee woman' who lived in a 'wee,

169

wee house'—how unfortunate had been the person charged with reading out this account of smallness so ambiguously expressed. At that time, Louis himself had almost forgotten the word wee wee. He hated Olwen's little sister no less for dragging him back to shameful, swampy memories of wee wee in his own past.

He hated her for much else besides. He hated her ludicrous smallness and her puny limbs. He hated her face; her dry, dead-feeling hand; her knobby knees. He hated her little skating outfits, her brightly-coloured jumpers and her raincoat with the hood. He hated her face for looking so stupid; he hated the parting that meandered among her hair-ribbons; he hated the eskimo on her dungarees-pocket, and the foolish mittens, tied together. He hated her common accent, that was Bermingum like Olwen's but infuriatingly quiet and bashful; and that way she pulled up her socks under the table, and said 'Moomy' for 'Mummy' and asked for 'egg on bread' and called a jumper a 'sloppy Joe'. What he hated more than anything else was her refusal to pronounce 'nougat' properly, as Nanny Belmayne said you should, however many times Louis corrected her. She just laughed, wrinkling up her nose in that hateful, silly way. Then, deliberately, she said it again: 'Nugget.'

'It's not nugget—it's nougat!'

'Nugget!'

'Nou-*gar*!'

He went around the club members as he had intended, explaining to each of them that he and Gaye were not really lovebirds—it was only Dad's joke to say so. He told his special friends that, one by one, in confidence, and with a sinking heart watched their faces become contorted into the same affectation of surprise.

'Oh? I gathered you was keen on her. Your Dad said you couldn't stop looking at her.'

'Well! That's not a very nice thing to say about someone you've got a crush on! You can't kid me, Lou. She's your lady-love. She makes your heart go pit-a-pat.'

170

'Do you believe me?' he asked in desperation.

'I believe you—thousands wouldn't.'

Out in the Gents', between the big, glazed wings, he felt his whole life undermined in the sea draught that blew up through the hole. He closed his eyes against the insults he had received and lowered his forehead against those which were still to come. A single thought gave him strength, standing here in the windy twilight—Nanny Belmayne was coming soon! Nanny Belmayne, one day, should learn of this.

Their taxi drove along Links Road, squeaking over potholes that lay hidden by the veined sunlight. It was Sunday-quiet here, although Friday and the bustling town were just a minute away. The trees formed a dark corridor, thick and over-arching like an old postcard view. Every so often they passed a seat mouldering on its stone tablet, unused since the days when Links Road was renowned as one of the prettiest local 'walks'.

To the left, sloping upward, were empty paddocks. To the right, the grand houses of Ryde lay hidden behind continuous fortification. Sometimes Louis glimpsed among the trees a flat-roofed observation tower, its windows turned away towards the sea. There was something frightening about these houses, their stepped boundary walls, their secrecy and silence. He remembered what his cousins had told him about a foreign prince who lived in Links Road, who collected wireless sets and was mad. And not far from here, along the beach, was Player's Copse, where people sometimes went to hang them-selves. Sitting in the taxi with his mother, he felt uneasy—and not only because they were going to lunch at Olwen's parents' house; nor even at the ordeal of lunch itself. The sun, dodging from tree to tree, made purple patterns flicker in his head. He stared out at the old green walls, the ruined seats, the mounded ivy, and with suddenly-refreshed horror, won-dered what became of people after they had died.

The taximan, whose neck was crooked from a War wound, stopped uncertainly in front of a wall that was greyer than the

171

others, lying along the bottom of a depression filled with dead
leaves. A basin, set into the wall and surmounted by an open-
mouthed stone face, was also full of leaves, as if the face had
sicked them up. 'This must be it—Parkfield Lodge', Louis's
mother said in the drawling voice that she had assumed for their
visit. 'Yes, *there* it is on the gate. Thank you *so* much, Mr
Attrill.' Passing the fare through to the taximan, she turned
to Louis with a frown, pointed to the big, quilted door and
commanded:

'Out.'

Why did she always try to make him look silly in front of
other people?

Behind the wall, the upper parts of a long, grey, turreted
house crouched in a sloping undergrowth of nettles and
bamboo. As Louis and his mother went down the path at the
side, a dog heard them and started barking. The only way in
seemed to be through a blistered porch, littered with old deck
chairs and card-tables. Louis's mother sighed angrily and
pulled at a bell-lever on a rusty iron arm, but no sound came
from within the house. They must be very near the beach;
he could smell something seaweedy and yellow. Or might it
be . . .? The terrible suspicion remained unformed as, through
the door-glass, lace curtains parted, and Olwen's face looked
out at them with what seemed to Louis to be a cold and triumphant little smile.

'Hello,' his mother said brightly. 'Was this about the time
we were supposed to appear?'

He had never imagined that Olwen came from surroundings
as grand as this. They were climbing a huge, red-carpeted
staircase that curved away from an entrance-hall, full of armchairs standing in groups; now passing a round window, inset
with coloured glass shields. Olwen went ahead of them, climbing carefully in her black suede heels and long, straight black
skirt, holding the cardigan of a bright orange twinset around
her shoulders with that usual chilly, shuddery, slightly hounded
air. At the top of the stairs, Louis and mother followed her
along a corridor through the open doors of which they glimpsed
172

big, high-ceilinged rooms full of armchairs and sofas and card-tables. The house was quiet, but for that same little dog, barking somewhere in a rusty squeal.

'Oh stop it, Pedro,' Olwen said under her breath.

In a room that was neither large nor grand, Olwen's parents, Mr and Mrs Rumsey, waited to be introduced. Mr Rumsey sat in an armchair, wearing a new suit and smoking a cigar. His face was just like Olwen's—he had the same flat cheeks, straight nose and downward-turning mouth. Slim, dark-skinned, unwrinkled, he seemed more like her brother than her father. Louis looked from him to Mrs Rumsey, in be-wilderment. For Mrs Rumsey *was* old. Not old, perhaps, to be 'Mum' to Olwen, but grotesquely old to be 'Mummy' to Gaye, who became visible now under the table, peeping out in a silly, sidelong way. Mrs Rumsey was stout and pale-skinned; off-white from her buttoned over shoes to her hanging sleeves and heavily-clasped cream handbag and the French poodle which sat in her lap shrieking so violently as to drown Olwen's formal introductions. The poodle barked and Gaye shouted, 'Moomy, Moomy', thrusting a doll up in a scene so noisy and confusing, so full of electric fire heat and piled up newspapers that one did not notice at first the smell of wee wee in the room.

Mrs Rumsey made it speedily plain that Louis and his mother were Olwen's guests and that she herself was disin-clined to let them interrupt her usual way of life. This con-sisted of sitting in her chair, with her handbag close by, as if she had just come in or was shortly to go out, and talking through clenched teeth in a Bermingum accent so much more pronounced than Olwen's that it emerged at times like a foreign dialect from her daffodil-shaped mouth. Her husband, whom she alluded to as 'Junn', sat with his jacket open, smoking his cigar, saying little and whistling slightly, for he suffered with his chest. Olwen sat at the table, holding her elbows, and Louis's mother, who had not been invited to take a seat, stood with folded arms, listening to Mrs Rumsey's plaintive account of a recent holiday abroad. In a bright, artificial tone she remarked what a lovely house this was,

173

and exhorted Louis to go to the casement window and look out. The room directly overlooked the sea, which surged and slopped a few feet below, littered with driftwood, dead seagulls, rabbits' heads—which were often mysteriously washed up by the tide—and seaweed, clotted like manure. To the east, the pier slanted out at an angle he had never seen before. He turned his face longingly to the hazy west where a car ferry, forecastled like a little Viking ship, made its way, drawn as though by invisible ropes towards the headlands of Fishbourne Creek.

Inside the room, Gaye had now clambered up to join the poodle and the handbag on Mrs Rumsey's lap. Louis looked at the handbag despondently, conscious that it contained no promise for him. 'Moomy, Moomy—I do loove you,' the girl bleated. 'I do loove you, Moomy.' 'Mummy', to Louis, was a vaguely thrilling word, evocative of someone young you could cuddle up to in bed. When he thought of cuddling up in bed with Mrs Rumsey, a cold shiver possessed him.

For lunch, served in the same small living-room—though dining-rooms and ballrooms and assembly and billiard rooms stretched empty all around—they were given chicken noodle soup. That was what Louis's mother called it anyway as she struggled to assert that Mrs Rumsey oughtn't to have gone to so much trouble. Louis, meanwhile, peered with horror into the pale, cloudy liquid which in colour seemed to resemble nothing so much as the contents of Nanny Belmayne's 'Edgar Allan' after it had stood unemptied under her bedstead for a day or two. And what could be those pale white things under the surface, shifting and waving as in a sluggish current? He remembered when Melody caught worms, and they had to follow her about and look into her number two until they found a thin, white slithery thing like these things waving about under the soup. 'Finish it up,' his mother said, looking at him across the table with a smile bereft of all recognition. 'It's nice chicken noodle soup.'

'Please may I have a drink of water?'

'It's bad for them to drink with meals,' Mrs Rumsey said.

'Moomy!' Gaye cried. 'I want a drink as well!'

'All right, sweetheart: you shall have eet.'

Later, in Gaye's underground playroom, Louis gazed upon the rubble of her toys, the volume of which had been increased by more old newspapers and by empty cream-pots and nail polish bottles from Olwen's dressing-table. The wee wee smell was even stronger down here: it seemed to impregnate the doll's house; to gush out afresh with the blink of the biggest doll's eyes and the buzzing voice that said 'Mama' if you tilted it. He tried to read but could not, for wee wee had got into the storybooks and melted the glue of their spines. Even the titles—*Jimpy* and *Mumbo Jingles*—seemed to belong to a wee wee universe.

With a new vividness of hate, he turned towards Gaye, who was kneeling on top of the rubbish, kissing a photograph in a frame. The photograph was of Olwen in uniform. She wore an Army cap with a peak; her hair came out underneath in two fluffy bunches. 'I do loove you, Moomy,' Gaye said in a crooning voice. 'I do loove you—you are loovely.' This was another silly thing she often did. She called Olwen her Mummy instead of her big sister.

Her idea of games was pitiful. She only knew how to play doctors and nurses, or 'falling in love'. If he tried to tell her a better game, she shrugged and said in a toneless, sing-song voice, 'I don't know what you me-an.' That was when Louis hated her most of all. He wanted to slap the vacant little brown face until she did know what he meant. Instead, even though it did smell of wee wee, he snatched the doll from her arms.

'Give eet me!' she whined.

'Not "give it me" . . .'

'Give eet me-e!'

'Not "give it me". Give it *to* me!'

She took hold of the doll's leg, wailing, 'Loose eet!' He could easily push her down.

'Loose eet!'

'Say "let go of it." '

'Loose *eet*!'

175

'I won't until you speak properly.'

Slowly, the tide went out, leaving a slimy green mark along the stone front of Parkfield Lodge. The driftwood and rabbits' heads now lay tangled together on the dark, inky sand. Louis had been deprived even of Gaye's company. Mrs Rumsey, lifting her and the doll away, looked suspiciously at him and said, 'Yow've to let her alone now. She's gowing to eat an egg.' Gaye was removed to partake of this extra-curricular meal and Louis sat down on the rubble, condemned to *Jimpy* again. A proclamation on the book's frontispiece announced that it belonged to 'Gaye Nevinson, Parkfield Lodge, Links Road, Ryde, Isle of Wight.' The stupid girl couldn't even remember her own name.

In the taxi on the way home he said to his mother: 'What's Jack's other name?'

'Nevinson,' she answered shortly.

'Olwen's Mrs Nevinson, is she?'

'Yes.'

So Olwen must have made a mistake as well when she signed herself in the skating club members' book as 'Olwen Rumsey'.

Another puzzling thought occurred to him.

'But old Mrs Rumsey isn't Gaye's grandma, is she?'

'No.'

'But she isn't her mummy either . . .'

'Yes she is. Gaye and Olwen are sisters. Gaye is Olwen's little sister.'

'She smells of wee wee.'

'I know.'

Louis sensed that they were in agreement. He remembered how his mother had kissed Gaye when they left Parkfield Lodge—quickly on the brow, and looking elsewhere.

'It's funny, isn't it? One sister's grown up but the other one's only a little girl. In fact, Gaye *could* be Olwen's daughter, couldn't she?'

'Well—she *isn't*.'

'But she could be, couldn't she?'

176

'Well she isn't, so for goodness sake, don't keep *on*!'

His mother was speaking in her real voice now. She stared angrily out of the taxi window, sighing cigarette smoke through her nostrils; at Parkfield Lodge she had smoked nearly a whole packet of Senior Service. He wondered if it were possible that she had not enjoyed going to lunch there, even though they had a private beach. But never mind, he thought: they were safely back in Union Street. Seeing the big blue drop-shaped chemist's jars in Gibbs and Gurnell's window, he felt certain that an epoch was closing. Jack and Olwen would not be family friends for much longer. Gaye would no longer come to tea on a Sunday. He would never have to go to Parkfield Lodge again.

A few days later he heard that Olwen and Jack would be moving into the empty flat at the top of The Creamery. Jack was to take over, on Dad's behalf, the running of the café.

going to the pictures in the afternoon

It happened one Sunday evening while he was in Margaret Mitchell's care. He had been to tea at Margaret's house, 'Dormers', in Elmfield, the lower class district of Ryde. Afterwards, on their way to the bus stop, they looked in on some kind of bazaar or garden party which was just at the point of shutting down. Trestle tables lay flat on the grass through a small orchard and people were kneeling around boxes and handing chairs into the back of a van. The only stall open was a Fortune Teller. Margaret, who was very superstitious, decided to have her fortune told, and she and Louis joined a queue that stretched through long grass, among the small, barren apple trees. In a few minutes, some other people were queueing behind them. The extraordinary thing happened while Margaret was talking to a friend she had met, and Louis stood behind them and watched some Sea Scouts pulling down a tent.

Turning impatiently, he saw Nanny Belmayne in the queue a few places back. The realisation that it was not Nanny Belmayne—it was a woman uncannily like her—came too late to stop his heart from toppling and crashing into smithereens of joy. Her face was exactly like Nanny Belmayne's. She had the same dark eyebrows and long, almost Oriental eyes; the same small, turned-up nose; the same kind, peaceful mouth, which so readily puckered up with mischief if a black man happened to pass. Even her coat was like Nanny Belmayne's— even her squashy corduroy hat. At the side of the queue Louis could see a shopping bag that *might* have been a string bag, and a big pointed 1920s lace-up shoe. Patiently, inquiringly, that was just how Nanny Belmayne would wait in a queue for a bus or at the Food Office, or to gain admittance to the Duke of Wellington's house.

She was not Nanny Belmayne, though in a few anguished and ecstatic minutes, Louis almost metamorphosed her. Indeed, in this lingering twilight, he could not be absolutely sure. He turned round secretly again to look, his whole heart flying to her, during the second or two before it became rude to stare. As the queue dissolved, moved forward again and settled, he searched in panic for her, found her, and sent off his love in another desperate volley. He was sure that in a minute she would recognise him—that the face he so tried to adore must itself reflect some image of adoration. Now she had turned to speak to someone out of sight—remarking, no doubt, what a time they had to wait for their fortunes to be told. He imagined the kind voice she had. Then she looked out along the queue again, and her eyes, at last, met his eager ones. He saw the face of Nanny Belmayne bestow on him no more than a stranger's indifferent frown.

The next day, life resumed its old servitude: the next day, and the next. Here he was in Ryde, walking through narrow streets, toiling uphill sometimes, or hurrying downhill. Here he was in John Street or Cross Street or Melville Street, watching the shopblinds pass, while shopkeepers' names paraded dully through his mind. Here he was getting up; going to school; having exams; breaking up—these things were as distant echoes, patterns of light blue and brown whispering faintly under the walls of a deeper preoccupation. Occasionally, he would be recalled from thoughts of Nanny Belmayne to

179

the present, as when someone at school touched his arm, and said 'You're He!'; he noticed the extraordinary number of freckles on Anthony Durham's face, and the trance returned. French lessons, Bible lessons, roller-skating, sweet coupons, a two shilling piece, even a slap on the bare leg, touched his mind's outer defences: he smiled, cried, laughed, put up his hand to vote, like someone hypnotised, while his brain, at its command post, measured the ability of happiness or unhappiness to use up all these terrible tracts of misspent time. Sunshine meant nothing to him, nor the School Captaincy election; the sea air, freshening in March, was tasteless on his lips. Only sometimes, at the top of Union Street, where Pack's the drapers' awnings formed a curve, did he sometimes open his eyes fully, and look out to the mainland across the high-banked sea, and think of London, and Nanny Belmayne, and feel a twisting despair inside, because of the terrible endlessness of now.

One of the things he dared say to Dad—without being spoken to first—was:

'Dad, isn't it nice when Nanny gives you a plate of cabbage by itself, with vinegar and pepper on the top?'

Dad, his fingers poised on the chair arm, said, 'Very enjoyable, Lou,' in a solemn voice, as if he, too, felt sad to think how far away from them Nanny Belmayne was this afternoon.

'Very enjoyable, Lou', Dad said again. 'Very, *very* enjoyable.'

He brought out his pipe and tobacco pouch, filling the bowl with fingers that seemed to kneel on the rim, then holding the match until the last second as he puffed, and skeins of blue smoke floated down to colour and animate the little sitting-room. In the savoury tobacco-smell, Louis's dread vanished; he sat inside Dad's parted legs, unafraid of tickles or sudden lunges—for this was a hallowed subject between them. This was the cherished *used-to* world.

'She always used to have an account at Roper's Café, in the Old Town. Know it: round on The Pavement? Uncle Cal and I used to go in there from school and have a slap-up tea whenever we wanted.'

180

'What did you used to have, Dad?'

'Ooh—pie and mash. Honey tarts, they used to sell. Two-pence each they used to charge for those. And we used to end up with twenty Gold Flake. She never used to mind. She always used to pay up without a murmur.'

Sometimes Dad told Louis about great opportunities which had come his way, and which might have made him rich, or taken him to live abroad instead of this little flat above a café in Ryde High Street. '. . . But, of course, I couldn't leave Nanny,' he explained, and Louis nodded, marvelling at the unselfishness which had guided Dad throughout his life. For if Dad had allowed himself to become rich, or gone away to Rhodesia in the Air Force, who would there have been to board up Nanny Belmayne's windows for her in the War? Who would there have been to lay crazy paving in her garden or build her a rockery up under the blue tin shed?

She was always near Louis during those endless months. He saw her each time he looked at a packet of Bisto. She was the larger of the two Bisto Kids—the one in ragged breeches, turning towards the gravy smell a blissfully-upturned nose. He saw her in the Atora suet box, in which a team of oxen seemed to drag along one enormous pudding; it reminded him of the olden days, and of her kitchen at midday, full of cabbage steam and her face turned round, glowing from the hot stove. The Tate and Lyle Golden Syrup tin, green and gold outside, gold and silver inside, reminded him of the trick she did with a dessert spoon—the column of treacle unfolding from it and slowly climbing down to his plate. He saw her in Murraymints, in Peter's Original Milk Chocolate, in Keiller butterscotch and Barker and Dobson's Butter Brazils, those products she commended for their wholesomeness; he saw her sweet-tin with the cavalier's face, and chips of nut and toffee and boiled sweet stuck around the inside. Once, at somebody's birthday party, he was startled to glimpse her face on a certain card in the Happy Families pack. He saw her even in newsreel films of the Maoris who danced for Princess Elizabeth on her New Zealand tour, with their elbows pumping and bottoms moving

181

to and fro a little like Nanny Belmayne's war dance with the potato-slice while she was cooking breakfast.

If anyone mentioned Clapham, the pictures in his mind gave actual pain. He saw the little domed Underground station, where, deep below, the Northern Line trains rushed in, from Stockwell, from Clapham South, on either side of the same platform. He saw the borders of the Common, the sparkling distances of the South Side, the little tributary roads around that dangerous paddling pool, and the trams, marshalled high and clanking over the main road. He saw Mr Brill's off licence, and Maritime House, and the big Elizabethan place which he hoped was called The Plough. He did not like to hear about any time in history when Nanny Belmayne's house would not have been standing at the end of Orlando Road, near the bomb-site. He was chilled, one day at the pictures, to see film of Victorian London, full of flickering, jogging carts and cabs, and to realise that, should he be suddenly reborn in the 1890s and make his way to Clapham Common, he will not find Nanny Belmayne there yet. For the same reason, pictures he saw of the General Strike were comforting and reassuring. He remembered what fun she said it had been; how the buses had been driven by students from Oxford and Cambridge, who would take you anywhere you wanted to go for sixpence. Were he ever to find himself back in 1926, he would only have to go and wait at the top of Klea Avenue. Sooner or later, she would come along, scarcely altered, sitting on top of a bus with an open-air roof.

He did not envy those at school whose grandmothers lived on the Island. Pam Boardman's even occupied the same house as Pam and her parents. Louis saw her at a birthday party, handing round cakes, and he felt sorry for Pam at the possession of so wan a specimen, whose grey hair and cameo brooch and bandaged knee—which showed when she sat down—all seemed feeble and somehow unconvincing; whose very name, 'Nana', was the slurred approximation of an ideal. Nobody could be like Nanny Belmayne, and yet every old lady he saw was a little like her. Nanny Belmayne appeared to him as a

182

monarch, ruling the whole race of old ladies, whose lives were regulated by her example who dressed corns or bunions, made pots of tea, suffered from bad legs, sucked peppermints, knitted egg-cosies, went to the Doctor's, bathed their feet, slipped covers over hot water bottles, stroked cats, took afternoon rests, drank Guinness, put false teeth in and discussed Rheumatism, Arthritis, Mr Churchill and the mild winter, with due acknowledgment and deference to the originator of these pursuits.

Once a month, at least, she sent him a parcel. It would arrive sometimes by post, at other times with Dad, if he had been up to London to see her. Dad frequently made these rather mysterious journeys to Orlando Road 'on business', which apparently involved taking Nanny Belmayne out in a boat. So Louis thought after he overheard his mother drily remark, during another of Dad's absences, that Nanny Belmayne would soon be having to bail him out again.

Nanny Belmayne's parcels were very large and lumpy. She made them from brown paper she had saved up in her kitchen wash-stand, and knots of hairy string, fortified by sealing wax which scattered dark orange crumbs over his name and address. Louis, who had stood beside her while she tied up many parcels —to be sent to the West Country, or to Uncle Harmer in Los Angeles—felt sorry he had not been there this time with his forefinger to hold down the knots. He pictured her with her sleeves rolled up, at her green tablecloth, wrestling energetically with the stiff paper, pulling out string from the special tin that had a hole in it. Then she would take down the sealing-wax from her high mantel, among the carved mugs and ornaments and back-scratchers. She would strike a match and hold it against the bar of sealing-wax that was like a blunt crayon. Sweetly acrid, the red blobs cooled over the knots she had tied.

Nanny Belmayne said you ought never to cut string. Always untie the knots and save it. Guiltily, Louis sent his mother to fetch her dressmaking scissors. His fingers wrenched open the thick paper, pulling out a box of New Berry Fruits, a bar of Peter's chocolate, throwing them aside in his eagerness to see

183

what else she had sent. However many things there were, the parcel always yielded just too little to his trampling and trembling hands.

Out with the bars and boxes fell a letter. She always used the same notepaper, Canadian Brand from Woolworth's, with a moose head on the cover of the writing-pad. The sheets were ready-ruled and so thin that all the kisses she had sent him showed through to the other side. Her writing was like a procession of spiky blue-black knights, swaggering in triumph along each line, or just below it, pushing and jostling to tell him how much he was loved and missed. Her signature always ran slightly out of control, like a long vehicle whose brakes have failed somewhere: overweighted with concluding endearments, it toppled over the line, righted itself again, swept forward again in an adoring subordinate clause until, confronted with the edge of the paper, it was obliged to ascend vertically into the margin. There were kisses in three lines, interspersed with 'hug' and tailing off into 'millions' as the need to kiss him grew finally overwhelming, and the ink dried on her nib.

Inside the letter was a postal order for half a crown, made out proudly to 'Master Louis Belmayne', crossed twice with such a flourish as to suggest that the whole Post Office had been taken into the secret of her love for him—that even the King, whose pale blue profile was shown in one corner, knew all about Nanny Belmayne, and could barely restrain a smile.

He opens his eyes to see rain, dashing sideways across his window, outside the three iron bars. He kneels out on his rug and looks down, across the narrow High Street, at Johncox's the fishmongers, through the wet smears shining in a blurred constellation; at the coats and hats, hurrying past; at the darkened traffic, the rain, invisible on glassy pavements, gurgling and snorting in hidden pipes, running in twists along the gutter, and spouting, with a regular smack-smack-smack from the rim of Johncox's blind. He loves rain for its power to make the world glitter and go fast. He feels happy first

184

because it is raining; then, another happiness breaks open in his mind—a happiness so immense, it almost makes him sad to think that nobody in the world can share it.

Nanny Belmayne is coming down from London today.

This afternoon, when the last bell goes, the rain will have dried to the middle of the long paving stones. At the gateway through the dripping hedge, where usually no one waits, she will be standing, looking for him as Partlands School swarms out. He will see her, as always, just before she sees him— her green squashy hat, her coat with the squares of light and dark brown, her face searching for him in the crowd. Then he will be smothered by her arms, and lifted up against her coat and her cold, dry, rosy face; he will smell the heavenly Nanny Belmayne smell and, deafened by the hugs, the kisses smacking, hear her chuckly West Country voice murmuring:

'Hello my little love! Hello my sweet! Hello my love; my loved one, my precious, dear loved one! Hello my little old bit of cobbly cheese, and how's my little bit o' fluff? How's my little bit o' fat? His Nan's so pleased to see him bless his dear face! She's missed you and missed you, she has!'

From school, she takes him straight to the pictures. She has brought along their tea to eat in the cinema—sandwiches and sausage rolls and pear drops and sweet cigarettes. She has also brought his rubber six-gun so that he can return the fire of bandits in the film.

They will be almost alone inside the cinema, eating their tea in darkness. Butter tastes funny in the dark; he can't see what's in his sandwich or which end he is eating of his sweet cigarette. It is hours yet to the place in the film where they came in. The hands on the square green clock hang motion-less. She nudges him with a bag containing invisible cake. He is so happy, he wants to be killed by a shot from the screen and to roll on the ground, through the iron legged row in front of theirs, then over and over, through all the seats to the foot of the sloping auditorium.

Once she spent the whole summer in Ryde, running The

185

Creamery for Dad. It was an epoch that Louis remembered
with incredulity—Nanny Belmayne there every day in the
little High Street café; day after day still there, presiding over
the tea urn, the fridge and the single slot machine, asking
customers if they took sugar, calling everybody she served
'love' or 'my duck', at night staying with Uncle Tony at the
Eagle Tavern in Green Street, just around the corner. Had
it truly happened? Each time Louis passed the Eagle Tavern,
he looked up at the sign of the rosy-faced man who advertised
Mew Langton's Ales & Stout, struggling to reconstruct that
wonderful time which had lasted so long, and yet still ended
too soon. He vaguely remembered being outside The Creamery,
walking from sunshine under a shopblind, and then suddenly
noticing her, in the cool depths of the café, biting an ice-
cream around the edge, winking and signalling for him to
come in and have one, too.

'*This time* . . .' he thought, shutting his eyes and clenching
his hands together to stop the minutes slipping through.

She couldn't stay at The Creamery—there wasn't a spare
room. Louis had written to her, suggesting she might sleep
with him in his small bed above the High Street. Nanny
Belmayne answered that it would be better if she and Uncle
Tony—who always accompanied her—stayed in Haylands with
Uncle Cal. It wasn't far away, she reminded him. They would
still be together nearly all the time.

But there now arose an awkward diplomatic question. Dad
and Uncle Cal were not on speaking terms at the moment.
After last summer, when Uncle Cal was still visible in the
business, something had happened—some disagreement between the two brothers as sudden as it was violent which
brought about the total estrangement of their two families,
though it did not inhibit Dad from continuing to 'help'
Uncle Cal. Had he not promised Nanny Belmayne he would?
And Uncle Cal, while being 'helped', had become increasingly
remote from the scenes of this endeavour. Sometimes in Union
Street, Louis would sight Uncle Cal's bulky figure, moving
along as it used to at the Pavilion—even on busiest days—
186

with profound dignity and disinterest. Louis, at such moments, felt worried that he might betray Dad by speaking to Uncle Cal, but fortunately, Uncle Cal gave no sign of recognition— he continued past under the full sail of his heavy chin or, on a sudden impulse, crossed over the road and passed Louis on the other side.

As Louis walked up the drive to Uncle Cal's house, he felt like the messenger in some medieval film, such as *Ivanhoe* or *Kings of Castile*, venturing into hostile territory under a truce flag, the efficacy of which had still to be tested. Instinctively, his footsteps became those of a horse; he heard harness jingle in his satchel, and one hand moved back to steady an invisible charger, which snorted nervously as the big white house where Uncle Cal lived came flickering among the trees. He reflected how unthinkable, a week ago, would have been this journey after school on the Haylands bus—how, but for Nanny Belmayne's presence, this would still be a forbidden place. It was funny to hear silence, broken only by the swish of a car in Upton Road; and to smell the charred wet country smell and see fields instead of the beach, and no pier, which-ever way he looked.

To this, presently, was added the odour of Uncle Cal's household—an odour somewhat like cake-mixture, yet contain-ing an element more sinister than cake. Though Uncle Cal lived now on the ground floor of this big house called Merlin-brook, with numerous French windows and wide lawns and grass embankments planted with daffodils, he had imbued his surroundings with the same strange, brooding atmosphere so noticeable at his previous house on Clapham South Side. Here at Merlinbrook had materialised the long picture of blue ladies with nothing on but 1920s hats, painted for Nanny Belmayne by an artist in her Chelsea days but given to Uncle Cal, doubtless as typifying the sort of thing he had seen on his unusual foreign travels. Here, in the passage, hung the picture of French dogs, wee weeing like men; there, in Uncle Cal and Auntie Rita's bedroom, Louis glimpsed the picture of the French boy wee weeing over the frog. He braced himself

187

to this world where wee wee was not rude if French, where
'Bones' (as in Uncle Cal's bedtime story) could follow you at
night, and where, if Uncle Cal felt humorous, it was perfectly
possible to find your dinner, as Auntie Rita had once found
hers, generously sprinkled with his toenails.

Louis sat, waiting for Nanny Belmayne, on a big sofa with
a lace cover over the back and a metal ashtray on the arm, held
there by a woolly-looking leather strap. Near his foot was the
round, quilted object which Auntie Rita called 'the humpty'.
On a table by his elbow stood a framed photograph of Auntie
Rita, in the days before her nerves became bad. Her cheeks
tinted salmon-pink, she was nursing Louis's cousin Terry,
peering closely into his scarcely visible face, as if to find some
authenticating watermark, while his elder sister Marie looked
towards the edge of the frame with a quizzical air that made
Louis impatient to see her again. But both Marie and Terry
were out at the moment: so was Uncle Cal. Uncle Tony had
gone for a lie-down in another part of the house, and Nanny
Belmayne and Auntie Rita were in the kitchen, having a private
word. Louis waited in the lounge, alone but for muslin curtains
billowing in from the opened French windows, and Judy, the
big, black, spiteful Persian cat who wouldn't stop making
messes.

That was another reason for Auntie Rita's bad nerves. If
not protecting her food from Uncle Cal's toenail clippings,
she would be clearing up the messes made by Judy—who was
old Judy, mother of the Orlando Road Judy—always in
awkward places, underneath the chair or the sideboard, and
always with terrible suddenness and a loud noise, like somebody blowing out a carnival squeaker. As a result, Auntie
Rita attended Catholic Mass even more devotedly and went
around with her hand laid on her heart, to still its fluttering,
or her fingers twisting and twirling the piece of green chiffon
tied round her wrist to hide the scars of her motor accident.
From the voices in the other room, Louis deduced that Auntie
Rita was having a further attack of nerves and that Nanny
Belmayne, as usual, was trying to placate her. Probably she

was telling Auntie Rita that, when Judy made a mess in the kitchen sink or in the bath, it was a sign of intelligence.

Marie came home first to Merlinbrook this afternoon. Finding Louis on the big sofa, she took his hand in her cool one and led him out through the French windows as if to tell him something too secret for words. She was tall and very slim, with black eyebrows and dark brown eyes and hair in plaits which lay on her coat lapels like two glistening ropes. Everybody said how beautiful Marie was. Nanny Belmayne, in particular, never ceased praising her dark eyes, her Belmayne dimples and the long brown hair which, like Nanny Belmayne's own, used to hang all the way down Marie's back. It was none of *her* business, Nanny Belmayne said, but beautiful hair like that should *never* have been made into plaits.

Louis did not mind about the plaits. It was nice to see Marie again after so long—exciting to be drawn aside by her like this, to hear something secret, or perhaps rude. Though Marie was three years older, he had always been able to make her laugh especially about things like dog manure, or blowing off. And when they all had to sleep together in one room, Marie sang 'Greensleeves' to comfort him when Terry said that a big hand was coming through the darkness to kill him.

Outside the French windows, she told him about things called milk shakes which you could buy at Dinelli's Café on the front. She told him that Mr and Mrs Read, the caretakers, were grumpy, and that she had been given a slap by a nun at school for drawing a fish with arms and legs. Then, with dimples tightening her cheeks, she told him the book joke. The following books had been written, she said, by authors with these appropriate names:

A Heap in the Road by G. G. Dunnitt.
Something Up the Wall by I. P. Freely.
The Tiger's Revenge by Claude Balls.
Accident on the Clifftop by Eileen Dover.

'*Dangerous* by Hugo First,' said a voice, and Terry, Louis's other cousin, stepped round the corner of Merlinbrook, where he had been hiding to listen. In grey short trousers that hid his knees, he sauntered towards them, smiling contemptuously and pulling at his bottom lip. His fingers were always at work in his nostrils or on his face somewhere, like a lattice over that falsely-ingratiating smile, modelled on the smile of Mexican bandits in cowboy films. In looks, he favoured Auntie Rita; he had the same long nose, the same cautious, preyed-on look. He, more than Marie, shared his mother's devout Catholicism. If you opened a storybook of his, there would usually be a note on the flyleaf, asking Auntie Rita to wake him in time for early Mass. Like hers, his nerves were bad as a result of an injury long ago. Down at Hornchurch, while he was a baby, he had pulled a saucepan of boiling water off the stove, onto himself. The skin all down his left arm below the elbow was one wrinkled whitish scar.

He was two years older than Louis. 'Silly old Lou-ie!' he used to chant. 'You're four f'four-four. I'm six s'six-six!'

Sometimes Louis was only a year younger than Terry—then, with a birthday in September, Terry mockingly forged ahead again. Their friendship, stretched paper-thin over the chasm of those two years, seldom lasted longer than an initial bartering of jokes.

'We're going to Saturday morning pictures at the Scala,' Terry announced defiantly. Marie went to the Presentation Convent, but Terry, despite Uncle Cal's fabled scholarship, had been sent to Green Street, the Council School. He knew rough boys in ragged grey, who rode bicycles along the pavement and shouted insults at Partlands people. Nobody had tried to discourage Terry from speaking with an Isle of Wight accent. He pronounced Scala in the lower class way, as if it had something to do with scales. All this time, he was looking at the skylark badge on Louis's blazer and smiling, behind his forefinger, like the Mexican bandit who intends to turn traitor in a moment.

'Terry, why do you chew your mouth like that?' Marie asked.

'M.Y.O.B.' Terry said.

190

If you told Terry to 'M.Y.O.B.', he said, 'M.Y.O.B. back.'

'Nanny's inside with Uncle Tony.'

'Tell me news,' Terry said. 'Not history.'

'Isn't he rude?' Marie said in despair. 'Be quiet, Terry, and don't make a noise because Mummy's nerves are bad, and Uncle Tony's having a lie-down.'

'It's not Scaler, anyway,' Louis said. 'It's Scala.'

Terry removed his finger from his nose and examined the end of it.

'Not *Scarla*', he said, mimicking Louis's voice. '*Scaila*!'

'Look at his dirty knees!' Marie said.

'It's Scala. You can ask anybody.'

A little nerve twitched between Terry's eyebrows.

'*You* ask anybody. It's Scala, so shut up, knowall.'

'You shut up yourself, Purple Tooth—anyway, *you* don't know. You only go to Green Street.'

'Purple Tooth?' Marie said, laughing. 'What was it you called him? Purple Tooth?'

Terry started forward and, in a voice curdling with rage, said:

'Don't you tell me I only go to Green Street! This is our house, anyway.' Louis felt a flurry of punches on his arm and saw Terry's eyes staring furiously into his. Then Marie came between them. With a protective 'Aah!' she whirled Louis round to the other side of her so that his nose pressed hard against her raincoat buckle. 'Get off, Stinker!' she ordered Terry.

He turned on her then. His eyes were quivering like the dark spots you shook up to form a pattern in some little sixpenny pocket game.

'What did you call me, Marie? "Stinker"?'

'Yes, but don't be silly,' she said, pressing Louis closer to her raincoat buckle and speaking quickly to ward off the punches. 'I'm Porky, don't forget. I'm Porky, aren't I? I'm Porky.'

They always quarrelled: that was why Nanny Belmayne did not have them all together to stay with her at Orlando Road. When Louis arrived, he would find empty Tizer bottles in the lower kitchen cupboard, or rabbit-shaped junkets half-eaten in the meatsafe, or the ticket stubs and programmes from places where Marie and Terry had been taken by Nanny Belmayne. She took Marie inside the Houses of Parliament and to Derry and Toms' roof garden to meet Enid Blyton, who signed a book for her. Terry was interested in boxing, so Nanny Belmayne took him to see the boxing match between Randolph Turpin and Sugar Ray Robinson. It was easy to picture her there, amid uproar, bright lamps and ringing bells, perfectly at home with her squashy beret and string bag. Now even boxers, like Randolph Turpin and Don Cockell reminded Louis of Nanny Belmayne. Their eyes, half-closed and swollen, were a little like hers. He thought she might well have taught them the comic little dance they all did in a sand box in the corner.

She had no favourites as she many times proclaimed : she loved each of 'the grandchildren' no more and no less than the others. She loved Marie for being beautiful—though it was *such* a pity about the plaits. Terry was her beloved underdog; she had made a little treasury of his dour and stoic sayings : to Nanny Belmayne, he was 'poor old Terry' or 'Dear old Tel' '. She loved Marie, and 'poor old Tel' '—of her inordinate love, Louis's was an exact third share. And yet in his heart he knew better. He knew that something to do with his littleness —something to do with how the world looked through his spectacle-frames—made his preciousness to her unique. She had to *say* she loved them all the same. But his was the embroidered egg cosy kept in her china cabinet; his the baby photograph displayed on her wireless cabinet next to the toucan on its perch. She told him of Marie's trip to Derry and Toms', of Terry's to the boxing match, with an underlying sense of 'Just wait—that's nothing to what we'll do when we get to the West End', so that, in the end, Louis pitied his cousins these expeditions, undertaken with only half of Nanny Belmayne's heart. She had a way of breaking off a sentence about Marie or Terry—of squeezing his hand in a significant way, and winking at him—sometimes, from a corner of her
192

mouth, almost saying what both of them knew to be true, but inadmissible:

'He's *still* top favourite with his old Nan, he is!'

It was agony to leave her—to go home from Haylands on the bus after tea while Marie and Terry could stay with her, and get ready for bed near her, and go to sleep in the very same house. He hoped that while she was staying at Merlinbrook, she would accidentally give something to Marie and Terry but not to him, for he knew how sorry she would be when she discovered what she had done; what presents she would shower on him in compensation; how much more she would love him after having been accidentally unkind.

Uncle Tony doesn't go about very much. Sometimes, in his grey City hat, he takes a stroll along the Eastern Promenade, stopping from time to time to consult his pocket watch, or look out over the seawall, across the sand flats to the floating fort where he was garrisoned in the First World War. Little else is known about Uncle Tony's life before he came to lodge at Nanny Belmayne's house. He is observable always to the rear of her, irritable and long-suffering, short-tempered and affectionate, shaking his head and wiping his eyes to think that anyone can be so good. As there is not enough room for him in Uncle Cal's flat, he has to sleep on a folding bed in a different part of Merlinbrook. Nanny Belmayne offered to sleep there instead, but Uncle Tony wouldn't hear of this. In the mornings, he sits alone on a stool at the Greyhound, the Wellington Tavern, the Nag's Head, the King Lud, the Hole in the Wall or the Marine. In the afternoon, because he sleeps badly at night, he has to have a rest in his dressing-gown on Auntie Rita's big couch. He dozes off, sitting up straight, his braided collar furled around his clean, red neck. If anything disturbs him, he jumps and his moustache bays quietly; in uncomplaining despair, he whispers, 'Cor—*luvaduck*!'

Behind Uncle Tony's back, enormous rows happen which leave their protagonists marooned, all over the house, in stiff attitudes awaiting Nanny Belmayne's return. One afternoon, when she brings Louis back, they find Terry locked in the garden shed, sobbing wildly beyond the old horseshoe that hangs crookedly on the door. In an arbour of the lounge, Uncle Cal sits hemmed in by straight-backed chairs like a baby in its playpen. Breathing heavily, his downcast features glower at his several chins. Auntie Rita, in the kitchen, is tearfully cutting up beetroot. It all began, she says, because a chair was digging into Uncle Cal. 'I told him . . . "*If* the chair's bothering you, move it away . . ." ' At that moment, from Judy's crouching black shape, comes another long, loud, squeaking, squelching noise. 'Oh—what's that?' Auntie Rita sobs, pressing her fingers to her heart. Nanny Belmayne answers in a soothing voice: 'There—that's nothing. Only the cat leaving its visiting card.'

The main trouble, Louis gathers, is Auntie Rita's Roman Catholicism, and her insistence that Marie and Terry must be Catholics also, and so grow up disapproving of their father —so Nanny Belmayne says—because he won't cross himself or eat fish on Fridays, or get up early to go to Mass. And of course all Auntie Rita's brothers and sisters in London are Roman Catholics, too. When Nanny Belmayne mentions Auntie Rita's brothers and sisters, she taps the side of her nose with her forefinger, or rubs the fingers of one hand together like someone counting money. 'They're all very *Jewish*-looking in that family,' she says. 'It's always the converts who are most fanatical, y'know.' Certainly, all Auntie Rita's brothers and sisters, in their newsagent shops in Wimbledon, have dark complexions and extremely prominent noses.

Of course, Nanny Belmayne would never say a word against Auntie Rita, whom she calls 'poor Rita' or 'dear Rita' or 'poor dear Rita.' It is always in a general way that she alludes to 'those Catholics', as to some illness contracted by Auntie Rita, drawing her black eyebrows together and wrinkling up her little nose at the smell of their religion. 'All that curtseying and crossing and singing through their noses . . . it's all a lot o' ballyhoo. *Amen*!' she says flutingly through her nose, to make Louis laugh. 'Priests coming round with their beggar-bowls while the Pope sits in Rome, counting up his gold bars! Ugh—they make me so cross!' In the street, she nudges Louis whenever a nun approaches. On his own, he is a little afraid of the oval face, framed in stiff white, like hard-boiled egg. Now, as the black robes swish past, he fights the urge to smile, because he knows that Nanny Belmayne is thinking the same thing—*currant buns*. Once, when they get back to Merlin-brook, a currant bun rustles by them in the porch, with a ghastly whiff of dust and Jesus. Nanny Belmayne, as usual, has to 'keep the peace' in the row that happens later when Uncle Cal finds out that Auntie Rita let a currant bun visit the house.

On her visits to Ryde she always buys a lot of things from secondhand shops—dinner plates, small potted shrubs, knee-bandages, nose-irrigation sets, and other useful things picked up in back streets at bargain prices, a sea of cartons and earthy newspaper parcels spread out like plunder round her bed. She always has her corns cut in George Street, declaring afterwards, in a continuing beatitude to the chiropodist, that she feels as if she's walking on air. This time, as well, she wants to buy herself a new winter coat at Pack's. She also shows interest in a metal standard lamp she has seen on the pavement outside Beany's junk shop. Though Dad tries his best to dissuade her, she goes striding in, still walking on air, through the archway of old refrigerators.

'Oh, no Mother . . . don't do it! You can't . . . *don't*, Mother . . .'

Dad is her adviser in all such matters. He meets her and Louis outside the Q Lending Library, a point half-way up the town apparently designated as neutral ground in the strife between Uncle Cal and him. He appears suddenly, shouldering out of the mid-afternoon crowd in a brusque, worried way, like a spy in a film, as if he intends only to say a password or hand over some secret plans. He is wearing his brown tweed overcoat—the one Nanny Belmayne bought for him. His hazel eyes look momentarily dismayed as Nanny Belmayne gathers him in her arms and kisses him with loud smacks,

195

heedless of shoppers ducking past to left and right of the fusillade. *Well*, she says . . . she's not afraid to let anyone see her give her boy a bit of love.

At Pack's, she asks his advice in the matter of the new coat. He thinks she should have the cheaper one, so she buys the one costing more than she meant to spend. He carries the bag with the coat in it, and a new lot of plants from Goble's Nurseries with their names lettered sideways on little sticks. The dimples open in his dark cheeks as she comes out of Beany's, carrying the metal standard lamp. Exasperation and fondness, mixed up together, make words almost too big to pass through his lips. 'Oh, Mother! Mother, *why* did you . . .? Mother, *how* are you going to lug it all the way back . . .? Mother, *why* . . .?'

They have tea at the Café Royal, upstairs, with flower pots on the floor around them, theirs the only table embellished by a metal standard lamp. When their tray is brought, Dad pours out the tea for Nanny Belmayne and Louis, then he adds more hot water to the half-empty pot. The odd thought occurs to Louis that it is Dad who plays the motherly part, while Nanny Balmayne takes the part of a loved but incorrigible child. Dad pretends to be still angry with her about the coat and standard lamp, but all the same he cannot help smiling and pressing her hand in his. Later on, he will describe how she paid too much for her coat, and how she gave sweets and sixpences to all kinds of people to help her carry the standard lamp back to Orlando Road.

At dusk, Louis waits in the garden at Merlinbrook until Nanny Belmayne is ready to take him home and put him to bed. His companion, when his cousins are out, is Long John, a knitted bear that belongs to them. Long John was intended to be Rupert Bear, but something happened to lengthen his trousered legs and greyish woollen snout to proportions more suiting a giraffe. He wears a blue jersey and a checkered scarf, thrown over his shoulder in debonair style. Louis has always loved him, and plays ostentatiously with him in the hope that one day Marie and Terry will say he can keep Long John.

196

Meanwhile, Long John is his patient partner in an endless acrobatic display, thrown high into the air and caught, or whirled by an arm and leg, faster and faster round and round and round and round until rushing trees and lawn and the whirl of the white house create a sort of flying stillness in his head. His mind is calm, clear, at one with the twilight and quiet trees. Happiness drops into it again, like the white water which he saw once, falling from a height. For he has seen Nanny Belmayne, in her coat and hat, coming out of the French windows. Now she is walking between the two stone vases, down the shallow steps in the grass embankment.

'Aren't you going to keep the peace tonight, Nanny?'

'No, I'm going to take you home and put you to bed with a nice story, and a sweetie to go to bed with.'

He can see the 'sweetie', a whole box of liquorice comfits, tilted in the mesh of her string bag. He hopes there will be no one at The Creamery when they get back. Then he won't have to wash his knees or clean his teeth. Nanny Belmayne lets him go to bed in his socks. She will sit on his bed, near the top, and tell him again about Glastonbury and Trowbridge and Shepton Mallet, and all those West Country places.

'Aren't you going to say Goodnight to Mr and Mrs Read even, Nanny?'

'I don't think so, my love. They're *not* such very nice people to know. That Mrs Read has turned misery all of a sudden.' They skirt the caretakers' windows—where yesterday Nanny Belmayne stood talking to Mrs Read, declaring her afterwards to be a 'nice little person'. A wheelbarrow bedded up with mown grass, the very rakes and flowerpots, now seem to Louis to decorate the lair of dangerous wild beasts.

'They're Catholics, too, y'know,' Nanny Belmayne says. 'It makes people turn very queer sometimes. All that chanting and ballyhoo, when they can cause *so* much misery in other people's lives. Promise Nanny that *you* won't ever have anything to do with any Catholics, or ever get married to one. Because I think you'd come to regret it *so* much, my love.'

'I won't, Nanny,' Louis assures her fervently. 'I won't marry anybody unless it's you.'

'Bless you my little duck!' She bends down, takes his cheeks between her hands and kisses him there at the end of the drive to Merlinbrook. 'Bless his dear, sweet face! His Nan's got a nice few sweets to give him when she gets him home. He's his Nan's dear sweet lamb, bless his old face in his spectacles!'

They sit downstairs at the front of the bus, where they can see themselves mirrored in the glass behind the driver's back. He watches himself in his school cap, his wound scarf, and thinks: 'This is now, after *Scaramouche,* with sausage roll taste in my mouth, and lights on inside the bus, and people getting off, and broken sweet cigarettes when I put my hand in my pocket. Please stop moving, time. Stay at the Swanmore Road Post Office. Don't ring the bell to move off again.'

'Would you like to come down to the West Country with Nanny in the summer?'

She asks him this while he is looking back, wishing they had not yet come to this last row called Alma House and Inkerman House and Balaclava House.

'Pardon, Nanny?'

' "Pardon Mrs Arden!" You remember Nanny always promised she'd take you down one day to see Glastonbury and Bath. We'll go down when you've your summer holidays, shall we?'

He can't believe his ears at first. He thinks, with short-circuiting joy, about boys and girls in Enid Blyton stories of whom it is said that they can't believe their ears.

'*Shall* we?'

'We shall. We'll go down on the coach—and what a time we'll have! Would you like that, my old duck?'

'Yes, *please* Nanny.'

'We'll go on the coach from Victoria, down to see Auntie Bessie Appleton in New Yatt. We'll pay a visit to Aunt Kate at Hungerford, and then go on and do Glastonbury and Bath and Shepton Mallet. Nanny'll show you the house she lived in when she was a little girl.'

198

'Where else, Nanny?'

'We'll see the Abbey. The Abbot's Kitchen. You shall sit in the Abbot's bath.'

'Can I ask them about it tonight?'

She leans towards him—how lovely the Nanny Belmayne smell is! Handbags and mothballs and rosy cheeks, and un-bathed skin. She shuts one eye and makes a secret-keeping face like the Idris lemon.

'Better not tell anyone yet, till Nanny's made a few arrange-ments. "Keep it under your hat awhile", like they used to tell us when we lived in Seattle.'

'Can't I even ask Mummy?'

'Better not. You never know who might try to nip these little plans in the bud. Just keep your own counsel a bit, love, and keep it under your hat a bit longer.'

In the reflection of the bus driver's back Louis sees himself pull his cap brim firmly down. Hatred for his mother darts through him to think she might try to interfere. He imagines her making difficulties for no reason. And supposing he were to fall ill in the meantime, and die without ever seeing Bath? He longs for the bus ride to be over; for *now* to be over, and all the hot, dead summer months that are to come. 'Hurry up, bus. Don't bother to stop in Upton Road!'

He was at school on the day she went home. Imprisoned in his half of a desk, he could only imagine her triumphant progress down the pier with all the flowerpots in newspaper, and the standard lamp. It was English Grammar with Mrs Aitchison. Under his exercise were written in red ink the words he had spelled wrong, to be copied out three times each. He copied out *babies, pennies, knives,* as the boat left the pierhead with Nanny Belmayne and Uncle Tony aboard, as the tumble of water under its stern grew fainter and wet ropes were drawn in, and its shape grew small, like a swimmer, breasting the long ripples of the tide.

That night, in an interval from crying, he constructed a little shrine of things to remind him of her visit. There was

199

the clockwork bus she had bought him at Dimmer's, surrounded by figures from a farmyard; there was his name, age and half his address, printed on a strip of tin from a slot-machine; two torn, joined cinema tickets; the liquorice comfit box, empty but for a single rattling sweet. He added the box to the shrine, vowing fiercely never to eat that liquorice comfit, not until the day he is setting off with Nanny Belmayne to the West Country.

These devotions were watched by Long John who had been handed on to him at last by his cousins. He picked up Long John, forgetting his grief for a moment as he spoke to the lanky bear in their private acrobat language. But the summer . . . all of it was still to come! Pressing his forehead against Long John's tapered snout, he prayed, through shimmering tears, 'Please God, give her back to me. Please God, let it rain over Whitsun as well.'

the allwyne de luxe

Summer showed itself first as a single face, among thousands. Not a human face, but that of a little sailor, cast in iron, smiling down on Louis with fat, jolly cheeks almost buried under silver scratches. The sailor was a slot machine—one of the oldest at the end of the pier. In all probability he had been there since Queen Victoria's reign He wore a scratched blue tunic and scratched white trousers which showed plainly the lineaments of a plump iron bottom. In the Pavilion, he stood opposite the entrance hall, raised high on a wrought-iron stand, his stumpy legs planted wide apart, his outstretched paws offering a trial of strength at the usual fee—a penny. To win a prize, you had to force his hands together. The prize, a single toffee in a small grey cardboard box, was seldom awarded. Through the iron torso ran ancient electrical wires which, when the sailor's hands were pushed into contact, sent quite a nasty shock up the customer's arm.

Gradually, too, Louis grew conscious of the sea in summer —of its brightness and thick greenness and ripe salt smell. High tide in July and August brought it up to within inches of the pierhead, a stiff, green lawn that sucked hungrily at the

201

plank-edge, spilling its life in the form of weed and wet drift-wood and tiny, transparent crabs. Cuttlefish lay milk-white and baking all day in the sun. At that time, Louis believed cuttlefish to be living sea creatures which swam through the glassy depths, directed by the meagre frill along their spines. He did not dare to pick up even a cuttlefish. He would kick it under the rail, out over the bright green, oily-smelling sea.

In the centre of the pierhead, the sea lay in an open trough, which filled and emptied through a labyrinth of posts and iron rods and platforms and jetties under the water. This reservoir was a private sea to the Pavilion, which towered at one end of it, screening it from the estuary where railway and tramlines diverged to their separate termini. Virtually land-locked, dangerous to boats and swimmers, the trough had no purpose save to measure the tide's incessant rise and fall, and provide an anchorage for flotillas of rubbish. Its name, among pierhead employees, was the Triangle.

Along one edge of the Triangle were slot machines in a cabinet fixed above the rail. Half of these machines were Dad's: the rest belonged to Mr Naylor at the rock shop. Next to Dad's machines, a short strip of unimpeded rail continued to the Pavilion steps. If the tide were high, a tram-driver named Frank would come and lower a conical net into the Triangle, tying it to the rail while he made his journey back to the Esplanade. Louis and other boys crowded round to watch when Frank returned, untied the string, and pulled and pulled until the net came up, dripping silver with a beard of dark slime at its tip. One day, he showed them a hermit crab he had caught in the net. It was frightening, like red fingers groping from a shell. The sand that caked it was black, like soil. A bigger boy caught hold of it then, and threw it in Louis's face. He remembered his own sigh of terror to see the red claws sailing at him. The bigger boy laughed and trod on the hermit crab, rubbing it to death under the toe of his plimsoll. It died without a sound, in smears of watery blood that dried against the Pavilion steps.

On Saturdays, Louis would stand on those long wooden

steps, watching the boats bring thousands of daytrippers across from the mainland to Ryde. The boats plied ceaselessly back and forth across sea lanes that were crowded, in high summer, with big liners and tankers, with battleships and high, grey, sidelong aircraft carriers. On busiest days, to aid the modern ferry fleet, old fashioned paddle steamers, brought out of retirement, would wallow across, oddly flat and wide in the sea, with people packed along the narrow promenades and around the black and gold-cased paddle wheel. As an old ferry sidled to its berth, Louis could hear the whirl and strump of the paddle wheel in its housing, beating up the sea into furrows of hissing, scalding, snowy, blue-black foam. That was the summer noise, mixed with the jingle of bottle crates in the First and Last, the voices by the thousand, yet muted in sea air; and Dad's voice, enormous over loudspeakers, yet speaking his announcement, somehow on a note of pessimism, as if he did not expect the crowds to listen.

'We are now serving hot or cold luncheons on the sun-roof or in the restaurant, upstairs. The entrance is on the tramway station. There is no queueing and no waiting. Make certain of your meal in comfort,' his voice rather sadly advised, '—before you leave the pier.'

On Saturday mornings, they used to get to the pierhead often before eight o'clock. The car park lay dry and deserted all around as the Wolseley nosed to a stop. The Pavilion, along its whole irregular frontage, stood far inside cold continents of shadow. Around at the long front steps, above the locked doors a signboard proclaimed the new age in letters of railway green on yellow:

HARCO LTD

AMUSEMENTS   RYDE CASINO   RIFLE RANGE

Dad let in the staff and unlocked the casino, then came up to breakfast on the sun-roof. It was the one meal of the day he regularly shared with Louis and his mother, among the iron furniture and shut umbrellas, at their special reserved table. The dome, one level higher, swelled like a whale's back into the new blue sky. Like Louis, Dad seemed to enjoy these breakfasts looking out across the railing-knobs over an empty Solent, in mild sunshine, with the sea still unflawed, like silver satin, gently-stirred. The sun warmed the egg yolks and the already warm lid of the hot water jug. It was nice and calm and empty and peaceful and still.

It never lasted long enough. At five past nine, the first boat that had met a London excursion train crept round on its arc, moving in on the pierhead from the west, almost wilfully slitting open the calm water. Dad got up from the breakfast table, leaving his crossword half-done, his pipe lying sideways on its bowl. On his way across the sun-roof, often he would stop and paw the ground with his sandaled foot, attempting to level out the ragged tarmac floor, but, to Louis's eyes, seeming to indulge in a stern incantation before battle. Then he vanished through the glass doors, made dark by direct sun; his rapid footsteps died away on the stairs.

The sun-roof was situated directly above the tramway station, from which, presently, a sly rumble announced the first tram's arrival. Beside the tramway station, a pair of loudspeakers were fixed into an alcove of the Pavilion, their trumpets close to where Louis and his mother sat. With a sinking heart, now, he saw the breakfast plates lifted away, felt the slide of the gate on the platform below, saw the first untidy squadrons coming through the ticket barrier and across the car park, bearing down on his defences of peace and quiet. Inside the loudspeakers, a buzz sounded, was quelled, and Dad's voice began its catechism for the morning.

'Morning coffee and biscuits are now being served on the sun-roof or in the restaurant upstairs. The entrance is on the tramway station. There is no queueing and no waiting. Make *certain* of your meal in *comfort* before you leave the pier.'

From now on, Louis saw little of his mother. She worked in the cash desk, shut up all day inside a dark, narrow room, sitting on a stool and looking out from a window, shaped like a mousehole, into the passage between the sun roof and the Ocean Restaurant. The waitresses stood on tiptoe, putting their bills on a little shelf in front of her, and trilling out 'Cash please!'

The waitresses wore red gingham frocks, to match the tablecloths. Little starched hats, like cuttlefish, were tied among their hair with elastic. Three or four of them worked in the Ocean Restaurant, with its narrow balconied windows open to the Solent. Another three or four of them worked out on the sun-roof. Outside the doors, they stood in a row, resting on their elbows along the wall of a small hut that had the stillroom behind it. When Dad and Louis and his mother came out to their reserved table, a little stir was observable among the waitresses. Then one of them came forward, as if she had been pushed, and said, 'What would you like?', smiling down at them with the sun in her eyes.

Waitresses were nice to Louis. They let him draw on their order pads with the funny, indelible pencils they carried tied to their aprons on string. They played games with him in a waitressy way, their roles as Red Indian or Cavalier, limited by the necessity of standing in one place, breaking off the duel to bring a cheese salad or heat up a baby's bottle. Ivy, the chief waitress, who came across from Portsmouth every day, told him he was her boyfriend; she said she'd like to take him home with her at night, and Ann, her stepdaughter, gave him all her sweet coupons every month. There was something about Ann—about the way her dress went at the front—that made Louis feel nervous and excited if he saw her in the Ocean Restaurant. For some reason, he wished that Ann would call him her boyfriend and offer to take him home with her at night. He hoped she would still be here at the end of the season, when a staff party was held. Perhaps there would be hide-and-seek, and he and Ann could hide together. He pictured himself hiding with Ann in the Breadstore—in the darkness together with all the loaves and buns, and the big red slicing machine.

Here, 'upstairs', where hot or cold meals were obtainable, where sun umbrellas fluttered outside in the sea breeze and plates clicked and clashed down the long kitchen passage, Dad's summer business maintained its most sensitive battle front. Nominally, Louis's mother had command. She did the cash desk, the wages, the ordering and checking of supplies. She typed the menus, and the forms which had to be sent back, with customers' ration coupons, to the Ministry of Food. She also worked in the kitchens, as there were seldom enough staff there. When Mrs Pike got the sack for fiddling, she did all the cooking on her own. She did not get any pay for this. Once, Louis remembered, she had asked Dad for a pay packet, like the other staff. He gave it to her, but as a joke, teasing her about wanting a pay packet. Later, he stopped giving her one again.

Her willingness to do so many jobs in the business ought to have made Dad grateful to her. On the contrary, it aroused in him deep misgivings as to her competence, even her trustworthiness. Each day in the restaurants was punctuated by the frequent appearance of Dad, coming up from his own province in the main Pavilion to ascertain that all was as it should be. By using several different routes, he maintained the element of surprise. He would appear suddenly in the doorway of the Ocean Restaurant, having tiptoed up the stairs from the tramway station. He might come that way, or up the grand staircase and through the kitchens, or around the promenade balcony, where teas were sometimes served. Always, as it was as if a trapdoor had opened, projecting Dad directly to the threshold, with his head thrust forward, his jaw compressed, his eyes dilated with an angry misgiving.

He had sometimes come up like this and caught Louis playing games with the waitresses. He had taken Louis aside and told him very gravely that he must not 'worry' people when they were busy. He must not 'worry' his mother in the cash desk nor go into the kitchens and 'worry' people there. That, above all, was a forbidden region, where Mrs Truman washed up in her bloomers, hidden only by a pinafore, and where Mrs Dibbens the new cook covered great ragged cold joints with warm gravy while her daughter June stood making salads at a floury marble shelf, endlessly drawing down the little guillotine which cut one hard boiled egg into twelve equal slices.

If the cash desk were empty for a minute, Dad went inside to hunt quickly through the restaurant bills on their spikes or pull out the cash drawer to examine the money kept there in shallow wooden bowls. Louis had seen with what great reluctance, early each day, Dad handed over the canvas bag containing the 'float' for the upstairs restaurants. He would pull open the door to reveal Louis's mother sitting in her stool as if that of itself were somehow devious.

'What's the total so far, Laura?' he would say, harshly.

When she told him, he would study her face closely, just as he did if he suspected Louis of having been deceitful.

'Are you *sure*, Laura?' he would say to her. 'Are you *sure* that's right?'

By ten o'clock, Louis felt hungry again. He went inside the cash desk and climbed up to his mother's empty stool. Its green plastic dome felt warm where she had been sitting. The little low-eaved room smelled of sunshine and stale ice-cream wafers. Outside the mousehole, a waitress tapped the ledge and shouted, 'Cash please!'

He fetched his mother from the kitchen, where she had been cutting off crusts. She wore her blue man's trousers, and the pink striped blouse she had had since they lived at St Neots. Her hair was in a turban, because she had no time to get it done. Her skin was shiny, and pouches hung under her eyes. Why couldn't she look pretty, he wondered. Melody the cocker spaniel followed her into the cash desk, settling peacefully down again at the foot of the stool.

'Can I have a pencil and paper?' he asked.

'Not while Mummy's busy.'

'—Cash please!'

'When will we be having lunch?'

'Not until later.'

'When, though?'

'Not until after the two-five boat.'

'Can I have a cake now?'

'All right—just one.'

'Cash please!'

He went down the sun-roof stairs and stepped out into the tram station, adjusting his eyes to its hot, yellow, light. The rush had now subsided, for a little while. The trams had taken everybody but for a few people, left queueing up to the gate which had been bolted against them. Louis followed their anxious gaze down the open tram line, all fresh-looking with sea breezes, to the dot of its far perspective where, in a few minutes, the tram's green front would slowly reappear. He wondered which tram of the two would come back next, and whether anything about his life today, or his far destiny, might be determined by his ability to forecast correctly which tram it would be. It might be Frank's tram, with the little white dog aboard which growled, if you tried to stroke it, like the tram's own rolling, rumbling noise. And Peter, the tramboy—or was his name Charley?—wearing a money satchel and his two silver cap guns in a ruby-studded belt.

The main hall into the Pavilion was cool and dark. One wide swing door, pinioned inward, did little to dispel the window-less winter Sunday gloom. It was almost as if Dad had striven to make this way into the Pavilion, under its low, barn-like portico as enigmatic and uninviting as possible. A few machines were fixed along the left-hand wall—games of skill, abstruse in execution, which Louis did not glance at as he passed. Below the grand staircase—which only kitchen staff now used—stood, on its pedestal, the queerest machine of all; the one which, Dad said, had been built by Polish prisoners-of-war. It was one of those machines in which you inserted a penny to watch a scene enacted by mechanical figures. Inside the cabinet glass was a castle, the gates of which parted to show black-caped policemen mounting guard over a man on a gallows. Deeper inside the castle, within a scarlet tinfoil inferno, watched by two more guards, a grinning but troubled figure crouched on what seemed to be a chamberpot. There was even a number-two, made of paper, hanging from his bottom by a thread.

208

Through the partition-doors, the iron sailor's outstretched arms welcomed the visitor into the main Pavilion. Louis stood on the threshold, uncertain which way to walk. There were so many possible avenues.

Machines now covered the whole Pavilion floor. That wide, wheeling space, that enormous rink of last winter, had disappeared under cabinets of every size, under legs by the hundred, fashioned of vinous wrought-iron, of gaudily-painted wood. The machines were laid out like a city, in double rows, parallel and intersecting. Punch-balls and pin-table score-boards were the spires of this city, its sky the empty dome which, from a remote stained glass freize, dwindling high in shadow, cast down over all the hoods and cowls and curly crests, a pale, dusty, yellowish light. The noise of the pierhead seemed far away, despite many wide-open doors. Customers, never numerous, moved unseen through the avenues, their presence betrayed by certain small, tentative sounds. You might hear the 'tick-tick' of a ball wandering slowly down some pin-table path; the bang of a punchball against its glass dial; the almost inaudible splash as a penny dropped.

Along the left-hand wall, in a bright red and yellow rifle range, Wilf stood, framed by a background of cut glass vases and twopenny sticks of rock. You got three shots for sixpence, using a weapon described, by the noticeboard above Wilf's head, as 'Genuine Remington .22 Precision Rifles.' The three shots taken, smoothing his fingers back through his flattened hair, Wilf brought the target to the counter to see the score, extract the little silk-topped darts with his pliers and, where appropriate, hand over a cut glass vase or stick of rock. At intervals, he retired to an adjacent cash-desk: in its window, his hand appeared, pushing towards the customer a sixpenny or shilling pile of pennies, between finger and thumb, very cautiously as if he were disposing of a wasp. If any fault were reported to him, he leaned forward among the airguns to listen, or else stood back near the targets, slowly scratching his head. Then, covering his open till, he left the rifle range and came out around the change desk to look for Dad.

Dad was to be found across the floor, past the juke-box and its suspended arrow, at the top of the staircase to what had once been a dressing-room beside the stage. Where pierrots had once donned their frills and greasepaint, Dad now kept the safe, and his roll-top desk, and the keys and identity-tags to hundreds of slot machines, hanging behind the door in two long, tarnished chains. Here also, in what he now styled 'The Amplifier Room', Dad broadcast his announcement over the pierhead. To interrupt him at this task was no small matter, as Wilf plainly indicated, hesitating outside on the stairs for several minutes until Dad had completed the bulletin of the moment. Then the door brusquely shut and opened again, and Dad came out holding one of the big key-chains. On the wall by the stairs, a painted Scotsman, eight feet high, grimaced lewdly and waved his whisky bottle, his gingery knees and roller-skates barely clearing the top of a machine called 'The Copper Mine'. Further along the wall, and behind the stage, the Welsh lady, the circus clown, the Zulu and Red Indian chief still cavorted on slapdash skate-wheels as Mr Boynton, the signwriter, had painted them.

Nobody had told Louis there would be slot machines at the Pavilion. He knew nothing until the day he arrived to discover them massed in their city underneath the dome. His first thought was that Dad had done it all for him. He wanted to run through the avenues, jumping and shouting, putting hundreds of pennies in.

That day, he exchanged a whole half-crown for pennies. The brown pillar of them filled up his hand, growing warmer, shorter, dwindling down through outposts of optimism—'Well, I've still got ninepence left.' 'I've got fourpence left, anyway.' The last penny vanished into an Allwyne de Luxe—the red-and-yellow striped one, long before he had discovered what an unlucky machine it was.

He went across to the Amplifier Room, and up the stairs. He did not know any better then than to say what was in his head. He looked round the door at Dad, who was standing at his microphone, staring out of the window, across the Triangle,

210

towards the main ferry berth. Dad's lips were close enough to the microphone to kiss. His eyes looked sad, as if he expected some tragedy to arrive with the eleven five boat.

'Dad—I put a penny in a machine on the other side, and it didn't work.'

He remembered the pause as Dad's face looked down at him, like the pause in the machine itself after his lost penny had dropped.

'These machines aren't put here for *your* benefit, Louis,' Dad said coldly. Then, pushing down a switch on the cabinet, so that a red light glimmered on, slowly and carefully into the microphone Dad said: 'We are now serving morning coffee and biscuits on the sun-roof or in the restaurant upstairs. The entrance is on the tramway station.'

'Old son—' he said, speaking to Louis again. 'This is a place of *business*. It's not somewhere for you to come and have a game. This is a place of *business*, Louis.'

Certainly, it was a serious matter when Dad, holding the long key chain that was like a dull fleece, its tarnished jingle echoing his rapid and irritated footsteps, came down the avenue towards the broken machine, where Wilf and the complainant together stood guard. They watched, and Louis did, as Dad, by a process known only to himself, selected the right key, from the numbered disc attached to it, and then—if this were a cabinet machine, like the Allwyne de Luxe,—opened it from the front, swinging out its glassed-over façade to reveal the mechanism glued on behind, and the cabinet empty but for some pennies lying on the floor in a shallow tin.

Dad's omniscience about slot machines was something people took for granted, the natural extension of cars and aeroplanes and guns and roller-skates. Any machine that was defective, he approached in equal certainty, with the key-fleece and swishing oilcan, and the little screwdriver that went, angrily, 'Click-click-click'. While mending the machine, he would play it continuously, but without pleasure, shooting the ball round its spiral while he studied the consequences internally, then making it drop out again for play—sometimes winning, so that the ball re-

211

turned by itself, and a penny appeared, to Louis's wild excitement, slyly, like a brown tongue in its brass tray. But Dad showed no excitement; he put the penny in again calmly and shot it, with his eyes frowning behind the machine-door, twisting his screw-driver with a click-click-click. As skilful as Dad was, he could not keep pace with every fault that occurred. Many machines, in a corner of their front glass, had a scrap of cigarette packet with OUT OF SERVICE printed on it in Dad's writing, as though they were aeroplanes temporarily unable to fly. One such notice remained stuck in the glass of a crane-grab, in which liquorice comfits were packed around stray half-crowns, for so many summers that the liquorice comfits lost their colours, becoming a uniform, bird's egg green.

'The Boxers' stood inside a pale wooden cabinet with windows to a three-sided prize-ring. Louis stopped and looked through the glass at them, sparring motionless before a crowd that was like an oil painting of people in a theatre. He had witnessed many bouts between the two sleek-headed antagonists, threshing forward wildly at each other from the iron rods that held them upright. He stood and thumbed the levers, set into the front of the cabinet, which raised each boxer's iron gloves in ineffectual defence. 'The Boxers', too, was a very old machine, though the little knitted jerseys, one blue, one red, had evidently been given to the pugilists at some recent date. The scene behind fascinated Louis, with its smoky dimness, its wide balcony and the glimmer of many white shirt-fronts. He thought it would be nice to be sitting up there, in the fragrance of brandy and cigars. People in paintings had no worries.

Other figures waited in the darkness of little rooms for the penny that would bring them light and life. In 'Sweeney Todd', Louis could see the outline of the trapdoor through which the barber's chair would fall and the man who waited round a corner to appear with a tray labelled 'Hot Pies'. In 'Bedroom Scene', the little night-shirted father stood ready to rock the baby in his arms and the muslin-draped cradle with

212

his feet, while his wife lay in her bed, her lacy bosom poised to twitch up and down. In 'The Uninvited', the miser sat at his table, which was stacked with bars of gold. Behind him in the galleried room, Louis could see bits of the ghosts and skeletons that would come out when the penny dropped. He could see a ghost in the chimney, in the linen-chest and grandfather clock, the skull in the chimney, the caped skull that flew up under the gallery floor. He could see his own face, like some extra, unscheduled ghost, reflected in the dark glass.

At the end of the next avenue, he stopped and stood still and listened. He had reached the Pavilion's innermost corner, at the far right of the stage, where Mr Boynton's freize concluded in a roller-skating Zulu. Only with some effort was this part of the Pavilion recognisable to Louis as the scene of his earliest skating lessons. The floor, under machine-legs, was etched with skid-marks; a balcony post still wore its protective green canvas jacket. He remembered when he had struggled with Phyllis the barmaid, up and down the vanished beginners' bars. Through the windows, the Pavilion's domed shadow darkened the sea which, further out, sparkled with sunny silver darts.

His wanderings, so carefully aimless, had brought him to the place where the windows stopped, and smaller cabinet machines hung bolted in a row along the wall. Each one had a name, suggesting some climax in slot-machine invention, inscribed within a wooden crest, in scarlet letters on mirrored glass. There was 'The Caley'; 'The Allwyne', and its indistinguish-able, but evidently superior, neighbour, 'The Allwyne de Luxe'. In each case, the principle was the same. You shot a silver ball around a coloured spiral on to a row of shallow cups. The dark-shaded cup at either end was the loser. If the ball entered any other cup, you received your penny back, and a free play.

These were machines in which Louis frequently invested. Unequipped for games of skill or the simplest manipulation, he could delude himself he had acquired some special knack

in bending the lever to launch the ball—some secret force of
will to guide it in its spiral, smacking round and round. For
him, in addition, there was the question of which machine
might intrinsically be a harbinger of good luck—absent from
the Allwyne, whose façade was red and yellow in a sunrise
pattern, but recurrently present in the Allwyne de Luxe, whose
plain yellow façade glittered like sherbet crystals. As Louis
moved in front of this machine, he had the strangest feeling
that it was alive, and capable of sensing the reverence he
felt for it. Twisting the *Coin Return* handle, he whispered
to himself, 'There's nothing there,' attempting to bluff God
as usual. Yet, for all his guilty excitement, somehow he felt
no surprise as the handle gave in his palm, and a penny,
abandoned by the last player, poked itself slyly into the
brass tray.

He put the penny back in quickly: at the bottom of the
spiral, a silver ball dropped out of a hole. His thumb bent
down the sprung lever that pulled the hammer back—he held
it there a moment longer, knowing the wrongness of what he
was about to do. From either end of the avenue, from the
avenue adjoining, he fancied he could hear footsteps, soft and
condemning, and the click of a long key-chain. The very
machine seemed to rebuke him with its brassbound injunction
For Amusement Only, its title, etched on mirror, a corroboration
of what Dad had impressed on him so many times about summer's formal and serious purpose. He shut his eyes, let go of
the hammer and, with eyes tight shut, whispered:

'It's lost. I know it's lost. It's no good . . . I assure you. I
assure you.'

He had won. He knew it before the racketing ball had lost
momentum and fallen on the row of cups, bouncing on the
metal rods between them, nervously to and fro, settling for
one terrible instant on the dark end-cup but then freeing itself to vanish into a plain winning cup near the middle. The
Coin Return handle yielded voluptuously in his palm, returning
the ball, and a penny to the tray. It was a different penny,
old and black, worn flat, and clouded with Queen Victoria's

face. Its coldness matched the chill of having committed theft from Dad. He hid it quickly to warm inside his trousers-pocket.

Walking outside a few minutes later, he sighted Dad half-way along the avenue where the juke-box stood, engaged with Wilf in the periodic emptying operation. Dad unlocked each machine in turn and removed the money-tin, or else he simply pulled out the loose pennies with his hands, spattering them into the ice-cream tin that Wilf held up. Seeing them, Louis made his legs swerve off quickly to the left, with one hand in his pocket to quiet the three misappropriated pennies which now lay there.

'Here, old son.'

It was Dad, coming after him.

I haven't done anything—don't blame me. I haven't been playing the machines. I promise.

'Here you are, old son. Go and have a game with these if you want to.'

Louis looked at the pennies, mixed with a few brass tokens, which Dad had poured into his outstretched hand. He said, 'Thanks, Dad,' feebly as Dad walked off up the avenue to rejoin Wilf, and he himself wandered out through the main doors, past 'The Automatic Palmist', in which a gipsy's torso, inside her curtained glass cabinet, waited to trace a fortune with the penholder between her chipped but elegant fingers.

The main rush stopped at about half-past two. Then Louis was allowed to have his lunch, up on the sun roof, alone at their reserved table. His lunch was the same every Saturday and every Sunday. He had salad with luncheon meat and mashed potato served from an ice-cream scoop, and Neapolitan ice with two wafers in a long green sundae dish. The day trippers had all arrived now, settling like bees on the shoreline half a mile away, filling the cafés and open door pubs, massing in a winged glitter along the beach. The ferries stood hove-to in the Solent, waiting for the homeward queues that would soon

215

begin to collect. During July and August, the queue in the evening often stretched from the ferry berth, round the edge of the pierhead and all the way down the planks to the Esplanade.

'Afternoon teas and high teas are now being served on the sun-roof or in the restaurant upstairs,' Dad's voice boomed patiently from the loudspeakers. 'The entrance is on the tramway station. Make *certain* of your meal in comfort before you leave the pier.'

For Louis, these afternoon tea and high tea hours, just after his own lunch, were the longest of the day. The pierhead grew empty but for occasional baggage-trucks, or a car out of season, crossing from the planks across the metal stud with a loud 'belp!' noise. The First and Last had closed its doors on the dozens of brown bottles left standing outside like sentries. It was quiet, but for Dad's voice, and the sea wind blustering in deckchair backs, rattling the stiff blind of the rock shop across the square. Even the trams seemed to die away. There was nothing to do but follow his own shadow wherever it chanced to stray over the baking concrete.

There were fishermen round the edge of the pierhead, stationed between its thick grey wooden posts. They did not seem to care if it was the busy season. They arrived just the same on their slow bicycles, guiding the front wheel clear of the crack along the planks. Their rods, balanced on small iron capstans, curved out to nothingness over the high green sea. Some wore little bells that glistened in mid-air. Their worms, dug up at low tide, lay in Oxo tins or nests of ragged newspaper. He peeped with disgust at the fat, shiny shapes that were dark brown or flesh pink, still alive and feebly writhing. He refrained, with some effort, from asking the fishermen if they had caught anything yet. For some reason, they didn't like it.

He lay down on a stone staircase that descended to lower ship berths. No big ferries docked on this shoreward side; only pleasure craft or, sometimes, a Naval launch. The stairs were concrete but somehow soft, like powdery sand made solid.
216

Below him he could see bright water, barred with the staircase shadow, where thousands of tiny fish swirled and flickered close beneath the surface. Through the sunlit depths were other levels, descending lower and lower, to the treacherous platform which revealed itself only at very low water. He was not supposed to go down there, but he had, several times, with Terry his cousin and some other boys. He had stood on barnacle-encrusted concrete bars, so slippery with silk slime that they seemed to move under his feet. The water that sucked between the bars was black. Transverse girders, draped with slime, stretched out across the black water in pathways to a dim death, through the ghost-grey forest of pier legs, where streams of water tumbled down from various public toilets.

Some bigger boys were swimming off the pier. Their clothes lay on the steps near Louis. They were only low class, yet some, he noticed, had underwear whiter than his. The tide was at its highest now: from that sunken berth, the bigger boys had only to step off a beam-edge to crash among the thick, green water, sending up splinters of white foam. Their pale bodies travelled underwater for a frightening long time— then, skirling their wet hair off their foreheads and sniffing huge sniffs, they stood up in the water and shouted at each other, their pale knees holding them there as on some invisible platform. They were swimming from the pierhead, across to the landing-stage where Captain House's pleasure launches tied up. As one of them climbed back on to the jetty, Louis saw a streak of bright blood down his leg. He must have cut himself on a sharp stump in the water.

The sun on his hot hair, the noise of the sea splintering and crashing as the big boys dived, brought about in Louis a sudden, surging, chilling wave of shame. He pushed his face further down between the warm steps and shut his eyes, to try to escape even the summer sound. He was eight and a half already, and still not able to swim.

At Partlands, Miss Stella, to teach them about tenses, wrote a summary sentence on the board. A pink strap had slipped

217

down across the arm-hole of her blouse. She wrote: 'I will go swimming after school today.' Turning to the class, she said: 'Hands up the people who *are* going swimming after school.' Bare arms arose with a rustle. Brown arms from short sleeves, straining proudly aloft. Everybody's. Even Julia Carter, the silliest girl, taunted at breaktime by the universal cry:

> Julia Carter
> Get in the larder!

even Julia Carter lived at Seaview, where you could dive from the rocks. 'Louis Belmayne! Is your hand properly up?' The class looked at him. Janice Bennett looked. 'Yes, Miss.' Summer brought, with the chill of insufficiency, the worse chill of telling Miss Stella a fib.

He had not lacked opportunity to learn. He had been taken on the Eastern beach with his cousins, when all Auntie Rita's brothers and sisters were down in Ryde, protecting her from Uncle Cal. Various half-uncles had offered to teach him, holding him around the middle while he moved his legs and arms. Sooner or later, the same thing always happened. A wave washed up his nose, scalding the back of his throat with a phlegmy saltiness that made him retch and cough. He had sometimes been sick on top of the sea. It looked horrible, floating there. So now, he just pretended. He moved through the shallows, kicking up a fine wake, while his arms groped guiltily, one by one, for the cloudy sand along the bottom.

'Afternoon teas and high teas,' Dad's voice continued, 'are *still* being served on the sun-roof or in the restaurant upstairs. There is no queueing', he insisted wearily, '—and no waiting. The entrance is on the tramway station, Make *certain* of your meal in comfort before you leave the pier.'

The four o'clock boat came in almost empty. A Red Funnel steamer from Southampton was also at its westward berth. The tram went off, carrying no one but the tramboy. A few

218

minutes later Louis saw his mother walking across the pierhead from the tram station. She was carrying a packet of cigarettes and a rolled-up towel. He pretended not to see her, but she knew he had, and called him by pointing angrily at her own shoe. He showed himself from the staircase where he had been lying. He walked towards her, following his reluctant shadow.

'Come on—we're going to the Rowing Club,' she said.

Steadying him by one arm, she produced a handkerchief, spat on an end of it and began to rub violently with it at the side of his face.

'Stand *still*, will you!' she sighed. 'Awkward little hound!'

The same words formed in Louis's mind as always: 'Don't blame me.'

'Have we got to?' he asked.

'Yes *you* have!' She spoke tonelessly, peering into his face, and yet not at him. Then she spat on the handkerchief again. It was less a wash, more a convulsive attempt to alter his features before he was fit to show to company.

'I'd like to stay here.'

'It's *nice* at the Rowing Club. You can go swimming off the slipway.'

They walked, with Melody, a little distance back along the pier, towards the pair of round-roofed green huts standing out from the walkway on stilts, with a long, crooked slipway between them. The hut nearest the shore belonged to a deep sea fishing club, whose members ventured in rowing boats out to the Solent forts, bringing back huge, shark-like fish that sometimes needed two men to carry them. The other hut belonged to Ryde Rowing Club: one of Dad's discoveries, for purposes other than aquatic. Deep inside the hut there was a little bar which, at weekends, stayed open all afternoon.

Louis and his mother went down some steps between the two huts, to a plank platform littered with overturned dinghies and fishing nets spread to dry. The entrance to the Rowing Club was a small door set into a bigger sliding one that was opened only when a boat had to be launched. Inside it was suddenly dark. They had to feel their way among the shapes

219

of boats which lay on the floor—and also hung from the rafters, side-by-side with long, shining oars. Louis heard Melody sniffing about among the boats, and a sigh of anger as his mother bumped herself on something. There was a smell of varnish and mould and gym shoes, and he could hear the water lapping close under the floorboards. In a moment, the bar appeared, shining faintly among the dark boats.

Dad was already there, in conversation with a man he called 'Old Pussy Inman', standing at the small counter where all sorts of people went behind to serve. Even this dimly-lit and dishclothy, faintly-damp recess held the taboo of all bars where Louis was concerned, his very approach provoking splut-tered cries of warning. Law and the Secretary would be satisfied if he sat half in the shadows, on the edge of an unsteady skiff. As usual, it was Dad who seemed most to regret this banish-ment. Dad came over to him at once with a bag of crisps and a mineral bottle with two straws hovering high in the neck. He looked down at Louis with a sympathetic smile, hiding the bottle behind his back. ' 'Want a cream soda?' he said, and smiled, broadly, affectionately, divining in Louis yet again some predictable and therefore lovable, quality.

Louis soon grew tired of sitting there. His crisps were not Smith's—they were Tony's, a local substitute, his first packet of which yielded only two wide, flabby, under-cooked crisps and one cindery fragment. His taste for cream soda had been widely exaggerated. Yet all the time, he felt an excitement as groundless as the boat-edge where he sat—a suspicion that Dad at the bar was advancing some plan for him; a scheme for his life as a grown-up, or some glorious, unimaginable treat. The same expectation was discernible in the other people, listening so avidly to Dad's stories that they seemed almost mesmerised—their hands, in particular, moving slowly towards their pockets when the till rang up. Dad re-strained them, kindly but firmly, by the forearm, and himself turned to pay for all the drinks again.

He *was* making plans for Louis. To the man who had gone behind the bar, Louis heard Dad say:

'Tom, old son: do one thing for me. I'd like you to bzz bzz my young son and heir. Bzz bzz. Can I ask you to do that thing for me?'

The man, who wore a white polo neck like a crown that had slipped too far down his head, looked across at Louis with no shred of fondness or recognition.

'Sure—any time,' he replied flatly. 'Just send him along; we'll fix him up.'

'Pussy!' Dad said, performing a grave little bow. 'Thank you for those words. What are you going to have?'

His mother, bringing Louis a second cream soda, whispered:

'What do you think! Daddy's going to make you a member of the Rowing Club!'

Horrified visions danced before his eyes of the boats he had seen launched from the Rowing Club in the evening. Grown-up men with long, pale, prickly legs. And bigger boys, their unkind faces spotted with freckles.

'But I can't row in boats,' he whispered.

'Daddy wants you to join. You'll be the cox. You sit in the boat and say "in out, in out".'

Along the outer edge of the clubhouse ran a narrow veran-dah like the boat-deck of a ship, with lifebelts tied to the rail and the skeleton of an overhead awning. People sat out sun-bathing all along here, in upright canvas chairs. Sweating, smiling faces turned towards Louis and his mother as they emerged. He recognised Mr Russell, who took Dad shooting on winter Sundays, and his wife Peggy, who always seemed to be recovering from an operation. Their eyes were behind sunglasses full of the sky's glare. They said 'Hello' in lazy, sweaty, glistening voices. Their twin skies left Louis and his mother, and moved to the man who had walked to the tip of a diving-board, extending from the verandah rail. He put his hands together—he was gone, with a fountainous splash that sprinkled the verandah with black spots.

For Louis there was no escape. His mother sat down in a canvas chair, pulling him roughly towards her. His yellow

221

'Chilprufe' vest, then his white school shirt, were forced over his head. He sank his chin down, trying to trap the shirt-neck, to seek refuge in the warm, white folds. His disrobing became a testy little pantomime for the amusement of John and Peggy Russell: she made him take off his spectacles, his khaki shorts and socks, leaving only his sandals and the red woolly trunks he had been wearing all the time. The rough, hot insides of the sandals stuck to his bare feet, and he could feel unemptied sand grating between his toes. She freed him at last, with an exasperated little push. The fresh breeze settled round his shoulders, making him cross his arms in horror over his little white ribs. There was a draught on his nose and behind his ears where the spectacles had been.

He glimpsed himself, reflected in the sunglasses of Peggy Russell. She was showing her legs, but it wasn't nice. Big bare legs from a pushed-back print frock. She had once showed his mother the stitches from her operation. Her sunglasses tilted to inspect Louis above a make-you-look-silly smile.

'Oh, Lou—you *do* look a sorrowful Jones. Cheer up, old bean. You're looking proper poorly.'

'Is he?' Mr Russell said. 'Are you, Lou? Are you proper poorly?'

His mother was patting cream along her arm talking to Peggy Russell. In a few moments, Louis was able to back away, into the shade of the boathouse where he generally awaited the end of these ordeals. Hiding from summer, in the corrugated shadow, he watched the figures who could sport without fear—the bodies splashing down at the slipway end, the heads that bobbed and glinted further out to sea. Some Pedalo boats had daringly approached the pierhead, with two people each in them sitting nervously upright behind their four pumping knees. Behind them, the Western beach sparkled under the crowds. He could see the wet smear of the walkway put out over the sea for speedboat rides. Every so often, somebody would dive from the board, showering the verandah near his feet. He shrank back into his cold lair, shut his eyes tight, and thought about winter. He thought of feather beds and hot-

222

water bottles at Nanny Belmayne's, with a warm pink flannel cover; of gas fires shining upward on the picture of Jesus. He thought of Nanny Belmayne herself as she came up to bed, slowly climbing the stairs: one at a time, sighing deeply with every creak.

A few minutes later, Dad came out to the verandah for a swim. He kept a pair of trunks always at the Pavilion, in a file drawer in the Amplifier Room, and swam off the pier whenever he could—sometimes late at night, so Louis had heard, with Olwen and Jack and a crowd of other people; and sometimes without any bathing costume at all.

His trunks were not like the ones Louis had to wear. They were dark blue with a white belt and, embroidered on one thigh, a little emblem of a diver—a badge, perhaps, for diving from brave heights. The black hair that matted his chest was fluffed and curled tight from the warmth of his clothes. But his legs were slender and white, and his shoulders white and pale, almost like a lady's. Standing up on the diving-board, he looked so big and strong that Louis shrank back into the shadows, ashamed of his own fair hair and little puny limbs, and because Dad always knew when he was being deceitful, and Dad never wore any pyjamas in bed.

After the splash, he went to the rail and looked down into the water.

Dad had surfaced a few yards beyond the shadow of the diving-board. He was standing upright in the water, pushing back his widow's peak with both hands, his knees shimmering white among the sea green, as he coughed with blown-out cheeks the way he sometimes did early in the morning. 'Buffalo!' his cough went. 'Buffalo!' Then he looked up to the verandah and caught Louis's eye. He rested his arms on top of the water, as if arranging it like a green counterpane around himself. He smiled up at Louis, and went 'buffalo!' again into his cupped hands. He shouted:

'Jump in!'

That must be a joke. Louis tried to laugh loudly and obviously enough for Dad to notice.

'Pardon, Dad?'

'You jump in, too,' Dad shouted up from the sea. 'Learn to swim.'

'I can't, Dad.'

'Yes you can. Jump in: I'll catch you.'

He looked round for his mother, but she had gone inside the boathouse. Only sunglasses watched him, full of indifferent blue sky.

He looked over the rail again at Dad's head, at Dad's hairy chest, at Dad's knees moving gently in the deep water.

'I—can't, Dad.'

'*Yes,* you can,' Dad shouted. 'Just get on the board and jump in. It's easy. I'll catch you. Learn to swim—it's the only way. Come on!'

This, perhaps, was how you died. You just set off like this from the midst of life, and nobody noticed. As Louis knelt up on the diving board, which was covered with a rough, stringy netting, he saw no flicker of change in the sunglasses that studied him. On the pier behind the boathouse, the world carried on as usual. A tram arrived; footsteps on the plankway pattered to and fro. Everything as before, but for him, standing up straight on the diving board with a cool breeze among his ribs—now walking out from the rail, across the sea. Here he stood in space, although he knew he couldn't do it. His shadow stood below him on the sea, at the end of the diving board shadow. Even in the instant before he jumped—and a man's voice said 'He's still got his shoes on!'—Louis found an instant to wish that his shadow belonged to another person.

How bright the sea is underneath. He can study it with wide-open eyes. He sees a greenness like wet, green grapes, and strips of pale weed hanging down through the water that sway and flicker as at the prompting of a gentle breeze. He watches these twisting, flickering strips with pleasure and disinterest. He does not remember his fall, nor the splintering crash with which he fell through the sea's surface. He remembers nothing of his existence before that vanished moment.

224

For as long as he can remember, he has been here, anchored wide-eyed before this grape-green window of a world.

There is paler green above him, where the sun shines. He tries to climb towards it, with legs and arms that move on their own, climbing higher with his legs and arms while his body sinks down, further and further, towards the bottom.

Oh well—it doesn't matter. Nothing really matters . . .

Just when he is about to touch the sea-bed, his head pops suddenly up through the surface.

His first feeling is of mild astonishment. He has not been drowned after all—how nice! He is surprised to discover how far he is from the Rowing Club and how close he has surfaced to the pier's legs—so close, he can look up and see shadows of people and cars. He can hear the squashy sound a car tyre makes, and the bouncy noise of footsteps walking overhead. All is somehow just as he imagined it would be if he looked up at the pier from the sea while he was drowning.

Somebody near him is shouting very loudly. No: somebody *inside* him is shouting very loudly. He is shouting loudly and gasping and shrieking because not one single breath inhabits his body.

'It's all right—I've got you.'

Dad is there, holding him up out of the water and saying:

'I've got you. I've *got* you. Now, swim! Swim!'

Dad's arms are round him. Underwater, he can feel Dad's legs around him, pulling him close to that wet, black, curly chest. Recoiling, he tries to touch the sea-bed with his foot. His leg, and then his face, sink down through layers of choking green.

His head comes up again, shouting. Dad's arms and legs are all coiled round him. Dad's voice says:

'Don't panic. Don't *panic*.'

'I . . . I . . .'

'Swim!'

'I . . . I can't. I . . .'

'Yes you can. I've got you. Now, swim!'

But he isn't. He can't. He is only carried by Dad through

225

the water, keeping his limbs still for fear of touching Dad again. The slipway breaks the surface a few yards away, sloping out of blackish water. He feels his foot stumble on a slippery edge. Dad's legs and arms release him. He is standing, in his sandals in shallow water.

'Sorry, Dad. Sorry, Dad,' he gasped.

Sorry, Dad. Sorry.

He stood down on the slipway later, feeling like something that had shrunken in the wash. Dad came down the slope towards him, dressed again, with a towel under one arm.

He expected to be told off about the sandals. But Dad, looking severely at him, said:

'You had pluck to jump in like that when I told you. That was plucky of you, old son. You're a real Englishman, Louis. I'm proud of you.'

close friends of the family

That summer, apart from Ryde Casino, Dad opened an outdoor skating rink. It was in the old band enclosure on the Western, next to the pier entrance, where the beach lay drifted in several small crescents around a low peninsula of public gardens and sea wall. The sand in these crescents, unwashed by the sea, was pale and granular and, as such preferred by holiday-makers to the wide, clean beaches east of the pier. Seen from afar, at high tide on a July afternoon, the Western resembled an overloaded raft, with its dunes swamped under deck-chairs and children, its margins aglitter with hundreds of bobbing heads. On that small, teeming curve of shore were to be found the Pedalo and speedboat rides, the Punch and Judy, the sellers of almanacs and plastic windmills and the old man in white who sang at the same time as playing a violin. Low tide brought out, in their turn, the embroiderers of seashells, the professional sandcastle-builders and Eade's ponies and donkeys, massed at the end of a concrete sewer-pipe.

The band enclosure, in the gardens above, had not been in use for several seasons. When Louis first came to Ryde, it

227

used to be filled with deck-chairs, and a concert party gave daily performances on the high-canopied stage. He and his two cousins would go every afternoon to watch the company—unaccountably called 'boys and girls'—who sang and danced, together or singly, to the accompaniment of one striving open-air piano. A man in sandals, with an air of ferocious boredom made flowers snap out of nothing; and a lady who showed her legs sang 'You Made Me Love You', pointing at Louis with such insistence that he supposed he *must* have made her love him. Reciprocating her love, he nerved himself one afternoon to accept the bored man's invitation to anyone who wanted to get up on the stage and sing. His chosen refrain—as on all such occasions—was 'The Teddy Bears' Picnic'. For a (consolation) prize, the compère asked him if he liked rock, then made a joke of the answer Louis attempted to give. ' "Yes thank you—No!" I've never heard that one before, have you, ladies and gentlemen? "Yes thank you—No!" ' His heart still swooned from the shame of it.

Louis did not know Dad had acquired the band enclosure: not until that day he rode in the van down the pier, sitting in the back among a cargo of skates from the Pavilion store. At the foot of Union Street, the van, unprecedentedly, mounted the pavement and made its way into the Western Gardens. Louis, in the back, felt wild excitement at this calm flouting of byelaws which prominently forbade even cycle-riding here. When Dad stopped next to the enclosure, opened the van doors, and he and Wilf gathered up an armful of skates each, he still did not feel it necessary to take Louis into his confidence. They carried the skates across the empty oval arena, to the right-hand corner of the stage, through a door marked 'Musicians Only', and stacked them in a stone-walled room, against a short flight of stairs that led up to the stage.

'What *are* you doing, Dad—'

'Nothing, Louis,' Dad replied evenly as he received more skates from Wilf and packed them with wheels interlocked close against the stairs.

*   *   *

228

The new rink opened at Whitsun, on a warm, grey evening which brought further proof of Dad's influence in the larger spheres of public entertainment.

Opening night was auspicious—as Dad's opening nights always were—with crowds all over the rink, and many more spectators than had paid sixpence for the privilege, looking in through the long windows on the beach side. Congas and rumbas and 'The Skaters' Waltz' played faintly over loud-speakers in little boxes set around the ornate iron verandah roof; at intervals, Dad's voice broke in, with patience exhorting skaters to move all in the same direction, proclaiming items of lost property, or vouchsafing, in his formal idiom, that light refreshments could be 'obtained' or were 'obtainable' from the snack bar at the entrance.

Louis was there, up thrillingly late in his long trousers and Hopalong Cassidy shirt. After one or two unsteady circuits, he found he could still skate as well and as fast as ever, although skating on concrete felt strange at first, as if the hard ground were rubbing his wheels away. The rink was as large as the Pavilion but its oval shape imposed more restrictions. After getting up a good speed down the side, you had to brake for the sharp turn past the stage. And going backwards was hazardous. You could catch your wheels easily in a sort of gutter around the edge.

'Ladies and gentlemen—' Dad's voice again interjected, 'will you clear the rink now? Ladies and gentlemen, will you clear the rink, *please?*'

Reluctantly the skaters drained away to the seats around the pavement edge Louis, as mystified as anybody, sat under a handrail with his skate wheels in the gutter. Nearby on this side was the little glassed-in announcement box where Dad, in his leather shooting over-jacket, stood by the gramophone and amplifier. Louis could read no clue in the sad eyes that looked out, above the microphone in Dad's hand.

'Ladies and gentlemen', his voice around the enclosure continued, 'we now proudly present, for your pleasure, high speed action and thrills, but no spills, with those stars of

H*

229

Stage, Screen and Bertram Mills' Circus—Jimmy and Jo: the Skating Sinclairs!'

To Louis's surprise, it was his mother, not Dad, who largely ran the outdoor skating rink. At six o'clock, after cashing up at the Ocean Restaurant, she would ride down the pier on an old bicycle she had bought, to take over from Wilf, who managed by himself during the afternoon. At the evening session they looked after, between them, the ticket office, the snack bar, the issue of skates and the gramophone records. Dad's arrival, on many evenings, was delayed until almost dark, when the time came to reckon up the takings.

Possibly it was this unwonted independence which made Louis notice how happy his mother seemed in this period. The Western at night seemed to dispel the fatigue and irritation of her pierhead day and bring back some of the prettiness he so wished to see in her. At the rink she wore a pair of dark blue slacks with a chalk stripe and—as it grew chilly—her camel hair coat, the one Louis liked so much with its belt and brown silk lining. The coat, though far from new, fostered a hope that it might form the *basis* of new clothes; that her life at last had begun to turn back towards the way it was in the time of 'We'll Gather Lilacs', when she and Dad used to be friends of Ivor Novello.

For him, these evenings with Dad away were pleasant, lenient and long-trousered. When he grew tired of skating, there was the Western outside, which he roamed now with an air of proprietorship. It seemed to him that Dad, with unceasing enterprise, was gradually assuming control of every major public site on or around the pier. Looking inshore from the Western, Louis felt it would not be long before Dad controlled Arcadia, the big rival slot machine place; the Royal Esplanade Hotel and the Marine; the Maypole and Dinelli's Café and the Ash Tree Restaurant; even that big place no one seemed to want, at the bottom of Union Street, with windows full of nothing but dust and sun-bleached chocolate box dummies.

230

He grew to know the gardens that spread from the pier, out behind the guest-houses of St Thomas's Street; and the beach below, with its pale, soft, unwashed sand. When the beach was deserted at evening, the sand grew cold and dank, its loose grains yielding up mummified dogs' mess to the most casually-digging fingers. Boys who lived around the Esplanade came down through the gardens then, to play raucous, lower-class, stone-throwing games next to the pier legs. One of them told Louis that, if you stood under the pier while a tram was starting out, you died of an electric shock. He was allowed to accompany them along the donkey tracks, around to the other beach, shut in on its western side by the Royal Victoria Yacht Club. The boys climbed the stone slipway and ran along the wall, where ancient black cannons pointed out to sea; but Louis did not dare to follow. Some premonition warned him there might be dead people at the Royal Victoria Yacht Club.

A spatter of applause from the band enclosure took him back there, although he was by now profoundly unexcited by the Skating Sinclairs. Jimmy Sinclair, a man like a film star, in a tight grey bullfighter suit, merely picked up his sister Jo and threw her around, much as Louis himself was accustomed to throw around Long John, the knitted bear. Sometimes Jimmy lifted Jo up; sometimes he swung her round by the arms, or by an arm and a leg. At the end, smiling his sinister white smile, Jimmy fixed a harness to his coat and spun in a pirouette with Jo hanging on by the arms. Then she dropped her arms and hung on, spinning, by her teeth. Every night, it was exactly the same.

Between performances, Jo would stand in the control-box with Louis's mother, chatting and smoking cigarettes. In looks the two of them were strangely alike: they had the same rather sad-eyed prettiness; even the same kind of coat, slung loosely on their shoulders. The difference was that Jo, under her coat, wore a tiny white, black-spotted skating dress. Her reddish hair, cut in a fringe, was crowned by the tinsel hat for her soldier boy skate-tap routine. Sometimes her skirt would slip open at the front, affording Louis a sudden view of legs,

231

bare all the way up to the white silk fringe that hung between them. It fascinated him to think that, here she was, talking and nodding about grown-up matters; yet in a few minutes, she would let fall her coat and be changed to that white, compliant figure at the top of Jimmy's arms, or sitting on his shoulders, gripping his face between her knees . . . Meeting Louis's eye, she seemed to sense his absorption in her. She hitched her coat more tightly round her, stamping her skate wheels to keep warm.

Outside the windows and the peering faces, the gardens dwindled into dusk. A chill moved in from the sea, pushing at the beach in the small, fretful waves which preceded the turning of the tide. Around the rink verandah, coloured lights winked and trembled against the failing indigo sky. Light quivered and ran in neon shapes along the frontage of the Esplanade. Lamps had been lit along the pier, all along, like grubs in their round globes, growing nearer together and fainter as the pier strode further out across the darkening water.

He could tell when Dad had arrived. Something in the very air seemed to change, sending a quick spider of expectation down his back, even before he had seen the little stir around the ticket office, and Nigger wandering up to the rink edge, and Olwen on her way round to the changing room on black suede high heels, unpicking the headscarf she wore. Nowadays, Dad invariably delivered Olwen to the rink in person.

Olwen's husband Jack worked hard at running The Creamery Café for Dad. All day, until late evening, the big, fair-haired man stayed patiently at the top of the town, selling scones and Bath buns, coffee made with Camp essence and tea from the spluttering urn. After school, when nobody was in upstairs, Louis would sit on a stool in The Creamery's back room and watch while Jack, in his steamy white shirt, with a damp tea towel over one shoulder, washed up or cut sandwiches or twisted the knobs of a greasy wireless to find his favourite
232

orchestra, The Bandoliers. He listened to Louis's conversation with a faint smile, at times shaking his head at the butter-knife and gently observing, 'You're as nutty as a fruitcake, aren't you Lou?'

Olwen, by contrast, enjoyed a prestige unlike any other employee of Dad's. Indeed, she could nowadays scarcely be counted an employee. Since passing her Bronze Medal test, she gave little or no tuition at the rink. She was, rather, an intimate and ubiquitous family friend; a somehow essential part of the migration ceaselessly carried on between the places where Dad did business. Louis, as a less essential part of the same migration, was aware of Olwen's always being given a lift which seldom appeared to end in her getting out of the car. Instead, she came on to tea, at Dad's chosen café of the moment—which, as it chanced was never his own café, The Creamery. And always it seemed to happen that, while Louis and his mother sat half-way down the table, Olwen would be summoned to the place next to Dad, to sniff with admiration his strong Gorgonzola cheese, or watch as Dad sketched on a Players' cigarette packet his next strategy involving points A, B and C. In cars, in cafés, in snapshots when they returned from the chemist's, Olwen always seemed to be there.

For Louis the most significant change in her status occurred when, in the spring of 1951, she went up to London to take her Bronze Medal for figure skating. Jack was busy in the café that day and, in any case, it seemed appropriate that Dad, as the sponsor of her training, should accompany her, catching the early ferry with her in his dark suit and Air Force squadron tie. Late that night, he rang up from London to say that Olwen had passed the Bronze Medal test, but they had missed the last train from Waterloo and would not be home until tomorrow. Louis, in dressing-gown and slippers, was sent downstairs by his mother to give the news to Jack. The late hour, the telephone call from Dad's remote night-time world, gave drama to the occasion: it seemed to Louis that a great crisis had passed. And Dad would not be coming home tonight. He

233

slippered his way back up the dark stairs, glad of this dividend of time alone with his mother.

Olwen's duties on the Western were extremely light. Each evening, between the Skating Sinclairs' two shows, she gave a short display of figure skating or roller dancing, the latter with Johnny Whitewood, from the skating club, as her partner. Mr Boynton the signwriter came down from his loft in Union Lane, with his stencil and fine brush, and Louis stood proudly at his shoulder as Olwen's name was added to the signboard that stood outside the band enclosure. Above the photograph of the Skating Sinclairs Dad pinned a picture of Olwen, taken by himself at some earlier date; Olwen on the Pavilion rink, standing up on her toe-stops, spreading her skirt and smiling her wintry little smile.

She was always there—yet Louis had not become accustomed to her. Still, in her company, he felt that shyness which arose partly from a suspicion that Olwen, in some quite ungrown-up way, felt similar shyness with him. He hated it if, at the meal-table, some incident happened to draw humiliation on himself, while Olwen was there. To her he seemed able to show only the side of himself that choked on swede and turnip, and hid fat ineffectually under his fork, or was slapped, for being rude, on the bare legs under the table. Olwen, at such times, added nothing to the general condemnation. She only sat and watched, with black-browed eyes that commiserated with nobody in particular. She herself attempted to impose no authority over him. She had offered him, in all these weeks, no word of censure, or of praise. Where he was concerned, she seemed to take her cue entirely from Dad. If Dad rebuked him, he became aware of Olwen's sharp features mildly reflecting the outrage that was in Dad's. And when Dad chided him for his more ridiculous vices—such as being a 'know all'—there, floating in the same hot blush, would be Olwen's face, her thin lips almost pursed in a smile.

Still, when she skated, he could not stop looking at her. He would watch, with the same uneasy fascination, as she gave her display on the outdoor rink, dressed in the red or the
234

dark green velvet outfit which Dad had bought for her, and the new white boots ordered by Dad for her from London. His mind continued to grapple with the contradiction between Olwen's stern face and prim front, and the big legs that fell out beneath, and the tiny, fluttered skirt-pleats revealing, with apparent unconcern, her taut dark green or red matching velvet knickers. At times, looking from her legs to her face, he would notice afresh that expression she wore, as if someone somewhere were still being very unkind to her.

'Olwen Rumsey, ladies and gentlemen—' the voice of Louis's mother said over the rink microphones. 'Olwen, you might like to know, ladies and gentlemen, has recently been up to London to take her Bronze Medal in the N.R.S.A. figure skating class. I'm sure we'd all like to congratulate Olwen on her achievement in passing this very difficult exam.'

Applause clattered from the sides of the rink, and Olwen gave a little speeding curtsey, smiling the smile that was also, somehow, a frown.

'Perhaps,' Louis's mother added, 'if we practise hard, one day we *all* may be as good as Olwen.'

It was Saturday afternoon, during Louis's Half-Term Holiday. He stood in the foyer at the Commodore cinema, waiting while Olwen bought their tickets at the paybox shaped like Nelson's flagship *Victory*. Ticket windows shone under the dusty casements of the captain's cabin. He loved this dark blue stern-castle, with its two lanterns, lolling at anchor, high under the ceiling; the wide, shiny-floored expanse all around; the twin silent staircases to Dress and Upper Circle; the soft-lit hush that was timeless yet vibrant with the excitement within himself, mingled always with a nibbling dread that some late intervention might still prevent him from going in.

His joy at finding himself at the pictures again was qualified by one hideous circumstance. It was the same hideous circumstance which nowadays marred his every pleasure. The hideous circumstance stood nearby in the Commodore foyer with its hair done in two chewy plaits, its brown socks pulled up tight under thin and knobbly knees. Wherever he looked, that hideous circumstance remained, in a corner of his eye. His try for happiness faded; it was with collapsing fury that he turned, from Nelson's cabin windows, back to Olwen's little sister, Gaye.

Scornfully he hissed at her:

'You can't skate.'

The effect was, as always, gratifying. The little brown, foreign-looking face grew blank with dismay.

'I can,' she wailed.

'No you can't. And you can't draw.'

'I can. I can draw a lady.'

'No you can't. You . . .' He stopped, for Olwen was coming back with the tickets.

If anyone were to ask him what he hated about her the most, it would probably, Louis thought, be the terrible things she did to pencils. He was amazed that people could give her, not only pencils but also Lakeland crayons, twenty graduated colours, which she just scattered from the tin and broke; because she didn't really *want* to draw—she *had* to say 'I want to as well' when he asked for a pencil and paper. Sheets of white paper, to his deep disgust, were also provided to be coated by her scribble. He himself marched off in contempt to some distant table-top and worked there with arms encircling his page, glancing round frequently to ensure that she kept her distance. But after that, somehow, his drawing never would come right. He bore down in fury on his pencil until the point snapped.

How stupid, how unutterably, heart-sinkingly *stupid* she looked on the Western, in the miniature white skate boots; the little grey one-piece skating dress which ludicrously parodied Olwen's own. He had tried in vain not to notice her there, nor observe her progress, from stumbling in and out of Olwen's legs to standing unaided—then moving forward with a confidence that grew each time, almost mockingly, a little more. He was outraged to see her learning to skate by

236

those very stages he had painstakingly formulated for himself. Skating, when she was there, ceased to be a trance of happiness since he was driven constantly to demonstrate the superiority on which she had not yet encroached. She could go backwards now—even crouch down on one leg, lifting up her other foot, That always used to be *his* speciality.

In his anger, his revulsion, he found himself alone. He watched with disbelief as people he had formerly esteemed bent down to speak to Gaye or lifted her up, possessed of this extraordinary, widespread delusion that she was pretty. Couldn't they smell the wee wee? Couldn't they hear the shrill cachinnations that ravaged his own nerves? Even Grandma Cussons, while down from London on a visit, put her arm round Gaye while they were on the pierhead station, waiting for a tram. Louis walked to the end of the platform, jumped down onto the flat luggage tender that was kept there, and paced around, stiff-faced with disappointment in Grandma Cussons, his mind forming over and over the contemptuous word: 'Women! *Women*!'

His hatred of Gaye did not diminish against her evident admiration of him. She was his devoted follower, ready at any time to fling her arms round his neck should he show signs of acceding to her dreary wish to play 'Mummies and Daddies'; in all things, subservient and credulous. If they had been given an ice-cream each, Louis would trick her by saying 'Let's have a race to finish first', letting her race alone and finish, leaving him with all of his to gloat over. But it was too easy. He glared at her as she nibbled obediently around her ice-cream with cold and hurried little bites. He wanted her not to exist. He wanted to cancel her.

'*You* can't skate', he would whisper, as Dad had sometimes whispered mockingly to him.

'I can.'

'You can't skate, you can't draw and you can't swim.'

'I ca-an.'

'—you break all your toys.'

'I don't', she wailed, stricken. 'Not all my toys.'

237

He tried to take her doll, Elizabeth. She even had a doll that wee wee'd itself. She held on to a leg, whining:

'Loose eet!'

'Not "loose it." Can't you speak the King's English?'

'Give it *me*!'

'Not "give it me". Give it *to* me.'

'—Here they are!' Dad said, coming with two cherryades. 'Here are the lovebirds, billing and cooing!'

His mother was his only ally. She took no part in the admiration of Gaye, or in the laughter when Dad pretended they were 'lovebirds'. When he confided in her about the wee wee smell, she nodded sympathetically, and said 'yes, I know.' He sensed that she, too, was not altogether delighted that Olwen—and Olwen's relations—had become such intimate family friends. She was unfailingly polite: it was, indeed, something in that very politeness to Olwen which often caused Dad's eyes to alight on her like angry wasps. For he seemed to consider Olwen a friend as much for her benefit as his: to keep her company when 'business' took him away from them both. It frequently happened that they sat together waiting for Dad, on the Wolseley's dove grey couch. Once, in Union Street, Dad returned carrying a box of Fortune chocolates which he presented, with a courtly flourish to them both. 'A little afternoon treat,' he announced, '—for the ladies.'

Parkfield Lodge, to which Louis had once so fervently bidden goodbye, was another regular consequence of being friends with Olwen. Under the terms of that friendship, he was taken there once a week, at least, and abandoned with Gaye for the afternoon. He had come to dread that journey in the car up St Thomas's Street, turning along Links Road, where the grey walls and mildewed seats and woodland and 'observation towers' began. He wished it could be a year ago, when he was able to look from the pier, along the shore towards Fishbourne, and not know that Parkfield Lodge was there.

Olwen's parental home absorbed him without welcome—almost without acknowledgement. Though summer guests were in residence now, they occupied a distant and sequestered

238

region, denoted by the periodic smell of a powerful and alien gravy. The grandest quarters remained still unused; and it was here that Louis would be obliged to spend the afternoon, in some chill assembly room with the furniture in dust sheets and paintings on the ceiling, and Gaye, and sometimes her cousin Warwick, also six, beneath one or other of whose nostrils there invariably nestled a two-colour bogey.

Old Mrs Rumsey most decidedly did not like him. He reached this conclusion with difficulty—for were not old people always kind to little children? It was puzzling to elicit, on Mrs Rumsey's pale face, only that faint frown; only those little crosses and creases of disapprobation. She seemed, for some reason, reluctant even to look at him—her small eyes passed over his presence, even at moments when she would rebuke him. 'That floor's only joost been polished, I don't want eet all footmarks,' she would object, to the world in general rather than to Louis; or, 'them banisters break if anyone plays on them.' Her French poodle sat on her lap: she patted it with a jingle of bracelets. Occasionally, this would make a thing jump out of the poodle, underneath, that was pale and pointed like one of Olwen's lipsticks.

Mrs Rumsey conveyed her dislike of him also by ostentatiously petting and pampering Gaye. As Louis stood by, feeling the envy that was like bruised and dirty knees, he would be puzzled afresh by this family that lived in such a big house, yet was so common; and in which such an old woman could be 'Mummy' to a girl of six, just as Olwen herself, a grown-up woman eminently suited to be Gaye's mother, was referred to so insistently as her 'big sister', Equally inexplicable was Olwen's own seeming inability to remember her surname—whether it was Nevinson, like her husband Jack's, or Rumsey, as it had been written by Dad in the rink visitors' book. The puzzle was compounded by Gaye's shrill invocation of 'Moomy', both to old Mrs Rumsey and to Olwen who, at those times would pick Gaye up and cuddle her fiercely, as if to smother the appellation.

As sisters, their bond was obsessive. Several times a week now, Gaye would be delivered to The Creamery to stay the night with Jack and Olwen in the top floor flat. Wee wee, thought Louis gloomily, seemed to be getting nearer and nearer.

Recently, yet another person had been found to take care of him. Her name was Marian. She arrived from the Mainland one sunny Sunday evening when the bells of Ryde's three churches were ringing all together and the Salvation Army band stood playing on the corner outside Timothy White's. In the top floor back bedroom, Louis stood and watched her take some mauve pyjamas out of a suitcase that was white. She had short, dark hair and a noticeable moustache. When she told him she lived at Petersfield, near Guildford, he pitied her. Guildford was only half-way along the main line to Waterloo.

He began to like Marian when he found her willing to bribe him to be put to bed at night. A Koola Froota ice-lolly became the fixed price of his co-operation.

One morning, when Marian called him into the lounge to breakfast, he found Gaye sitting at the table in her dressing-gown and slippers. She wore the most horrible pink dressing-gown and the most repulsive slippers, decorated with cotton wool rabbits' tails.

When Marian asked what she wanted for breakfast, she pretended not to know. She looked around the table until her eye fell on the honey that was Louis's personal and private property. Then she gave that maddening shrug of hers, collapsed sideways in her chair, giggled shrilly and answered.

'Toast and hooney!'

'Oh, Lou, don't be mean,' Marian said—for he had snatched the honey pot under the table.

'I haven't got it,' he growled.

'Oh Lou, don't be mean. Give her a little bit.'

'Why can't she stay at Parkfield Lodge?' he protested to his mother that night. 'Her granny's there, isn't she?'

'That's her *Mummy*. Gaye is Olwen's little sister.'

240

'But why has she got to come into our flat?'

'She'll have to when Marian gets your breakfast.'

'But Marian's supposed to look after *me*!'

Marian, it had been ordained, must look after them both. At night, she put Gaye to bed first, in the top floor flat. Louis crept onto the stairs to listen and ensure no untoward privileges were given.

When he himself had consented to undress and be washed, he said, 'Now can I have a . . . can I have a . . .' Not liking to ask Marian directly for the ice-lolly, he repeated the motto spoken by the black man on the frozen paper bag. 'Can I have a—"Cool, Refreshing, Good For Me"?'

She had to go out, to Jacqueline's, the other café, to fetch it. He lay in a torment lest she should bring one back for Gaye as well. The night she did so, he fancied that his Koola Froota was the smaller and frostier of the two. In a rage he pushed it through the top of his bedroom window. It was still there next morning when he looked; a faint orange stain on the pavement around a matchwood stick.

Marian had gone out on an errand for Jack. Louis was left alone with Gaye in the two empty flats above The Creamery.

The top storey flat had no front door; and Louis could come and go in it as he pleased. He had often crept up to investigate the low-eaved, oddly-unfurnished rooms in which Olwen, supposedly, lived with her supposed husband, Jack, Their bedroom, above Louis's own, looked out through similar iron bars, across the High Street chimneys. There was a dressing-table, covered with makeup pots, and a sea of flimsy silver and gold evening shoes. Beside the narrow bed stood a photograph of Jack in Navy uniform, with his shoulders at a slant, smiling in a gentle, cynical way. In Gaye's small bedroom, at the head of the stairs, a rubble of toys lay on her permanently-unmade bed.

He walked from room to room aimlessly, stamping his feet on the uncarpeted boards. He was torn between revulsion at Gaye's company and the desire to improve his solitary games by num-

241

bers. In all that he suggested she would eagerly concur. She would stand still in the character of explorer's wife while he, as Alan Quartermain, parleyed at length with hostile Zulus. The thought of Zulus reminded him of his idea for another game; and his heart beat so loudly, he could hear it.

In Olwen and Jack's bedroom, he turned and saw that she had been following him again. She held her doll Elizabeth in her arms, and was singing the words of 'Red Feathers'. Anger grew in him suddenly, like a balloon, because he could smell wee wee and because she was singing the words all wrong. He snatched her doll out of her arms.

'Give it me!'

'Give it *to* me!'

'Give it me-e!'

'I will when you say it properly. "Give it *to* me." '

'Give it to me.'

He threw the doll across the room into Olwen's gold and silver evening shoes. Gaye knelt down and cuddled it to her, rocking it in her arms.

'I don't want you to come anywhere near me now,' he said grandly. 'I'm going to draw.'

'So am I.'

'What are you going to draw?'

'A lady.'

'A lady!' he jeered. 'You aren't, anyway.'

'I am.'

'You're not. You can't draw.'

'I can,' she wailed.

'You can't.'

'I can.'

'You can't draw and you can't skate.'

'I can.'

'You can't, a million more times than you can say "I can".'

'I can.'

'Anyway: Marian doesn't like you.'

'She does.'

'She only likes me. She hates you.'

242

'She *likes* me.'

'I'm going to play cowboys. I'm the King of the Cowboys, Roy Rogers.'

'So am I going to play cowboys.'

'No you're not.'

'All right, you can be an Indian. Do you want to?'

'Yes.'

His face was throbbing as he said, 'I'm the King of the Cowboys, Roy Rogers. You're the Indian. You've got to fight me. Indians,' he went on quickly, 'don't wear any clothes. You've got to take your clothes off to be a proper Indian.'

Gaye gave a puzzled frown as she digested this.

'All my clothes?'

'All except for something round your middle. That's what real Indians wear.' He held his breath, but her face lit up with sudden understanding and she began zestfully to pull her 'sloppy Joe' over her head.

'Not here,' he said in alarm. 'We'll go down to the other flat. We'll make a fort.'

'All right,' she agreed.

They made the fort in the sitting-room, between the bookcase with King Rameses on it, and the back of Dad's armchair. Louis knelt and watched Gaye undress down to her shoes and socks and her greyish knickers.

In this state, she was more than ever hateful to him. He hated the faint, pale trees that were her ribs, and the little flat dots on either side of her chest. He hated just as much his own anxiousness that her undressed body should touch his clothed one. He wanted her to climb on his back or sit on his chest, pretending to stab him. He wanted her, despite the wee wee smell, to press her legs tightly on each side of his face, like Jo Sinclair did to her brother Jimmy on the rink.

Glancing up, he suddenly saw Jack looking down at them over the top of the armchair. Jack looked at him, and at Gaye kneeling up undressed in front of him, and then smiled faintly and murmured, 'I'd never have believed it of you, Lou.' That was all he said, even after it had been explained to him that Gaye

243

was wearing authentic Red Indian dress. He said, 'I never would have believed it of you, Lou.'

The next afternoon, Louis was standing on the outdoor rink, feeling happy because it was Friday—no school tomorrow, and easy homework about William Wilberforce—when he suddenly saw old Mrs Rumsey come in past the ticket office. She had probably come to see Olwen, he thought, and promptly forgot about her again, secure on his skates and in full view of other people. It occurred to him that Mrs Rumsey, this afternoon, might at last, belatedly begin to be fond of him. He would accede, he thought, quite graciously to that. It would be quite pleasant, when she searched inside her handbag, to think that something for him might be there.

When he looked again, he saw that Mrs Rumsey, in her poodly white coat and hat, was now on a diagonal course across the rink. He realised she was heading straight in his direction, and with a demeanour, even to his poor sight, unmistakably hostile. He stood, mesmerised, while she bore down on him, pointing at him and frowning along her finger like someone taking aim with a gun. At the last second, he noticed Gaye as well, clinging tight to the stirrups of her elderly 'Mummy's' coat.

'Ere, Oi've got a bone ter pick with you!' Mrs Rumsey said, looking directly at him for a change, her small eyes glaring. Her teeth clenched tight inside her daffodil mouth, she went on: 'yow've been getting on at Gaye, haven't you?'

He did not understand at first, because of the Berm-ing-gum accent. A part of him found time to marvel that Dad could have found the Berm-ing-gum accent amusing when it was so clearly full of complaint and hatred and menace. Cocooned in shock, he could neither speak nor move, could feel nothing but his face, looking up at her while his mind strove to comprehend the nature of the bone she was picking with him. He understood when he saw Gaye, peeping at him with a little brown smirk of victory.

'You know what I mean, so don't let on you don't,' Mrs
244

Rumsey said. 'Yow've been getting on at her all the time, throwing her dolly and tormenting her. You're not to do eet again, do you hear?'

Just then Olwen skated out of the changing room where she had been getting ready for her display. Her face, softened by powder, listened as her mother reiterated Louis's crimes. Surprisingly, however, she did not join in the attack. She drew her lower lip under her pursed upper one and, almost reproachfully, said, 'Oh, *Mum*!'

'Oi've told him, he's not to do eet any more.'

'Oh, Mum, you *know* what kids are . . .'

'Nasty little article. I've told him, I won't have eet . . .'

'—*Mum*, you *know* what kids are . . .'

And Louis stood between them, trapped and speechless, wishing with all his heart that Dad had not chosen people like this to be close friends of the family.

anthony durham

Every day at ten to one, the brown and blue Partlands crocodile
led by Miss King, with Miss Stella at the rear, walked down
Swanmore Road to lunch at the London Hotel. By five to one,
they would be passing the County Hospital with its terrible IN
gate and the long huts where you were X-Rayed, so Michael
Hambly said. The London Hotel, a square, dark building, with
its name lettered along its side in whitewash, stood on the
corner opposite. A special dining-room was set aside for the
use of Partlands School. At one o'clock, they would all be
sitting at their long table, watching the swing doors to the
kitchen, beyond which an ominous scuffling could be heard.
There was a dog in the hotel called Whisky—Michael Hambly
said its name was Biscuit—and sometimes the manageress
brought in an ugly baby to show them.

One wall of the dining-room was covered by an immense
carpet with a scene from an Eastern market woven on it, in
yellow and brown, thick and somehow gravy-like colours. In
the foreground, two figures walked, robed and turbaned, one
guiding the other by his elbow and indicating what a variety
was to be seen of stalls, jugglers, snake charmers, camels and
246

tall jars. Louis's place at the table faced the wall with the carpet, and his hatred of his lunch on most days led him to lengthy study of those two bearded Eastern gentlemen, who seemed fortunate in not being confronted, as he was, with the London Hotel dining-room at one o'clock—the hot air and white cloth and little water glasses; the green odour of cabbage, mingled with the yellow of clumsily-sewn broad bean; the clash of plates and babble of urgent voices pleading with Miss King or Miss Stella to be let off from finishing something or other.

It was at this table, below the outspread carpet, that Louis first became acquainted with Anthony Durham. They were sitting opposite one another, and had seized the opportunity to kick each other in a wild few seconds while Miss Stella's attention had been diverted by allegations of 'hard potato' on Jeremy Mitcheson's plate.

Anthony Durham had hair like a short yellow busby, with a chink on the right-hand side where his mother daily attempted to part it. His cheeks and nose and what could be seen of his forehead were covered with freckles. He had more freckles on his face than anybody else at Partlands School. His face, among the millions of freckles, was amiable and short-sighted, even though he did not have to wear glasses. He sat forward against the tablecloth, because his and Louis's legs were so entangled, and all his freckles at once seemed to twitch with hilarity over their invisibly-drubbing sandals. 'Ow!' he laughed—or rather, 'Ou!' for he always took the same care with his vowels. Little did Louis realise that within a week, Anthony Durham, would have become his best friend in the world.

It happened when his mother, meeting Anthony's somewhere, arranged that she should collect him from school in the afternoon when she collected Anthony. The next day, he found waiting for him a large, plump, rosy-cheeked woman with fluffy hair and a brusque manner which showed itself when Mrs Durham advised him to take off his blazer, he temporised, and Mrs Durham ordered him to stop arguing and do as he was told *this minute*. She had formerly been a nurse, so Louis's

247

mother informed him later with an admiration unqualified by Louis's account of Mrs Durham's impoliteness about the blazer. That, his mother replied approvingly, was 'not taking any back chat'; an evidently admirable and nurse-like quality.

Anthony had been brought up with such extreme strictness that his very name seemed to suggest a sort of confinement, its syllables polite, well-washed, worn smooth by obedience to unnumbered regulations. These regulations—covering bathtimes, sweet-eating, cap-raising and all points of pronunciation —held fast for each second of Anthony's life; though he never did anything remotely classifiable as wrong, reproof and correction continually rained upon him. His spine was straight, from perpetual exhortations; his socks were always pulled up tight; he walked, as though propelled at the small of his back, with little tripping, anxious steps.

And yet, for all the oppression of his home-life, Anthony contrived to remain both amiable and inquiring. He did not try to resist his drastically early bed-times, nor being obliged to wear sleeveless shirts made of pale blue towelling, and khaki shorts with an elasticated waist. He accepted Louis as philosophically as his unmerited reproofs, the curt answers given by his mother to his numerous questions. His mind remained calmly occupied with the establishment of knowledge, his lips within his freckles moving ceaselessly as he read out to himself the abbreviations to be seen about Ryde on shopfronts and canvas blinds. 'G.N. Key & Co., Ltd.', he would quietly murmur to himself, or: 'W. H. Dabell and Sons Ltd.' These abbreviations and their meanings were a source of perpetual fascination to Anthony Ronald Durham.

With Louis, Mrs Durham made no distinction, treating Anthony and him with impartial severity or irony, according to her humour. Louis discovered his wheedling and rhetoric to be useless on her; her physique was so formidable, he did not dare experiment with rage. He sensed that Mrs Durham, by some intuition given to nurses, could guess what liberties he had previously enjoyed, and with her merry, caustic smile, was challenging him now to try something of the sort. Swallowing his outrage, he did what he was told *this minute*.

She would meet them both in Partlands Avenue after school and instruct them to take off their blazers. They took off their blazers in unison, and Mrs Durham folded the two garments over her arm and placed them on top of the basket she had brought with her. Anthony and Louis accompanied her meekly down Partlands Avenue, not daring to drag at the hedge; along West Street, not daring to walk on the bus seat; past Ryde Cemetery and unfinished angels outside Ellery's, down to All Saints' Church, where the Solent reared like a wall from the bottom of West Street, and huge ocean liners hung by their hazy funnels in the sky.

Going on the beach with Mrs Durham had something penitential about it since she took care to lead them to a place on the Eastern Shore far from all amusements, and remained deaf to their appeals for ice-cream or beach equipment or 'goes' on the automatic telescope. On their way down Union Street she would have bought sweets, a quarter only of some stark and suitable variety like mixed fruitdrops, which she issued singly, like iron rations, once or twice an hour.

While Mrs Durham sat and read a book, Louis would wander with Anthony barefoot over the wet tracts, which were dotted with tens of thousands of worm-shaped coils of sand. Occasionally they would come to a place where fishermen had been digging for bait, and the sand was ploughed up into dark inky heaps. There was so much beach, yet so little to do. Far to the east, opposite a headland now stranded, the dark seaborne forts stood barely above the tideline. The pier, from this side, seemed thin and low-lying. The noise of a tram came through the thin air so clearly you could hear each girder it traversed on its journey to the pierhead.

Conversation with Anthony took an analytical turn. Would that be the *Queen Mary* passing, he wondered, or the *Queen Elizabeth*? When the sea drew back from Ryde so far, did it cause flooding and panic along the Portsmouth shore? What was the cause of those little worm-shapes on the sand? Could you conceivably row across the Solent? His eyes, faint blue within his freckles, pondered these weighty matters as he bent to pluck at one trouser trunk, where a slip of yellow underpant was permanently visible.

Later they sat on the hard sand and ate the tea which Mrs Durham brought from her basket, under their two blazers. There were sandwiches, the faintest darning of jam through bread that tasted of good behaviour; there was cake to follow, of a severely sultanaless kind. Anthony sat up straight on his towel, holding his sandwich in both hands, ever inquiring and careful with the formation of vowels.

'Mummy: is that the *Queen Mary* out there, or the *Queen Elizabeth*? Or is it the *Mauretania*?'

'Mummy: that's a submarine trap out there, isn't it? Almost out of sight.'

'Probably,' Mrs Durham said.

'What are those black things out there in the water?'

'I know what they are. They're forts,' Louis said.

'Now Anthony, darling, you're *not* to bite a sandwich from the middle like that. And don't *you* copy him, either. Bite it in the correct way, *both* of you.'

'Do the forts have soldiers on them?'

'They have dead soldiers on them; some do.'

'Now stop saying *absurd* things,' Mrs Durham said, with the breeze prettily ruffling her hair. 'They're just part of the old harbour defences.'

'Mummy: what *is* the difference between Portsmouth and Southsea?'

'But they *are* forts, aren't they?' Louis pleaded.

'I've *told* you! They're part of the old harbour defences.'

'Mummy: that's Spithead over there, isn't it? What's the difference between the Solent and Spithead?'

'Now stop asking questions and go away and play. You've got five and twenty minutes before we go home. And woe *betide* you, either of you, if you do anything silly.'

The Durhams lived in a flat half way up a big rambling mansion called Clyde House, near the top of Dover Street. It was there that Louis first met Anthony's father, a silent but unnerving man who was mathematics master at Highclere School and whose completely bald head, round spectacles and calm hollow-cheeked physiognomy powerfully suggested kinship with the Treens, that race of intellectually superior but perfidious Venusians against whom Dan Dare had fought so long in the *Eagle* comic. Mr Durham, of course, was not green, he did not have a body bound in gold hoops, nor did he say 'Pah! This is fruitless, Earthman!', nor owe allegiance to the Almighty Mekon. It was the rarity and compactness of his speech which suggested to Louis a superior but hostile intelligence, inscrutably contained by the deep, and indubitably treen-like groove between his eyebrows. His connection with Highclere School increased his aura as representative of an alien world. Terrible tales were circulated at Partlands of the cruelties practised at Highclere School—of rough games and callous punishments, of lessons like Arithmetic elevated to the horrifying plurality of what Anthony already called 'maths'. Anthony also employed Highclere School's brutal habit of calling boys by their surname only.

By now, because his mother was so busy, Mrs Durham had virtually taken charge of Louis. At night, she often took him back with Anthony to sleep at Clyde House. He had to have a bath almost every night or, at the very least, he had to wash his face, hands and knees. Afterwards, he and Anthony were put directly to bed, passing through the lounge on tiptoe because Mr Durham was there, helping a Highclere School boy with his mathematics.

'Is that Eddie Casale, Mummy?' Anthony whispered. 'Is it Gretton or Ghobadian? Ghobadian's from Persia, isn't he?'

Not until he was in bed, in Anthony's room, did Louis have time to resent this new epoch which, like Mrs Durham's vigorous bath towel, had irresistibly engulfed him. Now, under his breath, he completed all the protests which she had cut short; in his imagination, he firmly declined both bath and the pumice stone. Resentment became nostalgia for bedtime as it had been in Marian's time—for skimped washes and sweet-eating; the glass marbles clicking and rolling in the folds of his

251

bed rug at home. Why had Marian been given the sack? To-morrow morning at the Durhams' was a prospect equally uncheering. There would be further washing, and inspection, then little hard strips of streaky bacon and fried bread in rigid squares, eaten meekly under the silent, treen-like scrutiny of Mr Durham, in what was called The Breakfast Room.

His body grew rigid with the frustration of being in bed when daylight still clamoured beyond the fully-drawn curtain. He lay awake for hours in the unnatural dusk, staring at the stitches along the yellow blanket which covered him. The blanket had a label like the bedclothes at home—the war-time 'Utility' brand of two black circles with missing segments, like open mouths. That label always made him think of Dad. Where was Dad now, Louis wondered, and what would he be doing tonight?

A voice came from Anthony's bed.

'Louis?'

'Yes?'

'When we came along West Street, past the graveyards, you know where we cross over Argyll Road?'

'Yes.'

'You know where SWS is written on the wall? Those big letters, SWS?'

'Yes?'

'Do you know what SWS stands for?'

'No.'

'Does it stand for "Static Water Supply"?'

The blanket on the other bed heaved up, indicating that its occupant had decided to turn upside-down. In a moment Louis saw Anthony's feet emerge and settle on his pillow.

'Are you going to make a hole in the bottom of your bed?' Anthony enquired.

'Are you?'

'Are you?'

'Are you?'

*   *   *

Anthony spent a little time on Louis's territory. He would come to the end of the pier after school for tea on the sun-roof. It was Anthony who first raised the question of the ticket collector's notice at the pier gates. Why did it say 'All Tickets to be *Shewn*'? On the tram journey he read aloud from advertisement cards in the car. 'Barry O'Brien presents *Starlight*, nightly on Shanklin Pier: A Riot of Music and Fun; Visit the Buddle Inn, Paul's Evening and Mystery Tours; Dibben's Ltd, Removals & Storage.' He noted that the doors inside the tram opened outward while those in the open portion between the two cars had, for safety, to be pulled towards you. He wondered why it was that the tram on its outward journey travelled backwards, and what combination of forces carried it thus across open girders without slipping, and what the purpose might be of that large iron handle in the tramboy's forward compartment. Anthony knelt up in amazement on the slatted seat while Louis, indifferent to these familiar mysteries, stood midway in the rattling car with the air of one intent on a difficult feat of balance.

'How about comin' to the fair with me, Lewis?' the tramboy, Peter—or was it Charley?—shouted as he passed, clipping the tickets of those who had to pay.

'Whereabouts?' Louis shouted back.

'Over Pompey.'

'I can ask . . .' Louis shouted eagerly.

'No, don't do that,' the tramboy shouted, laughing as he went into his compartment and slid the door shut.

Dad liked Anthony, whom he would greet in the Pavilion with an ironic heartiness—'Hel-lo young Durham!' He seemed amused by the notion that Louis had a friend. Seeing the two of them together, Dad would start to chuckle for no discernible reason—merely at the foibles and gaucheries of boys as a species—and he would speak to them in a gruff, monotonous voice, intended to mimic theirs. Often he would subject them to some good-humoured ordeal, such as standing on the Pavilion stage and reciting through the inside loudspeaker system some poem which they had learned at school.

They recited, in turn, staring out at nothing, with short trouser trunks thrust out from the knees puckered in embarrassment, and speaking deliberately in the gruff, expressionless voices which Dad seemed to expect of boys saying poetry. Anthony quickly learned what Louis knew—that the more Dad laughed, the richer would be the subsequent rewards. He would give them handfuls of brass tokens to play on the machines, or take them upstairs into the breadstore, where big wooden bakers' trays of strawberries were stacked. Dad allowed them to take six strawberries each. He led them downstairs to the Tea Bar again, where he gave them bottles of cherryade and packets of crisps. All because they had spoken in expressionless voices, and because Anthony's underpants drooped out of his trouser-leg.

'Gould, Hibberd and Randal Gold-Medal Minerals and Cordials', read Anthony from the label of his cherryade bottle as the race to finish last grew slower and slower. Separate beads of cherryade hovered and fell inside their drinking straws. Each still held his first crisp, as yet only grazed by bared and giggling teeth.

At these moments Louis understood the luxury and privilege of his life in comparison with Anthony's. And he saw his good fortune in having Dad for a father, instead of Mr Durham—for Dad's good humour appeared timeless, the sun's warmth rose from his soft green shirt and he arranged miracles, before Anthony's blue eyes, with greater nonchalance than ever.

One day, when their mothers wanted to take them to Portsmouth to buy blazers, Dad arranged for them to cross the Solent in Captain House's red speedboat. Louis sat in front of the speedboat, lifted high off the sea, between his mother and Captain House. Mrs Durham and Anthony sat downhill in the stern, with silver spray behind them like the wings of a high-backed throne. The breeze raised Anthony's fringe, show-ing thousands more freckles on his forehead, above his half-shut eyes. It was an epoch of splendour, destined to fade as quickly as the spray spots on his shirt, as they rushed away
254

from the pier, bumping and bouncing across the waves that glided from big liners in the deep channel, moving towards Southampton.

The garden at Clyde House sloped steeply down to an overgrown spinney where the palings of a Victorian boundary fence glimmered black among dock leaves as thick as a false floor. From the back entrance, a flight of shallow steps ran down to a point half-way in the hilly lawn. Here, Anthony and Louis, with some rusty scissors Anthony had found, would crouch, waiting for a woodlouse to cross the flags. They would cut the woodlouse in half, slicing with the scissors through its soft, grey, gleaming armour, into blood that was as dark as wine. Death was to be seen in that garden in many forms—dead cats, dead birds; a rat with its belly torn open to show muscles of pulsing blue. The Sunday they saw the rat, unfortunately, Mrs Durham was cooking kidneys for lunch.

Sometimes in the garden they met a fat, squeaky lower class boy named Martin Leary, who whimpered in a gratifying way if you punched him in the soft part of the arm. They had good fun with Martin Leary, punching him or telling him that his mother had died suddenly during the last half-hour. They also met a bigger boy in long trousers who might reasonably have been expected to punch and terrorise them. Instead, he sidled along the path towards them, smiling deferentially. A few minutes later, he took Louis on one side alone and, in a polite voice, said, 'May I see your snooky?' By this he meant Louis's winkle. His manner was so affable, and his request so unsurprising to the other Clyde House boys, that Louis felt it would be churlish to refuse. So, behind a bush, he undid his trousers and showed his winkle to the bigger boy, who looked at it, smiling as if some harmless preconception had been borne out, and then inquired. 'Would you like to see my bottom?' He quickly undid his long trousers and bent down, looking over his shoulder and smiling as his large rather fluffy-looking bottom crack rose into view above his underpant rim.

255

He often appeared in the garden when Louis was there, and always made the same courteous request. His sole interest in life appeared to be looking at people's snookies, although Martin Leary said that he was also a gifted wood-carver, able to fashion soldiers from any period in history. He agreed to make some Roman soldiers for Louis, in return for yet another brief look at his snooky—a small enough price to pay if, as he promised, he could carve real armour and leggings and square shields and Roman helmets with crests. He must be hard at work carving the soldiers, Louis thought, when he was not out in the garden, looking at people's snookies.

Life at Clyde House gave ominous intimations of what school could be like outside the placid sphere of Partlands, Miss Stella and Miss King. The Durhams had another Highclere School master lodging with them, a tall, bony man called Mr Forbes-Jobson, with a long nose, a black moustache and an expression of contemptuous savagery which domestic life seemed barely to hold in check. Mrs Durham kept up her nursing by working as part-time Matron for the boarders, whose inconceivably miserable existence Louis and Anthony shared to some extent in perpetual washes and inspections, and meals unceremoniously served, to be consumed sitting up straight, without comment or negotiation. At night, as they prepared for bed, there was usually a big boy from Mr Durham's class being helped with his mathematics. Tiptoeing past, Louis saw, next to Mr Durham on the sofa, a figure whose hand, pressed to a tortured forehead, made his own spirit quail to think of the impenetrably difficult sums.

Anthony was soon to leave Partlands for Highclere School. He seemed undismayed at the prospect, and eagerly questioned his father and Mr Forbes-Jobson about the ordeals in store for him there.

'Shall I do Latin, Daddy?'

'Not until you're in the Senior School,' Mr Durham replied, in words that were like separate, scientific cane-strokes.

'There are three houses, aren't there, Daddy? Hanover, Trinity and Seaford.'

256

'And Westmont for the boarders.'

'I wonder which house I'll be in. They go to school on Saturday mornings, don't they?'

'Do they?' said Louis, aghast.

'In the Senior School they do. You'll find out soon enough,' Mrs Durham told him.

'I shan't. I'm not going to Highclere School.'

'That's all you know,' Mrs Durham said mysteriously.

He visited Highclere School under safe conduct, as it were, on Saturday afternoons when Anthony and he were compelled to accompany Mrs Durham to a cricket match there. He saw as an outsider—so he thought—the long, dark wooden classroom blocks which, though empty of boys, still seemed to resound with a terrible weekday noise in which the voices of Mr Durham and Mr Forbes-Jobson could readily be imagined, harshly uplifted.

He sat with Mrs Durham and Anthony on an embankment overlooking the great oval field where the match was being played. A dark, flat-topped privet hedge ran round the field, with the sea in a blue hill outside it. Away to the right, you could just see the tip of the pier.

They had to sit still on the hard seat for hours, watching the diagram of white figures whose imperceptible changes would periodically bring about the sudden hooking-up of a new number on the board outside the Assembly Hall amid bursts of feeble applause. Giants in batting pads came and went on the steps cut in the front of the embankment. Above it, lawns sloped upward to the grey mansion where the headmaster and the boarders lived. It was strictly forbidden to walk on the lawn or to play on the front of the bank. Further along the path, a group of boarders sat at a table, keeping the score in long green books, occasionally looking towards Louis and Anthony and laughing in a scornful way. Louis felt himself marked down by them as one of the vulnerable Partlands species. Perhaps they had guessed that he liked to read in bed and wear a bed jacket and be tucked up by his mother. But for Mrs Durham's protection, he felt sure he would have been set on by the

257

cricket scorers and carried away for initiation into their heartless and homeless world.

Anthony clapped earnestly when others did, his desire for facts, as ever, inexhaustible.

'Is that a four, Mummy?'

'Is Casale out, Mummy? Was it lbw? Who's the next batter going to be?'

'It's *batsman*,' Mrs Durham said fiercely.

When their fidgeting grew insupportable, she released them to go and play further along the embankment, where it dwindled to blue asphalt and a line of cricket nets. From here, against instructions, they wandered into the thick woods that lay sunken behind the cricket field—The Jungle, it was called—where groups of boarders could sometimes be seen, thrashing among the flat ferns in search of lost cricket balls. Once, with a whip of air, a ball actually flew through the boundary hedge and into the ravine, close to where Anthony and Louis stood. A moment later, several enormous figures in white came bursting through the hedge and down the earth slope almost on top of them. 'Did you see where it went?' a giant in batting pads asked, but neither Louis nor Anthony could muster a reply. When they returned to Mrs Durham on top of the bank, she handed them a Mars bar, angrily cut into two equal halves. 'This *isn't*,' she informed them, 'because you've been good this afternoon.'

On Sunday afternoons, when they went for a long drive in Mr Durham's car, Louis had to sit in the back next to Mr Forbes-Jobson, who wore for these outings a reddish tweed coat with leather elbows and an odour peculiarly reminiscent of Highclere School—of chalk and creosote and shoe-whitener and unswept leaves and inkwells and pine cones and cricket pads and books containing impossible languages or maths. Louis, racked by fear of car sickness, shrank away from Mr Forbes-Jobson's coat, putting his mouth as close as he could to the window he had secretly wound down a little way. They were driving out of Ryde, through Haylands, past Uncle Cal's front gate, and the stables where Marie went riding; past the bus

258

stop where he and Nanny Belmayne used to wait. Out along the old airport road, a black windsock strained in the sky. It could not nearly be over, Louis thought—it had barely even begun.

Mr Durham followed the same route across the 'Douns'—for he, too, took great care with his vowels—to remote parts of the Island where holidaymakers did not go, save on the most ambitious Mystery Tours; to lonely roads along the tops of chalk cloven white cliffs, where huge waves fell on empty beaches hundreds of feet below. Beyond the surf, the sea stretched, without a mainland, glittering, vacant. There was no pier; no boats could be seen over miles of wrinkled emptiness. No esplanades, no arcades or cafés: only fields of wind-furrowed and trembling yellow grass.

'Is that France, somewhere over there, Mummy?' Anthony asked.

'Mummy: if you started from here and kept going, would you come to America in the end? Look, Mummy—those are The Needles, aren't they?'

Louis glanced down at the headland where sharp, grey crags floated out to a stumpy lighthouse ringed with thick stripes. It all looked less exciting in real life than on picture postcards. He returned to his torpor, staring from the car with hopeless eyes at the absence of toyshops and ice-cream. Somewhere among these deserted cliffs and bays were places he had longed to visit—Alum Bay, with its coloured sands, or Blackgang Chine, where you could sit inside the skeleton of a whale. He pleaded to be taken there until 'please' had spent its force. Hopeless, expectant, he gazed at Mr Durham, seated sternly and erectly like a Treen handling some spacecraft; at Mr Durham's bald crown wherein the formula had been worked for missing Alum Bay again, and bringing them out between more sighing grassland and the view of another deserted bay.

Once, as they drove along a cliff road, he glimpsed an esplanade far below. It might have been Sandown or Shanklin. There was a paddling pool in the shape of the Isle of Wight.

259

His heart lurched to see coloured cars—real cars, but driven by children—moving slowly round an oblong arena.

'*Please*,' he said, taking his face from the window-crack. 'Can we have a go on those cars?'

'We'll see,' Mrs Durham said.

It was not, as he had expected, outright refusal. 'Oh good,' he blurted out. ' "We'll see" usually means "Yes".'

'No it doesn't!' retorted Mr Durham, Mrs Durham and Mr Forbes-Jobson all together. 'It means "it all depends how well you behave yourself".'

Eventually Mr Durham found a bay that was remote enough, and a beach empty and hard and clean enough to be suitable for their picnic. At Mrs Durham's command, Anthony and Louis undid their Partlands belts, stepping in unison from their fallen shorts in similar red trunks and matching white ribs. Mr Forbes-Jobson used a more complicated method of disrobing. He sat on the sand with a white towel wrapped tightly round his legs, and put on his trunks by working them gradually up inside the towel, moving a little further down the beach with each jerk he gave his trunks, so that he appeared to be riding on a rather slow and angry toboggan. Mrs Durham seldom put on a bathing costume, and Mr Durham never removed more than his jacket. He sat with one knee flat on the sand, the other knee raised with his thin elbow resting on it, and stared at the sea coldly as if the waves were whispering without permission.

Even the picnic was a kind of lesson. Afterwards Mr Forbes-Jobson, wearing his trunks, a flapping white shirt and his still damp black moustache, would suggest that he, Anthony and Louis should make a sandcastle near the rocks. In fact, only Mr Forbes-Jobson ever built the sandcastle. Anthony and Louis stood clear while he crouched down, modelling, between his high, bony knees, a complex fortification with numerous concentric walls, viaducts, bridges, moats and raised highways, hammered flat with Anthony's little tin red spade, 'a poorish sort of implement', as Mr Forbes-Jobson repeatedly called it. If Anthony or Louis took upon himself the building
260

of an excrescent wall or tower, Mr Forbes-Jobson dragged five angular toes through it and said, 'No—not like that old bean.'

They stood and waited until Mr Forbes-Jobson had finished the sandcastle and was walking away from them backwards, hollowing out an irrigation canal to the water's edge. As the sea rushed up, foaming brown through the moats and backwaters, Mr Forbes-Jobson wiped his sandy hands on his trunks and pulled his shirtsleeves down, smiling behind his cruel black moustache as if the flood had caused hundreds of innocent hostages to perish.

'I build wonderful sandcastles,' he said. 'Don't I, Anthony?'

'Yes. Do you think a *real* castle could have seawater in the moat?' Anthony asked. 'I bet it could if it was built at the seaside. Did Carisbrooke Castle have sea in its moat? In the olden days, I mean.'

On Sunday evenings Mrs Durham took Louis back to The Creamery and put him to bed in a flat that was empty but for Charles the Siamese cat. She tucked him in so firmly that his mattress bent up like a bow on either side, and then—an unexpected indulgence—unwrapped a toffee and slipped it into his mouth. The toffees she bought that summer were flat and knobby and wrapped in clear paper sprigged with little silver emblems. One evening she had no toffees with her, so she kissed Louis on the forehead—the only time she ever kissed him—and said, 'Double ration tomorrow.'

After she had gone, Louis slid out of his tightly-tucked bed and knelt on the rug, looking through his barred window, down into the High Street.

Though the sun had gone in, it was still day, as bright and motionless as early morning. No cars went by, and the few people who passed below walked carelessly down the middle of the road. He could hear voices talking and laughing on the pavement out of his sight. Further along, Nash's fish shop would be open, with the leathery balloon fish hanging in its window, and the blackboard outside which said FRYING TONIGHT. He envied the warmth and certainty in the words.

Further along still, he pictured the Scala's lighted front, and the old man in uniform pulling open the door. Evening had come to life everywhere but in the empty street below him and the empty windows facing his.

Sometimes his mother came back to the flat while he was still awake. She would come into his room, smiling conspiratorially, with a little bowl of lard she had brought back from the Pavilion kitchens. She brought him things to eat—a piece of cake or a Banjo bar or a packet of Wrigley's gum which she took out of her bag singing the song 'How I Love Chewing Gum'. He lay there, chewing gum, listening with pleasure to her movements around the flat. She sat on his bed and he described to her the fresh incivilities he had suffered from Mrs Durham. She listened attentively, sometimes nodding and agreeing: 'Well, yes, that's the point. That's the whole point.'

More often, nobody came. He formed the habit, after Mrs Durham had gone, of getting up and wandering about the flat—from the narrow bathroom to the back bedroom, where Dad's 'compactum' stood in yellowy dusk; from the kitchenette, with its empty dog bowls, back into the sitting-room. There he would climb on the drawers of the linen press to peep over the summit at a large black box with *Totopoly* printed on it. It was another present from Dad, put away until Louis was old enough to understand it, but hidden on top of the linen press so long that he had ceased to associate it with himself. Next to it on the cobwebby timbers lay Dad's double-barrelled shotgun, and the smaller shape that was a blunderbuss with a bayonet that flew out on a spring.

He saw Dad in the sitting-room wherever he looked—in the books about fishing and shooting, and copies of *The Field* spread along the window seat; in the bronze bust of Rameses, staring with sightless, sensitive eyes—his face as slender and thoughtful as Dad's own—standing on the ledge beside Dad's long unoccupied armchair. Above the panelled-in fireplace hung the picture of wild duck, taking off across yellow marshes. He remembered how, when he was younger, the wings skeined

262

against the cloud curve seemed to form themselves into Dad's face, brooding sorrowfully over the water and wind-bent grasses.

He knelt on the sofa-back and opened the top drawer in the chest. He picked among the shallow debris—screws and spent cartridge-cases, the silk-lined box for a Yard-O-Led pencil, and Christmas decorations, bought long ago, while they were still at the Cross Keys. He picked out a gold Christmas tree ball, weighing it in his hand as he stared at his swollen gold reflection and at the room behind him in a gold, distorted arc. The past had taken with it all happiness, all substance. The present was like this Christmas tree ball, dulled and weightless, musty with disuse.

Suddenly he heard water flushing at the end of the passage. Mrs Durham—who had not gone home: only to the toilet—came back into the sitting-room.

'And just *what* are you doing out of bed?'

It was another very hot afternoon.

Mrs Durham had met them from school as usual, and folded up their two blazers. They were walking, blazerless, one on each side of her, along the Esplanade, past the pier gates and Smith's, past the bus stops, interspersed with knobby, leafless trees, and the coach stops and coloured notice-boards for Evening and Mystery Tours. There were holidaymakers everywhere, queueing for buses or sitting on the wall along a shallow garden whose hedge shut out the Esplanade railway line. There was the noise of crowds and huffing trains and, further away, violins that squeaked flatly on the thin, blue after-school air.

Louis was thinking about ice-cream. All afternoon, during Elocution on the big field, he had been thinking, not of Vowels and Expression but of wafers and choc ices, and of cornets licked smooth with your chin wet, round and round. Everywhere he looked, he saw people buying ice-cream, unwrapping ice-cream, giving ice-cream to babies to plaster on their faces; he saw boards and banners that vaunted ice-cream; he saw fridges open on smoky tins, and scoops squeeze out dollops on topheavy cornets, and threepenny bricks slabbed into wafers and broken-up choc ices sucked from melting silver paper. A terrible famine seized his tongue and drained his mouth of moisture. It seemed madness at this moment not to be eating ice-cream. He looked without hope at Mrs Durham as she strode along with both arms in the basket where her purse lay, inviolate, under their two school blazers.

'I like Wall's ice-cream best,' he observed nonchalantly.

'I like Lyons',' Anthony said.

'I don't like Lyons'. It makes me feel sick. Lyons'—ugh!'

'I like Eldorado. Do you, Louis?'

'It always makes my teeth ache.'

'Do you like Farmers' Dairies?'

'No.'

'I do.'

'I don't.'

'I do.'

'I don't.'

'Now you're *not* going to have an ice-cream,' Mrs Durham interrupted. 'So you may as well stop talking about it.'

'I wasn't. I was just saying the ones I like.'

'Well, *stop* it. They're *all* extremely nice.'

She led them into the Eastern Gardens, firmly avoiding the beach tray counter that sold Eldorado ice-cream. They went along the path beside the Repertory Theatre with its four towers like dark green Chinese pagodas. This was the tropical part of Ryde Esplanade. The lawn next to the path was covered with short, dusty-looking palm trees, all leaning in different directions. Anthony asked if you ever got pineapples from palm trees. Or did pineapples always come from pine trees?

'*Breath of Spring*,' said Anthony, reading from the notice-board of plays at the Repertory Theatre. 'A Bright New Comedy in Three Acts by Peter Coke.'

'Daily Performances by the Ryde . . . Mummy, what does the next word spell?'

'Municipal.'

264

'The Ryde Municipal Orchestra. Mummy, what does Municipal mean?'

'It means "don't ask so many questions".'

They came round the corner of the Repertory Theatre, into the radius of the violins. On a stage, inside a geranium bed, the Ryde Municipal Orchestra (Leader: Henry Jolliffe, LRAM) played to an audience concealed by deck-chair backs in semi-circular rows. Out on a promontory, in sunshine, two violinists stood with handkerchieves under their chins, sawing busily at the sides of their crumpled faces and tapping their feet loudly on the boards. Other musicians were visible further back, notably a pianist in sunglasses who was large and plump and dignified, somewhat like Louis's Uncle Cal. Today, as they passed the bandstand, they saw another man push a xylophone out into the sunshine. He stood there with his sleeves rolled up and several small hammers in each hand, and said into the microphone:

'I should now like to play for you, ladies and gentlemen—"Twelfth Street Rag".'

The clonk and clop of the xylophone came faintly through loudspeakers fixed to the lamp posts along the seawall promenade as Mrs Durham urged Anthony and Louis on, past the bowling green, packed with straw hats, kneeling and standing; past the dark-veiled tennis courts; past the bookstall, the flower stall, the shellfish stall and the toffee apple stall; past the fortune teller's caravan and the giant weighing machine and the machine that stamped your name in metal; past the Putting Green, the Harbour Café and the Canoe Lake, sunken in its grass basin, across the road from a bleakly unadorned sea wall.

'Mummy: is it true that dead bodies are buried under the Putting Green?'

'Please can we weigh ourselves?'

'Not now.'

'Can we have some cockles and mussels?'

'*Please* can we have a go on a motor boat?'

'No you can't. Now go on the beach and play until I call you for tea, and woe betide you if you do anything silly, either

265

of you. And *don't* bring back any crabs this time. They only have to be thrown away.'

Mrs Durham sat back inside a deck-chair on the pavement. Louis and Anthony moved off at walking-race speed that made a feather of gold hair jump up and down on Anthony's head.

The seawall arrested their momentum and purpose. They walked along inside it, stepping on and off a drain filled with dead sand and dry black seaweed and empty ice cream tubs. Every few yards they passed a shelter with a green pagoda roof and holidaymakers sitting on all four sides of it, like the occupants of an Irish jaunting cart.

'That's Appley Tower over there,' Anthony said. 'You can walk along the wall all the way to Puckpool Park, I think. I've seen the place at Puckpool where the big guns used to be.'

In the distance, they could still hear xylophone music, and faint laughter, as from children in a game. But no children were to be seen on the wet brown plains, where shallow ponds shivered under diagonal tides. Portsmouth had come very close today. To their right, two black forts, slanted in the sea like gateposts, stood guard on invisible deeps. A tram raced out along the pier to meet the boat.

A coin-operated telescope offered views of the Solent and shipping. Louis and Anthony in turn stood up on the metal platform, tilted down the eyepiece and squinted through it in the hope that someone's threepence might have got stuck. Each squinted into the blackened lens, with sea and sky leaking coolly round the edges of the eyepiece.

They stood on the seawall together. Soft sand, not far below lay drifted against the wall's concavity. Above the sunny sand their shadows argued:

'I said it first.'

'I *thought* it first.'

'I am if you are.'

'I will if you go first.'

'I washed first this morning.'

'I bet I've washed first more mornings than you.'

'I bet you haven't.'

266

'How much?'

'How much do you bet me?'

'A million pounds.'

'I bet you ten million pounds. And anyway,' Louis said, 'I bet I'm the first one to jump off.'

Out on the sunny sand, some holidaymakers are sitting with their deck-chairs in a circle. Two or three of them looked at me when I landed. They think I was brave to jump off the wall.

I am kneeling where I landed, in the shadow of the seawall —on cool sand with a flat paving stone, half-buried in it, that I didn't notice before I jumped. The people in deck chairs are still looking at me. They don't realise I often jump off seawalls as high as this without hurting myself. I didn't hurt myself this time, except for the funny feeling when I landed on part of that paving stone, as if I had thrust my foot suddenly into a sock made of my own skin.

I'm starting to get up now, pushing away the sand with my hands and smiling a grown-up smile to assure them I'm 'quite all right', as a grown-up would put it; I'm wiping my hands on my trousers and beginning to walk away—but my right foot isn't there. Only a stump, pushing down into a sock made of my skin.

I've fallen down, not meaning to. The people are running towards me from their empty deck-chairs, kicking up the powdery sand.

They are kneeling round me, shutting out the sky.

Strangers' voices say: 'Are you all right, son? All right, sonny?'

'He jumped down off that wall. I saw him. He was up there talking to his friend.'

'—sprained it. Must have.'

'Let me feel it.'

'Feel it, Bob . . .'

'—we better get some cold water to put on it?'

Someone's hands lift up my foot.

'Does that hurt, son?'
Yes.
'Yes, yes, yes, yes, yes.'
'We ought to get some cold water to put on it.' The same voice keeps suggesting this, and, inside my screaming, I think: 'Where will they find any? The sea has gone miles out.'
'Here comes his Mummy.'
I can see Mrs Durham looking at me with an upside-down face. Her lips make red eyes; her eyebrows, a straight, bushy mouth. I hear the smack as her knees strike the sand behind my head.
'I can't walk,' I tell her.
'I can't walk, I can't walk, I can't walk, I can't walk—'
'How do you know?' is her curt reply. 'You haven't even tried yet.'

Throughout the turmoil that followed, Anthony remained motionless on top of the seawall. Louis, down on the beach, glimpsed him beyond the hubbub, plucking at one trouser leg and seeming to stare at something far away across the beach.

Anthony stood like that on the seawall as Louis was lifted up; as he established, by piercing screams, that he truly was unable to walk. One of the holidaymakers had smoothed away the sand from the paving stone on which he must have landed. Mrs Durham, still with an air of grim scepticism, pushed her basket past her elbow, then gathered him up and carried him towards the steps. Anthony watched, his freckled face vacant with embarrassment.

Mrs Durham did not really believe he was hurt. Even so, she carried him, as well as her basket and his shoes, all the way up George Street, the very steepest way to the top of the town. Anthony walked beside them, decorously, disinterestedly, as always maintaining a careful study of placards and hotel noticeboards. It was Louis's chief memory of that difficult journey—Anthony's blond head bobbing out of step and his lips moving in careful enunciation: 'The "Woodbine" Private Hotel. Under the personal supervision of Mr and Mrs. H. J.

268

Player. Newlands Hotel. Private & Commercial. Tariff on Request . . .'

Towards the end, he had begun to wonder if Mrs Durham might not be right. His hurt leg dangled loose above her re-solutely-advancing frock; his shoeless foot felt little more than cool evening air.

'Mummy,' Anthony's voice said. 'What does "Tariff on Request" mean?'

The disconcerting lack of pain continued after Mrs Durham had carried him upstairs to the flat, tipped him onto his bed and gone away to ring up his mother. He lay there irresolutely, listening to the quiet rustle of a page from the sitting-room, where Anthony was waiting and reading his comics with a detachment that now seemed infinitely enviable. The tears on his cheeks had long dried, so he refreshed them by thinking of very sad things—of a faithful dog's death; a she fox losing all her cubs. The latter produced two new tears, finely poised on their slipways as his mother's face looked down at him, and Mrs Durham, behind her, supplied an account notably lacking in the tragic element.

'I could hear all this screaming and yelling,' she said. 'And then I saw Anthony, standing on top of the wall and *gazing* down at something . . .'

His mother smoothed his forehead with her hand. He blinked, with impeccable timing, to spread the two new tears wide over his cheeks.

'Don't cry, Lou Lou,' she said sadly. 'We'll soon make it all better.'

He gave an elaborate sniff.

'Does Dad know yet?'

'Daddy's gone away for the night.'

'Where to?'

'Away on business. As soon as possible, we'll let Daddy know.'

Mrs Durham and Anthony receded in the quickening events. He was taken by taxi to the County Hospital—through that terrible IN gate and, in the taximan's arms, down a nightmare

269

passage, harshly lit, with a stinging, cut-you-open smell. He sat on a trolley on a red blanket while a doctor with warm thumbs felt all around his foot. The doctor, through a speech impediment, spoke just like a tiny boy in kindergarten. 'You're being ve' good. A ve' good boy. Does it hurt there?' The warm thumbs made a sock of skin overlap again. 'Yes, it does,' Louis replied calmly. 'It hurts ve' much.'

'I fink we'd better have an X-Ray,' the doctor said.

Carrying him out, with a right foot tightly bandaged, the taximan said jovially: 'Are you going to die? Or are you going tomorrow?'

'He's broken a little bone,' his mother said. 'Just a very little bone in his foot.'

'So you're not going to die,' the taximan said. 'You're not going to die, so you must be going tomorrow.'

After the taximan had gone, he began to scream and cry in agony. He continued to do so late into the night, kicking the bedclothes off himself and shouting:

'I want Nanny. Please get Nanny Belmayne—please get her. Ring her up or something. Please ring her up and tell her—*please*. Oh, please ring her up or something, *please*!'

Eventually, running out of tears, his body shook in long, dry juddering spasms.

'*Please* get Nanny—please ring up and get Nanny to come. Please oh—please. Ple-ease, get Nanny, send for her. Plea-ease . . .'

'I will send for her—I promise. I'll ring her up, first thing in the morning.'

'Wha-at time will you—you?'

'First thing in the morning I'll ring her up. Just go to bye-byes now.'

'I want—I want Nanny. I don't want you.'

'I know. I know. Only, try to go to bye-byes. Try to go to Bo-Peep.'

Her voice tried to comfort him with lullabies long disused.

She kissed his forehead, drew the covers over him again and went back into the sitting-room.

270

                              *   *   *

Nanny Belmayne arrived next day after lunch. She had set
off from Clapham as soon as she heard the news, stopping
only to make one or two necessary purchases.

She came into his bedroom like a strong wind that lifted
him off his pillow up against her big-squared coat, and he
breathed the beautiful Nanny Belmayne smell of clothes and
hair and skin and cornplasters and leather purses, while big,
smacking kisses rained on his face and head. Amid the swoon
of happiness and relief that she was here at last, he hoped
she had not brought him the kind of New Berry Fruits that
were all green ones.

'Bless him, *bless* him, has he hurt himself, the poor lamb?
Bless his dear heart, has he hurt himself, Nan's little loved
one? Nan's here love. Nan's here and brought him lots of
things, and going to take him down the West Country soon, bless
him—*bless* his old face. His Nan's missed him so much . . .'

In the doorway, his mother said: 'That's what I've been
hearing all night. "Send for Nanny; send for Nanny Belmayne". I suppose he knew you'd bring him things.'

Time was delectably out of step. There were lights turned
on everywhere; telephones ringing; voices at the flat door,
murmuring his name. There were New Berry Fruits and
Mitcham Mints, a late Easter egg from Eilian and Wilf, a
toffee apple sent up for him from Jack. In the sitting-room,
the wireless was turned up loud for him to hear. A voice began
the *Woman's Hour* story. '*Return to Jalna,* by Mazo de la
Roche . . .'

Toward the end of *Mrs Dale's Diary,* Dad came.

He did so at a moment when Louis had chocolate paper
and glass marbles all around him, and Charles the Siamese
cat asleep among the other new presents, and also his light-up
garage tilted on his ankles under the rug. Hearing the unmistakable rapid sound—as much like a pounce as footsteps—

271

he realised too late that marbles ill become a sickroom; that chocolate and a light-up garage are seldom adjuncts to genuine illness. His heart and his chewing stopped guiltily together.

But Dad smiled broadly at him, putting a thick roll of comics down on a chair. 'Feeling rough, old son?' That was all he had time to say before Nanny Belmayne, still in her travelling clothes and her green squashy beret, rose from the end of the bed and gathered him into a gigantic hug. 'Here's my Emmie,' she murmured in between kisses. 'Here he is: my little old Emmie.' She seemed to tower over Dad, to bury him in her arms. Then Dad stooped over Louis in bed, and kissed him and rubbed his rough cheek so gently against Louis's pale one that Nanny Belmayne's love seemed to be relayed to Louis through Dad. Then she hugged both of them at once, making them equal little boys, and murmured to each how much she loved him.

To Dad, Louis now discovered, he was a hero. The circumstances of his fall were forgotten amid glowing praise for his bravery under X-Ray—a pleasant enough procedure—and his further bravery while the doctor had, painlessly, bandaged his foot. The roll of comics which Dad handed to him contained, not only his usual weekly order, like *Eagle* and *Knockout,* but also unfamiliar comics with red and yellow covers and names like *Hotspur* and *Wizard,* in such profusion as to suggest the ransacking of many bookstalls, wherever Dad had been on business. And even this giant comic roll, Dad made clear, was to be regarded as no more than an interim tribute.

'Bless him!' Nanny Belmayne said, kissing Louis again. '*What* a good boy he's been.'

'I know he has,' Dad said, also kissing Louis again. 'A very good boy. A boy worthy of a reward.'

'How's he going to get about love? He mustn't put his foot on the ground for two weeks. You'll have to buy him one of the donkeys they ride on the beach.'

'Oh, Nanny!' Louis laughed, with one eye wasting his comics, and Dad said adoringly: 'Oh, Mother—be serious!'

'Or we'll get him an elephant with a howdah on top.

Howdah you do?' Nanny Belmayne screwed her eyes up tight
—her habit while savouring one of her own jokes. 'You'll have
to find him a bath chair to ride in, Dad.'

'A push-chair,' Dad corrected. 'We'll have to try to get a
push-chair for him.' And Louis sank back among his pillows,
thinking, 'O Joy!' just as Biffo the Bear did in *Beano* comic.
'Swoon!' he thought—the word printed in comics above people
when they fainted with delight.

'A push-chair! A *push-chair*! O Joy!'

The next morning, Dad went out early, returned with a
black, folding push-chair and unfolded it with great deliberation, kneeling next to it on the front door mat. It had four
thin grey tyres and a footrest with channels, like the Wolseley's
running-board. He did not mention where he had acquired it,
and Louis did not dream of asking. It was just one further
instance of Dad's power over all mechanised things.

Often, seeing babies and what luxury was wasted on them,
he had wished he could be transported back to the epoch of
his own push-chair or pram, never thinking it might one day
happen; never dreaming of this delightful progress on a
sunny morning, down through the Ryde High Street in the
borrowed push-chair, through crowds that fell back on either
side and looked down at him—at his rug and bandaged foot—
with pity and admiration. Dad himself wheeled out the push-
chair on its maiden voyage, which had as an additional object
the rewarding of the invalid for heroism. The invalid attempted
to compose his face into a look of patient valour, though his
spirits were dancing and dazzling within him. For they were
on their way—in Union Street now, against a steep blue sea—
to Mainstone's, to buy him the popgun he wanted.

Mainstone's was dark after the sun, and fragrant with the
smell of soft rubber. The assistants were ladies in funereal
black, notoriously adept at spotting the browser and dismissing
facetious inquiries while barely glancing up from the counter.
Today, though they knew Louis of old, the Mainstone ladies
smiled at him, and smiled at Dad as he wheeled the push-chair
from counter to counter, past Hornby trains and Meccano sets

273

and life-size pandas and huge rubber dinghies, past buckets and spades and soldiers and throwing rings and archery-sets and Bendy Bunnies and Mobos and pedal jeeps and tall yachts and miniature clarinets and so many other things that Louis fell into a panic to think how many directions his life could take. Though affecting to look for the popgun, he recognised this as one of the moments when Dad would buy him anything in the world.

'Well, what's it to be, old son?' Dad prompted gently, 'The popgun or a nice launch?'

His eye flickered to and fro once more in covetous despair.

'Um—um. The launch.'

It was a fishing boat: the Frog 'Drifter'. He changed his mind before the assistant had finished wrapping it up. He sat with the parcel on his knees, feeling dismal at the squandering of his wonderful prerogative. Now, too late, he realised what he really wanted. It was the little yellow powerboat with the real outboard engine. Or was it the rabbit whose limbs you could tie into knots?

He saw Dad striding back from the other counter with a second brown paper parcel. He knew all along that he would get the popgun as well as the Frog 'Drifter'.

'Extra salary,' Dad said, kissing him. 'Because of being very *very* good.'

The two weeks he spent in the push-chair were the happiest of Louis's life. He simply sat there, putting the brake on and taking it off, while the world showered presents on him. He remembered the epoch afterwards as one of neurotic luxury— of drawing books with half their pages wasted; of chocolate left inside gold and silver corners in his haste to break a new bar; of green and black grapes so plentiful, he only troubled to bite off the tops, then stuck them like wet, translucent busbies on his fidgeting finger-ends.

He begged to be allowed to go back to school in the push-chair, and did so in conquering style, a few days before the end of the summer term. Miss King herself received him at the gate and wheeled him into Form One amid a little gasp of envious commiseration. Patricia Wade held a chair out for him to sit down. Miss Stella made a little speech saying how glad they all were to see him. At breaktime everybody crowded round to offer him sweets. Even Claire Thomas gave him two sherbet lemons. Janice Bennett gave him a Turf cigarette-card and said, with a smile that made his heart turn over, 'You'll be Captain next term, Louis. I'm going to vote for you.'

After school, Miss King or Miss Stella wheeled his push-chair across the stepping-stones for the ceremony of handing him over to Nanny Belmayne at the gate. She waited for him every day in the same Esplanade taxi, driven by the man whose head was all to one side like a broken concertina. He had been blown up in the First World War, Nanny Belmayne said. She called him 'one of Nature's Gentlemen'.

She had been back to London once, but had returned again for a few more days, just to be with him. She wheeled him along the Esplanade, singing, 'Bumpety-bumpety-bumpety-bump, as if I was riding my charger . . .'

She wheeled him into the Eastern Gardens where, less than a week ago, he had walked beside Mrs Durham, the captive of good behaviour. Squeaky violins were relayed from the lamp posts, a hymn to his liberation. Three weeks from now, he would be back on holiday at Orlando Road. Two weeks after that, they were to set off on their journey to the West Country. Nanny Belmayne had made all the arrangements.

'Bumpety-bumpety-bumpety-bump—as proud as an Indian rajah . . .'

By the Borough noticeboard, she stopped the push-chair, put the brake on and bent to smother his face and head in big, dry, smacking kisses.

'Bless him! *Bless* his old face, his Nan's going to take him down to Bath and Glastonbury soon like she promised—and *what* a time we'll have ourselves! His old Nan loves him and loves him *so* much!'

'Shall we be going to the West End as well, Nanny?'

'We shall, my lamb. And to see a Walt Disney at the Cameo, and have a Welsh Rarebit at Lyons' Corner House. I said I was going to get you one of those ships off Chelsea Bridge for Christmas.'

'Please can I have an ice-cream, Nanny?'

'What, my love?' she said in astonishment. 'Of *course* you can have an ice-cream! Ten ice-creams if you can eat 'em, my little love. Nan'll have a cornet with you if it's Wall's.'

One Sunday morning, Dad took him out in the Wolseley to catch newts in a pond at Binstead. Louis sat on the running-board, with long grass nestling close underneath, and watched Dad circle the pond with the shrimping net they had bought on their way. The sun was hot on the old black car, and the green that coated the pond gave off an odour like cabbage cooking at the London Hotel. He kept shouting out to Dad, 'can you see any yet?' and Dad called back, hold your horses and keep your hair on and other such kindly exhortations to be patient. It felt like long ago, on the river at St Neots, when he had watched Dad fishing, and taking the fish so gently from the line. The past was all coming true.

He caught three newts for Louis that morning. They were put into a goldfish bowl and displayed in the sitting-room, on top of the high chest of drawers. The newts showed no emotion at their captivity. They lay, with bodies overlapping, in the dark pond water, their tiny legs motionless, their snake eyes never blinking, their mouths registering no more than faint disgust. At first Louis intended them to be founders of a whole city of newts, with streets and newt houses, some newts to be citizens and others policemen or soldiers. But in his frenetic convalescence, he forgot this plan. The newts were left for other people to feed. He remembered them only when, out in the push-chair, he looked at the popgun and Frog 'Drifter', lying on the foot-rest, and thought: 'I've got three newts at home as well.'

Then something peculiar happened. One by one the newts vanished from their bowl. Charles had eaten them, so Louis's mother told him, but he was reluctant, for some reason, to believe this. He wondered if the newts could have climbed out of the bowl and jumped down from the chest, and might therefore still be at large somewhere under the linen press or the sofa.

He sat in the hall, in the push-chair, waiting for Nanny Belmayne and pondering the mystery of the vanished newts. Could they even have jumped straight out of the bowl? He must ask Nanny Belmayne and his mother, after they had finished talking to each other, whether newts could jump.

Nanny Belmayne came out of the sitting-room first, and Louis leaned forward in the push-chair to take the brake off, ready for the pleasant experience of being bumped downstairs. Then his mother came out, holding an unlit cigarette in one hand and fumbling with a match. Her face looked shiny and bad tempered. Nanny Belmayne must have been trying to cheer her up. She must have been advising her to count her blessings.

'Yes—I might have known,' she said. 'You're always carrying tales back to Emile about me, aren't you? Oh yes, you do. You've done it before and you'll do it again.'

'No, my love—of course I don't.'

'Oh yes, you do.'

'No, my love—of *course* not . . .'

At first Louis thought she was paying Nanny Belmayne some kind of compliment—praising her for the speed with which some message or information had been conveyed to Dad. Yet Nanny Belmayne—for all that she tried to agree with everyone and pacify everyone—seemed reluctant to accept this particular compliment. She had paused by the flat door with one hand on the door knob and the toe of her lace-up shoe pointed, as though, in her grey 'costume' and green beret, she were posing for some full-length formal portrait like those on the staircase at the Duke of Wellington's house.

'No-o, my love. I never carry tales to anybody. Not to anybody, my love.'

Nanny Belmayne's voice, unfailingly gentle and kind, had a ripple of mirth running through it, to think that anyone could

277

accuse her of so petty and mortal a thing. In anguish, convinced that some terrible mistake had been made, Louis looked at his mother, beside the kitchen door, still standing her ground against all Nanny Belmayne's gentleness.

'Yes—yes. You can say what you like.' Her voice, in this forbidden territory, grew stronger. It was—yet how could it be?—almost angry.

'I know this'll be straight back down the pier to Emile. You're going straight down now, I expect, to tell him what I've said. Straight off to carry tales.'

Then, to Louis's amazement, Nanny Belmayne turned and went out of the flat without him. His mother had gone back into the sitting-room. He was left alone in the hall in his push-chair, still gripping the brake.

He stared at its crooked shaft for a long time, unable to give words to the thought which had come into his mind.

Was it possible . . .

Was it possible that his mother did not love Nanny Belmayne as much as he did?

the great west road

Nanny Belmayne shut the front door behind them, and Louis looked for one last time through the red and blue glass, along the narrow hall, with its wooden couch and buffalo horns, and up the dark stairs to the curtain at the top where for days he had rolled and tangled himself, waiting and wishing and begging God to dispose of the hours more quickly. He remembered yesterday: how interminable had seemed the morning and afternoon, how many hours last night he had lain awake, staring out of the big brass bedstead at the night-light; the wash-stand; the picture of Jesus, above the gas fire, sadly contemplating his crown of thorns. And he remembered how it had felt, at last, when he opened his eyes to see light in the window, beyond Nanny Belmayne's dressing table, and happiness had struck through him as he lay there, rubbing his toes together under the sheet and thinking the same words over and over:

'Today! It's today. We're going to the West Country today. We're going to the West Country. O Joy!'

They crossed over Orlando Road at the top, opposite the bomb site, and went down Klea Avenue next to houses with

279

high front staircases and piled-up bay windows and brickwork finished in red and white, tigerish stripes. No one was about yet but the milkman and one lady, in a turban and pinafore, who was kneeling and scrubbing her high front step. 'Good-bye', Louis thought, feeling sorry for her because her life would stay the same today, and tonight, while he was in the West Country, she would see only the usual yellow-tinged, roaring London sky.

He wore new black shoes, the first ever bought for him with laces and hard soles. His shoes felt heavy, and clattered on the pavement as he walked. Each step in the hard shoes seemed to jog his excitement and set it fluttering in his throat like birds; in his stomach, like waiting to race on Sports Day; in every single one of his bones, like an extra skeleton that tingled and buzzed as it marched along inside him.

Nanny Belmayne carried their suitcase. It was very large and old-fashioned, of a brown canvasy fabric, with darker brown corners, and much old string, and torn railway labels bunched around its handle. Inside it, Nanny Belmayne's clothes and Louis's were packed up all together—his vests and her satin knickers, her knitting needles, his popgun and the blue wool and a cactus for Aunt Kate, and so much else that, with her string bag to manage as well, the suitcase was almost too heavy for Nanny Belmayne. They had only gone a short way along Klea Avenue when she had to put it down and have a rest. Then she picked it up in her other hand and they walked on. They had almost drawn level with the flats being built for policemen's families. Nanny Belmayne put the suitcase down again, had another rest, then picked it up in her other hand.

'Hurry *up*, Nanny!' Louis thought as he waited for her, and his sock-garters, biting round his legs, implanted a terrible suspicion that something might happen to the West Country if they delayed any longer; that by tonight, it would have stopped being there.

Their coach was travelling away from London in a race of

traffic, past clean white factories set among lawns; past rows of modern shops with new flats above; past Tudor estate agents and lorry depots and garden-encircled Tube stations with newly-built, rural-sounding names. It was sunny and windy together, and the gushing coach and whistling wind, and clouds in the roof-window, tearing along overhead, gave everything a look of urgency, of flight down one broad road towards the same destination.

'Whereabouts are we now, Nanny?' he asked.

'This, my love?' she said, and he noticed how much deeper and richer her West Country accent seemed already.

'Why—this here's the start of the old Great West Road.'

'The old Great West Road' was a thrilling name to think. This must be the way she had travelled on that historic day when she left behind the life in the album-pages and set off to establish her London domain. Now, in his eyes, each strange suburb took on a familiar look. The factories and flats and florists and parked vans all seemed, in their way, to acknowledge and be proud of an unwitting place in the chronicle of Nanny Belmayne's life.

She nudged him.

'Come on, Lou, have a bit o'chocolate. And a Murraymint. Take two, my duck.'

Their journey was not destined, however, to be a happy one. They were sitting right at the back of the coach, on the long seat facing up the gangway. Louis had insisted on sitting here, despite Nanny Belmayne's suggestion that they would be better off near the front. At first, after the coach left Victoria, he had enjoyed the swaying and bumping motion. For lunch, produced from her string bag as the Houses of Parliament receded, he had eaten two big doughnuts, a cold sausage, a Blenheim apple, several Murraymints and Butter Brazils, some pickled onions, an orange with a sugar-lump in it and a piece of home-made lardy cake.

A little way further along the Great West Road, he suddenly began to taste pickled onions and lardy cake together. A funny feeling came into his eyes, as if the speed of the coach had

281

magnetised them and was pulling them inexorably out of focus. He looked for a window to open—it was too high; too far forward. They had stopped for traffic lights, next to a removal lorry, and he gazed with unspeakable envy at a man he could see, resting one elbow carelessly over the name written on the cab. The coach gathered speed again, clawing his eyes up closer and closer. Several people around him were smoking cigarettes. A dry patch had come into his throat; then he could not stop yawning . . .

He held his breath for shame as Nanny Belmayne set off along the swaying aisle to see the driver and ask him to stop because somebody wanted to be sick. He could see her at the front, holding tight with one sleeve to a silver pole and leaning down towards the driver as he answered her over his shoulder. The driver was telling her he had no time to stop, and Nanny Belmayne seemed to be replying he had better, if he didn't want sick all over his coach.

The coach stopped.

The road at that place ran between wide grass verges, through a forest of straight, dark pines. Louis climbed down the step next to the driver and walked slowly towards the forest, feeling himself watched by everyone in the coach. He discovered that he no longer felt sick. Embarrassment and fresh air had completely cured him.

He stood in the bushes for a moment, then he walked back, stumbling a little, towards the coach and the faces all along it, waiting for him. Just as he was climbing the steps, he remembered the lardy cake. He jumped down again, as the faces watched, and ran back towards the forest.

Late in the afternoon they reached Witney in Oxfordshire where Nanny Belmayne said they must change buses for New Yatt. As they left the coach, the driver asked her in an angry voice if she realised how much of other people's time she had wasted with all this stopping and starting—for Louis had been sick twice more along the Great West Road. Nanny Belmayne answered in ringing tones that it was better than having sick
282

all over his nice clean coach. Their heads held high, they marched off across the bus station—or half-way across it since in a moment Nanny Belmayne had to put the suitcase down, and pick it up in her other hand.

From Witney, a double-decker bus carried them, between winding hedges, across countryside timeless with evening sun. By now, Louis's travel sickness had all gone; his senses all felt light and sharp; he looked about him with excitement—at high fields and resting sheep, at the prettily-scarred cottages and deeply-drifted farms, where people must now be sitting down to lovely West Country teas. Everybody on the bus spoke with an accent like Nanny Belmayne's—even the conductor, whose 'Any more fez please?' had precisely the same inflection, jolly but gentle. People looked at Nanny Belmayne, seeming to recognise her: she looked back smiling, as if to say: 'This is my little grandson. He broke a bone in his ankle last month. I've always promised I'd bring him to the West Country one day.'

'Will Auntie Bessie Appleton be there to meet us, Nanny?' he inquired anxiously.

'She will, my duck. She wrote me how much she was looking forward to seeing you again. "How I loved him", she wrote.'

'What is she to me, though?'

'She's your auntie—not a real auntie, but one of Nanny's old, old friends. That makes her your auntie. She looked after you during the War. And she looked after your Daddy and Uncle Cal when they were babies, down at Bampton.'

'How old was I when she looked after me?'

'Just a baby, love. All the bombs were going on in London, and you'd been sleeping in the Underground under those dreadful bright lights. You were down here for ever such a long time. Don't you remember Uncle Jethro? He gave you a little bath all to yourself in front of the fire.'

They got off the bus in bright sunshine and walked along a straight road with no pavement and cottages on either side, each at the top of its own long, cabbagey garden. Every few
283

yards, Nanny Belmayne stopped and put down their suitcase, and sighed and then picked it up in her other hand. There ahead, in the bright sun, was Auntie Bessie Appleton, walking down the middle of the road to meet them. Louis ran towards her, with a loud cracking of his new shoes, and Auntie Bessie Appleton opened her arms wide to receive him.

He had forgotten the main thing about Auntie Bessie Appleton. He stared with fascination at her as they sat in her cottage after tea, in the place next to the front door which she called her 'little room'. For Auntie Bessie Appleton was, without a doubt, the fattest woman he had ever seen. Her body, as she sat in her armchair, put Louis in mind of nothing so much as the huge laundry bags used for table-linen at the Pavilion. Auntie Bessie Appleton seemed to have one such long and overfilled laundry bag hanging from each shoulder, reaching almost as far down as the gigantic lap in which her hands lay, scrubbed to a high pink and peacefully folded. Her legs were too fat even to look at. Yet her head was not fat at all. She had grey hair, tied up behind with a slide, and an overhanging forehead beneath which sheltered a little bright-cheeked, bright-eyed, jovial face. Her voice was like Nanny Belmayne's but squeakier. Nanny Belmayne called her 'Bessie' but she called Nanny 'Mrs Belmayne' despite all the years they had been friends.

On a table beside Auntie Bessie Appleton's chair stood a wooden box with a handle and a money-slot at the top. Louis asked what this box was for, and Auntie Bessie Appleton replied: 'That's the Poor Box. That's where I put the money I saves for my little black babies.'

Uncle Jethro, her husband, was now dead, and Auntie Bessie Appleton lived alone in the grey stone cottage with its rose-trellis and crooked front gate, its low-beamed, stone-flagged cluster of rooms. Her kitchen contained a scrubbed table, an easy chair with home-knitted patchwork cushions; a narrow mantel, on which were displayed two brass crucifixes, flanking the photograph of Uncle Jethro; a brass kettle, a coalscuttle, a work-basket and a stove like a little black green-
284

house with brightly-glowing doors. In the corner by the dresser stood an iron mangle draped with three tea towels. Downstairs, as well as the 'little room', there was Auntie Bessie Appleton's best parlour, a narrow hallway and a winding staircase to two bedrooms. A white lace coverlet lay on the bed in which Louis and Nanny Belmayne were to sleep.

Auntie Bessie Appleton did not have a bathroom. You washed at the sink in an outside scullery with logs stacked along the wall next to the old stove where Auntie Bessie Appleton fried chips in a black iron frying pan. The only toilet was half-way up her sloping back garden—just a tiny shed, half-buried in ivy and flat, translucent marrow-leaves, where you sat on an old wooden seat in company with garden tools and flowerpots and a notice on a rusty nail inside the door that said, in faded brown writing, *Please shut door as adders come in.*

That night, he lay in the small bed, very close to Nanny Belmayne, looking out through lace curtains at the single lamp that shone in the village street. No one was moving, anywhere in Oxfordshire. He listened to the deep silence until it seemed to shrill against his ears.

'Why's Auntie Bessie so fat, Nanny, do you think?'

'Ssh, my love. It's politer to say she's a bit stout.'

'But why is she, Nanny?'

'It's glands,' Nanny Belmayne's voice replied sadly.

'Is it because of having too many black babies?'

Nanny Belmayne did not answer, but only chuckled in the darkness.

Next morning, an extraordinary thing happened. Auntie Bessie Appleton, in a gigantic red dressing gown, brought them a tray of tea, put it down on the coverlet, then she got into bed with them. Nanny Belmayne did not seem to think this at all odd, and moved over to make room for her, propelling Louis, on his side, right to the edge of the bed. But for the tucked-in bedclothes, he would have fallen out.

'There's no room!' he muttered angrily.

Auntie Bessie Appleton described to Nanny Belmayne an

illness she had recently suffered—connected, one could only suppose, with her enormous fatness—and what terrible experiences she had had in hospital: the impolite doctors, the unkind Sister and nurses and, in particular, the roughness with which her 'dressings' had been removed. Nanny Belmayne's voice murmured in condolence and Louis, wedged on his side, pictured huge, long strips of pink Elastoplast being summarily wrenched and ripped from Auntie Bessie Appleton's agonised but uncomplaining figure.

Every so often, Nanny Belmayne moved over a little more, and he was propelled further into the sling of bedclothes. 'She's got a bed of her own, hasn't she?' he continued to mutter. 'Why can't she stop in her own bed?'

But Nanny Belmayne only chuckled, and Auntie Bessie Appleton stayed in their bed, and returned to it every morning, to enlarge on that trying illness, those uncivil nurses, the pain and shock when those dressings had been unsympathetically torn from her. She had much else to tell Nanny Belmayne about the years since they had last seen each other—about chutney and jam-making; about blankets knitted for the Witney Red Cross, about cakes baked for the Chapel she attended, and the enmities aroused by worship and what the Minister, Mr Berry, had said to her in confidence. She and Nanny Belmayne had much information to exchange on the subjects of Rheumatism and Arthritis—and an entirely new personality named Rheumatoid Arthritis—to say nothing of bunions and corns, and what was to be done about them.

They talked as well, about the dear little baby Louis had been when he stayed with Auntie Bessie Appleton during the War, and how much the deceased Uncle Jethro had loved him. Uncle Jethro had never recovered from his departure, so Louis gathered, and had died soon afterwards of a broken heart.

'I used to say your prayers with you every night,' Auntie Bessie Appleton told him. 'I hope you still says 'em.'

'How he used to love Jethro to bath him in front of the fire,' Nanny Belmayne said. ' "Let Uncle do it!" you used to
286

shout. And he gave you a little walking stick all of your very own.'

'What happened to the walking stick?' Louis asked with interest.

'I don't know, my lamb. I think you put it down a drain somewhere.'

They talked a great deal as well about Dad and Uncle Cal as children, when Auntie Bessie Appleton used to look after them—how sweet and good both were, but how especially adorable Dad used to be because of his speech impediment. That rival little boy, with his square-necked jersey, his cupid lips but imperfect enunciation, had come to the West Country with them.

'Remember how he used to shout out if anyone came to the door. "It's only that old carter-man. Letten in! Letten in!"'

'He used to relish my green tomato chutney,' Auntie Bessie said. 'And my Victoria plum jam.'

'I know, Bessie. I can hear him now, what he'd say if you asked whether he wanted some more. He couldn't say "Yes please". "Yeppease" was all he could say. "Yeppease, Bessie, yeppease"!'

Louis began to tire of all this talking. They hardly went out at all at New Yatt, because of Auntie Bessie Appleton's bad feet. In the evening they would walk through the village to see the Chapel or visit a Post Office which, to his disgust, stocked neither soldiers nor Venus pencils. They went on the bus one afternoon to Bampton, to look at the Talbot Hotel, where Nanny Belmayne had lived with Grandpa Belmayne, before he was torpedoed. After all the stories Louis had heard about 'when we were at Bampton', he was disappointed to be shown what looked like an ordinary pub, with cobwebby bay windows and many chimneys, straggling along the village street. They did not go inside because Auntie Bessie Appleton's religion forbade it. So Louis never discovered if Nanny Belmayne was still remembered there.

Towards the end of their stay at New Yatt, he grew restive and rather naughty. He took to drawing pictures of Auntie

Bessie Appleton, whom he depicted walking among clouds that bore signposts 'to Heaven' and 'to Hell'. He picked up the Poor Box and shook it, pretending to steal the money from her little black babies. He recited poems he had made up about Auntie Bessie Appleton, alluding to her great fatness. One such poem went:

> Auntie Bessie Appleton
> is so very very fat
> she could hardly play cricket
> without a cricket bat.

Auntie Bessie Appleton only smiled. Nanny Belmayne took the Poor Box from him and put it back on the table.

'Steady now, my love . . .'

'Steady!' he mimicked rudely. 'Steady! Steady!'

He was glad when she clicked the thumb on the gate-latch and they could start off again with their big suitcase down the road towards the bus stop. After they had walked a little way, Nanny Belmayne put the case down, had a little rest, then picked it up with her other hand. Auntie Bessie Appleton was still waving goodbye to them from her cottage gate.

Aunt Kate was waiting to meet them at Hungerford, in front of the Bear Hotel. She was Nanny Belmayne's cousin, from some branch of the family deep in the photograph albums. She was very old and shy and gentle and so wrinkled that, when she bent down to give him a kiss, Louis felt afraid of the scratches all over her skin and the two big drops of flesh suspended beneath her astonished-looking pale blue eyes. She wore a black straw hat with red and pink wax flowers along the brim, and a long, loose-fronted, black and white spotted dress with a greyish vest underneath it, stretched high across the rods in her neck. As Louis kissed her, he caught a scent that reminded him of Nanny Belmayne's wardrobe—a scent of mothballs and lavender and shoetrees and things put away for years in special boxes, lined with newspaper from another reign. Her nose was very long, and so was her chin;

her lips turned downward, and they moved, even when she was not speaking as though she were silently saying her prayers. 'Thank you moi dear,' she said in a faraway, bubbly West Country voice when Louis presented her with the cactus he had brought her.

They walked with Aunt Kate, very slowly, and with frequent rests, along the High Street, spanned by its heavy railway bridge; then, even more slowly, and with more rests to put down the suitcase, they climbed a steep road, lined with nettles and unripe brambles, that wound above the silent redbrick town.

Aunt Kate lived on the crest of the hill, in a house of that same red brick, perfectly square and with four windows of precisely equal size, like one of the china houses at home in Nanny Belmayne's cabinet. Below her back garden was the road to the Common, where an asylum stood; below that was the railway station, and the river that ran side by side with the canal.

Like Auntie Bessie Appleton, Aunt Kate had recently 'lost' her husband—in this case, Uncle Bill. It seemed to be the rule among all Nanny Belmayne's old ladies that they should have suffered this loss and also that, while undoubtedly most regrettable, and productive of long, melancholy pauses and stares into the spaces of quiet kitchens, having 'lost' one's husband should also provide a topic for conversation as interesting and satisfying in its own way as corns and bunions and bad legs and the War and rationing and the mild winter and Mr Churchill and the poor Duke of Windsor and what, on multifarious occasions, the doctor had said.

They sat with Aunt Kate all afternoon in her small back kitchen, which had a stone floor and a black cooking-range with a tiny saucepan fizzling gently on it. In one corner stood a grandfather clock with pale flowers on its face and a painting of swans set in a gloomy arbour above. As the clock ticked, the neck of the foremost swan waved slowly back and forth. The clock ticked loudly, with one light and one heavy tick; the little saucepan fizzed on the range. Aunt Kate stared out

289

of the window with her big, faded eyes, moving her lips in soundless prayer. You could see only sky in her windows, with thin clouds racing past. Louis pretended the clouds were still—it was really Aunt Kate's house that hurtled through the universe, its meteor-course registered by the stir of the breeze in old white lace curtains.

In the evening, Nanny Belmayne went to the off-licence and bought Tizer for Louis and, for Aunt Kate and herself, tall black bottles of stout. That was the black, bitter, creamy-topped stuff that old ladies drank to do them good. Nanny Belmayne enjoyed 'a glass o' stout' but had been deprived of it at New Yatt since Auntie Bessie Appleton's religion forbade stout. At Aunt Kate's there were also dark green packets of Churchman's No 3 on the table, which rather shocked Louis—he had not realised before that Nanny Belmayne smoked cigarettes. When Aunt Kate raised the glass of stout to her lips, her expression was calm but sad, as if she were reminded of the husband she had lost, or of how kind Jesus was. But when Nanny Belmayne drank stout, her cheeks grew even rosier than usual, and her chuckle became richer and more frequent. Once she gave a loud roaring burp, and then, without repentance, said: 'Pardon Mrs Arden.' She leaned from her armchair across the table, pulled a new bottle of stout towards her, twisted off the top and said to Aunt Kate: 'Shall I say "Pass your glass"? Or "Pass your glass, you silly ass"?'

Louis grew bored with all the talk and silences and Tizer. He took the tin of cigarette cards Aunt Kate had given him and went to sit on the back doorstep. He was not angry, knowing as he did that, though she might be drinking stout and discussing bunions with Aunt Kate, Nanny Belmayne's thoughts were still directed towards him. Her attachment to old ladies was, he knew, merely dutiful; in her heart she would have preferred to be with him, eating ice-cream, discussing the American Civil War, visiting the Duke of Wellington's house or the West End, for a Walt Disney, a Welsh Rarebit and a 'mooch round'.

Aunt Kate's garden sloped downwards. There were gravel

paths criss-crossing among beds of tall and stiff-necked flowers whose names Louis did not know. Over the fence he could see the clotted red Hungerford houses, the clock tower in the High Street, the slate roofs and sheds and washing lines, the railway station's yellow palings, the grey light of the river, then empty hills beyond, with bonfires darkly smearing the sky. The roses on Aunt Kate's trellis were almost over, like summer itself, bruised and flustered and shedding their yellow petals around the path. Louis, all at once, felt a shape in his mind— a sensation lighter than the breeze, that he had seen all this before, or was fated to see it again in some far future epoch, exactly as it was this afternoon, with overblown roses, the clock tower flatly chiming, and bonfire smoke, and Hungerford, very peaceful in the sun.

He sat on the back step, looking through the cigarette cards which Aunt Kate had kept for years in a tin once used for 'Nosegay' tobacco. There were whole sets, of cricketers, athletes, railway engines and 'Notable MP's,' held together by elastic bands or compressed into solid blocks by damp, so that their pictures tore when Louis tried to pull them apart.

All the same, he wished Nanny Belmayne and Aunt Kate would hurry up. They were going for a walk later, down to the Eddington Bridge to look at a house where Aunt Kate's sister used to live. Louis wanted the walk to be over and tonight to be over and tomorrow to be almost over. Even here in the West Country, in Nanny Belmayne's ancestral land, he had found a reason for willing the time away.

One of the stories which Nanny Belmayne used to read to Louis was of Theodore, 'the little bear who always means well'. Theodore, a Koala bear with hairy paws and a beak-like nose, lived a life of perpetual but endearing misapprehension. His adventures, printed below a set of three black and white illustrations, invariably recounted how Theodore, involved in a game with real life boys and girls, had made some elementary mistake in pronouncing or understanding a word. In one story, Theodore played cricket and was asked by the captain of his team to keep wicket. ' "But I don't want to keep wicket", the little bear said in dismay. "I want to keep good!" ' When Nanny Belmayne read this to Louis, she paused and looked at him in a significant way over the top of her glasses. Clearly because his own hated middle name was Theodore, she perceived some analogy of lovableness between the misguided animal and him.

Later on, Louis had read on his own the magazine which published Theodore's adventures. It was called *Woman's Weekly*. It had a pink cover with the title printed in light blue and underneath, a picture of two ladies wearing cardigans or jumpers, the patterns for which could be found on inside pages. *Woman's Weekly* was full of such patterns, for knitting, sewing, embroidery, as well as cookery recipes and directions for the unusual folding of serviettes. These were activities seldom, if ever, practised by Nanny Belmayne, yet she always took *Woman's Weekly*, approving of it, in theory, so warmly that, like the *Daily Express* or *Sunny Stories* it seemed to exist solely to be read by her, and to reflect her opinions and have its back copies hoarded by her in a deep pile under the kitchen wash-stand.

A few days before they started for the West Country, Louis had been lying in the big bed, eating Brazil nut toffee and reading yet another old copy of *Woman's Weekly*. The big bed was still unmade, its sheets and blankets thrown together over the brass towers at the foot. Open in front of Louis was the page to which *Woman's Weekly* readers applied for advice from The Friend Who Understands, a moustachioed personage shown by the illustration in the half-light of a desk-lamp and, to Louis, as familiar a detail of Nanny Belmayne's bedroom as the wardrobe, the green-tiled fireplace, the pictures of Jesus or the 'Edgar Allan', still brimful under the bed.

The next page had photographs of dolls which could be knitted by the reader at home. His eye, skimming over them, suddenly stopped. These were not ordinary dolls, for little girls or babies. They were male dolls, dressed in real uniforms. The reader could make a doll serving in the Army, the Navy,

292

the Air Force or the Red Cross. Patterns were provided for knitting the bodies and making the uniforms; there were pictures, all rather murky, of hands anatomising tiny torsos to insert stuffing. In a final dark photograph four dolls sat together, in an Army, a Navy, an Air Force and a Red Cross uniform, their arms stiffly outstretched, their flat woollen faces wearing benign but rather weary, stitched-up smiles.

As soon as he saw the Air Force doll, Louis wanted it with an intensity that made his breath come in little snorts and his heart beat in both ears like a hammer. It was as if, at that moment, an entirely new existence began, rendering obsolete and absurd all previous notions of what happiness might be. He knew he could have no peace until he possessed this knitted figure in its Air Force uniform exactly like the one Dad had worn—the same, indeed, which Dad wore in the photograph on Nanny Belmayne's dressing-table. The tunic of the doll had those same pleated pockets and winged insignia, even loops on the shoulders, one with a tiny forage-cap pushed through. Under its tunic, it wore a shirt and a tie. These, most of all, made Louis long for the Air Force doll—its shirt and its tie. Nothing of such perfection had ever graced his life.

Down in the first floor kitchen, Nanny Belmayne was giving Bobby a dose of flea powder. She had rolled back a corner of the green baize tablecloth, and Bobby stood there in a dense white cloud, his empty eye-sockets cast down, his flannelly coat vibrating in a low growl. As Louis came in, a big yellow flea jumped out of Bobby's back, and Nanny Belmayne struck fiercely at it with the brass back-scratcher she held in her other hand. Bang, bang went the claw-like hand on the table, but the flea hopped through its clutching brass fingers and escaped through the open window, or into the open meat-safe.

He showed Nanny Belmayne the page in *Woman's Weekly* and asked if she would make him the Air Force doll. She didn't answer for a moment. She took it and turned over, looking at other doll patterns, for prosaic knitted farm animals. 'Here's Bertie the Bull,' she said. 'And here's Clara the Cow.'

K*

'*Will* you, Nanny—*please* make it for me. Please, Nanny, oh, *please,* Nanny. *Please*!'

'I will, love,' she said.

O Joy, he thought. O Joy, O Joy, O Joy!

'When, Nanny, will you?'

'When we're away. We'll get the wool at Brixton. We'll go to the Bon Marché for it.'

'But *when,* Nanny?'

'Soon, love, I promise.'

Then she returned to giving Bobby his flea powder, and Louis walked along the passage, and rolled and tangled himself in ecstasy in the dark, damp catty-smelling curtain at the top of the stairs.

They went to Brixton, to the Bon Marché, and the night before their journey, Louis sat with his arms extended, holding up skeins of wool which, in his excitement, seemed an appropriately Air Force shade of blue. Nanny Belmayne wound it into balls by the light of her table lamp shaped like an owl.

She was knitting all the time on their journey to the West Country. It was an unaccustomed, not wholly congenial thing for her to sit still, with needles on her lap, but she persevered —on the coach first, then in New Yatt, while listening to the stories of Auntie Bessie Appleton's dressings. Louis was afraid at first that someone who knitted so seldom, and so peremptorily, might find the pattern of an Air Force doll too difficult; especially, he feared that the little pleated tunic and epaulets and collar and tie might make too great a demand on her skill. Nanny Belmayne herself seemed to harbour no such doubts. She continued knitting, with that same sense of having driven herself to it, her face frowning like a kindly cannibal's, at times giving the ball of wool in her lap an impatient little jerk.

By the time they reached Hungerford, she had finished one long blue, sleeve-like piece. He saw it, mixed up with her knitting needles and the pattern from *Woman's Weekly,* on top of the fruit bowl in Aunt Kate's front room. He turned and hurried away, not wanting to see it until he held it, finished

294

and fully-dressed and perfect, in his hands.

Nanny Belmayne had promised she would finish it in time for him to take back to Ryde at the end of the holidays. He had asked God to make the time go quicker until then.

Aunt Kate accompanied them on the journey to Glastonbury and Bath. Though this had been arranged long ago by letter, it was Nanny Belmayne's forceful presence, and possibly the stout and Churchman's No 3, which persuaded Aunt Kate to wind her grandfather clock, water her many cacti, shut the sky out of her back windows and, at last, step timidly through her front door in a long, dusty black coat and a dark blue straw hat and spotted veil. Burdened by two suitcases now, the three of them made their way down the hill, just as the clock tower in the High Street tolled a flat, slow nine o'clock.

Aboard the coach, Aunt Kate shut her eyes and her lips moved in prayer beneath the veil, which strained and billowed in the crosswind from several open windows. Nanny Belmayne sat beside her, reassuring her with talk of poultices and corns. Louis sat two rows forward, next to a lady who kept smiling at him in a friendly way. He had no time to smile back.

This was the Bath Road. From the Bear Hotel, it flew in an undeviating line through the rolled-back hills, its sole objective to reach with all possible speed the city of Nanny Belmayne's birth. The coach, too, seemed to understand how pre-eminent was their final destination, stopping by the roadside or in unimportant market places, waiting while people got on or off with the fingers of its engine tapping impatiently, then leaping away again down the Bath Road like a racehorse ahead of the field.

No qualm of travel sickness troubled Louis now. He sat erect, a breeze blowing in his face, holding on with both hands to the chromium rail—tighter and tighter as the coach, as Bath came nearer and all Nanny Belmayne's stories about it congregated in his mind. He pictured the bustles, the parasols, the dog-carts and 'chay-carts' and governess-carts; the beer and champagne, served to Nanny Belmayne's father, of which she herself always had a little taste; and the butter pats she had cut in the dairy, as big as the space between her finger and thumb. The Bath streets would, he thought, be flickering and yellow, like a Charlie Chaplin film, but there would be steep, lush meadows, where the dairies stood, and mansions, like the china houses in her cabinet and so, possibly, sharing the view with giant reproductions of Bonnie Prince Charlie, and piccaninnies eating watermelon, and pug dog faces and toy cannons and haughty Staffordshire greyhounds with parts of their legs and feet broken.

At another stop he saw Nanny Belmayne stand up and start pulling down her coat from the rack. 'We're here,' she signalled, to his amazement: he had assumed this to be just one more town on the way to Bath. But everyone in the coach was getting up, pulling bags down; a soldier retrieved Aunt Kate's valise while she sat there, still praying among the leeches in her veil. The rattling vibration, which had for hours nurtured his excitement, suddenly ceased. The friendly lady next to him made as if to rise with a smile for 'Excuse me.' They had arrived.

Outside, he could see no meadows or dairies or dog-carts— only a bus station. Slanted bays for buses and a neon-sign, *Buffet*. A street of shops, quite ordinary; unflickering crowds, mundanely-coloured. On the corner, as they waited, a beacon flashed at the usual intervals.

Nanny Belmayne had arranged for them to stay three nights at a place called The Roseville Private Hotel. She said they could walk to it easily from the bus station. Had Nanny Belmayne not been born in Bath, had she not grown up in Bath and been spiritually acquainted with it throughout her metropolitan life, one might have supposed she had lost her way. For it seemed to Louis they had been hours in toiling up this elevated pavement, past the gates of houses built on rockery walls, high into the sky. Every few yards, Nanny Belmayne stopped to put the big suitcase down and pick it up in the hand she had been using to consult the letter from The Roseville Private Hotel. Aunt Kate, her veil and small portmanteau,

296

followed with timid, thrush-like steps. Encountering a seat, they sat on it for a long time, their baggage all around them. Louis, in his hard shoes, paced distractedly to the pavement-edge, where car and lorry roofs—the same as in the everyday world —thundered to and from a concrete tunnel entrance.

A kind gentleman led them eventually to The Roseville Private Hotel—or, at least, two gateposts of that name, the hotel itself being hidden beyond yet another steep front garden. Climbing up past terraced lawns, Louis noticed groups of ornamental pixies occupied in motionless excavation work among model toadstools and storks, and a cut-out man in a red waistcoat who nodded briskly and jerked his knee up and down as the breeze spun a windmill above his head. Slowly from the summit, a building arose that was no hotel but an ordinary house of yellow brick, stained like a chapel with age or damp. Somewhere inside, a dog saw them and began to bark.

He lay in bed by himself at The Roseville Private Hotel. He had been given a room on his own, away from Nanny Bel-mayne, and had submitted to it, wishing to place no stress on Mrs Marksman's kindness. His room was at the back of the house: beneath his window, Bath revealed a large expanse of itself, not in meadows and dairies but in drab hills and terraces and yellow street lamps that threw steep banisters of light across the wallpaper above his head. Far below, he could hear lorries still thundering past the embankment where they had almost got lost this afternoon.

Bath had ceased to be his journey's end. He turned from the window to face the yellow-lit wall, and hid himself under the blankets, in the lair of a new dream. He thought about the Air Force doll until he fell asleep.

For breakfast there were boiled eggs so undercooked that the whites were still slithery water. Only Aunt Kate could bear to finish hers. 'Ugh! Auntie, how *can* you!' Louis cried, turning away as her jaws shut placidly over the teaspoon.

297

When Mrs Marksman brought the teapot in, she was accompanied by a large, grey, grubby dog with copiously watering eyes. The dog licked Louis's hand, sat on his toe and belaboured his chair-leg with a stump-like tail.

'What do you call him?'

'We call him Chummy,' Mrs Marksman said. 'That's what we call him if he's been a good boy. When he's been a bad boy, we call him Chum.'

She withdrew, with Chummy, amid the chorus of their thanks. For she had been so very kind, Nanny Belmayne said. Mrs Marksman's kindness, it transpired, had been manifest chiefly at the letter-writing stage, when her willingness to provide accommodation had elevated her to a postal sainthood in Nanny Belmayne's eyes. Such was the extent of her past kindness that they strove, at Nanny Belmayne's prompting, to impose no further on it. Mrs Marksman, a trilling, whiskery woman, for her part did her best not to be imposed on. Watery eggs, blood-streaked kidneys, towels no larger than face-flannels and baths at a shilling each were just a few incarnations of her kindness, while extra considerations—such as Aunt Kate's morning glass of hot water—could be procured only by the loudest eulogies. Mr Marksman, who toiled unseen in the kitchen, came out to meet them during their whole stay only once. He wore a pink eye patch, smoked a pipe that smelled of prunes and achieved an instantaneous reputation for kindness in Nanny Belmayne's eyes, mainly through having been born near Trowbridge.

They spent one whole day in walking around Bath, looking at the dull streets and squares which had overgrown Harewood House, the stables and coach-house and pigeon-loft, and every other part of Nanny Belmayne's father's original estate, even out to the field where, early one morning in the 1890's, Nanny Belmayne and her sister had picked a mushroom so enormous, it covered the floor of the governess cart in which it was taken home. They visited the churchyard where Nanny Belmayne's mother, who had died so very young, lay buried beneath a tombstone which, for all its age, seemed to bear out stories of her kindness and mildness, just as Nanny Belmayne's father's tomb-stone was more indicative of wildness and losing one's money; they discovered also the graves of several other ancestors who, for all the incidence of madness among them, and the tendency to put revolvers into their mouths, had all, by Nanny Belmayne's account, been the most wonderful and affectionate of people. There lay Louis's ancestors, under stones etched with separate portions of his hated name, without urns or angels or flowers to commemorate them, in a part of the churchyard where even the grass failed to grow. He left Nanny Belmayne and Aunt Kate talking, and wandered off, more interested in the brand-new graves, the silver-grey or black-veined oblongs, the bright-gold lettering of fresh grief.

The next day they went by bus to Glastonbury to see the Abbey. It proved to be ruined—from Nanny Belmayne's de-scriptions, Louis had not expected that. There was nothing to it but mounds of grass, littered with grey stone in clumps or corners or incomplete arches, filled with disillusioning present-day sky. There were also seats, upon which Nanny Belmayne and Aunt Kate took rests that seemed to Louis to grow each day more frequent and protracted. He urged them to their feet at last to visit the Abbot's Kitchen. They went inside the building that was like a stone beehive, and moved around in semi-darkness, looking at odds and ends of smashed pottery laid out on the ground behind a rope enclosure. After a few minutes, they reached a large stone basin, full of cracks and identified by a notice as the Abbot's bath. When the keeper wasn't looking, Nanny Belmayne lifted Louis over the rope and, wearing his new shoes and Partlands school cap, he sat in the Abbot's bath, just as she had always foretold. For an instant, as he sat there, it flashed through his mind that, although Nanny Belmayne had been born in Queen Victoria's reign, her character was independent of any age in history, having been on friendly terms with the Duke of Wellington; having conspired to place that stone cauliflower on Napoleon's winkle; and having now, it appeared, been acquainted with the Abbot, whoever he was, in centuries past when Glastonbury

Abbey had a roof. Indeed, it seemed likely that this Abbot had had a kitchen and had bathed in it in his cracked stone bath for no purpose other than to accord with what Nanny Belmayne considered humorous.

The day after that, they went to Trowbridge to visit a cider factory owned by some distant cousins of Aunt Kate. They were taken round to see the mountains of bruised apples, and all the bottles, wobbling along a belt to be capped by a machine that picked four bottles up at once and whirled them round like partners in a square-dance. Louis picked up dozens of red and blue and silver caps from the vinegary-smelling, wet factory floor, and also collected many cardboard mats advertising the cider made by Aunt Kate's cousins. The mats all had a picture on them of men fainting flat with glasses of cider in their hands, and a lady behind a bar saying: 'No doubt about it, boys—it's great stuff.'

Aunt Kate's cousins were four brothers who lived close to the cider factory in a street of five identical new houses. The fifth house was occupied by their widowed mother, Aunt Kate's second cousin on her mother's side. Aunt Kate's second cousin, whom Nanny Belmayne and Louis met at tea, was a very old lady, dressed all in black, and when she spoke, her teeth made a loud whistling noise. She gave them prawns for tea, which Louis could not touch, nor could he even look at the greasy pink shells, piled high around everybody else's plate. His attention was fixed on the loaf, with its crusty topknot— a West Country loaf such as he had always imagined. When the old lady in black took a breadknife and sawed the topknot from the loaf, he was sure she would pass it across on the breadknife, to him. Instead, the old lady put it quickly on her own plate.

His thoughts had abandoned the West Country to his reluctant feet. He found it frequently trying—and would have found it unbearable had his mind not been able to seek refuge in the prospect of the Air Force doll. He thought about the Air Force doll on the long bus ride to Glastonbury, and throughout their other bus ride, to Shepton Mallet. He thought
300

about it among the ancestral graves; as he sat in the Abbot's bath and later, as he peered with Nanny Belmayne and Aunt Kate through the windows of a dark cottage where someone significant in his lineage had lived or passed away. At the cider factory, he forgot the Air Force doll, then remembered it suddenly at the old lady's house, just as she was passing cups of tea, and then felt so doubly excited, he wanted to jump up and scatter the prawn plates and sing.

By now he had lost any firm idea of how the Air Force doll would look when Nanny Belmayne had finished it. He struggled to visualise its face in the murky photograph; its semicircular eyebrows and wan little sewn-up smile. All he could remember was the Air Force uniform which, as his mind's eye stared at it, grew vaguer around the perfection of its miniature collar and tie. Sometimes, inadvertently, he caught a glimpse of the knitting while Nanny Belmayne was at work on it. It bore no resemblance to his dream—naturally enough, since tunic and epaulets and wings and collar and tie would be added only in the final stage. For this reason, he did not question the cream-coloured piece which Nanny Belmayne was now knitting, joined up to the blue piece she had finished.

To allay his fidgets, she bought him a set of hospital figures—a doctor, a nurse, two stretcher-bearers and their patient. He stood them among the tea things, heedless of Aunt Kate who, for some mysterious reason, had taken to frowning darkly at him and reproving him in a bubble of inaudible words. On the third day, it rained all afternoon. Nanny Belmayne and Aunt Kate were upstairs, sitting on Aunt Kate's bed and discussing bunions again while Nanny Belmayne knitted. Louis remained downstairs in the lounge, with Chum the hotel dog, picking the cork discs feverishly from inside the bottle tops he had collected. Tomorrow, he told Chum, they would be leaving Bath; three days more, and he would be travelling back to Ryde. His dream had come so close that he was almost afraid. For, when the Air Force doll was his, what an anticlimax would seem the residue of his life.

'It won't be long,' he whispered, and Chum the dog looked at him with rheumy, hopeful eyes.

In the evening, they went for a last walk through Bath. Nanny Belmayne wore her beret and big-squared coat, and Aunt Kate, the collection of grey fur pelts and paws and faces that she called her 'lynx'. They walked down the embankment, beneath the huge yellow street lamps, down the hills around the bus station to buy fish and chips, if the shop was open. The shop stood on a hill: it was open: all the way up the hill, people stood in shop doorways, eating fish and chips out of newspaper. As they walked down, a man in a doorway said something, and his companions laughed. Were they making fun of Aunt Kate's lynx? Then the same man said: 'If we'd known you was coming we'd have baked a cake.' The others laughed, the newspaper rustled in their hands and Louis, smelling vinegar, thought: It won't be long . . . not very long now . . .

Nanny Belmayne fitted the key into the lock, and he saw again, through blue and red door glass, the long front hall where the wooden couch still stood on coconut matting under the curved black water buffalo horns. He saw the stairs: they were unaltered. Darkness began, as always, half-way up.

'There!' Nanny Belmayne said with a deep sigh, as if everything were peacefully at an end.

'Come on, Kate dear.' For Aunt Kate had travelled back from the West Country to Clapham with them to spend a few days.

Mrs O'Rourke heard them and came bustling from her kitchen, followed by several cats, to report how good Bobby the terrier had been, and Uncle Tony—she having issued meals to both—and how very good Judy and Amber and Toby, bless him, and Korky and the other Judy had been. She had dusted all upstairs and aired the beds and 'Paddy' had given the garden a good dig-over. Cats' feet thudded round them as they heard this; the tails of cats waved softly against their legs. The dark was the same with its smell of liver; the same below-stairs glimpse of Mr O'Rourke, sitting with rolled-up sleeves, waiting patiently for his dinner to be cooked.

It was the same—and yet somehow, to Louis, the house in their absence had grown a little less. The very hall darkness now seemed less deep and lofty, more easily penetrable by his gaze. The upstairs kitchen looked smaller than he remembered it. The green baize table, the wash-stand and high mantel, which his eye greeted as a rule so gladly, now seemed to conspire in the inexplicable flatness which had come over life. It was the same—all the same—further up. The banister knobs, the Masonic scrolls, the pot of dusty walking sticks, the sawfish and the umbrellas, the picture of Grandpa Belmayne, even the great brass turbaned bed, had lost their old magnificence; they seemed dull and small, like things one has nearly outgrown:

'Now Kate—we'll go up into the front room, and I'll find us a drop o' something.' Aunt Kate's presence was like one more undusted ornament.

Later, Uncle Tony came home, the same way from the Common along Klea Avenue, wearing the same grey Homburg; he kissed Nanny Belmayne and Louis with a rasp of his grey moustache: he had, as usual, 'called in' somewhere for a Brickwood or Whitbread. He heard all about their travels sitting collarless in his usual chair, shredding the tobacco from his cigarette ends to be used in fresh cigarettes tomorrow.

For Louis, those travels had retreated already to a remote epoch. He listened to Nanny Belmayne's account of New Yatt, of Shepton Mallet and Trowbridge and the five new houses, of cider-making and gravestones and Mr and Mrs Marksman's great kindness, disinterestedly, counting bottle-tops on the table-cloth, paying attention only when Nanny Belmayne proudly described to Uncle Tony his sickness on the Great West Road, his sojourn in the Abbot's bath, and his remark to her in bed about Auntie Bessie Appleton's black babies.

303

Uncle Tony and she were arguing, as usual, over which of them ought to wash up.

'No, Gerry dear—I'll do it.'

'No, Tony dear—I'll do it.'

'No, Gerry dear . . .'

'*No,* Tony dear . . .'

'Oh—*Gerry,* dear . . .'

While they were arguing, Louis turned in his chair and pulled aside a corner of the curtain. Beyond the meat-safe, London was still there, familiar yet mysterious, with its glowing night sky, its distant, infinite roar of traffic. That promise, at least had not diminished—nor his old yearning to follow the light that shone over the shed on the rockery at the bottom of the garden.

Bedtime, with Aunt Kate involved, was not as it ought to have been. In Nanny Belmayne's room, the overhead bulb shone harshly down. The wardrobe door stood open to reveal Aunt Kate's 'lynx', hanging below the shelf of bottled plums. In comings and goings with hot bottles and an extra 'Edgar Allan', the ceremonial due to Louis was overlooked. Awaiting devotion, he loitered at the end of the big brass bed. Nanny Belmayne came in again.

'That next door little bed isn't very aired', she said. 'I don't want Auntie to have to sleep on it, so Nanny's going to sleep in the other room just for tonight. You'll be all right won't you, love, sleeping in the big bed with Auntie?'

He looked with failing heart at Aunt Kate, dressed in a long white night-dress, with her hair in a pigtail, holding a glass of water in which her teeth were already asleep. She frowned warily at him. In the turmoil of light and tiredness, he heard a bubbly, far off voice say: 'Now—you aren't going to kick in the night, are you?'

This is the last tomorrow.

He sits in the kitchen at Orlando Road, in a morning which has no tonight. After lunch, Nanny Belmayne will take him on the Underground from Clapham Common, past all the

304

stops in reverse, through Clapham North, Stockwell, Oval and Kennington, to see him off at Waterloo. It is the last time he will sit here at her kitchen table, with his feet on musty footstools, looking at the humorous illustrations around the wall—at Alfred the Great, baking cakes on an electric cooker; King John beaming to see his jewels recovered from an electric washing machine . . .

He is pretending to draw, although his hand has no strength, his page is a scribble: he looks at it only to keep himself from looking across to the wash-stand, where Nanny Belmayne has begun to put the stuffing into the Air Force doll. He tries, but cannot help seeing, through lowered eyelashes, her elbows busily at work, and hearing the wash-stand jog and rattle with her exertions.

'There!'

Now she has finished that job.

She has moved Bobby's chair across, fetched the owl lamp and sat down low at the corner of the table. Her work basket stands on the cloth near her head. She is wearing spectacles, looking fierce in them, looking fiercely down at the thing on her lap she is stitching, and Louis's eyes plunge deeper into his page and his pencil zigzags out of control, lest seeing prematurely should have power to hinder the putting on of the uniform, the buttons and epaulets and insignia which she has made and collated in secret . . .

He hears her break a thread between her teeth.

'Here y'are, my sweet,' she says, not handing it but tossing it to him across the table in her gladness to be absolved of knitting and sewing.

It's there. Now. From now, all tomorrows start.

His eyes lift, like a dawn, to see what she has knitted for him.

It lies there on the green cloth.

It is not an Air Force doll.

It wears no uniform, no tunic, buttons, epaulets, wings, no collar and no tie.

He does not know at first what it is. He gazes at the

305

fat blue—Air Force blue—body, its cream-coloured under-belly, its four splayed, stumpy legs, its upraised tail, its face, featureless but for two lumps in alignment on its head.

He remembers then—the other page in *Woman's Weekly*—and he understands.

Nanny Belmayne has knitted him Clara the Cow.

skaters of all the world

At Portsmouth, the big ships lay all around, put away tidily in their inlets until the next War. Louis stood at the stern of the Isle of Wight ferry and saw again the Naval panorama of which the concomitant emotions, for him, were always melancholy and regret. The usual long time elapsed before the boat's departure, though, hauling his own case, he had run to catch it in desperation down the zigzag ramp. The boat hummed softly but still delayed; he leaned at the rail, sad beyond thought to see the giant aircraft carrier, the *Victory*'s three masts above a barrack building, the tiny Gosport ferry, packed with standing passengers, crossing the harbour on a journey immeasurably happier than his.

Paired minesweepers passed—the tumbledown waterfront inns—the rampart of HMS *Vernon*. *Victory*, the dockyards and railway jetty dwindled down the ferry's wake. In that tower over there, frogmen were trained, so Anthony Durham believed. Grey walls, steep shingle, folded back as harbour and coast grew indistinguishable. Sea cadets rowed by, urged on by a brutal voice. (At least I'm not a sea cadet, he thought.) To his left he saw the line of what must be Southsea, with its pleasure ground and the fun-fair of which the pier tramboy always spoke. He looked, as he always looked, to see if the big wheel was turning.

Now the open sea—the cargo ships, the tankers loitering along invisible avenues. A yacht sailed past, jerking wildly through the swept-off waves, its bright yellow crew beheaded by the sail. Two forts appeared, then a third, hovering faintly between. The nearest fort stayed black in its moats of sea: you could not tell if anything on it were alive.

He paced around below the deck and, though he was hideously sad, could not help striding in and out of the No Smoking saloon, comforted in some strange way by the ferry's spotless order; the polished pipes and black and white floor of the Gents'. 'Ashtrays are provided', he murmured. 'Please do not put cigarette-ends into the urinals.' Just as he had done on every voyage, since that first day they came across to join Dad, he leaned at the open door to the engine-room, looking down through bright, clean silver pistons; letting the warmth that smelled like hot ice-cream blow up and dry his eyes.

Ryde was unchanged beneath its three church spires. The pier, black as ever, moved out slantwise to meet him, half a mile from shore. There was a train announcement, but no voice from the Pavilion as the gangways were made fast.

A taxi had been sent to the pierhead to collect him. The taximan, by ill luck, was Nanny Belmayne's 'Nature's gentleman'. Behind the peaked cap and crooked neck, driving down the pier at 5 m.p.h., Louis repressed a gasp of desolation to see, unchanged, the cascade of Union Street, the Western beach and enclosure, the Royal Victoria Yacht Club, the woodland that marked the site of Parkfield Lodge.

'Back in time for the Carnival eh?' the taximan said. They were driving up Union Street beneath row after row of faded red and pink flags.

He lay on the same green lino in his bedroom, his face in the forecourt of his light-up garage, reading the miniature posters for Castrol and Exide. Under his window, the High Street was the same. Mr Johncox and his assistant had not moved from either side of the tilted marble slab.

His mother came in again to try to cheer him up. Charles the Siamese cat followed her and jumped up onto Louis's bed. His markings, his plaintive voice, were utterly and heart-crushingly the same.

'—and what do you think! Daddy's going to enter a float in the Carnival procession. And *you're* going to be on it!'

Louis removed his face from the garage.

'In fancy dress?'

'Yes,' she said with her sudden, sparkling smile.

'What sort?'

'Something to do with skating. It's all going to have something to do with skating. Daddy will let us know.'

'Where is he today?'

'Gone away on business.'

'Where to, though?'

No longer smiling, she fumbled with a cigarette and match.

'Somewhere to do with Daddy.'

The Carnival was less than a week away. He had scarcely thought of it until now, despite the flags that hung across Union Street, the new posters covering each Borough notice-board. He rushed between notice-boards now, reading particulars of the Grand Opening (performed by His Worship the Mayor of Ryde); the Selection and Crowning of the Carnival Queen and her Attendants; the Torchlight Charity Procession —featuring Ryde's Famous 'Buccaneers'; the Old Tyme Music Hall—Relive Those Good Old Days; the Fête, the Donkey Derby, the Children's Fancy Dress Parade; the Carnival Ball at the Town Hall (Dancing to Geo. Wilkinson & his Swingtet); the Adult Fancy Dress and Grand Parade of Decorated Floats.

One further item caught his eye, printed in smaller type since it occurred half-way through Carnival Week and was outside the official programme:

'Thurs, Fri, Sat: T. Wall & Sons' Fair.'

It was now the very end of the season. Ryde held its

309

Carnival last of all the Island resorts, to catch the holiday-makers in the final moment, before they trekked out to the boats. It was equally an attraction for Isle of Wight people—a last fling before winter's long sleep. The crowds thronging Ryde in Carnival Week were thus an augury of empty streets and beaches. Special late-night buses prophesied the time when buses would almost cease to exist.

At the pierhead, the Ocean Restaurant and sun-roof had closed, and their waitresses and kitchen staff dispersed for another year. 'Ryde Casino' and the Tea Bar stayed open—whether or not under Dad's supervision was not made clear. From the flat, and his family circle, he continued to be absent 'on business'.

Yet even the colder, flag-hung pre-Carnival days brought Dad into Louis's thoughts. He remembered that, long ago in St Neots, Dad had spared time from fishing and shooting to assist in organising a Carnival there. Dad's influence in these inland revelries had been undefined but powerful—for it brought the Carnival Queen into the hotel every night. Louis, dressed as a Red Indian, riding Snowy the pony, had won Second Prize in the fancy dress procession, but had been compelled to give it back because Dad was 'on the Committee'. Still wearing the hated Red Indian suit, besmeared in reluctant warpaint, he was ushered up onto a stage in the Market Square to receive his prize, even though he would have to give it straight back afterwards. The prize was a long envelope with shapes inside it which might have been half-crowns.

It seemed to Louis an extraordinary oversight that Dad had not been called on to organise Ryde Carnival. Reading of the Sports and Talent Shows and Old Tyme Dances to come, he reflected how vastly these things would have benefited from Dad's energy and imagination and unique way of phrasing things on notice-boards. Without Dad's help, Ryde Carnival Week seemed doomed to remain incomplete and somehow slipshod and ignorant of certain indescribable proprieties.

But still the misguided preparations continued. In the next

few days, men from the Council could be seen on ladders that were boxed-in like medieval siege-towers, putting up flags between the lamp posts along the Esplanade. Flags now hung from the Repertory Theatre's four green pagodas as far along the Eastern shore as the Canoe Lake, whirling and tossing defiance at Portsmouth on thousands of invisible lance-points. For, every day, the wind blew colder and colder.

He wondered what kind of fancy dress he would wear in Dad's Carnival float. He saw himself as a hussar, a fur-trimmed jacket slung from his shoulders, trailing a sword looped-up in gold. Janice Bennett watched as he passed in the procession. He pretended to be unconscious of her rapturous gaze.

'I can make you the kilt,' his mother said. 'I'll borrow Mrs Durham's sewing-machine. And I know where I can borrow a proper leather sporran, just like real Scotsmen wear.'

It dawned on Louis that he was not to be called on to play the part of a hussar.

'We'll have to get you a proper hat with a feather . . .'

His tongue found speech in the clouds of awful dismay.

'Have I *got* to be a Scotsman? Can't I be . . .'

'—and a velvet jacket. I've got a bit of velvet I think I can use.'

'But have I *got* to be a Scotsman?'

She explained that Dad's Carnival float was to portray roller-skating by a theme already depicted by freize around the Pavilion wall. People of foreign lands on roller-skates would express to the Carnival crowds Dad's belief in roller-skating as a pastime enjoyed throughout the world. Owing to shortness of time, the freize characters must omit Red Indians and Zulus in favour of those representing the nearer world, namely Scotland, Ireland and Wales. The Scotsman, with his leering face and freckled knees and tartan of hasty brushmarks—that, she said, was Louis's part.

'You'll *have* to be a Scotsman to be on the float,' his mother said. 'It's called "Skaters of all the World". And Daddy *wants* you to be the Scotsman.'

311

'Did he say he wanted me to?' Louis asked. Despite himself, he felt moved by Dad's reliance on him.

'Yes, he did.'

'When?'

'He rang me up and told me. "I want Lou to be the Scotsman" is what he said.'

Suddenly, without knowing why, Louis wondered if she was telling the truth.

'There's nothing else you can be, anyway. There's only going to be a Scotsman, an Irish girl and a Welsh girl.'

'Who's going to be the Irish girl?'

'Olwen is.'

'Is—' he gulped on a detested word. 'Is that—that . . . Gaye going to dress up?'

'I'm afraid so. We had to let her be a little Welsh girl.'

He could well imagine the tirade of silliness by which Gaye had obtained her place on the Carnival float.

'Isn't there going to be any other sort of skater?' he pleaded.

'We did hope Anthony Durham might be John Bull. But Mrs Durham didn't think it was a good idea.'

'I'll be John Bull.'

'There isn't a John Bull now.'

'I know! Couldn't I be Hopalong Cassidy? I could wear my—'

'There isn't going to *be* a Hopalong Cassidy. I've already started making you a Scotsman's outfit, so let's have no more of this creating and carrying on. It'll be *nice* to be a Scotsman . . .'

Carnival Week began. Dad continued to be away from Ryde on business. It was, after all, a week much like the preceding one, but for the overflowing pubs, the buses immobilised among huge crowds of people walking rapidly in pursuit of a small hub of celebration that was perpetually on the move.

On Monday afternoon, Louis stood with them, watching the Carnival Queen receive her crown on the slopes around the Canoe Lake. Festivities then transferred to Elmfield, a district

312

he had not the means to visit. He came home quickly, fearful of meeting his cousin Terry with a rough gang.

No Carnival had infiltrated the top of Ryde. The Creamery Café was devoid of pennants and flags. His mother was at home again this afternoon. As he climbed the dark stairs, he heard the noise of the sewing-machine she had borrowed.

'Mrs Russell's lent me these socks for you to wear', she told him. 'These will do for a Scotsman's socks, won't they?' She opened a creased brown paper bag. Inside were some pale grey socks with green tabs sewn into them.

'I've sent away for the real sporran', she said. 'And Daddy's promised to get you a real pheasant's feather to wear in your hat.'

Evidently, then, she was in communication with Dad in his place of business. It was possible that Dad's absence might be entirely concerned with making ready the Carnival float, in some secret place where no one could distract him.

'Whose socks are they?'

'Just another little boy's. Oh, Lou—cheer up. You'll look ever so smart. I'm sure we'll have a lovely time in the Carnival. And you can stay up late to see the Torchlight Procession. I *promise.*'

She could not assuage the revulsion he felt at having to wear another boy's socks. He had a horrible suspicion that the owner of the socks was the boy he used to see when Mrs Proctor took him to prayer-meetings—the monkey-faced boy, grimacing at him across a smoky hut while pretending to sing the hymn.

Bands marched past somewhere in the distance. He stood with a little crowd in Simeon Street, watching the Fair arrive at the Recreation Ground. First, around the corner by Read's Garage, came long lorries painted like roundabouts in green and scarlet, proclaiming on wide gold parchments *T. Wall & Sons' World Renowned Amusements.* Trailers followed, whose tarpaulin sheets gave a glimpse of dodgem cars, huddled together. Vans and tractors and motorcycles, old poster-plastery

313

buses and long white caravans, turned, one by one, down the lane between the houses, to the open space which lay beyond.

The Fair had come at last. Joy, O Joy! Nothing else mattered, so long as the Fair had come. This, after all, was his first and true and incorruptible passion.

It had begun on a night long ago in St Neots, when the Fair came and Louis stood dumbfounded at the sight of it, lit up at night on the Market Square. He remembered no music, or noise or even people—only the roundabouts as they whirled together, like dancers in skirts that crackled with light. As he stood there under the archway, Dad came out of the hotel door behind him. The sight of him, watching the Fair alone, had made Dad laugh and pick him up and kiss him, and carry him, laughing and still kissing him, out among the noiselessly whirling roundabouts.

Ever since that moment, he had loved the Fair. It was the single constancy in his life, unweakened from year to year; a longing, never satisfied, for the same ideal of bright noise, loud colour, incomparable enjoyment. His life, whatever else might temporarily engross him, remained at bottom a preparation for those moments, rare and fleeting, when the Fair would return; and when, he promised himself, he would enjoy it as never before, having saved up great stores of money to spend. With this aim, throughout the year, he began—and quickly terminated—innumerable small funds, parcelled out in advance for such and such a ride. He read stories about Fairs, feeling bitter envy towards the fictional boys and girls who attended them. His dream was of fairs in storybooks—roundabouts with horses on barleysugar poles; Hoop-La and swingboats; a Helter-Skelter, giant in the sky. Of all fairground rides, although heights usually terrified him, he loved the Helter-Skelter most.

At Southsea there was such a storybook Fair, not subject to the usual brief season but open all summer. Each time he left Portsmouth on the boat, he looked across the harbour to its far shore to find that giant wheel, sometimes still but often moving, its chairs tiny against the sky. He had abandoned hope of ever going closer. The ragged tramboy often suggested that Louis accompany him to the Fair 'over Pompey', but then always laughed and walked away. It was probably for the best, Louis decided. For, if he were allowed to go with the ragged tramboy to Pompey Fair, in what low-class and ragged, tramboy surroundings would he afterwards be required to sleep the night?

He stayed on the Recreation Ground until the Fair was almost built. It was the same Fair that came in every Carnival Week. There was one fast roundabout, with chariots and wooden motorcycles, ringed by high steps and thick balcony and scrolled lettering and myths of hurtling speed. There was a dodgem track; a Helter Skelter, not tall, still lacking its girdled chute. Towards the canal bank were swingboats and kiddy rides and Roll-a-Penny stalls, still blind with canvas. The whole Fair was, by some niggardly byelaw, confined to the Recreation Ground's Simeon Street end. Four-fifths of the grass stretched wide and empty but for football goalposts and swings in the distance, and people exercising dogs. In the centre, a square had been cordoned-off for the fireworks on Saturday night.

He knew how different it would look when the Fair was open, and loud tunes played as the fast roundabout rushed on its course within the balconies; when dodgems spun and battered, sparking on their poles, when rifles snapped and pennies rolled and ducks by the hundred jostled on their circular pool, when wheels of bright bulbs, with bright-lit spokes, were turning, all turning against each other, and light was wound in sashes around the Helter Skelter, drawing it up to its full height in the noisy evening sky.

He left the Recreation Ground at last, and walked away, past old ladies at front gates, nervously awaiting the transformation of the little street in which, before you came to the Fair, you could buy windmills and balloons and cardboard hats and grey fluffy monkeys on white elastic . . .

Please God: *please* let someone have time to take him to the Fair.

* * *

315

It was time to dress for the Carnival Parade. He stood in his bedroom, looking through the window down into the High Street where, heedless of Carnival Week, Mr Johncox the fishmonger and his assistant were busily attending to their respective queues. The life of Mr Johncox or his assistant at this moment seemed, to Louis, infinitely desirable.

His mother helped him on with the jacket she had made from one of her old black velvet skirts. He knew she had sat up late last night to finish it on the borrowed sewing-machine. Its lapels were faced with silver foil. She hitched the sleeves back to display his white frilled shirt-cuffs. This part of his costume was not disagreeable to Louis: he crooked his arm, liking the way the shirt burst from the narrow sleeve, and forgot for a moment the horror that was below.

'It's real tartan', his mother said. 'I got you Hunting Stewart.' She was struggling to close the large safety-pin which, she had repeatedly assured Louis, was the method by which all real Scotsmen fastened their kilts. She was getting cross now, murmuring under her breath that he was an 'ungrateful little hound'. On his bed lay a black Girl Guide beret with the long brown pheasant feather pinned to its side. The real leather sporran, offered for so long as redemption, had failed to arrive. Instead, he wore a sporran run up by his mother at the last minute and resembling nothing so much as a little fluffy white rabbit.

Another boy's socks clung tightly to his legs. He pictured the boy's face, laughing, toothless . . . And his knees! His *knees* were going to show.

'There now! *Don't* you look nice!'

His mother shook him angrily by the shoulder.

'Turn round and *look*!' He did so, but his eyes stayed blind.

'There now! You look really smart! You really do! A proper little Scotsman!'

The back streets were lined with Carnival floats, getting ready. Louis walked with his mother on what was normally his peaceful uphill route to school, but was this morning lined with mobile farmyards and African villages and South Sea Islands, and teeming with cowgirls and court jesters, pirates, sailors, saucepan men and human telephones, in turbans and rabbit ears and wind-stirred grass skirts, all hurrying to their places in the parade. Milkmaids, Dutch girls and Queens of Hearts stared down from their tableaux at Louis as he passed. 'O God,' he silently entreated, trying not to catch sight of himself. 'God—please don't let Janice Bennett be anywhere around.'

Dad's float was parked in West Street, next to the long cemetery wall. The long black Wolseley stood, like an extra novelty, directly behind it. And there was Dad himself, with Wilf and Olwen and another man Louis did not recognise. He and his mother crossed over, watched sadly by the angels outside Ellery's stonemason shop.

Among the motorised galleons and castles and dragons and giant shoes, Dad's float was straightforward to the point of austerity. It was a plain green Bedford lorry which made no attempt to disguise itself save by strips of red, white and blue paper, nailed along each side of its open tailboard. Two long white cotton placards hung from either side, lettered *Ryde Roller-Skating Rink* in the unmistakable script of Mr Boynton. A further small placard stood across the roof of the driving-cab, from which fronds of red, blue and white paper hung loosely, like mop-heads.

Louis and his mother stood at the end of this modest equipage, and waited for Dad to speak to them. He had noticed their approach, but had chosen to remain deep in conversation with Wilf and the unknown man, looking up at the float, sometimes moving his head from side to side as if making some fine mental calculation with his eye. He wore, as usual, clothes redolent of the countryside, all soft and complementary green tweeds, and the sleeveless leather over-jacket which furled at the back hem because of the way he thrust his head forward and kept his shoulders bowed. His dark blue cheeks were newly-shaved. A breath of nice soap came from them. He filled his pipe as he talked, digging with his thumbs into a tin

L

of Log Cabin; and Louis, for all the shame and dejection, felt a shout of happiness within himself, just to be near Dad again. Dad, he thought, must be very pleased to see him as a Scotsman. Dad had wanted it so very much.

It came as a surprise, therefore, when Dad did not even say 'Hello' to him, but looked straight over his head and said curtly:

'Well—did you bring it, Laura?'

'Yes, I brought it.' Louis's mother said. 'Only, I should have thought . . .'

'Never mind what you'd have thought, Laura,' Dad broke in.

'I'd have thought you'd left enough I.O.U.s in that till . . .'

'Not in front of other *people,* Laura,' Dad said, the protocol grinding in his voice as he took the roll of money from her. At the same moment, Olwen, dressed as an Irish girl, skated along beside the cemetery wall to join them.

The green skirt and white blouse, with a swathe of dark green thrown over one shoulder, brought out all of Olwen's grim prettiness. A wide green beret hung suspended at the back of her fluffy brown curls.

'Very nice,' Louis heard his mother say distantly.

With eyes lowered, Olwen said: 'Could you find me that key please, Emile? We'll soon have to be locking up the kids' skates.'

Some floats were already beginning to move. Louis's mother kissed him and disappeared. He was not to see her again for the rest of that day.

He sat with Gaye on the Wolseley's running-board, trying on the skate-boots that completed their costumes as 'Skaters of all the World'. Possibly it was her voluminous Welsh girl's costume—a good deal less unbecoming than his—which made Louis, on this Carnival day, long more than ever for a chance to criticise Gaye, or discountenance or wound her in some way. He forced in his toes wearily under a boot-tongue. The boots would soon be too small for him now.

'You can't skate,' he whispered, feeling a momentary elation

318

to see dismay empty the little brown face under the high black Welsh hat.

'I can.'

'No you can't! . . .'

He stopped as Olwen came and knelt down in front of them with a key to lock their skate wheels, to stop them rolling off the back of the lorry.

The day was windy and overcast, and the crowds lining every pavement seemed a sign, not of Carnival gaiety but of some disaster which, however imminent, has the power to fascinate its victims. Crowds, stretching steeply downhill and curling over every street-corner, stood motionless under the spell of huge, smeared clouds, stretching from Portsmouth across a sea like wind-hurried mud. There was no defence but the chains of flags which reined in every thoroughfare on one faded pink leash and provided a transit-system for the slowly-moving procession. They were still in West Street when Louis felt the first raindrops, thrown in a handful against his face.

From the beginning it had been plain to him that 'Skaters of all the World' was not destined to win the prize for decorated floats. He understood, or hoped he did, that the modesty of Dad's float was intentional—that Dad, having gone thoroughly into the matter of Carnival decoration, had reached a conception truer to the Carnival spirit—and equally, to finer considerations of gentility and good taste—than any of the large floats which were merely spectacular, realistic and expensive. It was too much to hope that the Carnival judges would appreciate the subtlety of Dad's mind. Not that anything undertaken by Dad could have as its object so inconsiderable a thing as a prize.

His position on the float was in front, facing forwards over the lorry's crested cab. He stood on his locked skates as Olwen had arranged him, in the attitude of a Scotsman about to dance the Highland Fling. Welsh girls, it had been decided,

319

would sit rather than stand—even a Welsh girl on roller-skates—therefore, an ice-cream tin, hastily disguised with crepe paper, had been provided for Gaye's use. She sat on it a little behind Louis, facing the tail of the lorry, visible to him only as a tall black hat. Of Olwen, and whatever pose she had selected to represent an Irish girl, nothing could be seen from this position.

Dad drove the lorry himself. It seemed to Louis character-istic of him that, having conceived the Carnival float in these sombre nuances, Dad should round off the feat by a dis-play of practical and mechanical expertise. He drove the lorry as he drove everything—with a care and smoothness and grave deliberation which Louis could feel, even in the laboured downhill progress of the motorised floats, moving at a pace dictated by those in the procession who were on foot, with frequent stops to allow stragglers to catch up. The cab of the lorry was round: it reminded Louis somewhat of Dad's high and brooding forehead. Occasionally he would glimpse, in the outside driving-mirror, a pale fragment of Dad's face. Be-cause of the mirror angle, his eyes seemed to be looking straight at Louis. But the eyes remained fixed eternally on other things.

They had come to the top of Union Street. Crowds on the corner outside Pack's and Timothy White's formed two dense arcs to receive them. Each pavement swarmed in the shop-blind shade. People leaned out of bay windows, two and three storeys above. Flags lay ahead, in a dense tangle which parted, skein by skein, as Dad drove down towards the sea.

Their place in the procession was well towards the back. Louis could picture Dad being pressed by the Carnival or-ganisers to take higher precedence, but demurring in such a way as to make even his modesty seem modest. As 'Skaters of all the World' began to descend Union Street, the leading floats had already reached the bottom and were turning along the Esplanade. The throne transporting the Carnival Queen and her two attendants; The Old Woman Who Lived in a Shoe; the Spanish Galleon, Wishing Well and South Sea Island village were all of this remote vanguard. Back here marched uneventful contingents of the Boys' Brigade; a lorry came afterwards on which blind people sat weaving baskets under a thatched roof. The bands, too, had all gone on ahead. Silver scraps of their music were faintly detectable among the grind of lorries in bottom gear, the swish of paper costumes, and feet, unnumbered, walking not in step.

Time for Louis adjusted itself to the slowness of the parade. The floats, the distant bands and flags all grew into habit under the darkened sky. His shame and disgust yielded to monotony, and the realisation that no one of the thousand faces seemed to be looking much at Dad's float or at him. Frozen in his Highland Fling, he might himself have been one more spectator, observing his surroundings from some private elevation. He watched the man dressed all in newspapers who walked below the lorry's tailboard; and the little boy, representing a cup and saucer, whose mother walked beside him, carrying a raincoat. His thoughts wandered far and wide, until the very noise had receded, like sea sound inside a shell and the lacy cuff, suspended beside him, became unrecognisable as his own. Once, as they were passing the Electricity Board, he caught sight of Dad's float in a long outside mirror—a scribble of colour, both surprising and futile. There, in the midst of it, was the face—that pale face, held sideways which ever passed through life beside him.

Now they had reached the bottom of Union Street. They were turning the corner, past St Thomas's Street and the Inquiry Office, where the Esplanade began. He saw the Western —its paths and flower-beds and low sea wall; its sea-mine and photographer's kiosk—an epoch walled-in; complete. Through the gap, and the ghost of the Royal Pier Hotel, he saw the pier where it burst from the land wall, under the tramway station's yellow canopy. Here, behind crowds, was the broad pavement up to the pier gates. He saw the two stone lodges with the glass roof between; he saw the turnstiles and wide car gates; the men at the IN turnstile, working behind their boxes as usual.

They had passed the pier-entrance, and Smith's, and the Southern Vectis office. They were passing the bus stops, the shelters and knotted trees, the shallow garden and flat-topped hedge, with the Esplanade railway beyond, looping out to join the pier. They had abandoned their nationalistic poses and were throwing paper streamers and cotton wool snowballs at the crowd. He awoke again to find his own arm, in black velvet, with a white frilled cuff, throwing a streamer which curled through the air to drop, unnoticed, in the steep gutter. Olwen was standing by him, offering him snowballs from a paper sack. Gaye was there also, her arm deep inside the sack. They were figures without voices; he strove to remember them, but could not. He drew back his arm with a snowball. Dreaming set in again before the snowball had left his hand.

He saw that they were nearing the white towers and banked lawn of the Osborne Hotel & Brasserie. Brassiere, brazier, brasserie—what was the difference? He could see the little opening into a steep street with a handrail, where Mrs Durham had carried him barefooted in her arms. He saw, with surprise, Patricia Wade, a girl from Partlands School, leaning from the upper window of a dark blue seafront cottage. They had reached the Repertory Theatre, in its garden of dusty palm trees. He remembered 'Breath of Spring, a Bright New Comedy by Peter Coke'. They skirted the large roundabout planted with flowers, and turned left along the lane behind the Hotel Ryde Castle. Rain had begun to darken the pavement and lorry boards, and to whisper among the trees that overhung the road.

This was where Louis saw and felt least—as Dad's float followed the Carnival procession behind the Esplanade, through streets which, very soon now, would provide the next, most nearly everlasting epoch of his life.

The rain fell quietly stronger, turning his black velvet to wet grey fur, slowly pulping the man who was made all of newspapers. They were stationary for a long time in Monkton Street. He glanced for a moment up Wood Street—up the straight cascade of gravel, to that corner, by the Tredegar Guest

House, where his future lay along the broken pavement to a dark, high, many-chimneyed house.

They returned along Monkton Street later, past the end of Simeon Street with the corner Post Office, where buckets and spades hung in bunches outside. The rain fell thicker, warm and invisible through the strings of flags. He shut his eyes to the rain, and to pavements he would tread so many times. They turned into The Strand, passing the high guest houses with long stone balustrades, heading towards the foot of Ryde's eastern hills. Here was the Appley Hotel; the Putting Green, where dead sailors were buried, so Anthony Durham said. They were back on the Esplanade again, the procession complete again as it circled the long Canoe Lake. Turning at the Appley end, their route rejoined the sea wall, the steep-roofed shelters, the beach, horizonless below a rain-dull sea. There was the pier again, racing out to try to touch Portsmouth.

Other people had now jumped on to the lorry with them. 'Skaters of all the World' was no more. They stood, with the sodden newspaper man and several Buccaneers at the edge of the tailboard, rattling moneyboxes for the Carnival fund, while people in the crowd threw pennies and halfpennies up at them. His arm, in wet velvet, shook a tin; 'Come on!' shouted a voice that was his. He knelt on the sodden boards, trying to pick up wet, cold halfpennies and pennies.

It's still Carnival week. The Fair started yesterday; this is after lunch on Friday. The Fair is happening *now*. Please, *please*, O God, let them finish their quarrel in time to take me to the Fair.

I'm sitting on the window seat, at the light end of the room. They're facing each other and shouting like a show before me —like actors, since they pay me no attention. The room grows darker behind them, to the black linen press against the opposite wall.

I'm looking away, through the bars, down into the High Street, and thinking: This is a mistake. I ought not to be in here now. I ought to be in my bedroom, hearing this through the wall, or late at night, down the avenue of half-open doors.

I don't know why they're quarrelling. It has suddenly overflowed and trapped me here. I don't understand the things they are shouting. I can only hear how angry their voices are, yet how wearied by the necessity of wasting words on one another. Their voices, the two elements in me, never meeting, never blending, always soaring apart, into higher and higher galaxies of hate.

'—no, I *didn't*, Laura . . .'

'—yes, you did . . . you . . .'

'—no, I didn't! No, I did *not*, Laura!'

I'm sitting on copies of *The Field,* Dad's shooting magazine, arranged along the window seat in an overlapping line. I can feel the corners, shiny against my legs at the back. I can see the black titles, ending in a picture of a spaniel, holding a pheasant in its mouth, but with a beautiful expression, as if it never meant to hurt the pheasant. I can picture advertisements for guns and picnic hampers, and beautiful country houses where we might easily be living now.

'Oh no, I haven't, Laura. No, I *haven't,* Laura!'

Perhaps our lives would be different if she had not stopped looking pretty. I do wish her mouth didn't hang open and her face didn't shine. I wish she wouldn't wear the same housecoat and have bags under her eyes. I'm angry now because Dad is, because she won't be pretty; and I'm looking into the High Street, hoping that Mr Johncox and his assistant can't hear all this noise. Supposing everyone heard! Crowds in the High Street, looking up at our window . . .

She has screamed out something which is so terrible, it makes Dad pause for a minute, and the black peak quiver on his forehead. Then something yellow seems to light up in his eye. He starts forwards as if to strike her. A tiny bunch of froth forms on his lips as they struggle to make a reply of adequate force:

'No, I *didn't* Laura! You've got it all wrong! I did *not*, Laura!'

324

'You did! You've been sleeping with her . . .'

(Is that all?)

'No, I have *not*! I have *not*, Laura. No, I have *not*, Laura!'
His voice drops suddenly.

'Now . . . look at you, Laura. Just look at yourself.' His
voice is almost kind. 'Just look at you, Laura—the way you
look, and the way you're carrying on in front of Lou!'

Neither of them looks at me.

'*I'm* not the one who's carrying on in front of Lou!'

'Yes, you are! Screaming and going on in front of Lou!'

'You're the one who's going on in front of Lou!'

'No, Laura—*you're* the one who started going on and
screaming in front of Lou . . .'

Dad says: 'I've had just about enough of all this, Laura.'

'That's right! Go!' Her face collapses—*why* can't she look
pretty? 'Walk out as usual! Walk out as usual!'

Dad comes towards me. He's pulling me up from the window seat by the arm. A page of *The Field* sticks to my leg
behind.

'Come on, son,' Dad says confidentially, while she screams:
'Leave him!'

'He's coming with me, Laura.'

Dad is pulling me along behind the sofa. She has caught
my other arm and is pulling me back towards the window.
They are pulling me to and fro by my arms and shouting at
one another over my head. Suddenly I notice the empty
bowl on top of the chest of drawers. I think to myself: whatever *did* become of those three newts we caught?

Dad, of course, is the strongest. He has pulled me away
from her and out into the hallway. Old Nigger the labrador
is lying there. His black eye looks up at us; his big scarred tail
thumps once on the coconut matting. Dad is pushing me ahead
of him, over the thick front mat and down the stairs. I can
hear an urn's hiss, the clink of cups from the café underneath.

We are hurrying downstairs, turning again and again in
the darkness, beside dimly ragged walls. She is calling after

325

us wearily, as if even her voice cannot be bothered to stand upright:

'Come back, Emile! Come back, Emile! Come back, Emile, come back!'

We've come out under the archway into street noise as sudden as if my ears had popped. I can see Mr Johncox across the road, a few yards away, in his straw hat and apron. I can hear his big knife thumping on fish. People hurry to and fro across the arch, unreally large, like figures on a cinema screen.

I'm sitting in the front seat of the Wolseley, where Dad always leaves it, on the waste ground behind The Creamery. I'm looking down the long, sun-faded bonnet to its silver emblem, where I can see Dad's face, turned sideways, jerking up with each swing he gives the starting-handle. I'm thinking:

'There's still time for her to come downstairs and rescue me. Perhaps she's called the Police. I hope not. The Police might blame me as well. This is the second swing . . . this is the third . . .'

On the fourth swing, the engine starts. All the ancient woodwork and torn fabric around me begins, gently, to shake. Dad is getting in beside me. He does not speak, or even look at me as he lets down the big brake near my leg. We're moving slowly, carefully, scrunching over bricks and broken slates, down through the archway with only inches to spare on either side. Mr Johncox's assistant has stopped the traffic to allow us out into the High Street. We go forward towards him, then back, obedient to his pushing palms, and mount the pavement. People are waiting on either side. She could still come out and rescue me. We are moving back again. Dad's arms whirl on the wide wheel; his hazel eyes stare over my head. We've done it this time. The crowds move on behind us. Dad gives Mr Johncox and his assistant a cheerful wave.

We're driving down through Ryde, under the Carnival flags. Union Street is crowded on both sides. There are people walking up and down the road. I can hear singing and bottles clinking through the open doors of hotels and pubs. We are following a coach—Paul's Tours—past Fowler's and Colenutt's, and Talbot's Saddlery, where the old man remembers Queen Victoria; past Yelf's and the Royal Squadron Hotel. The sea, stacked up ahead of us, has hardened into a deep autumn blue. Close to the sky, the *Queen Mary* hangs motionless on her way to Southampton. Or is she the *Queen Elizabeth*? I can't remember which ship has three funnels.

Dad hasn't spoken to me yet. I look at him sometimes, but he doesn't look back. He stares out, over his steady hands, his face set in concern for the people crossing the road. To begin with, I wondered what he would say to me about the incident in the flat. Now I know: he will say nothing. I should ask nothing. Not even where he is taking me now, though I know he knows. We are nearing Mainstone's now, and I can't help thinking that his purpose in carrying me off like this might have been to take me to Mainstone's and buy me the thing I want most in the world.

Now I know where he's taking me.

The Wolseley climbs the wide red pavement, moving gently among the bus and taximen who congregate at the pier gates. At the IN turnstile, the man recognises Dad and comes round to pull open the twin iron gates. As we go through—with inches again to spare—the ticket collector touches his cap-brim, and Dad leans forward and smiles and gives another cheery wave.

We are passing the cage-like wall, the yellow canopy of the tram terminus on one side; on the other, a whitewashed fountain, the back of the Western ladies', a sign *Speed Limit 5 m.p.h.* With a loud 'belp!' we cross the loose metal strip dividing the land from grey pier planks.

We are driving along the pier at 5 m.p.h., over wastes of gleaming sand. Boats lie littered on their anchors, sideways. There is no one along the pier but ourselves—no tram or train or pedestrian or other car. The empty planks stretch further ahead than I can see. They seem to shift and swing in front of us with the light that comes up through them from the beach.

327

On either side of us, the railings pass in their eternal lyre shape, with green knobs along the top. The knobs on our left pass slowly, on our right, quickly, like the same knob, whipped away and replaced by an unseen hand. Further out, beyond the tramline and the railway, runs an outer rail of black iron hoops. On every hoop a white gull stands, fluffed against the sea breeze.

Here comes the first pier shelter. Perhaps when we have passed it, Dad will say something to me . . . Oh well: that was only a little shelter. It hadn't even a roof. Here comes the large one, built out on a promontory, with seats on all four sides and a green pagoda roof. Perhaps he'll say something . . . oh, well: perhaps when we pass the signal box . . . the sign for Lipton's Tea. Here comes the Rowing Club. I can see its legs, its drooping slipway. Perhaps when we pass the Rowing Club, Dad will look at me and tell me what's to become of me today.

A boat will be in soon. Is he taking me to catch it? And then, beyond Portsmouth—what? Tonight, where will we be? Where will I sleep? What sort of house? What sort of room? What sort of light? Will it be left turned on? How will the darkness look? Faces in it? What sort of bed? O, no. No. I shan't have to sleep in a bed with Dad. Shall I? The same bed with him. The white shoulders, the black hairy body, the thick, dark winkle that floated on the bath water . . . O no. O no, I start to think about her, and about her camel hair coat with its brown silk lining; how gently she used to wash me, and the night I heard her singing. I think: 'No Mummy any more.' I think it again and again: 'No Mummy any more. No Mummy any more . . .'

As we come to the end of the pier—as the railway curves to its terminus, and the Pavilion is revealed on its stilts down the long estuary—I feel myself, at long last, beginning to cry.

'Oh, don't *cry,* Louis,' Dad said, in a voice suggesting that, of all courses Louis might have chosen, this was the least original or interesting.

328

Just then, with a 'belp', the Wolseley crossed the other metal bar, from planks to the pierhead concrete.

Dad turned into the usual space, beside the gate to the low-level quay. Fishermen stood all round that wing of the pier-head. 'Come on, old son,' Dad said shortly, and Louis slid out, across the wide running-board. Dad came round behind the Wolseley and caught hold of his arm again.

'Come on, old son,' he said again, in a voice that was gentler, and, somehow, forgiving.

His shadow led Louis's across the grey and sunlit ground. Ahead of them, the Pavilion waited—as, for both of them, it would always wait. The sun-roof had been cleared of tables and umbrellas. The restaurant casements were closed. The dome still basked in sunshine but the slatted yellow wood below, around all its conflicting angles, seemed dulled already by darker days. From further around it, through the Casino's unpinned doors, a breezy voice on the jukebox still sang:

> She wears red feathers and a hooly-hooly skirt
> She wears red feathers and a hooly-hooly skirt

One shadow stopped. Its sandal-straps curled out; a tie shadow fluttered on its shoulder. It bowed its head and began to cry again.

The grip on his arm relaxed. Big and small shadows merged; a hug softly crushed his shoulders.

'What is it? What is it, old son?'

'I want . . .' He wheezed for breath. 'I want my . . . Mummy. Mum.' For he had never known exactly by what name to call her.

The hug ceased.

'All right, Louis,' Dad said flatly; and he knew that he had given mortal offence.

He felt himself hurried, not to the Pavilion after all, but the other way, across the pierhead towards the ticket-barrier for the boats. Were they then leaving the Island without luggage—without even tickets? The ticket collector saw them coming; he recognised Dad and stood aside to let them through. At the last moment, Dad seemed to change his mind again. He turned Louis aside and pushed him into the telephone kiosk that stood next to the ticket collector's hut.

The door moved slowly into place behind them.

Dad put in three pennies and dialled a number which Louis knew, even before his finger began it, would be The Creamery —Ryde 3113. As the disc spun back to its digit each time, he noticed that there was sand in the corner of the telephone box, and that paint from its red ribs lay smeared like blood outside the glass. A sign against the rail outside said, *Visit the Buddle Inn.* Cars were arriving to meet the boat.

Inside the receiver dots, his mother's voice said 'Hello'. Dad pressed Button A with contemptuous force.

'All right, Laura—you win!'

He repeated, with greater emphasis, since she had not understood:

'I said, "All right, Laura—you win!" '

That was the sole clue to the war they had waged. Dad was stronger, but had elected to give way—and, by giving way, had shown better than victory could the utter rightness of his position. He carried on speaking in the vein of such a truce, but Louis did not listen, for—worse than when they had pulled at him—he was torn between the elements of himself. Half of him felt sorry for Dad, so vexed on all sides by screaming and tears. Half of him caved in with happiness to know that his mother had won. And yet . . . if he had not cried; if Dad had taken him into the Pavilion, what wonderful treat or new toy might have been waiting there?

Dad, who had struggled so hard to win him, scarcely seemed to notice him now. His face looked back, over Louis's head, through the glass and across the pierhead to the Pavilion. Some new plan for improvement there might well have occurred to him, for the yellow anemone had died in his eye; he listened, no longer angrily, nor with any visible emotion, as

330

the voice in the telephone asked what was to be done with Louis this afternoon.

'He can go to the Fair,' Dad replied, and again, impatiently, because the line was crackling, Dad said:

'He can go to the Fair.'